Praise for Two Surre...

"How could I not fall hard for these two?! Their chemistry and banter was off the charts. The passion between Gigi and Conrad could light an entire village."
—Gab Reads Romance, *Netgalley*

"Their relationship is tumultuous and ever so enticingly sensual."
—Pamela B, *Netgalley*

"I absolutely adore this duo, their irrevocably entwined souls, their journey and the stark contrast between raw passion and heartrending healing tenderness."
—Alexandra, *Goodreads*

"Steamy, witty, full of secrets, and funny."
—Leidy, *Bookbub*

"This was an all-nighter. I simply could not put it down. Fast paced with twists and turns, keeping the reader entertained and guessing, and the revelation of the ultimate villain was unexpected."
—Nazmin, *Goodreads*

"Grace Callaway does it again with her combination of spice, intrigue, family and banter."
—Cindy, *Netgalley*

"I just want to keep reading one more chapter, just one more chapter. Grace's writing is superb."
—Angela, *Bookbub*

"Irresistible and fiery chemistry."
—Nancy, *Goodreads*

"Another well written story where our heroine is so much more than the decorative accessory society would have had her be. She's got a brain and she uses it, not for personal gain but for the causes of this otherwise forgotten village. She is powerful and patient. Our hero cannot help but change his mind about his original ulterior motives. The reader will find themself changing their mind about him too."
—Pamela M, *Netgalley*

"Absolutely delightful...I loved watching these two match wits while fighting and then giving into their attraction."
—Melanie, *Netgalley*

"I'll read anything Grace Callaway writes, and I think she delivers so well on creating characters you care about and want to see more from... Gigi is absolutely the daughter of Marcus and Pandora, the way she is so scheming and confident while also endlessly caring and looking to do what's best for others, screamed daddy and mama Harrington. I love this family so any time we spend with them is a win."
—Nikki, *Netgalley*

"The banter between the two main characters, Conrad and Gigi, is absolutely hilarious."
—Jill, *Goodreads*

"A passionate, character-driven historical romance that offers more than just steam—it delivers genuine emotional depth and a touch of mystery, too. As a lover of historical romance books, this book is definitely up in my favourites."
—Sara, *Goodreads*

Also by Grace Callaway

BLACKWOODS
One Kiss to Desire
Two Secrets to Surrender
Three Chances to Cherish (Coming soon)

LADY CHARLOTTE'S SOCIETY OF ANGELS
Olivia and the Masked Duke
Pippa and the Prince of Secrets
Fiona and the Enigmatic Earl
Glory and the Master of Shadows
Charlotte and the Seductive Spymaster
Mrs. Peabody and the Unexpected Duke (Novella)

GAME OF DUKES
The Duke Identity
Enter the Duke
Regarding the Duke
The Duke Redemption
The Return of the Duke
Steamy Winter Wishes (Holiday Novelette)

HEART OF ENQUIRY (The Kents)
The Widow Vanishes (Prequel Novella)
The Duke Who Knew Too Much
M is for Marquess

The Lady Who Came in from the Cold
The Viscount Always Knocks Twice
Never Say Never to an Earl
The Gentleman Who Loved Me

MAYHEM IN MAYFAIR
Her Husband's Harlot
Her Wanton Wager
Her Protector's Pleasure
Her Prodigal Passion

TWO Secrets TO SURRENDER

BOOK 2

USA TODAY BESTSELLING AUTHOR

Two Secrets to Surrender © Grace Callaway, 2025.

Paperback ISBN: 978-1-960956-48-4

All rights reserved. Without limiting the rights under copyright reserved above, no part of this publication may be reproduced, stored in or introduced into a retrieval system, or transmitted, in any form, or by any means (electronic, mechanical, photocopying, recording, or otherwise) without the prior written permission of the copyright owner.

This is a work of fiction. Names, characters, places, brands, media, and incidents are either the product of the author's imagination or are used fictitiously.

Cover Art: Night Witchery

Formatting: Colchester & Page

*For my family:
you are my Chuddums,
the home I will always be grateful for*

Prologue

Lady Georgiana Flora Aileen Harrington—"Gigi" to friends—skipped through the autumn-kissed woods. Beneath her feet, the mossy floor was plusher than an Aubusson, and sunlight dappled through the leaves like a natural chandelier. She breathed in the scents of the forest, feeling more at home here than in the ballrooms of London. From the moment she'd arrived at Chudleigh Bottoms, she had experienced a sense of belonging. Her brother Ethan had taken up residence in one of the local manors, and while many viewed "Chuddums" as being downtrodden—local lore even claimed it was *cursed*—Gigi had instantly fallen in love with the village and its people.

She'd become great friends with Miss Leticia Caldecott, a lovely spinster who owned Chudleigh Bottoms's World Famous Roman Bath. Contrary to its name, the spa had been fading into obscurity, and Gigi had suggested refurbishing the place. Miss Letty had embraced the idea, and today the pair had cleaned out a room that generations of Caldecotts had used for storage space. Afterward, seeing that her maid had fallen asleep on one of the spa's benches, Gigi had decided to slip away to the nearby stream. She inhaled the forest scents as she passed by curious squirrels and scurrying partridges. In the distance, a woodpecker tapped out an enigmatic message. For a little while, freedom was hers.

Arriving at her destination, Gigi took in the scene with delight. The stream was clear, diamonds sparkling on its surface. Along its banks, wildflowers had lost their bloom, but the grass remained stubbornly verdant. An ancient yew tree, its gnarled trunk swirling with the secrets of time, stood like a sentinel. Boulders dotted the water's edge, some of them large enough to lay upon while one basked in the sun.

The beauty and warmth of the day was too splendid to ignore. Gigi adored swimming, and moreover—she gave herself a discreet sniff—a wash was not entirely optional. Glimpsing her reflection in the water, she smiled. Letty had loaned her a stained and threadbare frock to wear while cleaning, and with her raven hair plaited and covered by an old kerchief, Gigi looked more like a country maid than the daughter of a marquess. It reminded her of the carefree summers spent at the family estate, where she'd grown up swimming and climbing trees with her three older brothers.

She followed the brook to a secluded pool surrounded by large rocks. There, the water had a sudden drop, resulting in a small but delightful waterfall...perfect for rinsing off. She was untying her kerchief when a splash startled her. Her gaze flew to the liquid curtain of water, behind which a dark shape suddenly lurked. It was massive...*monster-like*.

Instinctively, she took refuge behind the nearest boulder. Her heart pounding, she counted to ten before daring to peer around it. The shape had disappeared. Had she imagined it? The form suddenly broke the surface of the pool, and she clapped a hand over her mouth to stifle her gasp. Then she realized how fanciful she'd been.

Why, it is not a monster. It—he—*is just a man.*

Although only the fellow's head was above the water, the refined savagery of his features caused her heart to thump against her ribs. His broad, slashing cheekbones and light, piercing eyes belonged on a Viking crusader. His nose was bold and arrogant, his jaw hewn with an unyielding edge. With a rough gesture, he swiped back the dark-blond hair plastered to his brow before diving under again.

Her pulse racing, she watched his shadow glide below the water. Suddenly, he surged upward, standing below the waterfall and giving her a view of his profile. Her heart broke into a gallop as, through the rushing curtain of water, she glimpsed a naked male for the first time.

Oh my stars.

He was exceedingly tall, and his taut, grooved derriere—just thinking the word made her blush—was visible above the pool's surface. Even though she knew she should look away, she didn't. She *couldn't*. His blatant virility was like a magnet to her curiosity. He was lean and muscular, with the kind of honed strength that did not require bulk. As he rinsed himself, cascading water sluiced off his broad shoulders, giving her peekaboo views of his contoured back.

He turned, facing her, and her lungs emptied in a dizzying whoosh.

Oh my stars and garters.

Her eyes widened at the sight of his manhood...because, of course, that was where her gaze went. Ogling a naked stranger was beyond improper, yet curiosity and fascination kept her gaze riveted. She'd seen the male anatomy depicted in classical paintings and sculpture and always thought this part of a man looked, well, a bit silly. Like a worm curled upon a wrinkly plum. Yet there was nothing silly at all about this fellow, and his thingamajig wasn't a worm but more of a...a snake. Thick and long, it swayed sinuously between his muscular thighs.

In truth, this part of him matched his outsized masculinity. Chiseled blocks covered his chest and narrowed into tight bands upon his torso. His hips were topped with a vee of sinew. Whorls of hair adorned his chest, narrowing into a trail down his abdomen that pointed straight at his... At that instant, he wrapped his hand around his thingamabob. It *leapt* within his fist, rearing up, its crimson head burgeoning beyond the reach of his grip. When he gave it a rough jerk, she squeaked in surprise.

He whipped his head in her direction. "Who's there?"

Like the crack of a rifle, his voice chased birds into the skies. Gigi ducked behind the rock. She held completely still; it helped that panic paralyzed her. Her thoughts, however, kicked up turf like the horses at the Royal Ascot.

Did he see me? Should I run? Hide?

Being a lady of action, she made a run for it. Staying low and hopefully hidden by the boulders, she moved as quickly as she could. The mud along the bank sucked at her shoes, making squelching noises that she prayed wouldn't give her away. Nearly at the yew tree, she risked a glance behind her. No sign of the man in the pool. Had he gone beneath the water again?

I'll take refuge behind the tree and decide my next steps.

Just as she reached the tree, the Viking materialized in front of her. She skidded to a halt, barely avoiding a collision with his dripping form. How on earth had such a large fellow moved with such stealth?

Not that it mattered: she was well and truly caught.

The realization quivered through her, and she trembled, pressing back against the yew's bark. The stranger faced her, his large bare feet planted in an aggressive stance, his hands braced on his hips. He'd tied a towel around his waist, but it hung rather low and drew attention to the girdle of muscle over his hips. He seemed unconcerned that he was mostly naked and wet, and she wished she could be as indifferent. Up close, she saw his eyes were a riveting sea green. His resemblance to a legendary Norseman was even more evident: he was all twisting sinew and rough edges, battle scars marking his chest and knuckles.

"I thought I heard something," he said.

His voice was husky and deep, less booming than it had been

moments before. This relieved her. She had a talent for reading people, and he didn't seem angry, which he would have every right to be, considering that she had been spying on him like some Peeping Tom...or Thomasina, rather. Since she didn't recognize him from the village, she guessed he was passing by: a sailor, most likely, whose ship was temporarily anchored at the Chuddums docks. Yet his polished accent didn't sound quite like that of a typical seaman...perhaps he was a captain? That would explain his aura of command. Her papa had been a lieutenant-colonel during the war against Boney, and he evinced that same innate authority.

Speaking of Papa, he and Mama are going to murder me if they find out about this.

"What is your name?" the stranger asked.

Apprehension seized Gigi. Everything about the situation spelled "RUINATION" in capital letters. She had to get away as quickly as possible, without this fellow discovering that the only daughter of the Marquess and Marchioness of Blackwood had shamelessly spied upon him while he bathed.

Think of a plan, Gigi. You're good at plans.

He cocked his head. "Don't you talk?"

At that instant, the solution came to her. Thanks to her outfit, she looked like a country maid who'd spent the day doing chores. The only thing that would foil her disguise was her accent.

The best way to protect my identity is to remain silent—to let nothing slip.

Widening her eyes, she shook her head.

He drew his brows together. "You cannot speak?"

She shook her head again.

He studied her. "But you *do* understand me?"

After a moment, she nodded.

"Well, I don't mind silence." A corner of his mouth tipped up lazily. "Truth be told, I could use more of it in my life."

Oh no.

He came closer. Every instinct screamed "*Retreat!*", yet she had nowhere to run. She was caught between the tree and his equally unyielding form. He leaned a big hand on the trunk by her shoulder. His proximity set off a chain of foreign sensations. Her blood rushed beneath her skin, and her bones felt oddly liquid. Even when waltzing, she'd never been this close to a man...never mind one with a bare, rippling chest. A rash of heat spread over her insides.

Her breath unsteady, she contemplated her next move. Screaming would be useless; there was no one to hear her. However, she was no wilting violet and had three older brothers who'd imbued her with useful knowledge. Owen, the closest to her in age, had given the simplest advice: *If some bounder tries to compromise you, poppet, you knee him where it hurts and make a run for it.*

She snuck a peek at the Viking's you-know-what.

Merciful heavens, is that a bulge beneath his towel? Did his male member grow?

On the bright side, the size of her target guaranteed that she would not miss. She tensed and prepared to execute the defensive maneuver.

"You're not scared, are you?" the stranger murmured. "Upon my honor, I've never forced a woman and never will."

Upon my honor. The phrase stayed the upward motion of her knee. When her brothers or papa uttered those words, it meant something because they were gentlemen, and honor was important to them. Was it possible that this fellow also had integrity? His uncouth behavior would argue against it...yet that would be a case of the pot calling the kettle black, wouldn't it? Being a fair-minded person, she knew her own impropriety had contributed to the present fiasco.

Should I trust in this man's honor?

"In exchange for giving you a show, all I ask for is a boon in return."

She squirmed against the tree. She wasn't certain which was

more mortifying: that she'd ogled a naked fellow or that she'd been caught doing it. But she wasn't about to add insult to injury by getting herself compromised.

"I am not asking for anything excessive," he said easily. "Just tit for tat."

Tit for tat? He must be mad. If he thinks I am going to remove my clothes—

As if gleaning her thoughts, he laughed. "I'm not expecting a show, sweetheart. Not that I'm averse if you would like to give me one."

She hoped her narrow-eyed look conveyed her reaction to his suggestion *and* his cheap endearment.

"No show, then." He held up his hands, looking as innocent as a mostly naked, sopping wet Viking could look. "How about a kiss, then? After that, we part ways, no debts between us. You have my word."

Chewing her lip, she considered his proposal. A kiss was a small price to pay to escape the situation and, at two-and-twenty, she wasn't inexperienced. She'd allowed a few suitors to kiss her, and the experiences had been pleasant, if not particularly memorable. She'd wondered why her friends had giggled and blushed as they'd talked about kissing...wondered if she had missed out on something.

Will the Viking's kiss be any different?

Hastily, she tamped down the thought. Obviously, she wasn't *interested* in kissing this stranger. She was only doing it for expediency's sake.

She held up her index finger to emphasize the terms of their bargain.

"One kiss," he confirmed.

A kiss, then I'm off. What could be easier?

She angled her chin up, closed her eyes, and pursed her lips.

She was prepared for the pressure of his mouth on hers. Instead, she felt his hand slide into her hair, his palm cradling the back of her head. Startled, she opened her eyes and saw the gleam in his as he lowered his head. She'd expected his kiss to match his exterior—to be rough and uncivilized—yet he subverted her expectations again.

His lips hovered over hers. While their mouths did not touch, the warm pulse of his breath made her lips tingle. Tension burgeoned between them, her heart hammering.

What is he waiting for?

His warm, masculine scent entered her nostrils and caused her to swallow reflexively. He smelled clean, with a hint of salt and musk, a welcome change from the pungent colognes preferred by most gentlemen. She was acutely aware of his hold on her and his looming strength. He could overpower her so easily. While she ought to have panicked at the realization, instead she felt a strange thrill. Her instincts told her he would not hurt her. He could, but he would not, and the recognition allowed her to melt into the moment.

She swayed, steadying herself with a hand against his chest. Beneath the steely bulge of his pectoral muscle, his heart was a fierce beat beneath her palm. The primal rhythm made her aware of the places where she was throbbing...the tips of her breasts and low in her belly. Startled, she jerked her hand back, her thumb accidentally grazing the flat nub of his nipple. His low growl made her tremble. She parted her lips to draw a breath, and in that instant, he claimed her mouth.

Claimed was the apt word, for she felt owned by this marauder's kiss. While he wasn't forceful, he was persuasive, his mouth learning the contours of hers with a confidence that blurred her thoughts. His kiss was hard yet tender, everything she hadn't known a kiss could be. His firm lips explored her while his grip in her hair held her in place. When he swept his tongue inside her mouth, she stopped thinking entirely.

The bold penetration set off a fusillade of pleasure. Sparks scattered over her skin, heat rushed in her veins, and her limbs shook as he enjoyed her mouth with masterful intention. His flavor saturated her senses—smoky and male, with a hint of unexpected sweetness...cinnamon. He was the most delicious thing she'd ever tasted, and she wanted more. Tentatively, she touched her tongue to his.

His growl reverberated down her throat, setting her insides aquiver. He deepened the kiss, demanding her participation. He licked inside her mouth, and it was so slick and hot and wonderful that she slid her tongue against his with growing confidence. Her senses whirled as he led the carnal dance. Never had she felt this alive, her entire being buzzing with desire...

"Christ, you make me hard."

At his husky words, her eyes popped open. Awareness crashed through her. She was wrapped around the stranger like ivy: her arms were flung around his neck, her breasts squashed against the hard wall of his chest. He had one hand knotted in her hair, and the other was cupping her *bottom*. He gripped her derriere, pulling her tightly against him. Through her skirts, she felt a hard object jutting into her...

Heavens, that's his—

"My cock is harder than a pike for you," he confirmed without a trace of embarrassment. "If we don't stop soon, I'm going to have you—right here, against this bloody tree."

His boldness plopped her back into reality. Horrified, she let go of his neck, shoving at his chest. She wasn't strong enough to move him, which meant she was putting his honor to the test. If he failed to uphold his end of the bargain...

Frantic resolve filled her. *If necessary, I'll revert to my earlier plan—*

"Too much, too soon, sweetheart?"

He released her and stepped back, holding his hands up. Unbelievably, he winked at her. He was *amused* by her discombobulation.

She narrowed her eyes.

Well, pardon me for being unaccustomed to kissing a stranger in the woods.

He, on the other hand, was utterly at ease. Perhaps seducing unsuspecting females was a hobby of his. He stood with his feet planted apart, his hands on his hips, and he made no effort to hide the prominent ridge in his towel. Was he always this supremely confident and, some might say, *arrogant*? The smug curve of his lips suggested that he was used to things going his way.

Come to think of it, he'd lulled her into complacency with his proposal of a kiss. He hadn't mentioned anything about the involvement of tongues, which surely put what they'd done in a different category than mere kissing. She didn't think normal people kissed this way; certainly, none of her admirers had. And the way he'd gripped her bottom, grinding himself against her...

Her face burned as she thought of what she'd permitted.

Of what the Viking had *tricked* her into allowing.

Unfortunately, she couldn't even give him a proper set-down since she was pretending she couldn't talk. She had to settle for an annoyed huff. His sea-green eyes crinkled at the corners as if he found her fuming entertaining.

Get away, Gigi. Before more damage is done.

Her head held high, she walked past him. When he made no move to stop her, she told herself she was relieved. She'd almost made it to the woods when he called out to her.

"I'm sorry we didn't have more time. Things were starting to get interesting."

Pivoting, she risked a glance back. The man hadn't moved, although his amusement had faded, replaced by a look of genuine regret...and something else. Something dark and feral. Something *hungry*.

She felt an answering flutter in her belly. Fear—that had to be it. Shivering, she shook off his snare and fled into the safety of the trees.

Chapter One

Three months later

"Do have a care, dear." Leticia Caldecott's anxious voice floated up to the top of the ladder, where Gigi was precariously balanced. "If you were to fall from that height—"

"There is no need to fret, Miss Letty. I have everything in hand."

Although Gigi spoke in reassuring tones, she wisely did not tempt fate by looking down at her friend. The ladder *was* rather high and rickety, and she needed to concentrate on her task. She was attempting to clean the walls of the spa's bathing hall. Nearly a century ago, Letty's great-great-grandpapa Tobias Caldecott had built the spa. A visit to Bath had shown him the pecuniary potential of water, and he had decided to create his own mecca in Chudleigh Bottoms.

The fact that no Roman had settled in Chuddums did not deter Mr. Caldecott's entrepreneurial spirit. He believed that his property's natural hot springs guaranteed success. He built a Romanesque temple around it, and what his design lacked in authenticity, it compensated for in flamboyance. Chudleigh Bottoms's World Famous Roman Bath boasted more columns and statuary than Bath's Temple at *Aquae Sulis*, and in its prime had attracted crowds who bathed in its pool and took the waters in its pump room.

Unfortunately, over the years, the spa's fortunes had dwindled, and the place had fallen into disrepair. At present, the bathing pool was dry, cracked, and caked with dirt. Letty had drained it so that the stonemason could patch the basin. Behind the pool was a wall covered in a sprawling relief; Gigi was attempting to scrub off the grime that decades had layered onto the sculpted surface. Like the columns around the rectangular bath, the relief was fashioned from wood and plaster rather than expensive stone, and this made cleaning a delicate task. Yet the appearance of hygiene was essential for any business that promoted health, and she was determined to get every inch of the place spotless in readiness for its grand reopening.

As Gigi cleaned, she was getting her first close look at the top portion of the wall. From the ground level, the scene had looked like a typical rendering from Roman mythology. Venus and Mars presided over an idyllic wedding feast in the middle of a forest, with various gods and goddesses present at the banquet table. Cherubs and nymphs danced in celebration.

Upon closer inspection, however, Gigi noted the insidious presence of other guests in the background. Satyrs, horned creatures who were half-man, half-goat, lurked behind rocks and trees. They were lying in wait for the nubile nymphs, whom they chased throughout the scene. Sometimes the females escaped, swimming away in a stream. Other times, the satyrs captured them. Entangled limbs—one pair hairy, the other smooth—protruded from behind several bushes...

The memory of the Viking pounced upon Gigi. Although three months had passed since their encounter, he was a frequent visitor in her dreams. Night after night, he pursued her through the woods. The scenario ought to have been frightening, yet it wasn't fear she felt as she raced through the forest. Or when he caught her, trapping her against a tree. Caged by his bulging arms and sculpted chest, she would stare up into his tempest-tossed eyes.

"*I have you where I want you, sweetheart,*" he'd growled. "*This time, you're going to do more than watch...*"

"Are you certain this is necessary?"

Letty's query broke the spell. Drawing a breath, Gigi shook off her wayward fantasies. She should count herself fortunate that she'd escaped with her virtue intact. For days afterward, she'd both dreaded and anticipated running into the stranger in the village. She hadn't, and if he was a passing sailor like she suspected, she was unlikely to see him again...which was a good thing.

A young lady did not dally with strange seamen, and while Gigi did not strictly follow the rules of propriety, she was careful to maintain the appearance of doing so. Her family had enough troubles to contend with. Since her brother Owen had gone off to war a decade ago, nothing had been the same, and turmoil had besieged her close-knit family. She yearned to help, but since she was the youngest and a female, her parents and brothers insisted on protecting her. They wanted her to enjoy life, unburdened by its harsher realities.

She tried to be the good and proper girl her family deserved. Yet her energies needed an outlet, and during finishing school, she'd dedicated herself to worthy causes. Deciding to raise funds to help children who were forced to do dangerous factory jobs to survive, she'd sold corsages to family and friends. When she couldn't make them fast enough to keep up with demand, she'd recruited peers to help. Eventually, she'd added embroidered handkerchiefs and other items to the group's repertoire. By the time Gigi graduated, she'd organized an annual Charity Bazaar that funded dozens of scholarships for children to learn more desirable vocations.

These endeavors gave Gigi a sense of purpose, and she'd felt that way the first time she had set foot in Chuddums's Roman Bath. She'd also had an inexplicable feeling that her future and that of the spa were somehow intertwined. By helping Letty and Chuddums, she might also be finding her own destiny.

"First impressions are important, Miss Letty," she declared. "Now that the spa is gaining recognition for its waters, visitors will be chomping at the bit to visit the site itself. We must put our best foot forward."

"Thanks to your idea for the 'Chuddums Water Cure,' the spa has been more successful in the past month than it has been in decades," Letty said with gruff appreciation.

Gigi risked looking down and smiling at her friend. A handsome spinster in her fifties, Letty was tall and dignified, her angular figure clad in a practical bombazine dress. Her frizzy, greying hair was bound in a knot, drawing attention to her intelligent blue eyes.

"I didn't come up with the idea for the water," Gigi said modestly. "I borrowed it."

She'd been inspired by her visits to Malvern. The bustling resort town had a dedicated following among the upper and middle classes, who flocked there to partake of the "hydrotherapy cure." Local businesses flourished, and factories employed dozens of workers to bottle the famous Malvern water for export. Her Majesty the Queen famously refused to travel without a supply of her favorite mineral water.

"Whatever the case, you have given me hope," Letty said. "For the first time in years, I believe I may be able to save this place after all."

"You will," Gigi promised. "The spa's reopening will be a smashing success. And no one deserves that more than you."

When Gigi had first seen the spinster in the village, the latter had been dressed in a raggedy frock and bonnet, humbly asking Loretta Pickleworth, the greengrocer's wife, if there was any damaged produce available. The good Mrs. Pickleworth had promptly filled Letty's sack, and Gigi saw her slip in a few perfect apples, too. Letty had made the rounds in the village, purchasing cut-rate goods from the merchants. She'd paused to peer wistfully into the window of the Leaning House, Chuddums's tea shop, before continuing with her shoulders slumped but her head held high.

When Gigi asked about the mysterious woman, Mrs. Pettigrew, the owner of the Leaning House and the village's kindhearted gossip, had filled her in.

"*Leticia Caldecott is the last surviving member of one of Chuddums's oldest families,*" Mrs. Pettigrew had said. "*Miss Letty is a good woman who, through no fault of her own, fell upon hard times. If she sold the spa, her life might be easier, but she refuses to give up her family's legacy.*"

Gigi understood the importance of not giving up on one's family. The Harrington motto was *Ad Finem Fidelis*—faithful to the end—and over the years, that adage had been tested time and again. Determined to help, Gigi had introduced herself to Letty, and despite their outward differences, friendship had blossomed. When Gigi had proposed working at the spa, Letty had been surprised but open to the idea.

Gigi's parents, however, had been less keen.

"*Gigi, darling.*" Mama's violet eyes—eyes she'd given to Gigi—had shone with concern. "*A young lady of your station does not have a job. It simply isn't done.*"

"*This is important,*" Gigi had pleaded. "*Miss Letty needs me.*"

"*Help her in some other fashion,*" Papa had said. "*A donation, perhaps—*"

"*She will not accept charity. Please, let me do this—I have such splendid ideas for how to revive the spa. This will help not only her but Chuddums. Coming here healed Ethan—brought him and Xenia together. Our family is indebted to this village, and it is our duty to help it survive.*"

When her parents had exchanged looks, Gigi had felt a surge of triumph. She knew she'd won with that last point, for a

Harrington always paid his or her debts. In the end, her parents had allowed her to volunteer at the spa, but she had to bring along her maid.

"*I know how you love your projects, Gigi,*" Mama had sighed. "*Try not to get too carried away, all right?*"

Gigi had gone to work straightaway, implementing the first phase of her plan: gaining recognition for Chuddums's mineral water. Malvern's water had become famous after a physician named Dr. Wall declared that it was so pure that it contained "nothing at all." Gigi had set about getting a similar testimony from her family's physician. Once obtained, the next step had involved figuring out the best way to promote the product. Gigi and Letty had tested their ideas on friends and family, but nothing had seemed quite right...until Gigi had hit upon using Chuddums's famous legend, which involved a murder and a curse.

When her brother Ethan had purchased the local manor known as Bottoms House, he'd had difficulty hiring servants because the original owner, a man named Thomas Mulligan, had been shot dead there some eighty-odd years ago. Mulligan's ghost, dubbed "Bloody Thom," was said to haunt the place. According to village lore, Mulligan had offended a witch who'd cursed him and the entire village. In the years since, the decline in Chuddums's fortunes, which included the malignant growth of a criminal element, had been blamed squarely on the curse.

However, Ethan and his housekeeper-turned-bride Xenia had proven that sightings of Bloody Thom had been a hoax perpetuated by the Corrigans, a notorious gang of thieves and cutthroats. Together with the good folk of Chuddums, they had ousted the villains from the village. Now storefronts that had lain vacant for years were reopening with new businesses, and visitors who had once passed Chuddums by were stopping to sample its unique offerings.

Xenia had also unearthed secrets about the origins of Bloody Thom. According to Chuddums's oldest resident, Mr. Walford—

known affectionately as "Wally"—the witch of the legend wasn't a witch at all but a beautiful traveling woman named Rosalinda. As a boy, Wally had seen Rosalinda and Thomas Mulligan together by the stream (the one, as fate would have it, where Gigi had encountered the Viking). To Wally's young eyes, the pair had appeared to be in love. Yet after Mulligan's murder, the villagers, led by prominent citizen Langdon Pearce, had accused Rosalinda and her family of witchcraft. Soon thereafter, Pearce was found collapsed in his house, the cause of his death unknown. The villagers were certain it was because of the witch's curse. But Rosalinda and her family had disappeared, never to be seen in Chuddums again.

As an aficionado of gothic novels, Gigi found the legend thrilling. One night, she'd awoken from a feverish dream—one so intense and real that it hadn't felt like a dream but like a *memory*. Grabbing her drawing pencils, she'd sketched a scene of Mulligan and Rosalinda standing on opposite sides of the stream, gazing at each other like star-crossed lovers. She'd shown Letty her idea for the label, along with the accompanying slogan:

The Chuddums Cure: water as pure as true love.

They printed the label, affixing it to the bottles of water they'd collected from the spring. On her next trip to London, Gigi had taken the samples with her, distributing them to those who came to call upon her and her family. Everyone seemed impressed when she'd told them about the water's health benefits (everyone but her eldest brother James, who'd teased her for having the ability to sell hay to a farmer). Ignoring him, she'd focused on her task, and her efforts soon bore fruit.

The first success came with her friend, Miss Amelia Stanley. After four years on the marriage mart, Miss Stanley hadn't attracted any offers and feared she was destined for the shelf. To inspire her friend, Gigi had shared the tale of Mulligan and Rosalinda, which demonstrated that love could strike when one least expected it. Before she'd finished the story, Miss Stanley had uncorked the bottle of water, gulped it down, and confessed her unrequited feelings for Lord Alvin Neale.

A numismatist, Lord Alvin was known to pay more attention to his coin collection than people. Contrary to Miss Stanley's belief that Lord Alvin found her unattractive, Gigi suspected that he merely hadn't noticed her—or any female—and needed a nudge. Thus, Gigi had filched a coin from her papa's collection and suggested that Miss Stanley use it to strike up a conversation with Lord Alvin. It had taken coaching on Gigi's part, but her shy friend finally took her advice.

Gigi's plan worked better than she could have imagined. Within a month, Lord Alvin proposed, and Miss Stanley was over the moon. She thanked Gigi profusely...and, to the latter's bemusement, attributed her newfound love to the "Chuddums Potion." Miss Stanley shared her experience with friends, and news spread like wildfire through Society. Before Gigi knew what was happening, debutantes, widows, and bachelors alike were knocking on the door of her parents' town house, inquiring after the water. While James had rolled his eyes, Gigi had happily dispensed the rest of her supplies.

Seven more love matches took place.

Gigi began to believe that the water *did* have special properties. After all, when Ethan had retreated to Chuddums after being jilted by his former fiancée, he had sworn off love. Yet within weeks, he'd found his soulmate in Xenia. As Gigi became acquainted with the villagers, she'd also discovered that many of them had found their lifelong loves. Moreover, there was the dream Gigi had about Mulligan and Rosalinda meeting by the stream. The pair had been the most unlikely of lovers, yet their bond had felt so tender and passionate, so *real*...

The Chuddums Potion craze took hold of London, and in the weeks that followed, Letty could scarcely keep up with the flood of orders. She hired a team of women from the village to bottle the water and glue on the labels. She'd also decided to channel the profits into refurbishing the bath for a grand reopening.

Satisfaction filled Gigi.

Everything is going according to plan.

"I think you've done enough cleaning, my dear," Letty said. "Why don't you come down from the ladder?"

Gigi eyed the part of the relief she'd yet to clean. The sculpted surface was buried under mildew and cobwebs. Stretching, she managed to reach the corner, wiping away a layer of dirt.

"I shall," she said. "After I finish cleaning this section."

"Do have a care—"

"I'm fine." She excavated more of the relief. "Tell me how the ledgers look this week."

"Our profits are up. A young lady from London ordered ten crates."

"We must be prepared for an increase in demand," Gigi declared. "Once the Season starts, everyone will want our water."

"I don't know how I'll manage when you're gone."

In two months' time, Papa would be returning to London for the start of the Parliamentary session, and Mama and Gigi would be accompanying him for the social season.

Sensing Letty's worry, Gigi gave her a reassuring smile. "You have employees to assist you, dear. And while I'm in London, I shall promote the spa."

"Shouldn't you be focused on finding yourself a husband?" Letty asked.

Gigi waved her cloth. "There is plenty of time for that."

At two-and-twenty, she'd had her share of offers from eligible *partis*, but none of them had interested her. She was certain she would know when the right fellow came along. Marrying for love was a family tradition, and luckily, her parents wanted no less for her. In the meantime, she had more important matters to focus on.

While Letty wandered off to handle correspondence, Gigi continued scrubbing at a stubborn patch of dirt. From beneath the grime, a long, tubular shape emerged... Her cheeks burned when she realized what lay beneath her hand. Attached to the hairy groin of a satyr, the plaster member was huge and meticulously detailed with veins. Its mushroomed tip thrust toward the ceiling. Not long ago, she would have laughed at the ridiculous proportions of the body part. But the Viking loomed in her mind's eye, and her blood thrummed as she realized that this part of him had been equally sizeable—

"You'll never believe this, Lady Gigi!"

At Letty's voice, Gigi jerked her hand away—too quickly. Her abrupt motion sent the ladder swaying backward, and she held on for dear life as it teetered on rickety legs. Gasping, she leaned forward and tilted the ladder back against the wall. She descended the rungs on shaky limbs. Prepared for an *I-told-you-so* lecture, she was surprised when her friend didn't let out a peep. Looking over, she saw why: with her head bent over a letter, Letty had missed Gigi's death-defying experience.

"What have you there?" Gigi asked.

"It's a letter from a solicitor," the spinster muttered, scanning the page. "I've had an offer."

"An offer for what?"

"For the spa." Letty looked up, her blue eyes glinting with shock. "Someone is offering a fortune to buy it."

Chapter Two

A month later

Conrad Godwin was a man who did not accept failure readily. At one-and-thirty, he had fought for everything he had—literally, since the initial stake for his business had come from his days as a prizefighter. In the ring, he'd never backed down from an opponent, big or small, and he'd taken that philosophy with him into the boardroom. Seven years ago, he'd established his investment firm, Godwin & Co., and his ability to discern a winner from a loser had made him richer than Croesus.

A few months ago, he'd made the move to London, setting up a plush office near the 'Change. He filled it with men of business he'd trained to provide counsel on lucrative schemes. Toffs were curious about him, and his competitors wanted to know his plans, yet he deliberately stayed out of the limelight. Enigma added to his mystique, and the years in the ring had made him a bit of a showman. He would reveal himself, his true self, when the time was right.

When every part of his plan was in place. When he had both

his enemies against the ropes and begging for mercy. Only then would he execute his vengeance.

Anticipation simmered. He was close to achieving the goals he had been working toward for years. A spa, of all things, stood in his path, but he was taking care of that problem in the time-honored tradition: he'd instructed Ezra Marvell, his trusted solicitor, to buy the damned place. The offer was beyond generous for the ramshackle property, but no cost was too great for justice.

While Conrad couldn't claim many virtues, patience was one of them. He'd been plotting his retribution since the ripe age of eight and could wait a few weeks for his schemes to come to fruition. In the meantime, he sought out diversions such as tonight's visit to the Temple of Flora. The exclusive bawdy house was hosting an orgy in celebration of the Roman goddess of fertility and flowers. The *trompe d'oeil* mural on the walls and ceiling transported the viewer to a forest meadow, the effect enhanced by potted plants and silky green carpets.

Like the other patrons, Conrad wore a loose robe and mask to preserve his anonymity. He was seated on a private dais staged to resemble Roman ruins with fallen columns and crawling ivy. He'd reserved the platform because it provided the best view of the room, and he demanded the best. He watched as lightskirts wearing only crowns of flowers danced, flirted, and showed off their skills.

A few feet away, beneath the bower of a fig tree, a woman in a curly red wig was on all fours between two patrons. Her generous breasts jiggled as the men skewered her mouth and cunny. Despite the tasks that occupied her, she noticed Conrad watching and lifted a hand, crooking a finger at him. He had to admire her ambition...and her balance. As he was presently engaged, he shook his head. The whore acknowledged his refusal with a good-natured wink, her attention claimed by another fellow who joined her group.

That was the thing Conrad appreciated about orgies: they

were both intimate and impersonal. One could feel the spark of connection, then nothing at all. There were no ties, no lies, no empty promises. He appreciated the honesty, a rarity when it came to relationships.

Looking down, he clenched his hand in the blonde locks of the naked woman kneeling between his thighs. Isobel Denton's mouth was painted the red of ripe cherries, and she was putting it to good use sucking his cock. Moreover, she'd surprised him by recruiting a lightskirt to share in the task. With his other hand, he sifted through the brunette curls of the prostitute skillfully licking his stones.

As a man who prided himself on self-control, even the combined ministrations weren't enough to make him spend unless he allowed it, and for now, he enjoyed the indolent pleasure. Isobel drew on his shaft, making slurping noises before releasing him with a wet *pop*. In the holes of her red mask, her brown eyes had a lusty glow, and she licked her glossy lips.

"Do you like that, darling?" She breathed the words against the flared dome of his cock. "Two mouths on your meaty prick?"

He assumed this was a rhetorical question. However, during the month they'd been casual bedpartners, he had learned not to trust Isobel's generosity, which usually signaled a desire for something in return. As Isobel liked to be the center of attention, he was certain that her willingness to share came with a hefty price. While he didn't mind *quid pro quo*, he despised manipulation. In business and in life, he never agreed to anything without knowing the terms.

He raised his brows. "Was there something you wanted in return, sweetheart?"

"Must you be so distrustful?" Isobel made a moue. "Why can't I simply want your pleasure?"

"But you want something else as well."

Isobel studied him, obviously debating whether it was time to show her cards. She was a comely widow with ash-blonde hair and a curvaceous figure. Like many bluebloods, she possessed an excellent pedigree but no money to speak of. The first time Conrad had tupped her, she'd mentioned coyly that the lease on her town house had increased and was coming due, and wouldn't it be a pity if she had to leave London? He'd gotten the hint and taken care of her year's rent. Soon thereafter, her modiste's bills had started arriving at his residence, and he'd taken care of those too. He was a generous man when it suited him, and he was, after all, getting what he wanted in return.

He liked high-kick ladies—their soft hands, expensive perfume, and eager cunnies. During his prizefighting days, he'd had his share of them as they'd enjoyed the illicit thrill of dallying with a lower-class lover...which they'd assumed he was. None of the affairs had lasted long. After the women had had their fill of rough and wild between the sheets, they'd left him to search out another novelty, which was all he'd been to them.

Only once had he been stupid enough to want more. From that debacle, he'd come to understand that relationships were no different from business dealings. Everything was a transaction: a negotiation for power or resources. While females might prefer the candy-coating of romance, they knew exactly what game they were playing. Unfortunately for Isobel, he was in no mood for games... at least, not with her.

The country maid darted across his mind's eye. Over three months had passed since their encounter, yet he recalled every detail. God's blood, she had been a looker—easily the most beautiful woman he'd ever laid eyes on. Almost too beautiful to be real. That day, he'd been traveling incognito to surveil Chudleigh Bottoms, which played a vital role in his revenge, and he'd stopped to bathe in a stream. The last thing he'd expected was to run into a water nymph.

At Creavey Hall, the reform school where he'd spent his youth, a lad named Ratterby had smuggled in an erotic book featuring stories from Roman mythology. Ratterby had charged a hefty "borrowing fee," and Conrad had bartered his meals for a week to get his hands on that volume. He still remembered turning those pages with trembling hands, his blood heating and his cock swelling at the explicit words and illustrations.

The maid by the stream had been the spitting image of the heroine of his favorite story, "The Naughty Naiad." The tale told the adventures of a water nymph named Pearl, who was ruthlessly pursued by a satyr named Prickonus. Despised and unloved, lonely old Prick had roamed the countryside looking for a mate, and from the moment he saw Pearl, their fates were sealed.

Each chapter followed a formula. The peerless Pearl would tease the randy satyr, then lead him on a merry chase. Their lusty cat-and-mouse scenes always ended the same way: with Prick capturing Pearl and fucking her in creative variations until she cried her surrender. The story would conclude with Pearl wrapped around the hairy beast, her elegant fingers teasing his untamed mane as she promised never to leave.

Of course, she fled at the first opportunity.

Those illustrations had fueled Conrad's lustful adolescent dreams. He couldn't count the times he'd feverishly frigged himself to images from the book. He had two favorites. One was of Pearl against a tree, her wrists captured in the satyr's powerful grip, her features blissful as he impaled her upon his massive shaft. In the other, she was on her hands and knees, and Prick was shafting her from behind, his hand fisted in her hair as she arched in ecstasy. While the poses were undoubtedly arousing, it was Pearl's expression—one of sweet surrender—that had captured Conrad's imagination.

For those fleeting moments, the nymph had truly belonged to the satyr.

The country maid had shared Pearl's nubile figure and sublimely animated features. He'd wager his fortune that if freed from those thick plaits, her hair would flow down her back in a dark, silken river, just like the nymph's. While the black-and-white drawings hadn't shown the color of Pearl's eyes, the maid's gaze—a shade that made him, a proudly unsentimental man, think of violets in the rain—was mythical perfection. In short, she was his fantasy come to life.

Which was why he hadn't gone back. Fantasies were dangerous. They distracted one from reality and made one vulnerable to folly and failure. He couldn't afford entanglements when all his attention needed to be on his purpose—on getting what he was owed. If he wanted a fantasy nymph, he could purchase the services of one of the whores prancing about. Hell, Isobel would play the role if he asked, especially if he gave her that diamond bracelet she'd been dropping unsubtle hints about.

"Darling," Isobel said throatily.

Kneeling between his thighs, she held his turgid cock, feeding it to the lightskirt. Yes, he decided, he would get her that bracelet. While she didn't have Pearl's willowy form, her arse had a nice jiggle when he plowed her from behind. Perhaps, if he asked, she would even run from him, for nothing aroused him like a good chase. His brief pursuit of the maid through the woods, for instance, had made him harder than rock. Yet he'd promised not to take more than a kiss, and he was a man of his word.

"Hmm?" he asked indulgently.

"I want to share your bed this eve."

He stilled. Isobel continued to pump him languidly while the brunette applied her oral skills.

"I beg your pardon?" he asked.

"I said I want to go home with you tonight."

Frowning, he gave the prostitute's hair a gentle tug. Given the sudden turn in conversation, he didn't want to be distracted—or manipulated—by her talented mouth.

"That's enough," he said.

"You don't find me pleasing, guv?" she asked.

At her crestfallen look, he felt a moment's regret. He did admire her talent.

"You've a delightful mouth, sweetheart," he said. "Tell Mrs. Moddesty to add fifty pounds to my tab for your services."

"Thank you, sir!"

Beaming, the lightskirt headed off...straight into the arms of another customer. Watching her rub her tits against the man's chest, Conrad thought philosophically, *On to the next transaction.*

"It's not such a surprising request, is it?"

Isobel breathed the words against his cockhead. When she swirled her tongue across the broad tip, he grew harder despite himself.

"We've been together for weeks now," she said sultrily. "And I've never set foot in your town house."

That was by design. Conrad saw no reason to bring Isobel into his sanctuary. They usually met at a venue such as this one; on the rare occasions when they rendezvoused at her home, he never stayed the night. What was the point in lingering after the deal was completed? Moreover, after a good fuck, he was relaxed and magnanimous, and prior partners had taken advantage. Aftermath had cost him a fortune in jewels, furs, and other gewgaws.

Isobel, however, had yet to make him come, which was a tactical error on her part. When he was aroused, his mind was sharp and clear. He knew exactly what she was up to.

"We agreed from the outset," he said. "We are casual bedpartners, nothing more."

Isobel pouted, and he had to admit she was good at it. She released his erection, letting it slap against his chiseled stomach. Rising, she crossed her arms under her breasts, the calculated pose pushing up her tits and showing them to distinct advantage.

"I am not asking for a lifetime commitment," she said sarcastically. "Just to stay the night."

"Why?" he said bluntly.

"Why what?"

"Why do you want to spend the night in my bed?"

He was genuinely curious. She was no more a sentimentalist

than he was, and he knew for a fact that she'd shared her bed with others during their time together. So had he. As he was neither a possessive lover nor a hypocrite, he could give a farthing whom she swived. But why angle for intimacy when neither of them were suited for it?

"I want to get to know you better," she said.

He had no interest in knowing Isobel beyond the Biblical sense. He was focused on his goals: on bringing his two enemies to their knees. At present, Chuddums—a ridiculous moniker that suited the mudborough—was a thorn in his side. The success of his plan hinged on the village's downward spiral, and he'd nearly had the place where he wanted it—at rock bottom—when an unexpected resurgence began to unfold.

His neck muscles tightened as he thought of the latest report he'd received. Five new shops had opened in the square, and the local inn was nearing full capacity. The local economy was on the rise, and there was an air of optimism amongst locals who, not long ago, had been despondent about the future. The report attributed the change to two factors. The first was the arrival of some toff named Harrington who'd bought a manor locals believed to be haunted and proved that there was no bloody ghost after all.

Conrad wanted to snort. If the Chuddumites believed in ghosts, they were even stupider than he believed. Yet the "breaking of the curse" had given the villagers dangerous new hope.

Second, the village's oldest business, a spa, was undergoing a revival. Somehow, water from its mineral spring had caught on amongst the fashionable set, and here in London, claims swirled that it was a love potion. Thanks to the success of the water, the owner, Miss Leticia Caldecott, was planning a grand reopening of the bath.

Conrad had acted quickly and expected his solicitor to return soon with good news. He could not allow the spa to flourish and draw in tourists. Tourists brought money. Money brought new businesses, which would fill up the storefronts. An improved economy brought workers and tenants to fill rental properties. The value of Chuddums would be on the rise, and the noose Conrad had carefully slipped around his enemy's neck would loosen.

Not if I can help it. That bastard is going to pay for what he did to my mama and me.

"For heaven's sake, I'm not trying to deprive you of your precious freedom." Obviously assuming his frown was aimed at her, Isobel pouted, planting her hands on her hips. "It's not as if I'm asking you to drink that Chuddums Potion, for heaven's sake."

He gritted his teeth at the mention of the troublesome water.

"You don't believe in that claptrap, do you?" he said coldly.

Isobel sniffed. "What do you take me for, a fool?"

Her lack of sentimentality reassured him. That was why he'd chosen to bed her. That and her sexual appetite.

"I have no desire for love," she said. "I just want to spend a night together. One night. And if you take me home with you, we can do *anything* you want."

The fantasy of fucking the nymph on all fours flitted through his head.

"Winter nights are cold, darling," Isobel coaxed. "Wouldn't it be nice to share a warm bed?"

He didn't know if it was her beseeching expression or the way she was stroking his cock, but he felt himself yielding. He prided himself on self-sufficiency and didn't mind solitude. However, even he had the occasional desire to not wake up alone. What harm could a tumble between his own sheets do?

"One night," he said. "And it changes nothing between us."

"You won't regret it, darling," Isobel cooed.

Chapter Three

"*You're a worthless mongrel. A blight on the bloodline.*"

Although the jeering words filled him with rage, there was nothing he could do. Not with his face in the dirt, his tormentor's boot on the back of his neck. Even if he could get up, he wouldn't win—not against the three of them, all bigger, stronger, and more powerful than he was.

"Your mother's a whore. Say it."

He wouldn't. Not even if they killed him. The heel of the boot cut into his neck, and he felt wetness trickle, his blood mingling with sandy gravel. The boot's downward pressure increased, cutting off his air. Gasping, choking, still he said nothing. Suddenly, he was jerked up to his knees. While one bastard held him by the throat, the leader stood before him.

"Nothing to say, rat?" Robert's gaze blazed with the joy of cruelty. "Kiss the ring, then. Kiss it and say you're sorry for existing, and I'll let you go."

He stared at the ring—the gleaming oval ruby, the scrollwork on the heavy band. It would be easy to give in, but he couldn't do it. Powerless as he was, he could choose not to yield. The kick to the stomach came without warning. Agony exploded.

"Hold him steady," Robert said. "The little sissy needs a lesson."

I will not cry, he told himself. Whatever they do to me, I will not cry.

In the end, he screamed.

Conrad opened his eyes, fully alert, his hands fisted and ready to swing. However, a quick glance revealed that violence was unnecessary: he was alone in his bedchamber. Exhaling a slow breath, he let the shadows fade. He rubbed his hands over his face, relieved that Isobel was not presently beside him. He'd brought her home from the Temple of Flora, and they'd played out one of his fantasies, but the scenario had fallen flat. There'd been nothing nymph-like about Isobel, and she was a shoddy actress. She'd been too lazy to run and too fussy about comfort to enjoy being swived on the carpet.

"The rug will chafe my knees. Forget the games and fuck me," she'd cajoled.

He'd given up and obliged her. She bore no resemblance to his fantasy female anyway, and no amount of chasing her around would change that. Thus, he had plowed her in bed and, after they both spent, rolled to his side of the mattress and fallen asleep.

Sitting up, he ran a hand through his hair and wondered where Isobel had gone. Seeing the closed door of his attached bathing room, he guessed she was inside. His gaze veered to the pile of clothing on the carpet. Noting her garments entwined with his, he sighed. It had been too much to hope that she was getting dressed and ready to leave. The chamber smelled of sex and cloying rose perfume. Isobel had wanted champagne at some point, and the sour note of alcohol added to the pungency. The mix of smells was familiar—what he privately termed *Eau de Regret*.

Grunting, he flopped back down and draped an arm over his

eyes. He cursed himself for giving in to Isobel. Now he had to deal with her in the light of day when she was someone he only got on with in the dark. He'd had a rare moment of weakness last night, and he knew the cause of it: the country maid. Dwelling upon her had stirred his adolescent fantasies...desires he hadn't felt in a long time. Not since his ill-fated affair with Lady Victoria Jordan five years ago. He knew the folly of his secret longings. Life had taught him repeatedly not to trust a woman's promises, even—nay, *especially*—if the woman claimed to love him.

I'll come back for you, his mother had said. *I promise, darling. Your stay at Creavey Hall will be temporary.*

Temporary had turned out to be ten years, and he'd never seen her again.

Annoyed at the direction of his thoughts, he turned onto his side. What the bloody hell was wrong with him? He was no maudlin fool, yet that country maid clung to his imagination like the sticky, reddish streamside mud had to his boots (his valet had complained for weeks after). She stirred up stupid, irrational longings. It was her fault that he'd taken Isobel to his bed because he'd wanted, in that moment, to feel less...less alone.

Less like an unwanted beast running around in the dark with a raging cockstand.

Now he would pay for his decision because he was stuck with Isobel. At minimum, courtesy dictated that he should offer her breakfast. Talking to her would be unavoidable, and he'd never enjoyed her conversation, which consisted mostly of gossip. Outside of bed, they had little in common.

No, he didn't have the patience for her this morning. Then the idea struck him, and he felt instant relief. Yes, jewelry would do the trick. He would say that he had to leave for an early meeting and, in lieu of his company, he would send her to Garrard to pick out a trinket. She would be dashing out the door in no time.

Pleased with his stratagem, he wondered what the hell was taking her so long in the bathing room. He decided to hasten the process and went to rap on the door. When no answer came, he looked inside.

No Isobel.

His nape prickled, and since his instincts rarely steered him wrong, he shoved his feet into slippers, donned a robe, and exited his bedchamber. He descended the mahogany staircase, listening for unusual sounds. He followed them to his study, and his tension grew when he saw that the door was ajar. He pushed it open. Isobel, dressed in one of his dressing gowns, was at his desk, rifling through one of the drawers. She jerked upright as he crossed the navy and gold Kidderminster carpet to face her.

"What the bloody hell are you doing?" he demanded.

"Conrad." She gave an uneasy laugh. "You startled me."

"What are you looking for?" he said coldly. "Who paid you to spy on me?"

She regained her composure with an ease that made him revise his earlier assessment of her acting skills.

"I don't know what you are talking about, darling," she said coyly. "Since I woke up early, I couldn't resist giving myself a tour. I didn't think you would mind. Your home is so grand that I got lost and wandered in here—"

"And decided to pick the lock to my desk?"

Tossing her hair over her shoulders, she traded her mask of innocence for one of outrage.

"How dare you accuse me of such a thing?"

He'd definitely underestimated her dramatic ability. If only she had applied herself more while playing the role of the nymph.

"I always secure my drawers," he said evenly. "If I were to search your person, would I find a lock pick?"

Fear flashed in her eyes, but she held onto her bravado.

"You are an unfeeling bastard," she hissed. "I will not stay and be slandered in such a fashion."

When she tried to move past him, he blocked her exit.

"You are not leaving until you tell me who hired you to snoop in my affairs." He took her by the arm. "Was it Trowbridge? Smedley?"

Fellow industrialists Arnold Trowbridge and John Smedley were Conrad's fiercest competitors, and both had bones to pick with him. Last year, Conrad had outmaneuvered Trowbridge during a deal involving factories in Sheffield. The tidy profit he'd made selling off the works had resulted in the other man barging into his offices, uttering threats. As for Smedley, Conrad had gotten wind that the other had sent spies to infiltrate his business. Conrad had deliberately circulated false information, and when Smedley had acted upon it, he'd lost a fortune. A few weeks later, a blaze had erupted at Conrad's offices in Manchester, and while he'd lacked concrete proof of Smedley's involvement, his gut told him the fire had been no accident but an act of retaliation.

"I don't know those men." Isobel's breath hitched. "You... you're hurting me."

He realized that he'd tightened his grip on her arm. With an oath, he released her. He did not hurt women, and Isobel was merely doing someone else's dirty work. Luckily, she'd only gained access to a drawer of his desk. He secured his most important documents in a strongbox hidden in the wall.

"I have a message for whoever you are spying for," he said.

Her gaze darted, a telltale sign. "I told you I'm not spying—"

"I will find out who they are. And they will regret it when I do."

She blanched.

He yanked on the bell. Within moments, his butler Yardley appeared. He'd hired Yardley for two reasons: the fellow's discretion and the fact that he was built like a brick tower.

Yardley bowed, his thick, brown hair gleaming. "How may I be of assistance, sir?"

"Keep an eye on Mrs. Denton while she collects her things," Conrad said. "Then escort her out."

"This way, madam," Yardley said.

Isobel kept her head held high as the butler marched her out.

When the door closed behind them, Conrad examined his desk. Nothing looked out of place on the organized blotter. The drawer that Isobel had managed to open contained a report he'd asked his chief manager, Lionel Redgrave, to compile on failing works that might be worth investing in. All of it was public information, and even if Isobel managed to recall the dozen-plus businesses and conveyed them to Trowbridge or Smedley, it would not be the end of the world. However, Conrad's jaw tautened when he saw the file peeping beneath; it was labeled "Chudleigh Bottoms Spa" and contained his research.

Did Isobel see this file? Will she mention my interest in the spa to the bounder who hired her?

Exhaling, Conrad told himself it mattered naught. Even if his competitors learned of his interest in the spa, they would assume it was for business reasons. No one knew about his personal motivations. Not even his solicitor Marvell, who knew more about his past than anyone since he had needed the fellow's legal expertise on the matter of his birthright. While he had thoroughly vetted Marvell and the others who worked for him, he furnished only the necessary information. As far as he was concerned, less was more when it came to knowledge about his private affairs.

His secrets were his own…until he chose to reveal them.

He went upstairs to get ready for the day. His valet was putting on his cuff links when Yardley informed him that Marvell had arrived.

Finally, some good news.

The solicitor's early return from Chuddums must mean that he'd negotiated the purchase of the spa. With the business under his control, Conrad could shut it down and seal the fate of Chuddums.

"Tell him I'll be down shortly. By the by." Conrad cocked a brow. "Did Mrs. Denton go quietly?"

"I believe she had a few opinions." Yardley cleared his throat. "About the status of your parentage. Or, ahem, the lack thereof."

He smiled without humor. "I've been called worse. In case I did not make it clear, she is not to be allowed on the premises again."

"Understood, sir."

When Conrad strode into his study, Marvell shot up from his seat. Despite being in his fifties, the solicitor had no grey in his short, brown-black hair. He'd always reminded Conrad of a mole with his pale, twitchy nose and habit of squinting through his spectacles. Marvell's looks belied the fact that he was a top-notch negotiator who had a habit of getting things done. However, he looked more nervous than usual, and Conrad's mood soured.

"Don't tell me that Caldecott woman refused to sell?" Conrad demanded.

Marvell scrunched his nose. "I did all that I could, Mr. Godwin. After she rejected the written offer, I personally delivered a higher bid to her. She turned that down, too. When I doubled *that* offer, she said, and I quote, '*I will never sell this spa.*' Rather dramatic, I daresay, but those were her words."

Bloody hell. If you want a thing done, do it yourself.

"Never say never," he said.

The solicitor blinked. "But she ejected me from her property and told me not to return—"

"You are not going to the spa, Marvell," Conrad said grimly. "I am."

Chapter Four

"The place is shipshape, Miss Letty." Abel Pearce looked around the spa's pump room with approval. "You have restored it to its former glory."

A stocky fellow with thinning fair hair and an aggressively large mustache, Mr. Pearce was the largest landowner in Chuddums. Most of the businesses in the square were his tenants. The villagers treated him with deference due to his economic influence and his status as the head of one of Chuddums's oldest families. When he and his wife Dorothy had stopped by on an unannounced visit, Letty had dropped everything to give them a tour, and Gigi had followed along.

"Thank you, sir." Pride filled Letty's voice, which echoed in the high-ceilinged space. "My greatest wish is to make my great-great-grandpapa proud."

Gigi thought her friend had accomplished that and more. Once again, the pump room had an air of grandeur with large, sparkling windows and columns soaring to the upper gallery. Atop the columns were statues of Roman gods and goddesses. Jupiter, Hera, Minerva, Bacchus, Venus, and Mars formed a ring around the room, staring down at visitors with majestic grace. The parqueted wood floor had been polished to a gleam. At the far end, the pump, newly repainted a glossy black, was primed to dispense warm mineral water directly from the source.

"It isn't easy living up to our esteemed ancestors," Mr. Pearce said. "When my own great-great-grandpapa, Langdon Pearce, built his textile mill here, he brought prosperity to our village. He was great cronies with Tobias Caldecott, I'm told."

"I remember my papa telling me the two had an entrepreneurial spirit in common," Letty said fondly. "Apparently, your relative was the only one who didn't laugh at mine when he announced his plans to build a spa, complete with a caldarium."

"What is a caldarium?" Gigi cut in.

"A heated chamber," Letty explained. "The Romans used them for relaxation and purification purposes. But they require a feat of engineering, and if my great-great-grandpapa ever started building one, it must have been destroyed by the fire that nearly claimed this place some eighty years ago."

"You can't blame a fellow for dreaming big, can you?" Mr. Pearce said heartily.

"Thanks to my husband's generosity, Miss Letty," his wife said in her nasally tone, "your wish to preserve your family legacy may indeed be coming true."

A thin spike of a woman, Dorothy Pearce was possessed of an unshakeable faith in her own importance. Today she wore an excessively ruffled, flounced, and beribboned dress of fawn-colored velvet. Feathers exploded from the bonnet which sat atop her coal-black ringlets. Her outfit matched the ostentation of her husband's, which included a blinding constellation of gold fobs and buttons.

"I have always appreciated Mr. Pearce's support," Letty said humbly.

Letty had told Gigi that, a few years ago, she had taken a sizeable loan from Mr. Pearce to keep her doors open. Since he was charging interest at the rate of twelve percent, he was hardly running a charity, despite what his wife was implying. Even with the spa's current profitability, it would take Letty years to pay off what she owed.

Yet fate had given Letty an easy solution: a solicitor named Mr. Marvell, representing the interests of Empire Investment Co., had recently offered her a thousand pounds for the spa. Gigi had asked her eldest brother James, who had the financial brains in the family, to look into the company. All he could discover was that it had a history of purchasing failing businesses at low cost and selling them off for profit.

Progress at the expense of people, James had said with disgust. *That seems to be the way of it with these industrialists and financiers.*

If Letty had accepted that offer, she would be rich and carefree. Instead, she'd chosen to protect her family legacy. She believed in the value of the spa to the community and in Chuddums. From Gigi's perspective, it was Mr. Pearce who owed Letty, not the other way around. Rumor had it that he was mired in debt due to years of vacancies and plunging land values, as well as his profligate lifestyle. There was fear that he might have to sell off his properties piece by piece, destroying the fabric of the village. Luckily, the spa was bringing commerce back...even if he and his wife were taking credit for the positive change.

"Chudleigh Bottoms is indebted to my husband," Mrs. Pearce declared. "Dear Mr. Pearce has campaigned tirelessly on behalf of the village, touting its finer attributes to his influential friends in London. You have him to thank for your gala guest list, Miss Letty."

Gigi had to bite her tongue because *she* had sent dozens of invitations to her family's friends and acquaintances in Town, many of whom had promised to attend.

"I believe that is why my project to honor my husband as a living hero of this village was so well received," Mrs. Pearce went on. "Indeed, Lady Georgiana, I was particularly gratified by your brother's donation. Because of Lord Ethan's generosity, the tribute to Mr. Pearce was constructed of the finest Peterhead granite."

Since Gigi knew that Ethan would pay any amount to be rid of Mrs. Pearce's company, she said blandly, "He was happy to contribute."

"The presence of your family elevates our little village," Mrs. Pearce gushed. "Will your parents, the marquess and marchioness, be returning soon?"

"Yes, ma'am. Mama and Papa are vacationing in the Cotswolds for a few weeks, but they promised to be back for the reopening of the spa."

"How splendid." Mrs. Pearce gave her a conspiratorial look. "Between you and me, Chuddums could use more of the Quality and less of, ahem, the other sort."

Despite her discomfort, Gigi managed to keep her polite expression in place. This came from years of dealing with social climbers. She didn't know which she found more irritating: Mrs. Pearce's need to douse her with the butter boat or to put down decent folk like Letty.

"I must compliment your promenade dress *en redingote*," Mrs. Pearce prattled on. "The salmon-pink merino paired with brown velvet piping is ever so becoming. It is from London, I assume? The work of Madame Dubois, perhaps? I've attempted to get on her waitlist several times, but, alas, it is *always* full."

"Actually," Gigi said brightly, "this dress is the product of our very own Mrs. Sommers. Is she not talented?"

Mrs. Sommers owned the village dress shop. She and Mr. Duffield, the draper, kept abreast of the latest fashions and ensured that Gigi's locally made garments were as stylish as any from London. Gigi looked forward to her visits to the dressmaker not just because of the lovely clothes. Mrs. Sommers had an inexhaustible supply of nieces who cycled through her shop as assistants. The young women were lively, full of gossip, and obsessed with beaux and flirtations. Mattie, the current niece-apprentice, always had amusing stories to share.

"You should take your cue from this young lady, Mrs. Pearce." Mr. Pearce winked at Gigi. "By patronizing our local shops, you'll save me those outrageous bills from London. There's nothing wrong with keeping the wealth here in Chuddums, eh?"

<hr />

"Well, that was exhausting," Gigi said.

"Are you tired, dear?" Letty fretted. "You've overtaxed yourself on my behalf—"

"I was referring to Mrs. Pearce."

"Oh." Letty's lips quivered. "She has taken a rather keen interest in you."

"If she invites me one more time to her 'Ladies of Quality' meeting—which, I'm told, spends its time discussing all those who *don't* belong to the group—I shall throw myself over a bridge," Gigi vowed.

Letty laughed. "If you plan on getting soaked, I have a better suggestion. Would you like to be the first to try the bath? You still have a half-hour before your sister-in-law comes to fetch you."

She gestured at the pool, which the village stonemason had restored to its former glory. The limestone basin had been scrubbed clean and leaks in the lining patched and filled. The pipes had been opened, and water filled the long rectangular pool, steam drifting lazily toward the skylights above. The spectacular scene was completed by the pristine columns and relief.

"I was hoping you would offer," Gigi said gleefully. "I brought a bathing suit with me."

"Enjoy yourself, dear. You've earned it." Letty patted her cheek. "None of this would be possible without you."

While Letty went to conquer her to-do list, Gigi changed into her bathing suit. The ensemble consisted of two pieces: a navy, knee-length flannel tunic with long sleeves and a pair of pantalettes that extended to her ankle. The top and bottom were decorated with jaunty yellow ribbon rosettes and ruffles at the cuffs and hem. Returning to the pool, Gigi eagerly descended the wide steps that led into the water. She made a sound of delight as warm, silky water engulfed her.

Unfortunately, when she tried to swim, her heavy costume bogged her down, and she had to satisfy herself with prancing along the length of the pool. After a while, she grew tired of the restriction and yearned to move more freely. She was an excellent swimmer. As a girl, she'd snuck off to swim in the stream on her family's estate, wearing just her chemise. Of course, there'd been no one to see her...but who was here to see her now? The spa was closed, and Letty wouldn't care if she removed her pantalettes.

Getting out of the pool, Gigi peered around furtively before untying the flannel pants and stepping out of them. They made a rude sound like passing wind as they fell to the ground, and she snickered. Feeling a hundred pounds lighter, she went to the deepest side of the pool and dove in. She cut cleanly into the water, hardly making a splash. Although the tunic was restrictive, she could at least move her legs, propelling herself through the water. She did a few laps, exhilarated by her newfound freedom. When she got tired, she turned over onto her back and floated. Gazing up at the rising columns and flickering wall sconces, she lost herself in a daydream.

She was a Byzantine princess, enjoying a bath. Unbeknownst to her, one of the Varangian guards—Viking warriors who served as mercenaries for the king—was spying on her bathing. She experienced a frisson of excitement at being secretly admired. One day, he would step out from behind a column and say in his deep, gravelly voice, "*I have been waiting to declare myself to you, princess...*"

Her pulse thrummed as the star-crossed lovers' romance

unfolded in her head. Every day, they would meet at the bath. Then, one day, they would share a kiss...

Suddenly, a face came into her view.

She blinked...*but the Viking was still there.*

His wild-as-the-sea eyes glinted down at her as he flashed a wicked smile.

"Well, if it isn't the water nymph," he said.

Conrad's annoyance faded the instant he saw the young woman in the pool. He recognized her immediately: she swam like he imagined a naiad would. Even hampered by a bathing suit, she moved gracefully through the water...although, oh ho, it appeared her legs were unencumbered. As he stalked her through the columns, he caught the flash of her long, slender limbs.

By Jove, she has a fine pair of legs.

What an unexpected treat this was. He'd been looking for a stubborn spinster and instead found a nubile, half-clothed nymph. Was the girl a servant here? Sneaking in a swim while her employer was away?

Then and there, Conrad reversed his prior decision to avoid her. Bedding her was clearly a superior strategy. Once he had her, his interest would wear off, the way it had with other lovers. This woman was like any other, one who might prove a pleasant diversion during his hopefully short visit to this godforsaken village. He would invite her to supper and back to his room at the inn. When she flipped over, floating gracefully on her back, he made his move and went to the edge of the pool.

"Well, if it isn't the water nymph," he said.

Her eyes, the same vivid violet as they'd been in his filthiest fantasies, widened. The next instant, her exquisite legs vanished from view with a splash. She stood, staring up at him.

"What in heavens are *you* doing here?" she asked.

Oh ho, again. His nymph did speak. Her voice was as beautiful as the rest of her…and, he registered with a frown, *cultured*. Her accent was undeniably the product of generations of breeding, the kind that elocution lessons could not buy. He knew this because, to please his papa, his mama had tried desperately to polish up her accent. She'd succeeded to some degree, but certain vowels always betrayed her. His stepbrothers had mocked her, saying she sounded like a shopgirl.

"I said, what is your purpose here?"

If this young lady's accent hadn't betrayed her origins, then her expression would have. Even though she was standing in a pool dressed in a wet tunic, her damp tresses tumbling down her back, she carried herself like a duchess.

"You talk," he murmured.

"And you, sir, apparently do not answer questions," she retorted.

Yes, a duchess through and through.

Enjoying her spirit more than he should, he said easily, "Before we get to that, introductions are necessary, don't you think? I am Conrad Godwin."

She canted her head. "The name sounds familiar."

"I am an industrialist, and my projects have done passably well. Perhaps you've read about me in the papers."

After a moment, her gaze turned speculative. "I have read about you. You're *that* Godwin."

Used to having his accomplishments recognized, he bestowed a genial smile upon her. "Indeed, I am—"

"The one who tore down three blocks of tenements in London to build factories and left hundreds without a roof over their heads."

He stopped smiling. "Those buildings were fit to be condemned—"

"The one who bought those mills in Manchester and closed

them down, costing dozens of workers their livelihoods. Your actions caused riots."

"The workers caused the riots," he said, annoyed. "*I* simply took over businesses that were not performing and made them profitable."

"By shutting them down."

"By establishing lucrative enterprises in their place."

"Rather cold-blooded and mercenary reasoning, don't you think?"

"I think," he said through his teeth, "that a lady like yourself would not understand a man's business."

She crossed her arms over her bosom. Thanks to her clinging tunic, he could see her tits were perfection. Unfortunately, he couldn't claim the same about her attitude.

"That solicitor who came. Mr. Marvell," she said. "Does he work for you?"

She wasn't stupid, he'd give her that.

He saw no reason to lie. "He does."

"Well, Miss Caldecott already refused your offer."

He cocked his brow. "How is that any business of yours, Miss...?"

"I am Miss Caldecott's friend, and I know how much the spa means to her and to this village." She gave him a look that would have put Joan of Arc to shame. "I will not stand by and watch some unfeeling financier destroy it for the sake of profit."

When she lifted her chin, he didn't know if he wanted to shake her or swive her. Who *was* this woman? Someone who had a reputation to protect, he guessed. Then again, so did he. The last thing he wanted was to compromise some milk-fed miss and find himself caught in the Parson's mousetrap. He needed every ounce of his focus on one thing: achieving his vengeance.

Inhaling, he took a step back. "Don't you have a chaperone?"

"I didn't need one until you interrupted my private swim," she said loftily.

"What about that day at the stream?"

He had her there, and she knew it. The roses in her cheeks acknowledged his point.

Nonetheless, she didn't back down. "If you would kindly turn around, I shall restore myself to rights."

"By restore yourself to rights, do you mean you'll put on your drawers?"

Her eyes flashed. "Must you be so crude?"

He didn't know why he was enjoying needling her. If he were wise, he would let her get dressed and find the spinster. Then he would buy the spa and get out of this bothersome place. Yet he found this woman irrationally intriguing. She had spirit and fire... and, if the abandoned drawers by the pool's edge were any indication, an enticing streak of impropriety.

Beneath his frock coat, he was getting hard.

"It is the nature of cold-blooded mercenaries such as myself, I'm afraid." He issued a mocking bow before turning around. "My back is turned as requested."

Hearing the sloshing sounds she made, he paused before twisting his head subtly around. To be fair, he hadn't promised not to sneak a peek. As he admired her shapely legs, which she was trying to hurriedly jam into the wet, uncooperative drawers, she lost her balance. She hopped, one foot caught in the pantalettes, the other losing purchase on the slippery surface. Arms flailing, she let out a squeak as she toppled backward toward the pool.

He moved, catching her in the nick of time. Their gazes locked, and he felt every inch of her wet form plastered against his. Her curves fit perfectly against his edges. One hard edge, in particular, was jutting into the soft cove between her legs...her *naked* legs.

His blood pounded in his veins. Her tunic had ridden up, and she was straddling his thigh. Bleeding hell, was that the soft, damp heat of her pussy he felt through his trousers? He was tempted to find out...but unfortunately, she seemed to be in a state of shock.

"Are you all right?" he murmured.

She gazed up at him, and he was mesmerized by those fathomless violet pools. Then she let out a breath, and his gaze was drawn to her mouth. It was the color of a rose-flavored Turkish delight and, he recalled, even sweeter. When she parted her lips, heat surged through him, for he knew an invitation when it was offered.

Ravenous for another taste of her, he bent his head and took her mouth. Devil and damn, she was even more delectable than he remembered. With a hungry growl, he deepened the kiss, sweeping his tongue inside her dewy cavern—

A voice rang through the chamber. "Gigi! What in *heaven's name* is going on?"

Chapter Five

As the carriage rolled away from the spa, Gigi saw her sister-in-law's mouth open.

"Please don't lecture me, Xenia," Gigi blurted. "I know what you witnessed was highly improper, and I was a ninny for allowing it to happen."

Smoothing out her muted tartan skirts, Xenia gave her a wry look.

"As I am your senior by a mere year and no paragon of virtue myself, I was hardly going to deliver a sermon."

Gigi exhaled, grateful that she'd gained both a lovely relation and a friend in Xenia. Sensible and sweet, the petite redhead had once worked as Ethan's housekeeper. She had resisted the relationship because she felt she did not fit in her employer's upper-class world. The pair had tried to hide their attraction, but Gigi had sensed their connection and tried to nudge things along.

In marrying for love, Ethan had followed the family tradition. Thinking of love, Gigi squirmed against the velvet squabs. That was certainly *not* what she felt for the Vik—that is, for Conrad Godwin. Yet she'd allowed him to kiss her...again. Why had she done that?

Because you're a hussy? her inner voice suggested.

She decided to contemplate that revelation about herself later. Or perhaps never. While she didn't always adhere to the rules of propriety, she tried not to cause her family worry. They had enough concerns, and she didn't want to add to their burden.

"As I promised your mama that I would look after you in her absence, I must ask what happened." Xenia studied her with earnest brown eyes. "Who was that man? Do you know him? Why were you so, ahem, familiar with him?"

"His name is Conrad Godwin, and he just introduced himself to me." This was not a lie; she *had* only learned the Viking's identity. "I was testing out the pool, and he appeared out of nowhere. He was looking for Miss Letty as he wants to buy her spa."

Gigi gnawed on her lower lip. What if Mr. Godwin convinced Letty to sell? He struck Gigi as a man who was used to getting his way.

"Oh, Xenia, I do wish you had let me stay and support Miss Letty—"

"You were scantily dressed and in a stranger's arms. How could I let you stay?" Xenia's brow pleated. "While I don't come from your social sphere, Gigi, even I know this situation could cause irreparable damage to your reputation. This is my fault. I shouldn't have left you alone. I don't know how I shall tell Ethan. And your parents—"

"But you don't *have* to tell them, do you?" Gigi said beseechingly.

Xenia frowned. "You're not suggesting that I keep a secret from Ethan?"

"Of course not." Gigi sighed; she would never wish to be a source of conflict. "But Mr. Godwin and I were alone, and no one else was there—"

"Do not remind me," Xenia muttered. "Your mama would have my head if she knew about my lapse in chaperonage."

"Mama would never blame you. She adores you. We all do."

Xenia's tremulous smile spoke volumes about what it meant to her to be welcomed into the Harrington fold. Knowing how Xenia had suffered at the hands of the woman who'd birthed her, Gigi didn't blame her one bit. Nonetheless, she pressed her advantage.

"My point is that there was no one to witness what transpired between Mr. Godwin and me, which I assure you, appeared much more incriminating than it was. I slipped, you see, and he caught me—"

"And his mouth accidentally landed on yours?"

Gigi had the grace to blush. "Um..."

Xenia drew her brows together. "You are not interested in this fellow, are you?"

"Of course not. How could I be? Like I said, we were only introduced today."

While Gigi hated not being entirely truthful, she couldn't bring herself to disclose the encounter at the stream. It felt too private. For months, the Viking had fueled her secret fantasies—fantasies that were too wicked and mortifying to share with anyone, even Xenia.

Although the object of your fantasies is not a Viking, is he? Her inner voice was awfully chatty today. *Conrad Godwin is a ruthless businessman who has his sights set on Letty's property. While the offers his solicitor made seemed generous, he must believe that he can sell it at a profit. Perhaps he means to tear the spa down to build factories or some such thing. For financial gain, he would destroy Chuddums without a second thought.*

"He seemed rather taken with you," Xenia said.

"It was an accident. At the time, he was trying to help... although now he is probably trying to fleece Miss Letty out of her property. Please, *please* can't we go back and—"

"We are almost home. We shall talk to Ethan about the situation, and if he agrees to escort you back—"

"He will never agree to it," Gigi said darkly. "He's more likely to call Mr. Godwin out. Then we'll have to worry about Ethan getting hurt."

"Ethan can take care of himself."

At Xenia's tart tone, Gigi wanted to kick herself for being thoughtless.

"I didn't mean to imply that he couldn't," she said contritely. "Despite his injury, I know Ethan is capable of managing things."

Three years ago, during a drunken fit, Owen had injured Ethan's hand, ending the latter's career as a piano virtuoso. The rift between the two had nearly torn the family apart, and while Gigi had yearned to help her brothers patch things up, neither took her, their baby sister, very seriously. She'd hated watching the people she loved suffer and being helpless to do anything about it.

Truth be told, the feeling was not new. When Owen had bought his commission and left to fight in Afghanistan, she'd only been twelve years old. After the disastrous retreat from Kabul, he'd been declared missing and likely dead, along with the rest of the English army. Despite their grief and shock, the family hadn't given up on Owen. Gigi's parents and brothers had taken turns searching for him in Kabul. Despite begging to be included, Gigi had had to stay home and wait. All she could do was pray every night for Owen's safe return.

The day Owen returned was one of the happiest in her life.

However, she and the rest of the family soon discovered that the Owen who'd come back to them was not the same one who left. Not that it mattered. *Ad Finem Fidelis* was the Harrington motto, and she would do anything to help her brother heal. After Owen had injured Ethan, she'd done her best to bring the family back together again. Since Ethan had become a solitary curmudgeon and retreated to Chuddums, she'd concocted a scheme to follow him there.

To her delight, she'd found Ethan improved, thanks to his pretty new housekeeper. Gigi had managed to pull the other family members to Chuddums, and secure in his newfound happiness, Ethan had forgiven Owen for what the latter had done...even if, Gigi suspected, Owen had not forgiven himself. Nonetheless, it was a step in the right direction, and Gigi hoped that, with time, her family's wounds would be fully healed.

"I know you have faith in Ethan, Gigi." Xenia's expression softened. "Which is why you must tell him about this Godwin fellow. As I've said, I know next to nothing of the upper crust's rules, and if your brother judges that the situation will not harm your reputation, then I am certain he will escort you back to the spa himself."

"Mr. Godwin could be gone by then. With the deed to the spa in his pocket!"

"While I do not know Miss Letty as well as you, she strikes me as a woman who knows her own mind. She will not be pushed in to doing something she does not wish to do."

Letty *did* have a spine of steel. Nonetheless...

"What if he offers her gobs of money? From what I've read, he's richer than Croesus."

"If Miss Letty wants his gobs of money, don't you wish for her to have it?"

"I suppose." Gigi expelled a breath. "What sort of friend would I be if I didn't support her choices? It is just that she and I have worked so hard to restore the spa. Now it's nearly ready, and I know if given a chance, the place will thrive *and* bring Chuddums the recognition it deserves."

"You've grown attached to Chuddums, haven't you?"

"From the start, coming here felt like coming home," Gigi admitted. "I cannot explain it."

"You do not have to, dear." A smile tucked into Xenia's cheeks, and she reached over to squeeze Gigi's hand. "For I felt the same way."

As Brunswick, the butler, ushered them into Ethan and Xenia's beautifully restored manor, Gigi immediately felt the tension in the air. For years, locals had claimed that Bottoms House was haunted, and even after the sightings of Bloody Thom had proved to be a hoax, Gigi believed that there was a *presence* in the manor. It was like an invisible, spiritual miasma that heightened one's awareness of feelings.

Gigi had always been intuitive, but here in the manor she felt everything more keenly. The passionate and nurturing love between Ethan and Xenia. The abiding devotion between her parents and their relief that Ethan had found the woman of his dreams and happiness at long last. Gigi even sensed undercurrents from James, who typically hid his emotions behind stoicism and dry wit. Honestly, it was unsettling to realize that her confident, eldest brother and responsible heir was a bit…lost.

It was Owen, however, who concerned her the most. Before the war, he'd worn his emotions on his sleeve, and now his youthful exuberance had been tempered into something darker and harder, with lethal edges that could hurt anyone who dared to come near…as Ethan had learned at great cost. Most of the time, Owen's pain was a blade turned inward, and at that moment, in the unnatural stillness, Gigi felt his emotions bleeding through the manor.

"Has something happened, Brunswick?" Xenia said worriedly.

Gigi was not surprised that her sister-in-law sensed it too. Brunswick, who'd been with Ethan for as long as Gigi could recall, was a mastiff of a fellow with deep wrinkles and sagging jowls. His gruff manner belied a gentle heart. When she was younger, he'd given her comfits whenever she visited Ethan in London.

"I'm afraid there was a disagreement, my lady," Brunswick said gloomily. "Between the master and Lord Owen."

"Is Ethan in his study?" Gigi asked.

Xenia did not wait for an answer, hurrying toward Ethan's private sanctuary without bothering to remove her gloves or coat.

Alone with Brunswick, Gigi said, "How bad was it?"

"Not the worst it has been," Brunswick replied.

"I hope that is not your best attempt at optimism."

The butler sighed. "But it is the worst argument they've had since Lord Owen came to stay."

"What did my brothers fight over this time?" she asked quietly.

Brunswick hesitated, his loyalty ingrained.

"The master had planned to go riding with Lord Owen this morning," he said. "When Lord Owen did not come down, Lord Ethan went to his bedchamber. From what I could gather, Lord Owen had been drinking last night."

Icy dread percolated through Gigi. While Owen's moods had been unpredictable since returning from war, alcohol brought out the worst of his demons. It made him belligerent, angry, and self-destructive. Often, he would go on binges, drinking heavily and indulging in behaviors she wasn't supposed to know about but did because she'd eavesdropped on Papa lecturing him to stay away from brothels and gaming hells. More than once, Mama and Papa had taken Owen to the country seat in Hertfordshire to keep him away from bad influences. Owen would become sober and abstain for months, but then something would trigger him to start drinking again.

Since his return from Afghanistan, Owen had repeated this cycle...until he came to Chuddums. Five months ago, he, along with the rest of the family, had come to help Ethan in a time of need. In Chuddums, Owen had been different, and Gigi had *felt* it...felt her brother's desperate desire to change and make amends to Ethan. He hadn't touched spirits the entire time, not even at the wedding, and Gigi had been hopeful that he'd finally turned a corner.

"He promised he was done with drinking," she said haltingly. "After Ethan and Xenia wed, he made a vow in front of the family. He...he made a joke of it, saying that he was taking Ethan's lead and shackling himself. Not to a wife but to sobriety."

"Yes, my lady."

"He *promised*."

"Sometimes, when a man is not in full possession of himself, he cannot make such promises," Brunswick said with obvious care.

"If Owen cannot make the change, then *who* can? Who can do it for him?" Shaking her head, she went to the stairwell. "I must speak with him."

"Are you certain that's wise, Lady Gigi? He's in a state—"

But she was already halfway up the stairs, her skirts swishing with the urgency of her mission. She had to talk some sense into Owen. Had to make him understand the damage he was doing to himself and the family. Had to find some way to get through to him...to help him.

She traversed the paneled corridor to the guest bedchamber where Owen was staying. She was about to knock and stopped, her hand raised mid-air, when she heard a sound coming from within. Her pulse racing, she pressed her ear to the door. The sound of anguished weeping brought heat to her eyes, and her fist melted, her fingers brushing against the door.

"Owen?" she said, her throat tight. "It's me, Gigi. Let me in."

A pause before Owen's hoarse voice emerged. "Go away."

"Let me in, and we can talk—"

"There's nothing to talk about. I want to be left alone."

"But you shouldn't be alone. And I am here," she said helplessly. "I want to help."

"You cannot help. You're a sheltered girl who knows nothing of the world and how bloody brutal it can be."

"I can listen. I can understand—"

"You cannot possibly understand. I am not one of your goddamned projects. For Christ's sake, just *leave me be*."

Hearing the threads of rage woven into Owen's voice, Gigi knew further argument was pointless. Instead, she sank to the ground. Laying her cheek against the door, she listened to her brother's despair and wept silently with him.

Chapter Six

Conrad woke up to the familiar scent of *Eau de Regret*—minus the cloying perfume.

He was alone at an inn in Chudleigh Crest. Situated a few miles from Chudleigh Bottoms, the larger village had advantages that its downtrodden neighbor did not. For one thing, it had been built at a higher elevation, which made the Thames a pretty view rather than a constant threat of flooding. The businesses and people he'd seen in passing looked far more prosperous. The inn where Conrad was staying offered polite hospitality, spacious suites, and privacy. His original plan had been to celebrate his purchase of the spa here with a bottle of bubbly (and perhaps a local lightskirt) and return to London the next day.

Of that plan, he'd only accomplished one thing. He'd imbibed an entire bottle of champagne and now had a megrim to thank for it. The rest of his agenda had turned to shite as well. After the mysterious "Gigi" had been dragged away by a pretty redhead who'd looked daggers at him, he'd told himself it was just as well—he didn't need the distraction. Not that his focus did him much good. Leticia Caldecott was like a dog with a bone...that bone being her stupid spa. No amount of money—and hell's teeth, he'd offered her a king's ransom—could persuade her to sell to him. He'd left empty-handed, something that hadn't happened since his early days in business.

He had returned to the inn to plan his next moves. He'd ordered up supper, and the wench who'd brought it up had been dark-haired, buxom, *and* available. Yet for some bloody reason, he'd turned down her advances. Actually, he knew the reason. He'd been panting after his nymph...no, *Gigi*. Her name suited her: playful yet sensually elegant. She was even more beautiful than he remembered. She was also a meddlesome spitfire who ought to mind her own business and stay out of his. Nonetheless, an entire bottle of champagne hadn't erased her from his head.

Instead, he'd taken matters into his own hands...literally. Frustrated and randy, he'd relived the moment Gigi had straddled him: when he'd felt her warm, wet pussy kissing his thigh. In his soused state, the setting of the ancient Roman temple had melded seamlessly into his dark fantasies of Pearl and Prickonus. He'd imagined catching his little nymph emerging from her bath. When he cornered her, naked and dripping wet, anticipation had sparkled in her violet eyes.

Rub that needy little cunny against my leg, he commanded. *Make yourself come.*

With a plaintive whimper, she obeyed, masturbating against his thigh. Soon, she was riding him with delightful alacrity, moans escaping her rose-petal lips. He played with her breasts, enjoying their perfect shape and weight. When he tweaked her nipples—the same pretty hue as her lips, he fancied—she came with a gasp. The slick gush against his thigh made his erection leap against her belly.

With a growl, he pushed her to her knees, and she went with willing grace. Winding her wet raven hair in one hand, he used the other to feed her his prick. The swollen head, glossy with pre-seed, looked almost too big for her mouth. Yet she gamely opened for him, and he thrust into the tight, wet ring of her lips. He withdrew and drove inside again, and when she started to suck, he felt his eyes roll toward the back of his head.

Take my cock, he growled. *That's my good girl.*

Her muffled moan swelled his balls. He sheathed himself to the root, again and again. Her peerless violet eyes teared with effort, yet she urged him on with a sweet, feminine passion that shattered his self-control. He shot his seed, his release seeping through his clenched fingers and staining the sheets.

That had been last night. Now, he looked down and saw his erection tenting the bedsheet yet again. Grunting, he threw an arm over his eyes. A morning cockstand was hardly novel, but his obsession with Gigi was. While she was undeniably gorgeous, that did not justify her hold on him. She was just a woman—and one who spelled trouble for his ultimate goals.

Get your head on straight, Godwin. You didn't come this far to be stopped in your tracks by some toothsome chit. Concentrate.

In the past, his ability to adapt had allowed him to turn defeat into victory. First, he had to accept the reality that Leticia Caldecott was not going to be motivated by money. This meant that he would have to obtain the property by other means…or, alternatively, he could ensure that the spa failed. Then Chuddums would continue its rapid downward spiral, exposing his enemy's jugular.

Then I will go in for the kill.

The thought made Conrad's cockstand jerk against the bedsheet. Bloody hell, he might have to bring himself off again. He wanted to have a clear head as he tackled his new agenda: to determine the best approach to take with the spa…and, if he saw her again, the mysterious Gigi.

Arriving in Chuddums, Conrad grimly noted the improvements since his last visit. While the low-lying village lacked the tidy respectability of Chudleigh Crest, it flaunted a certain slapdash charm. He noted the patchwork quilt of frost-glazed roofs and the new coats of paint sprucing up worn buildings. As his carriage took him into the square, he passed a tearoom called the "Leaning House"…aptly named since the building was visibly tilting. With each of its three stories painted a different pastel shade, the establishment resembled a giant, lopsided wedding cake.

The other shops along the square were equally eccentric. Some buildings were tall, others squat, some narrow, and others wide. There was no rhyme or reason to the design. Nonetheless, business appeared to be thriving. There was a line out of the butcher's shop…at least, Conrad assumed it was the butcher's shop since the proprietor hadn't bothered to put up a sign. Passing the window of a snug establishment named "Hatcherds"—was the misspelling intentional?—he saw patrons curled up in chairs by the fireplace, nibbling on refreshments as they leafed through books.

When he'd last surveilled the village, many of the storefronts had lain empty. The street had looked like a smile without teeth. Since then, new shops had cropped up, and while there were still gaps, the new plate glass windows, brightly lit interiors, and painted doors conveyed cheerful optimism. Despite the chilly day, people bundled in winter coats wandered the square, their baskets full of purchases.

This is bloody unacceptable.

Conrad alighted from his carriage. Exploring on foot would give him a better sense of what was behind this inconvenient resurgence. In the center of the winter-touched green, he came upon a large tree with ghostly branches that seemed to claw at the overcast sky. He'd seen it last time, along with the small, rust-red stone that bore a plaque memorializing a member of Chuddums's most influential family:

> In memory of Langdon Pearce
> Hero and Soldier of Justice

> May He Rest in Peace

However, another monument had sprung up next to it. Constructed of pinkish granite, the obelisk was massive, thrusting into the withered branches of the tree. It resembled a giant prick... which was fitting, given who it was dedicated to.

> In honor of Abel Pearce
> A living Leader and Benefactor of Chudleigh Bottoms

Coldness crept through Conrad as he remembered his first visit to Chuddums over two decades ago. He'd been so young and afraid that he had taken little note of his surroundings. All he recalled was his mama using the last of her money to get them to an imposing house, slicking down his wayward forelock and straightening his jacket as they waited on the doorstep.

"*We must make a good impression on Mr. Pearce,*" she'd said.

"*What if he won't help us?*"

Even at age eight, he'd been no fool.

"*He will, dear. Although he and I are descended from different branches, we are family, after all. He will do the right thing and allow us to stay in the cottage that is my birthright.*" Her voice cracked with desperation. "*When he sees we have no one else to turn to, he will help us.*"

Conrad had refrained from pointing out that "family" had put them in this situation to begin with. Blood ties were no guarantee of kindness or compassion; his half-brothers had delighted in heaping pain and punishment upon him. Thus, it had come as no surprise when this new relation had listened indifferently to his mama's tale of woe, refused to honor her deed to the cottage, and had his butler escort them out.

"*There's nothing I can do.*" Abel Pearce had spoken in the impatient tones of a busy man who had better things to do. *"I'm sure you understand."*

Despite his tender age, Conrad had understood. Completely. His mama, however... His gut churned thinking of how callously Pearce had snuffed his mama's last hope and broken her spirit.

"Good day to you, sir!"

Shoving aside the memories, Conrad turned and saw a wizened fellow in a bright-green checked overcoat hurrying toward him... hurrying in a relative sense, that was. The old codger leaned heavily on a walking stick, his steps requiring obvious effort. If he were in a race with a snail, Conrad would bet on the mollusk.

"Welcome to Chuddums, sir. I am Wally," the old fellow announced breathlessly.

Above the red muffler that covered half his wrinkled face, the old man perused him with twinkling black eyes. Conrad had hoped to conduct surveillance incognito, but if this nosy nonagenarian had noticed him, then he'd probably been noticed by other villagers too. Being rude would likely garner more unwanted attention.

"Conrad Godwin, at your service," he said reluctantly.

"Miss Letty was right." Wally studied him. "You *are* a handsome devil with a stubborn jaw."

So much for incognito. News travels fast in this backwater hamlet.

"May I assist you with something?" he asked.

"You've got it turned around, sir." Wally chortled. "I am here to assist *you*."

"I do not require assistance—"

"Ah, but I can see that you do." Wally tapped the obelisk with his cane. "For instance, I noticed your interest in the newest addition to our square."

"It is hard to miss," Conrad said curtly.

"The monument does command attention, doesn't it?" Wally agreed. "The erection was spearheaded by our very own Mrs.

Pearce. She kept the design hush-hush, and now we must all live with it. Then again, I suppose no one deserves this stiff tribute as much as her husband."

When Conrad slanted a gaze at the old man, the latter blinked innocently back.

"Now about that tour," Wally said.

"What tour?"

"I thought you'd never ask. Come along, lad." Wally tugged him forward with surprising strength. "The delights of Chuddums await you."

Chapter Seven

Mr. David Duffield—"Duffy" to intimates—poured a cup of tea and set it on the counter in front of Gigi. As the draper, he owned one of the most popular shops in Chuddums. Women from around the county patronized his establishment and not just because of his exquisite taste in fabrics. In his early thirties, Duffy was a dapper blond Adonis, and his current ensemble—a forest-green frock coat, striped waistcoat, and pair of tan trousers—showed off his fit physique. While the ladies secretly, and some not so secretly, swooned over his looks, they also basked in his attention. For Duffy was unfailingly patient and kind, and when one visited his shop, he made one feel like a long-lost friend.

At least, that was how Gigi had felt the first time she'd come in. She and Duffy had hit it off immediately. Being a man of fashion, he was versed in the latest London trends and gossip, and they shared a similar sense of humor and view of the world. Over time, their friendship had deepened, and she'd confided in him about personal matters. He'd done the same with her. Now he was one of her closest friends, and she trusted him with the secret burdens of her heart. Thus, she'd come during the half-hour when he was closed for lunch to seek his counsel. Her maid, Colette, discreetly wandered the aisles, giving Gigi and Duffy privacy to catch up.

"Lord Owen hasn't left his room?" Duffy's hazel eyes were warm with empathy.

"No. He was still there when I left."

Picking up the porcelain cup patterned with cornflowers, Gigi took a glum sip as she looked around the shop. She took comfort in the cozy space, which smelled of newly cut velvet and lemony wood polish. Bolts of fabric were sorted by type and color and beautifully arranged on the walls and along the aisles. Scattered tables allowed Duffy to unroll fabrics for his patrons' perusal. At the counter where they were seated upon plush, upholstered stools, Duffy kept a pot of tea and plate of biscuits at the ready.

"He didn't even come out when Ethan went to knock on his door," she said. "Given what happened between them, that was an act of grace on Ethan's part."

Duffy nodded. She didn't have to explain because, little by little, she'd confided her history. He understood because he, too, came from a loving family that nonetheless had its struggles. A few years ago, he had left his parents' London home to strike out on his own and ended up in Chuddums.

"You tried your best," he said gently. "One can only lead a horse to water."

"I thought things were getting better." Gigi hated the hitch in her voice, which made her sound and feel like the little girl she'd once been. "Ethan is finally himself again, and he and Owen are on speaking terms. When James visits, we have merry times like we used to. Owen hasn't touched alcohol for months, and Mama and Papa trusted his sobriety enough to take a much-needed vacation. But now we are back to where we started."

"A setback does not erase the progress that's been made. You mustn't give up hope. Your brother will come around in his own time."

"I want him to come around *now*. I miss him," she admitted. "I miss our family...and the way things used to be."

"I know, my dear."

She blew out a breath. "But I cannot make Owen's choices for him, can I?"

"I'm afraid not."

"Instead, I should focus on something I *can* control?"

"A splendid idea. Whoever came up with that suggestion must have been one clever fellow."

Since Duffy had given her this advice on multiple occasions, she laughed. "The absolute cleverest. Now that I've bent your ear with my tale of woe, are there any catastrophes in *your* life you'd care to discuss?"

"No catastrophes." Duffy's smile faltered. "Just missed opportunities."

Duffy didn't have to explain because he'd, little by little, confided *his* history and the events that led to his departure from London. He'd been wary about opening up, and Gigi understood why. As a Harrington, she'd been raised to value love and loyalty in all its forms. It was the gravest injustice that society would not permit a man with Duffy's generous heart to love as he wished.

"You haven't talked to Mr. Keane?" Gigi asked quietly.

A recent arrival to Chuddums, Mr. Keane had opened a smithy three blocks away. Dark-haired and brawny, he wore a patch over his right eye that enhanced his piratical appearance. He was also stoic, prone to grunts and one-word replies.

"I tried." Duffy sighed. "Last week, I went in just before he closed and asked if working at the forge made him thirsty."

"And?"

"He said yes."

"Yes, meaning he wanted to get a pint at the tavern?"

"I haven't the faintest. His exact reply was, 'Yes,' and when I waited for him to say more, he started pounding on a horseshoe as if the conversation was over. Perhaps it was for him."

"Oh, dear," Gigi murmured. "I see how that could be confusing."

"Confusing and risky, if I misread his interest," Duffy said somberly. "Well, I've given him sufficient cues. I'd best take my own advice and focus on more productive matters. In fact, Miss Letty came in earlier this morning to check on the order for towels, which should arrive later this week. She mentioned that the two of you had a visitor yesterday."

Botheration.

Even Duffy didn't know about her kiss with the stranger by the stream, and she wasn't keen on sharing her recent kiss either. Especially now that she knew the man she'd secretly fantasized about for months was a notorious industrialist. Luckily, Gigi had received word from Letty saying that she'd turned down Godwin's offer.

"What did Miss Letty say about Mr. Godwin?" Gigi asked warily.

"That he is intent on buying the bath." Duffy's brow pleated. "Do you know why he's interested in Chuddums, of all places?"

"I assume it's part of some money-making scheme," she said darkly. "If he were to get his hands on the spa, he would undoubtedly squeeze every drop of profit from it. Or raze it to build something even more profitable. According to the papers, Mr. Godwin's *modus operandi* is increasing revenue at any cost. Even if that means destroying lives in the process."

"His reputation is rather cold-blooded. They say that he's calculating and enigmatic. What is the fellow like in the flesh?"

The mention of Conrad Godwin's flesh caused a flutter in Gigi's belly.

"He is just a man," she said dismissively. "Like any other."

"Really?" Duffy arched a brow. "According to the wags, he oozes animal magnetism."

"Mr. Godwin possesses no special powers, I assure you. He's an average fellow with deep pockets."

"Wealth does inflate a man's reputation, doesn't it?" Duffy said sagely. "The industrialists I encountered in London were pale, spindly coves hunched over from too much time at the desk. And do not get me started about the dukes—"

The bell over the door tinkled.

"How strange. I must have forgotten to lock up." In a genial voice, Duffy called, "I am afraid we are closed for lunch…"

His gaze widened, his jaw slackening. Twisting around on her stool, Gigi saw what—or *who*, rather—had caused this reaction. Dressed in a rich navy overcoat, a smart hat dipping rakishly over his brow, Conrad Godwin strode in like he owned the place.

She rose, ready to face her nemesis. Duffy got to him first.

"Welcome to my humble establishment, sir." Duffy bowed as if he were greeting a king. "How may I be of assistance today?"

"As it happens, I have found what I'm looking for." Godwin locked his sea-green gaze on her. "Good afternoon, Miss Harrington. I am delighted to see you again."

Somehow, she wasn't surprised that the blackguard had discovered her identity. He was the sort of man who went into battle prepared.

"I am surprised to see you, Mr. Godwin," she said coolly.

Her reply was meant to be an insult. However, his mouth merely quirked as if he found her…*amusing*? She narrowed her eyes.

In the tense silence, Duffy cleared his throat. "*You* are Conrad Godwin?"

As Gigi went to the back of the shop, she caught Colette's worried expression and Duffy's knowing one. The latter raised his brows and mouthed, "*A man like any other? Average?*"

Rolling her eyes, she said, "This will only take a few minutes."

She closed the velvet curtains and, squaring her shoulders, faced her adversary. The space served as Duffy's storage and work room, with bolts of fabric heaped on large worktables and trimmings overflowing from cabinets along the walls. With his outsized masculinity, Godwin ought to have looked ridiculous standing next to a dressmaker's form draped with pink satin and lace, but he didn't. The blasted man had the confidence to look at home anywhere.

Admittedly, Godwin was far from average and not just because of his self-assurance. He exuded a force more potent than mere charm. His calculating Viking's gaze held one captive while his striking virility overpowered one's resolve. He was the kind of fellow who would pillage your village and make you think he'd done you a favor.

In other words, you must tread carefully. Discover why he wants Letty's property. Try to dissuade him from his plans, and failing that, impress upon him that the spa is not for sale.

"What are you doing here?" she asked stiffly.

"I've asked myself that question countless times in the last hour. There I was, minding my own business in the square, when I was taken hostage by some old codger who insisted on giving me a tour."

At the mention of the "codger," Gigi smothered a grin. Wally was the village's oldest and friendliest resident. Although age had slowed him down, he remained spry and took his self-appointed duties as Chuddums's one-man welcoming party seriously. His infamous tours could last for hours, filled with minutiae that could be fascinating or deadly dull, depending on one's perspective.

"You've met Mr. Walford, I take. Did you enjoy his tour?" she asked innocently.

"I thought I might be his age by the time it ended."

At Godwin's unexpected wit, Gigi felt a quiver of amusement...which she quickly quelled. The fact that he had a sense of humor didn't make him any less cold-blooded. And while she could bend the rules of propriety, she couldn't ignore them completely. She only had a few minutes to settle matters with him. As antagonism hadn't served her well the last time, she would try a different approach.

Remember this, dearest Gigi. Mama's words flitted through her head. *It is easier to catch flies with honey than vinegar.*

Dear God. Papa had given Mama a wry look. *Our daughter already has your looks. If you teach her charm as well, the gentlemen won't have a fighting chance.*

Gigi put on a beguiling smile, one that usually had gentlemen scrambling to do her bidding. "I wouldn't think a place like Chuddums would hold any interest for a man like you—"

"What sort of man is that, Miss Harrington?"

When he lifted his brows, her cheeks warmed. Since her debut, she'd been celebrated for her poise and breezy command of any social situation, yet this fellow wreaked havoc on her equilibrium. Around him, she felt as if she were tottering on too-high heels, constantly trying to find her balance.

"An accomplished man of business." She made a graceful recovery. "Stories of your professional prowess precede you, sir."

"The last time we spoke, my prowess didn't seem to impress you. I believe you accused me of instigating riots and destroying lives."

Dash him and his memory like an elephant's.

"We got off on the wrong foot, and I apologize for my part in it," she said smoothly. "Be that as it may, there is no need for hostility between us. In fact, I believe we can find common ground."

"We have, and it's called the Chudleigh Bottoms's World Famous Roman Bath," he countered. "Convince your friend to sell it to me, and I'll give her a price she won't get anywhere else."

"It is not about money—"

"Everything is about money. Or power. Which is, essentially, the same thing."

She drew her brows together. "How did you get to be so cynical?"

"I've lived, sweetheart. I'm thirty-one, and I've seen more of the world than you have."

He reached out a gloved hand and tweaked her chin as if she were a *tot*. Before she could recover from her shock, he sent her reeling again.

"Given your sheltered existence, your innocence is understandable, and I won't hold it against you. But your little games will stop. Now."

Her temples began to pound. "I am not playing any games—"

"Then what is this?" Reaching into the pocket of his greatcoat, he removed a bottle of Chuddums water.

"Where did you get that?"

"It was a gift from Wally. He insisted that I sample the 'love potion' that saved Chuddums's spa. He also credited you with being the brains behind the racket."

While Gigi adored Wally, in this instance, she wished he did not talk *quite* so much.

"It is not a racket," she said stiffly.

"Please." Godwin curled his lip. "You're peddling a bottle of water that costs three times a pint of ale. You're robbing folks blind with this clever swindle of yours."

"It is not a swindle if it's *true*."

He laughed humorlessly. "Don't tell me you've fallen prey to your own ridiculous scheme."

"It is a point of fact that people who've taken the water have found their true love," she said hotly. "As of last count, I know of a dozen happy couples in London and at least as many here in Chuddums—"

"That is claptrap, and you know it. No damned water exists that can bring about true love." He paused, sneering. "And true love's probably a figment of the imagination as well."

The man was *unbelievable*.

She clenched her hands. "If you're certain that neither love nor an elixir for it exists, then I am sure you have no qualms drinking the water."

He quirked an eyebrow. Uncorking the bottle, he downed the contents in several swigs. He clanged the empty vessel onto the worktable.

"Satisfied?" Mockery glinted in his eyes.

"We'll see who has the last laugh when you fall head over heels in love," she retorted.

"Wait." He paused, placing a hand over his heart. "I do feel something. Something strange..."

She tilted her head. While she believed in the potion's power, its effects were usually not this immediate. "What do you feel?"

"Never mind. It was dyspepsia." He flashed strong, white teeth. "Probably from the hashed mutton the Briarbush Inn served for lunch."

"You are a *cad*."

"And you are a privileged young woman with too much time on your hands," he said flatly. "Find another little hobby to occupy yourself with, my lady, and stop meddling in my business. If you continue to stand in the way of progress, I cannot be held accountable for my actions."

Until that moment, she'd never understood the meaning of seeing red. All her life, she'd struggled to be taken seriously—to not have her abilities and ideas discounted because of her gender and age. Godwin's patronizing tone caused a scarlet cloud to fog her brain.

"Is that a *threat*?" she gritted out. "You, sir, are no gentleman."

His lips twisted. "Never said I was, duchess."

"Do not address me in that manner. I am not a duchess."

"Right. You are merely the daughter of a marquess. A lady with a reputation to protect."

His wintry-green gaze was that of a marauder: cold and

shrewd. She shivered, knowing that he was assessing her weaknesses so that he could exploit them.

Her pulse racing, she said, "If you're insinuating that you intend to blackmail me—"

"I'm not a man who insinuates. I say it, or I don't. And I am not going to blackmail you."

"Because you are above extortion?"

"No." He shrugged, her insult pinging harmlessly off his steel-clad arrogance. "Because anything I would use to blackmail you would incriminate *me* as well. I have no desire to pay the matrimonial piper for our little indiscretions. Delightful as they were."

Pay the matrimonial piper? While she didn't account herself a prideful lady, she'd had dozens of proposals since her come-out, from men of rank and wealth. They'd considered her a prize, not some dashed price to pay. Moreover, Godwin's trivialization of the intimacies they'd shared was more than a little insulting.

Her fingernails bit into her palms. "I wouldn't marry you if—"

"Is it necessary to finish that sentence? We both know how it ends."

"You are the most *insufferable* man I've ever met."

"So I've been told."

"I hate you!"

"Yes, well, I have that effect on people. Listen, sweetheart." His gaze hardened even as his voice strangely gentled. "You don't want to take on a man like me. You're meant for better things. For ballrooms and blue-blooded blokes who'll serenade you with poetry and shower you with jewels. Why do you care about a stupid country spa? Go back to London like a good girl and find another hobby. Leave the dirty business of life to others better suited for it."

A. Good. Girl?

Something in her snapped. Before she knew it, her hand was flying toward his face. He caught her wrist in an iron grip. She swung with her other hand, and he grabbed that one too. The next thing she knew, he'd backed her up against a wall, pinning her hands above her head. Although she struggled, he kept her manacled in place.

Her bosom heaving, she glared up at him. "Let me go."

"You don't want to play games with me," he warned.

"I'm not playing games. And this isn't some *little hobby*," she hissed. "Miss Letty is my friend, and I will not let you destroy her birthright. Why do you want her spa, anyway? A man with your predatory nature surely has bigger game to hunt unless...unless the spa and its waters are worth more than you've let on?"

"No one will pay her more for that damned place than I am willing to," he said with soft menace. "My reasons for wanting to acquire it are my own. Now I am telling you politely to stay out of my way."

"This is *politely*?" Pointedly, she tugged on her wrists, pushing her face into his. "You're nothing but a brute!"

"I *am* a brute." He leaned over her, as if to prove his point. "Which is why you ought to heed me, duchess."

"For the last time, do not call me that!"

"Stop acting like a spoiled brat whining about a lost toy, and I will."

The unfairness of his accusation made blood rush in her ears.

"You're the most arrogant, heartless, callous *bounder*—"

"But you still want me."

"I beg your pardon?"

"Your lips say one thing, your nipples another."

Even as her jaw slackened at his uncouth assertion, she became aware that her bosom was surging violently...against his chest. Beneath her bodice, the tips of her breasts *were* stiff and throbbing. Even so, with the layers of clothing between them, he couldn't possibly ascertain the state of her anatomy.

"You can't possibly..." She failed to find a genteel way to argue her point.

"Feel your nipples? No, I can't, and more's the pity. But I'm right, aren't I?" he said in a low voice. "They're full and aching, ripe as berries."

He leaned into her, the friction of his hard chest turning the tingles into dangerous sparks. She couldn't break her gaze from his, which was no longer smoldering with antagonism but with something hotter and hungrier. Deliberately, he slid his chest against her breasts, back and forth, and a helpless sound broke from her lips.

He bent his head, his breath warm against her ear. "That feels nice, doesn't it, duchess?"

Pleasure swirled over her skin.

"No, it doesn't," she lied.

"Almost as nice as the last time you rubbed yourself against me." His voice was low and hypnotic. "Christ, that felt good. I can't stop thinking about how wet and sleek you were, little nymph. Truth be told, I've done more than think about it."

Although she didn't understand his admission entirely, his tone left no doubt that what he'd done was wicked. Recalling her own naughty fantasies, she shivered.

"You're so sweet when you submit to me," he said.

She stiffened. "Submit? I'm not submitting to anything—"

"If you are wise, you will. Get out of my way, Gigi. Before we do something we both regret."

Duffy's voice came from the other side of the curtain. "Er, is everything all right back there?"

Coming to her senses, Gigi yanked her hands from Godwin's grip, and this time he let her go. Scooting away from him, she hastily put herself to rights. He took undue care adjusting the front of his coat.

"All is well," she called out.

Duffy poked his head through the curtains, his gaze bouncing between her and Godwin. "I have patrons rattling the door to come in, but if you need more time—"

"We're done," Godwin said. "I hope you'll take my advice, Miss Harrington. Good day to you both."

With a smart bow, he strode to the back door and let himself out.

She debated the wisdom of chasing after him and kicking him in the shin.

"By Jove." Duffy fanned himself with his hand. "Is it just me, dear, or has the temperature suddenly risen?"

Chapter Eight

"Where are you taking me, my sweet Rose?" he asked.

"Somewhere safe," she said. "A place where the world cannot reach us."

She knew her actions would be judged as wrong and wicked, but she didn't care. With Thomas, she felt safe for the first time—safe to be who she was. That feeling of security awakened her dormant recklessness. Because of her family, the villagers believed she was wild by nature, but she wasn't. At heart, she was shy and quiet. She preferred the woods over the village, plants over people. She'd been innocent in the ways of men...until she wasn't.

But she wouldn't think of him now. She wouldn't desecrate the few precious moments she had with Thomas. With him, she had only one thing on her mind: love.

She took his hand, which bore the calluses of the life he'd led before he'd retreated to the world of the scholar. They were alike in their craving for solitude. Nonetheless, destiny had given them something better, something she hadn't known to wish for until he came along.

A soulmate. The other half of herself. Although they came from different worlds, with him she could be her true self. As she *led him down, down into the deepening darkness, she shivered despite the growing heat. While he made her whole, was she tearing his existence apart? She brought danger to his life—burdens he shouldn't have to carry. He deserved peace, and she was anything but.*

It was too late. They entered the secret space, as warm and humid as a womb.

"I did not know about this," he said in wonder.

"Few people do," she whispered. "Mr. Caldecott didn't manage to get it working until my da tinkered with it. Now it works but only in fits and starts."

"It is working now," Thomas murmured.

He gathered her face in his hands, sweeping his thumbs over her cheeks, which were damp from tears or the humidity...she didn't know which. She didn't care because he kissed her then, her Thomas, not a buttoned-up bachelor any longer but a fierce and demanding lover. She let him in, wanting everything he had to give.

Passion surged over them, a swelling tide that made them moan and writhe, anchored only to one another. Even after, when the ravenous need had ebbed, they remained intertwined, bound by sweet words and even sweeter promises. Yet pounding footsteps made the stone walls shudder, booming threats reaching them even here.

You are going to burn, witch.

She clung to Thomas as the world caught fire. Her sanctuary was built on water, yet the blaze of rage reached her and her lover even there. Smoke and flames had her gasping for survival. Thomas was fighting with everything he had, but it was not enough.

If I cannot have you, I am going to destroy you. You'll be mine in hell, witch. Mine.

Rocks tumbled loose, pelting her before Thomas covered her body with his own. Yet he couldn't protect her from the water that rose from the pool. Higher and higher, reaching their knees, their chests. It was too hot, no escape.

Please God, don't let it end this way—

Gigi shot up with a gasp. Perspiration sheened her face, moisture trickling down her neck. It took her a moment to register that she was in her room in her brother's manor. Her heart pounding, she realized that she'd had a dream.

It was more than a dream. The thought shivered through her. *It was a...a memory.*

The encounter between Rosalinda and Thomas had blazed with authenticity. Just like the image Gigi had had of the lovers standing by the stream, the details had felt *real*. Panic poured through her as she felt smoke clogging her lungs and the heat of rising flames. Although the exact location where Rosalinda and Thomas had met was foggy, Gigi somehow knew the lovers had been at the spa. Sudden fear gripped her: something dreadful was happening there *right now*. The vision was a premonition—a warning.

Oh my stars, Letty sleeps like a log. She wouldn't know if the spa was on fire. Wouldn't know if the flames spread to her little cottage...

Fear catapulted Gigi out of bed. She thought about rousing her brother, but what if Ethan didn't believe her? What if he forbade her from going? She was already on thin ice where the spa was concerned. Over supper, Xenia had let the cat out of the bag about Gigi's encounter with Conrad. Although Gigi had pleaded that nothing had happened, Ethan had set his foot down.

"Until further notice, you must stay away from the spa." Ethan's face had been grim with big-brother fury. *"Conrad Godwin is reputed to be a ruthless man, one who will do anything to win. No hobby is worth compromising your future for."*

After futile resistance to her brother's ultimatum, Gigi did not want to waste precious time arguing with him now. She couldn't risk another moment with Letty and the spa in possible peril. She had to go. If there was nothing happening at the bath—if what

Gigi had experienced was just a dream—then she would spare herself the embarrassment of looking like a ninny. Of being the silly baby sister whom no one took seriously.

I'll ride over and take a quick look. If there's a problem, I'll alert Letty, and we'll summon help. If everything is normal, then none will be the wiser about my jaunt.

Decision made, she donned the shirt, waistcoat, and trousers she'd filched from Owen's adolescent wardrobe. This had been her favorite ensemble for romping through the woods at her parents' estate, and when Owen had been lost at war, she'd worn it to feel closer to him. Next, she contemplated the options for a stealthy exit. She could take the stairs or... Her gaze homed in on the large oak outside her window. Its sturdy branches seemed to beckon in the darkness.

Perfect.

Arriving at her destination, Gigi didn't know whether to be relieved or disappointed. Through the gate, she saw that the building was dark: there was no sign of fire. No smell of smoke, no glowing flames. Moonlight silvered the roof of the spa, its drawn curtains giving it a sleepy-eyed look.

Good thing I didn't wake Ethan. I would never hear the end of it.

Nonetheless, she thought it prudent to make sure everything was as tranquil as it seemed. She secured her mare and headed up the path to the bathhouse. In the moon's glow, the surrounding garden had an ethereal, almost magical, ambiance. She expected to find fairies cavorting in the fountain or gnomes popping out from the bushes. Yet nothing interrupted her journey, and she quickly made her way to the spa entrance.

Taking out the key that Letty had given her, Gigi slid it into the lock, her breath stuttering when the small momentum caused the door to swing open. The door was already unlocked...*open*. Someone had gone in and left it slightly ajar.

I knew that dream was a warning. I knew something was amiss.

Her heart racing, Gigi crept stealthily into the entry hall. Although it was dark, she didn't dare light a lamp and alert the intruder to her presence. Was it a burglar? A crafty criminal who planned to make off with Letty's hard-earned possessions?

Not on my watch.

Determination overrode Gigi's fear. She had two advantages over the prowler: she knew the spa inside and out, and she had the element of surprise on her side. Hearing sounds of shuffling coming from the bathing area, she dashed to a nearby hearth and grabbed a fire iron. The heavy, solid weight of her makeshift weapon bolstered her courage. Staying close to the wall, she advanced to the pool.

Peering around the entryway, she saw him. The burglar. Dressed all in black, he was about twenty feet away. He had his back to her, his hair hidden beneath a dark cap, and he was crouching next to the pool. Turned low, the flickering sconces cast more shadow than light, and she couldn't identify him from a distance. He had opened one of the grates on the ground that led to the piping system and appeared to be fiddling around.

Outrage lit a fire in Gigi's belly. *Is the bounder tampering with the pipes? I will not allow some saboteur to ruin Miss Letty's business.*

Tightening her grip on the poker, she inhaled for courage. Then she ran over, weapon raised and ready to strike. At her approach, the burglar shot to his feet and spun around. She had an instant to recognize the glittering green eyes before the poker struck home. The impact jarred her...though, obviously, not as much as him.

"Bleeding hell!" Godwin roared.

He grabbed his shin, his face creased with pain. Her initial plan had been to strike the crouching intruder across the shoulders, but since he'd moved and, to be honest, her aim was more enthusiastic than accurate, she'd struck his leg instead.

Rather hard, too. The impact was still singing up her arm.

Uttering oaths that made Gigi's brows rise even though she'd grown up with brothers, Godwin hopped on one foot, still holding his injured shin. He was dangerously close to the pool's edge, which was notoriously slippery (look at what had happened to her the last time). Before she could warn him, he slipped, hitting the water with a splash.

Chapter Nine

Swiping water from his brow, Conrad glowered at Gigi with as much dignity as he could muster. Which, given the fact that he'd fallen into the damned pool, wasn't much. God's teeth, she was a troublesome female. He couldn't believe that she'd *attacked* him. His leg throbbed like the devil; he was lucky that she hadn't broken his shin bone. He couldn't blame himself for being snuck up on, however. It was three in the bloody morning: no one should have been at the spa.

"Why in blazes are you here?" he growled.

"I beg your pardon. Allow me to explain."

He instantly distrusted her honeyed manner, and her next words proved why.

"I have a key, you see, along with permission from Miss Letty to enter her premises. Can you say the same?"

Well, she had him there.

"What, precisely, is the purpose of your trespass?" she said accusingly.

She crossed her arms, and he had to admire her boldness. And her outfit. Damn, she was a sight to behold in men's clothing. Her graceful throat rose from the open vee of her shirt, her unfettered breasts surging temptingly beneath her waistcoat. And those trousers... He swallowed. They displayed her lower half to perfection. Her hips were slim yet shapely. Her bottom looked perky and firm. Long and slender, her legs would wrap nicely around a man's hips, and he shuddered, imagining her delicate heels digging into his arse while he plowed her.

The throbbing in his shin gave way to the hotter, stronger pulsing in his groin.

"Well?" Gigi demanded. "What do you have to say for yourself, sir?"

Oh, he had plenty he wanted to say to her. To *do* to her. Nonetheless, he had to get a handle on the situation. He hadn't clawed his way up in the world to be stopped in his tracks by some little minx, no matter how alluring she was. He'd sweated and bled for his revenge, and now that he was close to getting what he wanted, he was going to *get it*.

One way or another, I will get what I am due. No one is going to stop me. Not even a tempting chit who is too big for her britches.

Wading to the steps, he emerged from the pool. He advanced toward Gigi, water sloshing from his coat pockets and his shoes making squishing sounds with every step. He didn't care if he looked ridiculous. When it came to his personal qualities, determination came second only to ruthlessness, and right now he had one goal in mind.

He stopped mere inches from Gigi, stabbed a finger at her.

"I do not answer to you," he growled.

She stood her ground. "Would you rather answer to the police? I can summon them, you know."

"What will you tell them?" he asked acidly. "That you came to the spa alone in the middle of the night and found me here?"

Seeing the rapid flicker of her eyelashes, he realized with grim satisfaction that she was recognizing her own predicament.

Compared to most well-bred misses he knew, Gigi seemed rather oblivious to her own fragility—that of her person and her reputation. Recklessness was her Achilles' heel, and he made note of it.

"Even your papa the marquess couldn't protect you," he taunted. "If word got out that you were alone with me. That you met me in the dead of night, wearing trousers..."

He took a step closer, and she retreated an equal distance. What she did not do, however, was back down.

"I did not *meet* you here."

While Conrad had had plenty of women scowl at him, he'd never until this moment thought a female could look adorable doing it. Yet Gigi managed to do so, probably because her face was obviously not made for anger. She had the face of a naiad: beautiful, expressive, meant for beaming joy upon the world. Her plump lips were naturally tipped up at the corners, and she had to work to pull them in the opposite direction. Even the twin furrows between her curving brows were cute.

"And what, pray tell," she said through her perfect, if gritted, teeth, "do my trousers have to do with anything?"

"They entice me," he said.

Her eyes widened.

He advanced, and this time she took a couple of steps back. Finally, she was understanding who was in charge of this cat-and-mouse game. He kept stalking toward her, and she kept retreating. The chase stirred his filthy desires, and he was hard before her back hit the stone relief on the wall. He planted his hands next to her shoulders. Feeling the odd shape beneath his right palm, he glanced over to see what lay beneath.

A satyr's bearded face grinned at him. How apropos. He leaned into Gigi, so close that he could see the fire of the sconces leaping in her eyes.

"I warned you to get out of my way," he said. "Instead, you throw yourself in my path at every opportunity. Tonight, not only do you attack me with a poker, but you do it while flaunting the prettiest legs I've ever laid eyes on."

"I did not throw myself at you," she said with an annoyed huff. "I thought you were a burglar, which is a reasonable conclusion since you are dressed in black and skulking around. I was defending my friend's property, which is why I pummeled you—quite deservedly, I might add. Finally, although it is no business of yours, the reason I am dressed this way is because my exit from my brother's manor involved the scaling of a tree. I also made far better time riding astride than sidesaddle."

He stared at her. "You climbed a tree?"

"Anyone can climb down," she said airily. "It is the ascent that requires skill."

"A skill you happen to possess?"

"I may have done it once or twice."

Right. Her smug expression betrayed that she was an expert tree-climber. In addition to "reckless" and "naughty," he added "daring" to her list of traits.

"A singular female, aren't you?" he murmured.

She narrowed her eyes at him. "Do not try to change the subject. We were discussing your purpose here tonight. Were you attempting to sabotage Miss Letty's piping?"

He was more worried about his own piping. Specifically, the amount of pressure that was building up. It couldn't be healthy for a fellow.

"I was not."

Only because he hadn't gotten that far. His plan this eve was to get the lay of the land—to find the spa's weaknesses. Only after a thorough evaluation would he strategize a plan of attack. Tonight, he wouldn't have done anything simply because he was too methodical and meticulous for such rash behavior.

"I don't believe you," she retorted. "I saw you with your hand down there. You were feeling around the pipes—trying to cause them to burst, no doubt."

He shut his eyes briefly. Unfortunately, that did nothing to block out the image her words had seeded...

For the love of God, do not go there. Regain control before this situation blows up—Christ. Before it explodes in your...goddamn bloody hell.

Her scent tickled his nostrils. It was fresh, floral, and subtle, the opposite of cloying. She smelled carefree and fun, like a springtime walk through the woods.

I want to walk through her woods.

"Well, were you?" she demanded.

He tried to clear his head. Which was novel because his head was always clear...except when he was around *her*. Why did this chit have such an effect on him? A thought flickered in his head—*Could this have something to do with drinking that damned Chuddums water?*—before he firmly snuffed it.

He sent her a surly look. "Was I what?"

"Trying to cause a pipe to explode."

That does it.

"My pipe was fine until you came along," he growled.

She wrinkled her brow. "Your pipe? I don't understand..."

Her huge eyes and the "o" of her lips conveyed her sudden understanding. She dipped her gaze downward. The wet wool of his trousers was plastered over the massive bar of his erection, and he could feel himself straining the seams. He'd never been harder in his life.

"Happy with yourself?" he asked darkly.

She yanked her gaze up. Even in the dimness, he saw the roses in her cheeks. Then, God help him, she wetted her lips like the naughty naiad she was, causing his arousal to border on painful.

"Enjoying your little game?" he asked.

"I'm not playing any games," she protested.

Her denial was breathy, the feminine awareness in her eyes drawing him closer. He leaned toward her, bracing more of his weight against the relief. As he did so, he heard a click and felt something give way beneath his palm. He jerked his hand away and saw that the grinning face of the satyr had receded into the wall.

"What the devil?" he muttered.

A rumble started in the wall, and he grabbed Gigi, shoving her behind him. His muscles bunching, he watched as a section of the sculpted scene separated from the rest. It swung open like a door, releasing a puff of steam. As the mist cleared, Conrad saw that the panel had concealed a staircase that led into the bowels of the spa.

"A secret passageway," Gigi breathed. "Just like in my dream."

Before he could stop her, she dashed around him and down the steps.

⁂

Trembling with excitement, Gigi descended the steps of the tunnel.

My dream wasn't a dream. It was *a memory. There is something down here...something to do with Rosalinda and Thomas. Something I am meant to discover.*

Feeling Godwin's presence behind her, she flashed back to Rosalinda leading Thomas into the darkness. Was this ruthless magnate somehow part of Gigi's destiny? She shivered at the thought. She wouldn't trust him farther than she could toss him and yet...

And yet.

He had a powerful effect on her senses. No man had ever affected her in this manner. He was blunt, crude, and stood for everything she despised. At the same time, when his voice got growly and those emerald flames lit his eyes, everything in her responded. Everything in her *melted*—

"Stop," Godwin commanded.

They'd reached a door.

"I will go in first," he said.

In the flickering glow of the candle he'd had the presence of mind to bring along, his face was carved with resolve.

She lifted her brows, stepping aside. "Be my guest."

He tried the doorknob. When it didn't turn, she felt a rush of disappointment.

Godwin handed her the candle.

"Hold this," he said.

Removing a pouch from his pocket, he upended it. Water gushed out (at his grimace, she hid a grin), followed by metal objects that clattered into his large palm.

"Lock picks?" She gave him a saccharine smile. "Came prepared, did you, Mr. Godwin?"

"I am always prepared."

"Even for trespassing."

At her jibe, he shrugged. "For anything."

Godwin inserted the picks, and while she might be concerned about his morals (or lack thereof), she had to admire his expertise. He unlocked the door within seconds, and taking the candle from her, led the way into a small antechamber. A risqué statue of a satyr embracing a nymph stood next to a stone bench. There were hooks on the walls and two shelves stacked with what appeared to be aged toweling. When Gigi picked up one of the linens, it disintegrated, pieces fluttering to the ground.

Godwin prowled around. "What is the purpose of this place?"

"I think it is a caldarium," Gigi said slowly.

He twisted his head to look at her. "Beg pardon?"

"A heated chamber that ancient Romans used for relaxation," she explained. "According to Miss Letty, her great-great-grandfather had dreamed of building one. She assumed that if he had started constructing one, it had been destroyed by the fire that nearly burned the entire spa. Yet it was right here all along. Literally hidden beneath our noses."

"This place feels more like a closet than a chamber for relaxation," Godwin muttered. "A man can hardly move around in here."

"Not all men are as big as you."

"So I've been told."

At his smug look, she felt her cheeks flame.

Why does he have to be so crass? As if there were any doubt about the size of his manhood. The only thing to rival it is his arrogance.

She decided to rise above. "This seems like an antechamber. Do you see any entrances that might lead into the caldarium?"

Godwin held the candle up, examining the walls.

"Here." He pointed to a seam in the stone from which sporadic wisps of steam escaped. "But where is the mechanism to open it?"

They both looked at the statue.

"The corridor to the caldarium was revealed when I pressed on the satyr's face," Godwin said. "I'll try the same with the statue."

He pushed on the bearded visage. Gigi heard a click, then a rusty squeal. As some inner mechanism worked, there was the sound of metal grinding against metal. Slowly, in fits and starts, a section of the wall parted, revealing an inner chamber.

"The caldarium," she breathed.

Eagerly, she raced inside. The air was warm and humid due to the round pool in the middle of the room. By some miracle, the hot springs had continued to feed the pool, steam curling from its surface. Next to the pool was a stone platform large enough to fit three or four people. The angled backrest allowed guests to recline as they soaked up the heat. Along the caldarium's perimeter were private alcoves where bathers could relax upon benches.

Gigi did a gleeful turn, taking it all in.

"I cannot wait to show Miss Letty," she exclaimed. "This secret caldarium will be her *pièce de résistance*. It will guarantee the spa's success."

When Conrad shot her a look, she remembered belatedly that he was her adversary. Despite their inexplicable chemistry, they were at cross purposes. Moreover, they were opposites in personality: he was callous and calculating, the least sentimental man she'd ever met. She didn't even *like* him. And from his perspective, she was a silly, naïve lady with too much time on her hands.

As he opened his mouth, probably to say something disagreeable, a screech tore through the chamber. She cringed as the sound of metal-on-metal grated across her eardrums. The next instant, the door to the caldarium slammed shut, sealing them in darkness.

Chapter Ten

"Bloody hell," Conrad bit out.

"Can you open the door?" Gigi peered over his shoulder.

"If I could, would we still be trapped inside this goddamned cauldron?"

"It's a caldarium."

Gritting his teeth, he planted his feet and pushed at the door, trying to slide it open. It didn't budge. He pushed harder, his muscles bulging against damp seams. He put all his power into it, calling upon his years of strength training as a prizefighter. The chamber was sweltering, heat radiating from the pool and the ground. Sweat poured from him as he shoved at immovable stone.

With a frustrated oath, he gave up. "The mechanism used to open and close the door is broken. Based on that unholy sound we heard, a chain probably snapped, and the door is too heavy to move without it."

In the candlelight, Gigi's eyes were huge. "We are trapped?"

"For now. In a few hours, Miss Caldecott will undoubtedly discover where we are. At that time, she'll have to fetch someone to break through the door."

"But I will be ruined if I am discovered here with you," Gigi moaned.

He resisted the urge to kick the door, which would accomplish nothing except possibly injure his foot. Disgusted, he said, "If there is a problem, I will take care of it."

Although he did not wish to bear the consequences of compromising the well-bred chit, Gigi's look of utter horror grated on his pride. Bloody hell, she could do worse—*a lot* worse. While she didn't know that his pedigree was, in fact, a match for hers, she was aware that he was wealthy as sin. Plenty of women would give their eyeteeth for the privilege of being Mrs. Conrad Godwin.

For him, revenge came first, which was why he'd vowed not to marry until his objectives were met. Now he found himself in a situation where his honor might make him break that vow, yet the reason for his conflict did not appreciate his sacrifice one iota.

"Take care of it?" she echoed.

"If worse comes to worst, I'll marry you." Saying the words gave him a heady feeling; it had to be the heat. "You could suffer a worse fate."

Apparently immune to sarcasm, Gigi began to pace. "None that I can imagine. If we were discovered together, my papa or my brothers will have my head—or yours, rather. It will be pistols at dawn or some such thing, and your blood will be on my hands."

"Why do you assume that it will be *my* blood that is shed?" he asked coldly.

"Because the men in my family are excellent shots," she rejoined. "And if you were to wound them, it would be just as bad! All of this is my fault. I should have never come—"

"On that, we agree."

"But you shouldn't have been here either." She glowered at him. "If you weren't trespassing, we wouldn't be in this mess."

He felt a muscle twitch near his eye. He was willing to do the honorable thing—the *right* thing—and this was her response? Not gratitude or, God forbid, some small show of excitement? Instead, she was pelting him with accusations.

"I was carrying on fine until you attacked me with a poker," he said curtly.

"*You* pushed me against a wall."

"Well, you strolled into this bleeding cauldron as if it were Hyde Park."

"*Caldarium.* And you were right behind me!"

They were standing toe to toe. Her chin was tilted at a mutinous angle.

"This situation is at least *half* your fault," she informed him. "I dare you to deny it."

The heat in the chamber was oppressive, but his blood felt even hotter. It rushed like molten lava beneath his steaming skin. Skin that was uncomfortably trapped beneath heavy, sodden layers.

"I don't deny anything," he bit out. "I acted foolishly. Lust clouded my judgment."

She blinked, swallowing. "Lust has nothing to do with it—"

"This is *all* about lust," he snapped.

Suddenly, he was done. Done with trying to control this out-of-hand situation and done with reining himself in. Done with sparing her delicate sensibilities, too. He stripped off his coat, tossing it to the ground.

"Wh-what are you doing?" Gigi gasped.

"Getting comfortable. It's hotter than hell in here." Grimly, he tore off his neckcloth and unfastened his waistcoat.

"You cannot just...just *disrobe*!"

"Watch me." His waistcoat joined his coat on the floor.

"You are no gentleman—"

"We've established that already."

He started on the buttons of his shirt.

"Stop," Gigi said in a high voice. "Stop right there."

He scowled at her. "You feel no lust toward me, correct?"

Wetting her lips, she said, "Of course I don't."

"Then seeing me without a shirt shouldn't prove a problem for you."

He shucked the sodden linen. Christ, that felt good. During his days as a prizefighter, rumors had flown that he felt no pain. In fact, the opposite was true. He was a highly sensual man, and the only reason he'd fought on with broken ribs, knuckles ripped to the bone, and eyes swelled shut was because he'd willed himself to. Courtesy of the "lessons" forced upon him by Grimshaw, the headmaster of Creavey Hall, he could push himself past normal limits of endurance...but that didn't mean he felt nothing.

Conrad felt *intensely*: pain, pleasure, and everything in between. It was why he enjoyed swiving—the sensual build-up and release, that fleeting sense of rightness in his own skin. On the other hand, the feel of wet fabric plastered to his chest had been torture. Shedding that layer was a physical relief. In fact, he was tempted to remove his trousers...but even he had limits when it came to toying with a virgin.

If he were honest, though, Gigi didn't look as shocked as she ought to. He'd deliberately kept his back from her—he didn't feel like explaining his scars—but he'd given her a good view of his chest. When she wasn't pretending not to look, he saw the curiosity in her eyes...the same sparkle she'd had when peeping at him at the stream. A sparkle that somehow combined innocence with feminine hunger. It made him instantly hard. Or *harder*, rather.

Yet he was a man in control of himself and the situation. To prove it, he sauntered past her and settled on the wide stone platform. He lounged against the back, welcoming the feel of warm stone against his spine, and stretched out his arms and legs. With satisfaction, he noted that Gigi was avidly watching him while pretending not to.

"Might as well settle in." He quirked a brow. "Care to join me? There is plenty of room here."

"Not for you, me, *and* your arrogance."

Despite his simmering lust, he had to stifle a smile at her cheekiness.

"Suit yourself." Leaning his head back, he closed his eyes. "I'm getting a bit of shut-eye. We have a long night ahead of us."

Eyeing the half-naked Adonis lounging in front of her, Gigi recalled her mama's advice.

The mark of a lady is not the absence of impulses, dearest, but the ability to make wise choices despite them.

Given the urges currently swarming her, Gigi made the prudent choice to put as much distance between herself and Mr. Godwin as possible. She made a beeline for one of the alcoves. Dropping onto the bench, she crossed her arms and tried to unsee the sight of his bulging biceps and rippling torso. His body hair had formed an intriguing pattern, sprinkling across his wide upper chest before narrowing into a line between the stacked muscles of his stomach. It drew the eye to his waistband and the thick, unmistakable ridge just beneath.

Stop thinking about his you-know-what. You're in enough trouble as it is.

The sweltering heat didn't help. She was warm, damp, and sticky; unlike Godwin, however, she couldn't just shuck off what made her uncomfortable. Hearing a snore from his direction, she blew out an annoyed breath and shifted on her hard seat. Perhaps she should try to rest; she would need energy to deal with this mess in the morning…

She must have dozed off, for a voice startled her awake.

"Don't touch me, you bastard."

Blinking groggily, Gigi sat up.

"No. *No.* Stop."

The pain in Godwin's voice propelled her from the alcove. She found him on the platform, still asleep, his head rocking back and forth against the stone headrest. Lines slashed across his brow and around his mouth. His jaw was tight, his eyes twitching behind closed lids.

"Stop," he gritted out. "Going to kill you—"

The sound that came from him was inhuman—an animal howl that made Gigi scramble onto the platform next to him. He thrashed his head against the unforgiving rock, not seeming to feel the impact, gripped in the greater agony of his nightmare. When another pained sound scraped from his throat, she could bear it no longer.

She placed a hand on his shoulder. "Godwin, wake up."

Beneath her palm, his skin was hot, nearly feverish. The muscles of his shoulder bulged, but he did not awaken. Demons from his past held him fast; he was trapped by terror that time had not healed. Understanding squeezed her heart, for Owen suffered from a similar affliction. When Godwin gnashed his teeth, smashing his head against the rock, she cupped his jaw with both hands.

"It's just a dream," she said firmly. "*Wake up.*"

His eyelids flew open. The nightmare stared back at her, blowing his pupils wide, obscuring any hint of cocky green. A chill passed through her as she realized she was looking straight at his demons. Yet she'd never been one to back down when someone needed her.

"You're awake," she said gently. "It's me, Gigi. We're trapped in the caldarium, remember? You had a dream, but you're safe. There is no one here to hurt you."

The darkness slowly receded from his gaze. She saw the instant he came back to himself, his storm-filled eyes taking her in. He reached a hand to his jaw, trapping hers beneath his callused palm. She understood his need to anchor himself and didn't pull away.

Even though his grip was strong, it was his slight tremble that held her captive.

"You're all right," she murmured. "I'm here, and I have you."

"You're here," he repeated. "And you have me."

His eyes flashed with a different kind of need. One that her female instincts recognized and responded to. Her heart raced, her breath hitched, her skin prickled with awareness. Every nerve tingled when he cupped the back of her neck, dragging her close. She tumbled atop him and had an instant to brace her palms against his hard chest before he claimed her mouth.

His kiss was as hot and hungry as she remembered. Yet the flavor this time was more than desire: it was pure need. He needed *her*, and he had no qualms about showing it. His intensity lay waste to her inhibitions. Insight flashed that *this* was what she'd been waiting for: this all-consuming feeling. This electrifying call to discovery. It was like unfurling hidden wings, and guided by instinct, she took the leap and soared.

His hunger was like tinder: she kissed him back with the passion that he'd sparked at the stream—that only *he* had ever elicited in her. When he licked the seam of her lips, she parted them readily. His essence flooded her senses, wild and forbidden and delicious. The thrust of his tongue seemed to reach beyond her mouth, stimulating her sensual core. She felt his velvet stroking at the tips of her breasts and between her thighs. She whimpered, squirming with need.

"Christ, I want you."

The growl in his voice made her squirm even harder.

"You want me too, don't you, sweetheart?"

Captivated by his stark hunger, she couldn't lie. When she nodded, the glittering triumph in his eyes caused a flutter of anxiety.

"But while we may feel a certain, um, mutual attraction, that doesn't mean we should—"

"I won't hurt you, Gigi," he said. "Whatever happens between us, you can trust me on this. Your virginity is safe with me."

When she stared at him, he drew his brows together.

"I assume you are a virgin?" he asked.

"Of course I am," she said with a small huff.

"Then rest assured your maidenhead is safe with me."

"Even so." She tried to think clearly. "It isn't proper."

"As long as we don't do anything incontrovertible and no one knows, who gives a damn about propriety?"

There was something wrong with his reasoning, but the way he was running his thumb along her cheekbone, staring at her as if she was the only thing that existed in the world, was muddying her thoughts. He drew her to him, kissing her until she was limp and breathless.

"If it reassures you, we'll keep our clothes on," he said against her lips. "No consequences, only pleasure. Say yes, Gigi."

Fully clothed and my virginity is safe. No one will know. No consequences...only pleasure.

How could she resist?

The word escaped with her next breath. "Yes."

He kissed her again, and only then did she realize that he'd been holding back. Now he unleashed his desire, his hunger, and her world went topsy-turvy—literally. Before she could regain her bearings, he flipped their positions, and she was lying on her back, sandwiched between the stone and Godwin's equally rigid length.

"Feel how well we fit together," he said huskily.

It was impossible not to. His hard edges pressed into her curves, setting off tingles of delight. She ran her hands over the bulging contours of his shoulders, and at his shudder, she felt a jolt of confidence.

"We do fit," she marveled.

"You were made for me, little nymph. Made for pleasure."

Her reply melted into a moan when he turned his attention to her ear, catching it between his lips. His flicking tongue scattered goosepimples over her skin. When he suckled her lobe, her breath hitched. Pleasure sizzled through her veins, shooting to the tips of her breasts.

"You're so sensitive," he muttered. "So bloody lovely."

His mouth was on hers again, his tongue delving deeply. When she licked him back, his groan of encouragement unraveled any remaining inhibitions. He led, and she followed, their tongues entwined in a timeless dance. He caressed the column of her throat, and she arched to his touch as they devoured one another. Then he palmed her breast, his heat seeping through the linen. His eyes on hers, he grazed the tip with his thumb, luring a gasp from her lips.

"Absolute perfection," he said. "That's what you are, Gigi."

At his blatant admiration, she felt a leap in her chest...and in her lower regions. And that was before he began strumming her nipple, adding to the ache at her center. She squeezed her thighs together, trying to quell the throbbing, and he laughed softly before kissing her again, filling her with his tongue, groaning when she sucked on his offering.

"Hungry girl," he rasped. "I know what you need."

Then he was kissing her neck, prickling her skin with his night beard. He kept going, and to her shock, she felt his mouth on her clothed breast. Before she could push him away, he closed his lips over the throbbing tip. Wet heat engulfed the sensitive peak as he suckled her through linen.

She didn't recognize the sound she made. "Oh my stars, Godwin—"

"Call me Conrad," he said. "I want to hear my name on your lips while I suckle your sweet tit."

When she gasped his name, the intimacy of it burned her tongue. Yet his was even hotter. She writhed with bliss as he laved, flicked, and teased her engorged bud.

"Rose-flavored Turkish delight," he muttered.

Her head spun. "P-pardon?"

"Your nipples. They're the same color as my favorite confection." His eyes gleamed down at her. "However, you are far sweeter."

He moved on to her other breast, consuming her as if she *were* a treat. Whimpering, she gripped his hair, lost in the slide of rough silk between her fingers and the masterful pull of his mouth. He played with her other breast simultaneously, rolling the swollen tip between his finger and thumb. The sensations spread from her breasts, building and building, until every fiber of her vibrated with need.

"Let go, Gigi," he said thickly. "Go over for me."

Before she could ask what he meant, he pinched her nipple while drawing the other deep into his mouth. The bite of pain and heated suction tugged at the knot at her center, and it suddenly *released*. Unraveled by bliss, she cried his name, and he growled, covering her mouth with his. Pleasure crested, rolling through her in luxuriant waves.

Slowly, she drifted back. She felt warm and lax, as if she were wrapped in a cloud. Touching his jaw, she felt the contrast between its hard edge and the tender press of his lips. He lifted his head, a gilded forelock dangling upon his brow. It added boyish charm to his handsomeness, and she couldn't resist brushing it back.

"Was that good, duchess?"

There was nothing boyish about the knowing rasp in his voice.

"It was," she said shyly. "I...I've never felt anything like it."

"That is just the beginning."

She felt her eyes widen. "There is more?"

He cupped her between her legs. She jolted at the intimacy, the way he casually laid claim to a part of her that no man had touched. As if he gleaned her thoughts, his lips curved in a wicked smile that made peril feel like passion and risk seem like reward. He rubbed his palm in a circle, and her thighs quivered anew.

"Oh, there's more," he said.

Chapter Eleven

Gigi awakened to flickering darkness. Her eyes widened as she registered that her cheek was pillowed by Conrad's hard chest, her trousered leg thrown wantonly over his. He held her close, his hand on her hip. His even breathing told her he was asleep—peacefully, this time.

Oh my stars. What have I done?

Even as panic began to set in, she couldn't regret her actions. As promised, Conrad had shown her "more." He'd stretched atop her, and the memory of being covered by his sleek, muscular form sent a thrill through her even now. Despite the layers of clothing, the thrusting friction of his heavy, turgid length had made her moan and buck her hips.

"*That's right, duchess,*" he'd coaxed. "*Rub that sweet little pussy against my cock. Do you feel how hard I am for you?*"

She'd felt him, all right. He'd ground his steely cock against her peak, showering her insides with white-hot bliss. He'd done it again and again, and she'd clung to him, wrapping her legs around his hips, trying to get closer.

"*You're so wet.*" Feral intensity had sharpened his features. "*I can feel you soaking through your trousers and mine.*"

She'd felt a jolt of embarrassment. "*I'm sorry—*"

"*Why in blazes are you sorry?*" he rasped. "*I love how wanton you are. I cannot wait for the day when I get to be inside you—to feel your drenched pussy squeezing my prick.*"

A combination of shock and pleasure had cut off her reply. He'd thrust harder, faster, and awash with need, she'd held on to his shoulders, chanting his name. Pleasure crested, this pinnacle even more intense than the last...especially since it was shared.

"*Bloody Christ,*" he'd roared. "*Gigi.*"

The tendons of his neck had stood out in stark relief, the muscles of his chest bulging. He'd lunged heavily, as if he wanted to pound her into the stone. In that instant, no matter how wrong it was, she'd wanted more. More of those guttural sounds from his throat, more of his harsh breaths, more of the wonder blazing in his eyes.

Of course, that had been the heat of the moment. Now reality was beginning to creep in, along with worries about the future. About consequences.

How will I escape this situation with my reputation intact? Although Conrad said that he would "take care of it"—whatever that means—he cannot control everything. If we are discovered, I will be ruined. My family will be devastated. The only solution would be to marry Conrad, but he obviously doesn't want to marry me. And I don't want to be married either...at least, not out of necessity. Not because "worse came to worst"...

A high-pitched trill interrupted her spiraling thoughts.

Is that a bird? In here?

Carefully, she tried to extricate herself from Conrad. Even in sleep, he held her tightly, and as she attempted to scoot from under his arm, his lashes lifted. With his hair tousled and eyes sleepy, he was so attractive that her heart tottered against her ribs.

"What's the matter, duchess?" he said alertly.

"I, um, heard something." Flustered, she said, "It sounded like a bird."

He sat up, running a hand through his dark-blond waves. Waves that had been mussed by her own hands as she'd clung to him in the throes.

"In here?" he demanded.

"I think so."

He was already on his feet. Donning his dried shirt, he prowled around the caldarium. She grabbed a dusty candle from the stash they'd found and joined him in the search. When a series of chirps broke the silence, Gigi followed the sound to an alcove that she hadn't explored. There, perched on the stone bench, was a small bird with a yellow breast and black markings on its head.

"However did you get in here, little one?" Gigi exclaimed.

The bird cocked its head, then darted upward. Gigi held the candle up toward the ceiling. Squinting at the cavernous roof, she saw no sign of her feathered friend.

"Did you find the bird?" Conrad's voice came behind her.

"Yes." Focused on the shadowy ceiling where the bird had disappeared, she added absently, "It was a great tit."

When silence greeted her, she twisted her head in Conrad's direction. His lips were twitching.

"What is so amusing?" she asked.

"I believe that was my line." Smirking, he lowered his gaze to her bosom.

The man owns half of England...and has the humor of an adolescent.

She sighed. "Don't be crude, Godwin."

"Back to that, are we? After what we shared, one would think we could be on more familiar terms."

She didn't trust herself to answer, especially when he moved close behind her. Although he made no physical contact, his virile heat kept her in a state of quivering awareness.

Now is not the time to become a ninny. Concentrate, Gigi.

"The great—the bird flew up to the ceiling, then disappeared from sight," she told him. "It is either hiding up there...or it escaped through an opening. I am guessing the latter since the bird had to get in here somehow."

"There must be a vent."

Conrad held his candle next to hers. The added light revealed a rocky ledge in the ceiling about thirteen feet above the ground. If there was a vent, it was cleverly concealed.

"The opening must be hidden beyond the ledge. I think I can just fit through the space between the ledge and ceiling," he muttered. "Once I get up there, I'll locate the opening and get us out."

He set down his candle, eyeing the ledge. She did her own calculations, informed by years of tree climbing. Unfortunately, she concluded that the rocky shelf was out of reach, even for him.

"It's too high—" she began.

He crouched, his thigh muscles bulging before he jumped. His athleticism was a sight to behold. As she'd predicted, however, the destination was too far up, and he landed with a frustrated grunt.

"You cannot reach it this way," she said. "I have a better idea."

"I can do it."

Again, he leapt...and missed.

"If you would just listen—"

"Stand aside," he ordered.

Seeing the stubborn set of his jaw, she raised her brows and moved out of the way. Conrad backed up, pawing his feet against the ground like an angry bull. He sprinted at full speed, taking off with an impressive leap. Bemused, she had to admire his determination as he soared through the air. Her breath caught when his fingertips brushed the underside of the ledge.

Close, but not quite there. He landed in a crouch, letting out a string of expletives.

She tapped the sweaty bulge of his shoulder.

"I almost had it." He rose, his hands clenched. "I'll try again—"

"We don't have time for your heroics," she informed him. "This time, we'll try it my way."

"Don't be afraid," Conrad said. "I've got you."

"I'm not afraid." Gigi's voice floated down to him. "Hold steady and stop distracting me."

He gripped her delicate ankles, providing stability as she rose and stood upon his shoulders. Damn, but she had the grace of an acrobat. The fearlessness of one, too.

"You'll have to bring us closer to the ledge," she said.

Given his precious cargo, he took the steps with care. Sweat beaded on his forehead as she wobbled, her bare heels digging into his shoulders. Sometime soon, he was going to feel those heels digging into his shoulders again—only this time, she would be on her back, moaning his name while he plowed her snug little pussy. The thought of being skin-to-skin, of being the first to claim her virgin territory, blazed fire up his spine.

Even fully clothed, she made him hotter than hell. He hadn't spent in his trousers since he was a fourteen-year-old lad. Ratterby, the enterprising bastard, had smuggled a leathery whore into Creavey Hall. For the price of a fortnight's meals, Conrad had been granted five minutes with her. Even though she'd smelled of sweat and onions, she'd expertly frigged him with her chapped hands, cackling when he spent a mortifyingly short time later. That had been his first experience of intimacy.

Shaking off the memory, he tightened his hold on Gigi.

"Almost there," she said.

Christ, he liked when her voice had that breathless quality. She'd cried his name in just this fashion when she came, and he'd never heard anything sweeter.

"You can lean forward." He braced her knees. "I've got you."

"I'm touching the ledge," she said excitedly.

"Good girl," he muttered. "Can you pull yourself up?"

"Not quite. I shall have to jump."

Concern jolted him. "That's too risky—"

"I'll be fine," she assured him. "But you'll have to let go of me."

Like hell I'm letting go of you.

The thought invaded him, along with a foreign feeling of possessiveness.

Frowning, he said, "It's too dangerous. If you don't make it onto the ledge, you could fall—"

"Then I'll just have to make it, won't I?"

Peering down at him, she winked. Christ, she was a handful. If he didn't keep a firm grip on the reins, she'd snatch them up at the first opportunity.

"I'll give you a boost," he said decisively. "When I do, *then* you jump. Picture yourself getting onto the ledge but have no fear. I will catch you if you fall."

"I know you will."

The trust in her bright eyes pierced him to the quick. The pain was fleeting and exquisite. He couldn't recall a woman ever looking at him that way.

Frowning, he focused. "On the count of three. Ready?"

"When you are."

Following his own advice, he kept his gaze on the ledge and envisioned Gigi's safe landing. "One, two, *three*."

He catapulted her. She coordinated her leap with his movement, and his lungs seized as she flew through the air. He braced to catch her...but she landed on the ledge, lying on her front, her feet dangling.

"Are you all right?" he demanded.

"I'm perfectly well. And there *is* a tunnel." Her elation was contagious. "I can see light at the end. I shall figure out the exit then come back for you."

"Be careful—"

She'd already disappeared. He kept his eyes fixed on the ledge, his ears pricking at the slightest sounds. Soon it was quiet...too quiet. When he called her name, she didn't reply. Perhaps she couldn't hear him? He tried again: still nothing. Minutes ticked by, and tired of calling for her, he braced his hands on his hips, staring at the empty outcropping of rock.

Gigi's fine. If she wasn't, she would call for help—

Then it hit him. What if she had escaped...and left him there?

It wouldn't be the first time a woman left you hanging.

The past crawled beneath his skin, grabbing his heart and smacking it against his ribs. Raking a hand through his hair, he tried to calm himself. To give Gigi the benefit of the doubt. She wasn't like the others. She wouldn't betray him. She wouldn't use him the way Isobel, Vicky, or other lovers had. Nor would she break her promise the way his mama had.

But as the minutes passed, he cursed himself.

How could I be so bloody gullible?

He hardly knew Gigi. Why would he think for even a moment that she would come back for him? Their relationship, such as it were, consisted of a few heated disputes interspersed with kissing and groping. He knew better than anyone that a night of pleasure meant nothing. Hell, she was probably galloping home right now, laughing to herself because she'd gotten away with an indiscretion, and her reputation was safe.

In the meantime, he was stranded in this hellhole.

I'll come back for you. I promise...

Desperation sucked at him, but he fought it off with fury. With icy logic, he contemplated Gigi's next moves. What strategies he, himself, might employ in her situation. She could, for instance, summon constables to the spa on the pretense of discovering a break-in. When the authorities knocked down the door to the caldarium, even Conrad would be hard-pressed to come up with a reasonable explanation for his presence.

"Fucking hell," he bit out. "The deceitful b—"

"Conrad?"

He jerked, his gaze shooting up to the ledge. Gigi was smiling as she peered down at him, and he choked on a breath. Relief flooded him...along with anger.

How could I have given her such power over me?

"What took you so long?" he said tersely.

"I was looking for something to help you up." She threw down a dirty length of rope. "Luckily, I found this in Miss Letty's shed. I've secured the other end to a tree; it should hold you."

"Aren't you ingenious?"

At his surly tone, she frowned.

"What's the matter with you?"

He was in no mood to share. He'd trusted her with too much already. He was appalled by how readily he'd let down his guard—by his own stupidity.

"Nothing's the matter," he muttered. "Except that I've wasted hours trapped in this stinking place."

She drew a breath. "Do you need help climbing up?"

"No, I do not need your bloody help." He snatched the dangling rope. "You have done enough. You're the reason I'm here in the first place."

She jerked as if he'd struck her.

"The reason you are here is because *you* decided to vandalize my friend's property." Her stare was harder than diamonds. "Well, I wish you the best getting out on your own. And by the by, *you're welcome* for the rope, you ungrateful clod."

If there was such a thing as stomp-crawling, she managed it. Her knees thudded irately overhead as she made her exit.

Jaw clenched, he grabbed the rope, tested that it could take his weight, and began his ascent.

Chapter Twelve

Walking through the village five days later, Conrad nodded brusquely as villagers greeted him by name. It didn't take long for a man to be recognized here, and if he'd been smart, he would have left. He would have returned to London and worked out another stratagem for ruining Abel Pearce. Instead, he'd done the opposite. He'd hung around the village, hoping to run into Gigi. He'd briefly considered calling upon her at her brother's house but discarded the idea because of the two most likely outcomes: she would refuse to see him, and Ethan Harrington would call him out.

Tired of staying at an inn, Conrad had leased a property in Chuddums called Honeystone Hall and sent for his London staff. When he wasn't working or staking out Gigi, he found himself brooding: he wasn't used to feeling like a bastard. While a few prior lovers had accused him of being one, he normally did not agree with their assessment. He prided himself on being clear about what he had to offer in a relationship and what he expected in return. He did this to protect both parties; after Vicky had shredded his heart, he had no wish to repeat the experience. If somewhere along the line his lover became dissatisfied with the terms, that was her problem. It wasn't his fault that she'd changed her mind. His usual response had been to terminate the arrangement.

To his knowledge, he had never treated a woman unfairly... except Gigi. The one woman who'd held up her end of the bargain. Who was the bravest, cleverest, and most spirited female he'd ever met.

The shimmering hurt in her eyes gnawed at his gut, reminding him of the hearty kidney pie he'd ordered for lunch. Actually, he hadn't ordered the dish: the cook at the local tavern, a fearsome matron by the name of Mrs. Thornton, had plunked it in front of him, declaring, "*Eat it or starve, it's up to you.*"

He'd appreciated her honesty.

Truth be told, he wished he could be as blunt with Gigi. Wished he could go up to her and apologize for acting like an ass. Wished he could thank her...and ask for a second chance. Yet he hadn't acted on his instincts because, for the first time in his life, he didn't know what he wanted from a woman. That is, he knew he *wanted* Gigi—Christ, he frigged himself several times a day, thinking about her—but he didn't know how to fit her into his plans.

There was only one way to have a well-bred virgin. But marriage meant commitment, and he was already committed to vengeance. He didn't want any distractions. Moreover, Gigi stood squarely in his path: she was determined to save the spa while he was equally determined to see it fail.

There is no way to make it work. Cut your losses and leave. Stop acting like a namby-pamby.

But he couldn't.

He could still taste her. Smell her. He could feel the way she'd trembled during her climax, rubbing her pussy so desperately against his cock that he'd gone off like a cannon. Moreover, how could he leave knowing that she was angry at him and rightly so?

Seeing Wally up ahead—thank God the fellow favored garish

colors that made him easy to spot—Conrad hastily ducked into the nearest shop. Wally had cornered him several times in the last few days, bending his ear about the legend of Bloody Thom. Although Conrad didn't believe in ghosts, a bad luck curse would explain a few things: since his arrival in Chuddums, nothing was going his way.

"Welcome to Hatcherds, sir."

Conrad turned from the window, where he'd been surveilling Wally, to see another elderly fellow smiling up at him.

God's teeth, what is it with friendly codgers in this village?

"I am Mr. Khan, the proprietor of Hatcherds." The man was as wrinkled as a prune, with snowy hair and eyebrows. His eyes twinkled behind thick spectacles, and he was holding out a tray dotted with exotic-looking sweets. "May I offer you refreshment whilst you browse?"

Since it would be churlish to refuse, Conrad took a small, pale confection studded with slivered nuts. He popped it into his mouth, his eyes widening as creamy, spiced sweetness melted upon his tongue.

"That is exquisite," he said.

"Thank you. I made the *barfi* myself." Mr. Khan beamed at him. "Have another."

Conrad didn't have to be asked twice. Before he knew it, he'd consumed the entire tray and found himself having a cup of tea with Mr. Khan at the counter. The bookshop owner was as chatty as Wally, and Conrad used this to his advantage, subtly milking the other for information.

"I'm told a family from London moved here recently," he said casually.

"You must mean Lord Ethan Harrington. His new bride, Xenia Harrington, is a gracious lady and dear friend," Mr. Khan said fondly. "She inspired me to reorganize the shop—"

"I think I've made her acquaintance." Conrad reined in Mr.

Khan before the other could meander. "Is she dark-haired and slender, with remarkable violet eyes?"

"No, you've mixed her up with Lady Gigi, Lord Ethan's younger sister."

"My mistake," Conrad said smoothly. "I saw Lady Gigi in the square the other day, and she reminded me of someone I met in London."

"It is possible that you met our Lady Gigi during the London Season, for she is a popular debutante," Mr. Khan said proudly. "She wintered here at her brother's house and is a friend of the village. She has helped Miss Letty to refurbish her spa...but then again, you know about the spa, don't you?"

The astute gleam behind Mr. Khan's spectacles reminded Conrad that while affable, Chuddumites were not ignorant bumpkins, and it would behoove him to remember that fact.

"News travels fast, I see," he said easily. "It's true that I hoped to purchase the spa, but as Miss Letty informed me that she has no interest in selling, I shall have to seek out another venture."

"It is for the best," Mr. Khan agreed. "The success of the spa means a great deal to our village. With the grand reopening less than two weeks away, we expect an influx of visitors that will benefit everyone in Chuddums. I, myself, have restocked on stationery and plan to make extra batches of sweets."

"An excellent idea, I'm sure." Conrad racked his brain for a covert way to ascertain Gigi's routine. "As a fellow Londoner, I should like to introduce myself to the Harringtons. Are they in the village much?"

"Xenia Harrington does the rounds on Mondays and Thursdays and always makes a stop here," Mr. Khan said proudly.

Goddammit. How do I ask about Gigi without being obvious?

"And, er, the rest of the family?"

"Lord Ethan often accompanies his wife. Being newlyweds, they don't like to be apart, eh?" Mr. Khan winked. "The rest of the

Harringtons—Lord Ethan's siblings and parents—join them from time to time, most often for tea at the Leaning House."

Conrad could hardly barge in on the family tea and ask to speak to Gigi. After further probing failed to yield results, he thanked Mr. Khan for the hospitality, purchased several packets of sweets, and left the shop. He exited the square, thinking a walk might clear his head. He hadn't gone far when jeering voices snagged his attention.

"Stop sniveling, you sorry scrap. We ain't barely started with you."

Hastening his pace, Conrad followed the voices to a back lane. A small, sandy-haired boy stood shaking against a brick wall. He had a shiner over his left eye. His smart woolen jacket and trousers were streaked with dirt, and his fashionable felt hat lay on the ground between him and the brutish, pug-nosed boy facing him. The leader was flanked by two other bullies—one blond, the other ginger-haired.

"This is what you get for being a tattle-tale," the ginger-haired bully spat.

"I d-didn't tattle," the boy protested.

"Then 'ow did the schoolmaster know that you've been giving us your lunch, eh?" the leader demanded.

"I d-didn't say anything, I swear—"

"Liar, liar, fancy pants on fire," the blond bully taunted.

"Let's teach this runt a lesson."

When Pug Nose stomped on the victim's hat, grinding it into the dirt, Conrad's nape burned. He stalked over, grabbing the surprised leader by the scruff.

"Pick on someone your own size," Conrad said coldly.

"Unhand me, you bastard," the bully yelled. "Help me, lads!"

The other two charged. Skills honed from years of prize-fighting kicked in, and in a matter of moments, the three lay in a groaning heap.

"Leave this boy alone, or it will be worse for you next time," Conrad warned. "Now get out of here."

The bullies limped away.

Conrad turned to the boy, who was staring at him, one eye bright blue, the other swelled shut. When a tear trickled down the lad's freckled cheek, he wiped it away with his sleeve.

"You all right, lad?" Conrad asked.

The boy shook his head, snot running from his nose.

"Here." Conrad took out a packet of Mr. Khan's sweets. "Medicine for that shiner."

The boy peered into the bag. "That's not medicine. That's Mr. Khan's *barfi*."

"It's medicine if it makes you feel better."

While the boy ate one of the treats, Conrad picked up the crushed hat and handed it to him. "Unfortunately, this looks damaged beyond repair."

"My mama can fix it. By the by, I'm Kenneth Sommers. You can call me Kenny."

At the boy's proper bow, Conrad stifled a smile.

"Conrad Godwin." He returned the courtesy. "Now, Kenny, you'd best run along and have your mama take a look at your eye—"

"How did you learn to fight like that, sir?" Kenny asked.

Years of being bullied just like you.

"I did some prizefighting in my day."

"You were a prizefighter?" Kenny gazed at him as if he'd taken a stroll over a lake. "Could you teach me how to box?"

Conrad shook his head. "I haven't got time, lad. I won't be in the village long—"

"It won't take long. I'm a fast learner."

"Ask your papa—"

"My papa's too busy for me. Mama says he has a long-standing appointment at the tavern." Kenny's bottom lip quivered, his good eye shimmering. "Just one lesson, *please*?"

Christ.

"I have to be somewhere—"

"Tomorrow, then. Please, Mr. Godwin? I've saved up money from doing chores at Mama's shop, and I'll pay you."

Seeing the boy's desperation, Conrad couldn't turn away.

What harm could it do to teach the sprat a few defensive maneuvers?

"One lesson." He sighed. "And you don't owe me anything."

In his study at Honeystone Hall, Conrad was reading the latest report sent by Redgrave, his chief manager, when the butler alerted him to a visitor. At the mention of the man's name, Conrad's pulse started to thud.

What does he want? Did he hear of my interest in the spa and guess my intentions? Does he know who I am—are my plans compromised?

His chest constricting, Conrad maintained his outward calm. "Send him in."

Moments later, Abel Pearce entered the study. Conrad rose, noting that the passing years had been kinder than the bastard deserved. Pearce was fuller in the middle, thinner on top, but was otherwise little changed. He still dressed like the pretentious ass he was and had the same grating, falsely hearty manner.

Despite the twenty-odd years that had passed, Conrad could have picked his distant relation out of the crowd. He tensed as Pearce studied him with keen eyes.

Does the blackguard recognize me?

"Mr. Godwin." Pearce's bow was deferential. "I hope I am not intruding. Although we are not acquainted, my family has a long legacy in Chuddums, and I take it upon myself to extend a welcome whenever a gentleman of quality joins our fold."

Relief loosened the knots in Conrad's chest.

Of course, Pearce doesn't know me. He couldn't get rid of my mama and me fast enough. He didn't think twice about throwing us out...about withholding what was rightfully ours.

"I am glad you came, Mr. Pearce." Conrad waved at the chair across his desk. "Have a seat."

"I don't mind if I do, sir." Pearce's eager manner gave off a whiff of desperation. "May I ask what brings you to our little village?"

"I sought a change from the brisk pace of London."

"Ah, yes. Chuddums is an oasis from modern life," Pearce agreed. "My great-great-grandfather, Langdon Pearce, was an industrialist like yourself. He built a mill here—which still stands, though it has long been abandoned. A man of great vision, he had a hand in developing Chuddums. The village owes much of its charming character to him."

Charming character? What a joke. Chuddums is a sinking hole and you know it.

Conrad rearranged some papers on his blotter. "A quaint slice of history, I'm sure."

After an awkward pause, Pearce said, "The truth is, I have an ulterior motive for my visit."

Why does that not surprise me?

"Oh?"

"Your financial prowess precedes you, Mr. Godwin, and I was hoping to get your advice on a matter. Confidentially, of course."

Just like that, the solution presented itself to Conrad. It was simple, elegant, and, best of all, removed the spa from the equation. The strategy would allow him to have his revenge *and* Gigi. Exhilaration filled him, and he clenched his hands beneath the desk, reminding himself not to show his cards.

Looking his enemy in the eye, he said, "I would be glad to be of assistance."

Chapter Thirteen

Two days later, Gigi was taking tea with her brothers and sister-in-law at the Leaning House. The group included her eldest brother James, the Earl of Manderly, who'd come from his estate a few hours away. At thirty-three, he was a younger version of Papa with his bronze-colored hair, grey-blue eyes, and brawny frame. Ever the impeccable heir, he had nary a wrinkle on his charcoal frock coat and black wool trousers, and his claret cravat formed a perfect knot beneath his square chin.

Mrs. Pettigrew had given them the best table next to the bow window, which offered privacy and a view of the square. Unfortunately, the view now included a large monument. The obelisk dedicated to Abel Pearce dominated the scene; the wintry sunlight gave the stone an unpleasant glow that made Gigi think of fleshy worms after a rain.

"What a remarkable addition to the square. And to think, Ethan." James raised his cup of Assam tea. "We have you to thank for it."

"How was I supposed to know what the monument would look like?" Ethan grumbled.

Of her brothers, Ethan was the one Gigi most physically resembled, as they'd both inherited their mama's coloring. As a girl, Gigi had gone to Ethan first when she had a problem for, despite his overprotective nature, he was the most understanding of her siblings. While his injury had, understandably, turned him into a brooding curmudgeon for a few years, his marriage had restored his disposition.

"Didn't Mrs. Pearce inform you?" James inquired.

Ethan scowled. "Her voice is like a badly tuned piano. Whenever she speaks, my ears close. It is instinctual—an act of self-preservation."

Beside him, Xenia giggled, and a wry smile tugged on James's lips.

While Gigi was happy to see James, she found it worrisome that he hadn't brought his wife, Evie. When the pair had first wed, the sweet, shy blonde, had accompanied James everywhere. In the past year, however, Gigi had seen less of her sister-in-law, and whenever she asked James about it, he brushed it off or claimed that his wife, a budding botanist, was busy with her greenhouse.

Gigi sensed something was amiss with the pair. Just like she knew that Owen, who sat beside her, was still struggling with his demons. At times like this, her intuitive nature felt like a curse. Like the Cassandra of mythology, her ability to predict disaster was overshadowed by the fact that no one listened to her. She was forever treated like the baby sister who was loved and coddled but not taken seriously. Because she knew her family's protectiveness came from a place of love, she didn't hold it against them. But for Conrad to underestimate, nay *demean*, her abilities...that was too bitter a pill to swallow.

How dare he treat me so shabbily? It was not as if I expected gratitude, but a word of thanks or a "well done" would have sufficed. And I was beginning to...to like him, too.

A week had passed since their rendezvous in the caldarium. Luckily, no one knew about their indiscretion...except for Miss Letty. Out of necessity, Gigi had awakened her friend that morning and confessed to the events leading to the discovery of the caldarium (minus certain intimate details). While Miss Letty had been ecstatic over the existence of the secret chamber, she had also grasped the scandalous consequences if word got out that Gigi had been alone with a man. The spinster had vowed to take that secret to the grave.

Gigi's reputation was safe for now. If only she could say the same for her sanity. Her righteous fuming over Conrad's behavior was constantly interrupted by other memories of that night. The hot flick of his tongue, the teasing suction of his mouth, the way he'd ground his...his cock against her. Just thinking the word made her hot all over. She'd never felt anything like it...never known such pleasure *existed*. At night, she tossed and turned, trying to get those memories out of her head. Trying to ignore the ache between her legs. To block out his rough and undeniably arousing words.

I cannot wait to feel your drenched pussy squeezing my prick.

In the shadows of her bower, feverish curiosity had consumed her. If what he'd done on the *outside*, with layers of clothing between them, had felt so blissful, how would it feel to have him doing such things *inside* her?

It wasn't just the pleasure she remembered. There were also the demons that had chased him through his dreams, and the vulnerability she'd glimpsed beneath his pitiless exterior. He was a complicated man with hidden depths, yet for a brief instant, he'd seemed to be letting her in...

It doesn't matter. He's made no effort to contact you, even though he has taken up residence in Honeystone Hall. You mean nothing to him.

Through the village grapevine, she'd learned that Conrad had leased a manor not far from the spa. She didn't know his intentions, and she told herself she didn't care.

"You are awfully quiet, Gigi." James's voice cut through her thoughts. "What mischief are you plotting, I wonder?"

She started, realizing that all eyes were upon her.

"I'm not plotting," she said hastily. "Nor am I involved in any mischief whatsoever."

James arched his brows. Growing up, she'd found him the most intimidating of her brothers, not only because of their age difference but also because he was the most proper...and perceptive.

"Me thinks our sister doth protest too much," he drawled.

Gigi fought her rising blush. "I am not protesting. I haven't been up to any trouble."

"Stop teasing her, James."

Surprisingly, it was Owen who came to her rescue. While he had apologized to Ethan and patched things up, Gigi felt his residual brooding over the matter. Ethan, on the other hand, was too busy flirting with his wife to be grumpy. His dark head bent, he murmured something for Xenia's ears only. She, in turn, gazed at him as if he'd hung the stars in the sky for her. It was clear that the rest of the world had ceased to exist for them.

It was like that with Conrad in the caldarium. For a little while, he was different. Then he had to ruin everything by reverting to his boorish self.

"It was an honest question." James rotated his cup a precise quarter-turn in the saucer. "By 'mischief,' I was referring to our Gigi's 'job' at the infamous bath."

Oh, right. He's talking about the spa. He doesn't suspect my, ahem, other activities.

Sensing an opportunity, Gigi decided to take it.

"Miss Letty and I *were* making excellent progress," she said brightly.

James took the bait. "Were?"

She gave him an innocent look. "Until Ethan barred me from going there."

"Why would he do that?"

James addressed the question to Ethan, who was too occupied with Xenia to take notice.

"Will this newlywed phase never end?" Casting his gaze heavenward, James cleared his throat loudly. "Ethan, old boy, did you see the pig that flew by?"

Ethan tore his gaze from Xenia.

"Pardon?" His indigo eyes were distracted. "Something flew by?"

"Never mind. I was just trying to get your attention," James said. "Given my charming competition, that is a Herculean task."

Xenia blushed, looking charming indeed in her red wool walking dress, which matched her fiery curls. Looking rather smug, Ethan picked up Xenia's hand and placed a light kiss on her knuckles.

"Why don't you stop flirting with my wife and tell me what you want?" he said mildly.

"I was asking why you would prevent Gigi from going to the spa," James replied.

Ethan's expression darkened. "Because I am her older brother and she is my responsibility, that's why." He lowered his voice. "And I will not allow some scoundrel to dally with her."

"Scoundrel?" James's urbane façade vanished in a blink. "What's this about, Gigi?"

You opened this Pandora's box for a reason. Make it worth it.

"It was a misunderstanding," Gigi said quickly. "A fellow named Mr. Godwin was visiting Miss Letty's spa, and there was an accident. He caught me as I was about to fall into the pool. Xenia saw us at an inopportune moment, but nothing happened."

She turned pleading eyes to her sister-in-law. "Please, Xenia, won't you vouch for me? You know how much Miss Letty and her spa mean to me. In this final stretch before the reopening gala, she needs my help more than ever."

Xenia bit her lip. "The reopening *is* important—"

"Nothing is more important than Gigi's well-being," Ethan said.

James nodded. "On that, we agree."

"Hear, hear," Owen added.

Perfect. The one time these three agree on anything, it is on restricting my freedom.

Gigi scowled at her brothers. "Why must I be treated like a prisoner? Why can't you trust my judgment? It's not fair. I am twenty-two years old. At my age, James was on the Grand Tour, Ethan was giving concerts all over England, and Owen…"

Too late, she realized her slip. In the heat of the moment, she'd referenced the painful period in Owen's life that had the power to trigger one of his explosive episodes. Filled with guilt and dread, she shot a wary look in his direction.

Owen's storm-colored gaze met hers. He was as handsome as her other brothers, but the ordeal he'd suffered had left its mark. Lines aged his face, permanent shadows smudged beneath his soulful eyes. Although he'd gained some much-needed weight since coming to Chuddums, he was still too thin. His brown hair was shaggy and needed a trim.

Hitching his shoulders, he said, "Life isn't fair, is it?"

Seeing that his expression was ironic rather than haunted, she let out a slow breath. As did everyone else at the table. Except for Owen, who took a gulp of tea and popped a bite-sized ham and mustard sandwich into his mouth.

"We do not make the rules, Gigi." Now that disaster was averted, James took up the refrain. "As an innocent young lady, you are bound by the dictates of society."

I am not that innocent. Rebellious pleasure quivered through her. *And what if I am tired of society's stupid dictates?*

"It is our duty as your brothers to keep you safe." Ethan added his brick to the tower they were building around her. "We are looking out for your best interests, Gigi. You know that."

Dash it all. Was there any explanation more annoying than, *It is for your own good?*

"Surely there can be a compromise," Xenia said. "What if, in place of Colette, *I* accompany Gigi to the spa and promise to keep an eye on her at all times?"

"You wouldn't mind?" Gigi breathed.

"Not at all," Xenia said warmly. "I know how much the spa means to you."

"What about the sonata you were helping me with?" Ethan asked. "I compose better with you by my side."

"I can do both. I shall accompany Gigi during the day and help you in the evening."

"Then I shall look forward to your nighttime assistance, my love."

At Ethan's devilish smirk, roses bloomed in Xenia's cheeks.

Before Gigi could celebrate her victory, James said, "Who is this Godwin fellow?"

Botheration.

"It's Conrad Godwin," Ethan said.

James's expression hardened. "The industrialist? The cove's a shark in his business dealings. Not to mention a rake—"

"That's the one," Ethan said dryly. "You see why I kept Gigi away from the spa?"

"Is he still here? Have you paid him a visit?" James demanded.

"Ethan has not," Gigi burst out. "Because I begged him not to make a mountain out of a molehill. And will you *please* stop talking about me as if I weren't here?"

James looked briefly nonplussed. "We were doing no such thing."

"I'm a grown-up and capable of handling myself. *Nothing happened* that day. My reputation is safe, so please don't go looking for trouble."

"Regardless, it's not safe for you to go to the spa," James insisted. "Even chaperoned by Xenia."

Her frustration boiling over, Gigi opened her mouth, but Owen spoke first.

"I'll escort Gigi and Xenia," he said.

Everyone stared at him, including Gigi. While Owen did occasionally venture into the village, he didn't stay long. He preferred the solitude of Ethan's estate.

Gigi drew her brows together. "Are you certain you are up to it?"

"It is not as if I have anything better to do." Shrugging, Owen bit into a jam tart.

After tea, Gigi and Xenia stopped at Mrs. Sommers's small but tidy dress shop. Gigi had an appointment for a fitting of the gown she was to wear to the spa's gala. Along the way, they collected Duffy, whose opinion was invaluable in such matters.

Exiting the dressing room, Gigi twirled to show off her new dress.

"What do you think?" she asked.

"That ball gown is perfect on you," Xenia declared.

"You've outdone yourself, Mrs. Sommers." Duffy circled Gigi with a critical eye. "The design is exquisite. The embroidery at the hem mimicking waves of water is an inspired touch. Brava, madam."

"Your suggestion of the pale-blue satin gave me the idea, Mr. Duffield." Mrs. Sommers, a petite lady whose manner and appearance were as neat as her shop, bowed her head. "We both deserve credit."

"If I may make a further suggestion?" Duffy asked.

"Please do," Gigi said.

"What do you think about lowering the slope of the bodice by half an inch?"

Mrs. Sommers pursed her lips. "A bit more dashing but demure, nonetheless. An improvement, I think. Lady Gigi?"

"I put myself entirely in your and Duffy's capable hands," Gigi said happily.

When Mrs. Sommers went to show Xenia some gloves that had just arrived, Gigi had a moment alone with Duffy.

"Any news from Godwin?" he asked quietly.

During her last visit to the draper's shop, Gigi had disclosed most of her dealings with Conrad. Duffy hadn't been too surprised when she admitted her attraction. His exact response had been, "*Well, look at the man. Who could blame you?*"

"No," she said. "And I've decided not to spare him another thought."

"Good for you, darling. He doesn't deserve you."

"How about you? Any developments?"

"As a matter of fact."

Seeing Duffy's hazel eyes light up, Gigi had to squelch an excited squeak.

"You spoke to him?" she said in hushed tones.

"When Oscar threw a shoe"—Oscar was Duffy's dappled stallion—"I took it as a sign that I should give things one last chance. I went to the smithy, and it was just me and Mr. Keane. I made chitchat while he worked on the shoe. He didn't say a word, of course, and I was despairing that I'd made a mistake when out of nowhere, he said, '*Patrick*.'"

"I don't follow."

"Neither did I. Until he clarified." Duffy's chiseled features glowed with elation. "He wanted me to call him by his given name —Patrick."

"Oh my stars."

"And garters," Duffy agreed happily. "I asked if he will be attending Miss Letty's gala, and he said yes. And then…"

"Then what happened?" Gigi asked breathlessly.

"He said, '*See you there.*'"

They sighed at the same time.

She touched her friend's shoulder. "I'm *so* happy for you."

"That makes two of us. Now I must get back to the shop." Duffy winked. "Hopefully, I'll have more news soon."

With a smile on her lips, Gigi returned to the dressing room. Mrs. Sommers's niece and assistant, Mattie, was pinning the bodice for the alteration. Seeing the twinkle in the buxom brunette's eyes, Gigi sensed that Duffy was not the only one for whom love was in the air.

"You look like the cat that got the cream," Gigi said lightly.

"I've a new follower, milady." Mattie pinched a pin between her fingers, her eyes dreamy. "But please don't tell my aunt about it. She's already cross with me, saying I pay too much attention to beaux and not enough to what I'm doing."

Eyeing the sharp pin hovering by her decolletage, Gigi cleared her throat.

"Perhaps it is better to focus on the task at hand," she said. "Don't worry, I shan't breathe word of your follower."

A few minutes later, Gigi was returning to the front of the shop when a small, sandy-haired boy appeared in the corridor. It was Kenny, Mrs. Sommers's youngest.

Seeing the purpling bruise beneath his eye, she gasped. "What happened, dear?"

"Bullies," he said succinctly.

"Oh. I'm sorry." Her heart ached for the little lad even as she inwardly raged at the brutes who'd hurt him. "Your mama knows about it, I assume?"

"She does, milady. But a man must take care of his own problems."

Seeing the way he threw back his thin shoulders, she was tempted to smile.

"While that is true," she said with care, "a man must also know when he needs help."

"I have help," Kenny said. "I also have this...for you."

Pulling a crumpled note from his pocket, he handed it to her and scampered off.

"What on earth?" she murmured.

There was no name on the front, and the decorative wax seal did not identify the sender. Brow furrowed, she broke the seal.

Duchess,

Of all the words in the English language, these are the hardest for me to say: I am sorry. While I don't deserve another chance, I nonetheless humbly ask for one. I owe you an explanation for my behavior, which I would like to give in person. Would you do me the honor of meeting me outside your home at midnight? If you choose not to come, I will understand and bother you no more.

I remain your servant,
  C

Chapter Fourteen

At a quarter past midnight, Conrad stood in the shadows and watched the front of Bottoms House. He could no longer deny reality.

Gigi is not coming. I've lost her. If I even had her to begin with.

His chest felt oddly tight. Rationally, he knew there was no reason for him to feel this sense of loss, but— Too late, he heard a rustling behind him. He whirled around, fists raised.

"It's me."

Gigi's whispered words were rather unnecessary, since he would recognize her anywhere. She was wearing trousers again. With her hair in two glossy, thick braids, she looked like a mischievous sprite who'd stolen some lad's outfit. In a heartbeat, Conrad's aggression morphed into arousal.

"I've been watching the front door for an hour," he said. "How did I miss you?"

"I didn't leave through the door. I climbed out my window and down a tree."

"You what?" Assessing the height from the second floor, he turned a scowl upon her. "You could have broken your bloody neck."

"I told you, descending is easy." She wrinkled her nose. "I must say, if this is the apology you promised, I might as well climb right back up."

"This isn't the apology," he muttered. "My carriage is waiting. We'll talk there."

"Let's get on with it, shall we?"

Turning smartly on her heel, she headed for the front gate. He followed, his irritation fading at the sight of her long, slender legs. If he had his way, she would wear trousers *all the time*.

He handed Gigi into the carriage and instructed his groom, Ainsley, to drive around until further notice. As they rolled off, she sat in the corner farthest away from him. Her arms were crossed, and even in the flickering lamplight, he saw that her expression wasn't the friendliest.

"How did you get Kenny to deliver the message to me?" she asked.

He frowned. "I didn't twist his arm, if that's what you are implying. I saw him being besieged by bullies and intervened. He asked me to teach him how to fight, and seeing as he could be blown away by a strong wind, I agreed. After I gave him a few pointers, he insisted on repaying the debt. I refused his savings, of course...but then he mentioned who his mama was. I saw no harm in asking him to deliver a note."

"Hmm."

When she did not elaborate, he drew a breath. "Thank you for meeting me."

"Did you think I wouldn't?"

"I wasn't certain you would show. I wasn't certain I deserved the chance," he admitted.

She arched her brows. "Then pray do not waste it."

Despite her delicate beauty, she had a spine of steel. He liked that about her. He liked that while he inspired fear in grown men, she wasn't intimidated by him—by his wealth or power.

She was a duchess through and through. *His* duchess.

The recognition flowed through him and illuminated the path forward.

"The apology first," he said brusquely. "I acted like a bounder at our last meeting."

"Yes, you did."

"When you carried out that dashing escape and came back with the rope, I was unforgivably rude. I offer my sincerest apology for the way I acted."

"Why *did* you behave that way?"

Of course she would ask.

He studied a crease in his trousers. "Perhaps I thought you would not come back."

"You thought I would leave you stranded?"

Hearing her surprise, he looked up. "It would not be the first time I found myself in that situation."

She drew her brows together. "Someone abandoned you in your time of need?"

"Not someone. Most everyone." He smiled humorlessly. "Especially the females in my life."

"You shall have to explain."

While Gigi's tone was firm, he took her softening expression as a positive sign. He gave her the story he had carefully prepared. All of it was true, even if certain details were glossed over.

"My papa died when I was not yet eight years old, and my mama was not able to raise me on her own. It wasn't her fault, for I was young and she was without resources. She left me in the care of a guardian, promising she would come back for me. I never saw her again. She passed away before she could make good on her word."

"Oh, Conrad. I'm sorry."

From anyone else, pity would have been intolerable. Yet Gigi was different. The empathy in her liquid eyes reminded him of what he'd felt when he looked at an engraving of Pearl, kneeling naked amongst the leaves. Not just lust but a feeling of connection —of not being alone in the dark, dark forest.

He nodded gruffly. "Like I said, it wasn't her fault."

"What about the other females you mentioned? Were they your...um, lovers?"

He liked the hint of asperity in Gigi's tone. Jealousy meant she cared.

"Yes. I haven't had the best luck when it comes to my liaisons," he said blandly. "Do you know how I made my living before I began investing?"

She shook her head.

"I was a prizefighter. I spent five years taking whatever fights were offered, saving up my winnings so that I would have money to invest."

As she digested that information, he added, "It isn't unusual for prizefighters to have female admirers. Women are drawn to the primal nature of the sport."

"And you had your fair share of admirers, I assume?"

Hiding a smile at Gigi's tartness, he nodded. "I did. None of the relationships lasted long. Most of the women wanted a taste of the forbidden—a roll between less civilized sheets—and once they had it, they moved on to the next novelty."

"Surely you were more than a novelty," she said quietly.

"When I became rich, a few women did want me for the comforts I could afford them." He thought of Isobel. "Or as means to some other ends."

Gigi frowned. "That is horrid."

"That's life, sweetheart, and I didn't mind because the transaction was mutual." He shrugged. "Except with Victoria. I met her at one of my prizefights and thought she was different. She was a widow. Her parents had married her to an old toff when she was eighteen, and when he died a decade later, she was ready to exercise her freedom. I fell in love with her, and she told me my feelings were returned. When I proposed, she said yes."

"What happened?"

"She changed her mind and married another toff. According to her letter—which she sent rather than meeting me in person—she'd enjoyed our time together but needed a more conventional life than I could offer. I suppose the idea of being wed to a fellow whose main prospect was his ability to pound his opponents to a fare-thee-well had lost its shine. She married a title...a baron, I think."

After all these years, the pain was no more than a sting. He realized that if he'd wanted Victoria badly enough, he would have told her the truth of who he was. But he hadn't because some part of him had known that she wasn't worth the risk of compromising his revenge. Now he was mostly embarrassed by how readily he'd been taken...by how weak and gullible he'd been. To his surprise, Gigi crossed the swaying carriage to sit next to him.

Her expression solemn, she said, "You are more than what Victoria—what any of these past lovers—believed you to be."

He was stunned by the pleasure her simple words evoked. Stunned by how much it mattered that she believed this of him. That she saw past the ugliness of his history to recognize what no one else had.

"None of them matter," he said hoarsely. "I'm telling you about my past not to excuse my behavior but to explain why I acted as I did. You...you're different from other females I've known. In the past, I implied that you were nothing but a spoiled chit acting out of boredom, and I was wrong. You are a clever, brave, and resourceful woman, and when you came back for me, what I ought to have done was express gratitude and admiration. Instead, I snapped at you like a rabid mongrel."

"I forgive you."

At her tremulous smile, relief burgeoned in his chest.

"Thank you. You cannot know what that means to me."

Taking her hand, he brushed his lips over her knuckles. Then he tucked her hand against his thigh and felt her tremble at the intimacy.

"Where does this leave us?" she asked hesitantly.

"I want to court you, Gigi."

Now that he saw a way to have what he wanted, he wasn't about to beat around the bush.

"You mean as a prelude to *marriage*?" Her eyes nearly popped from her head.

"What else?" Annoyed by her response, he said, "You needn't look so shocked. Do you think I am not good enough for you?"

"No." Twin lines appeared between her brows. "That's not it at all."

"Then why is the prospect of marriage to me so inconceivable?"

"To begin with, we hardly know one another—"

"I've just shared more of my past with you than I have with anyone. Lover or otherwise."

Her expression grew wistful. "I do appreciate your trust. That you see me as brave and resourceful—"

"And beautiful," he muttered. "Don't forget beautiful."

"There is no denying the physical attraction between us, but..." She bit her lip, her gaze searching his. "We're enemies, Conrad. When it comes to the spa."

Relieved at the nature of her perceived obstacle, he said firmly, "We are not enemies. We merely have differing agendas."

"What is the difference?" She shook her head. "You want to take over the spa, and I will fight until my last breath to help Miss Letty preserve her legacy."

"I like that about you."

Her forehead pleated. "Like what?"

"Your loyalty to those you care about. I want that from you," he said frankly. "That loyalty and steadfast care. Which is why I am willing to give up my plans for Miss Letty's property."

"You are?" Disbelief and hope warred on her exquisite features. "But you have a reputation for getting what you want."

"I want *you*. More than anything."

"But the spa." Her gaze was astute. "It is worth a lot, isn't it?"

He knew she meant financially. She wouldn't know that his interest in the place had been solely related to vengeance. Now that he'd set an alternative scheme in motion to ruin Abel Pearce, he no longer needed the spa.

"You are worth more," he said. "For you, I would gladly give it up."

"Oh, Conrad. You would do that…for me?"

The warmth in her gaze was worth exposing his past and changing his plans. While there were different ways to achieve his revenge, there was only one Gigi.

"Yes," he said tenderly. "I would."

"Then yes," she breathed. "I would very much like for you to court me."

Triumph rolled through him. Before she could change her mind, he snatched her onto his lap. She giggled, winding her arms around his neck.

"Then our courtship begins now," he told her.

Chapter Fifteen

Sitting on Conrad's lap in a swaying carriage, his mouth moving tenderly over hers, Gigi felt an inexplicable sense of rightness.

I'm meant to be here with him.

His honesty—his willingness to let her in—was a form of persuasion she could not resist. Not only had he apologized for his prior characterization of her as an indulged miss, but he was also demonstrating it through his behavior. By sharing his past, he was treating her like an equal...like a grown-up capable of handling the information and deciding her own path forward. She understood that he didn't trust easily, and as she now knew, he had good reason for it. The fact that he'd exposed his vulnerable side filled her with giddy hope.

Furthermore, he was relinquishing his plans for Letty's spa for her sake. Because no matter how much the water or land might be worth, he valued her more. He wished to court her...to *marry* her. Gigi was as surprised by his proposal as she was by her own reaction. For the first time, the notion of matrimony intrigued her. Past offers had lost out to her desire for freedom, but a future with Conrad brimmed with the promise of discovery and adventure.

There was much to contemplate when it came to the future, and for now, she wanted to focus on the current exciting escapade. On the hunger in Conrad's kiss. On her own desires, which turned her blood molten and made her squirm restlessly on his lap.

He chuckled softly against her lips. "Impatient girl. Ready for more, are you?"

Emboldened by his earlier honesty, she confessed, "I missed you. I have thought about our time together in the caldarium constantly."

"Have you now?" He shifted her so that she was sitting with her back to his front. His mouth roved hotly above the collar of her shirt. "What did you think about?"

Voicing her naughty fantasies was a bit *too* bold, even for her.

"Um…"

"I'll tell you what. Why don't we play a game instead?"

Hearing the catch of amusement in his voice, she asked, "What sort of game?"

"I'll guess what you thought about. All you have to do is tell me if I'm correct."

That sounds easy enough.

"Um, all right."

When his mouth engulfed her ear, she jerked in surprise. Winding one of her plaits around his fist, he held her steady. He licked and sucked her sensitive lobe until she was wriggling against his thighs.

"Did you think about this?" he murmured.

"Yes," she sighed.

"What about this?"

He reached in front of her, and the sight of his battle-scarred hands undoing her shirt increased her shivering. A part of her couldn't believe the risk she was taking by having this midnight rendezvous. In Conrad's presence, however, her sense of propriety gave way to more primal desires. Her need to be a good and proper girl was overcome by the more pressing need to be…to be *herself*.

Or whoever this wanton creature was. The panels of linen parted, and for the first time, her breasts were exposed to male eyes. Even in the dimness, she could see how swollen the tips were.

"Your breasts are even prettier than I imagined," he said thickly. "In your fantasies, did I do this?"

When he cupped her aching mounds, she whimpered her answer. He hefted her breasts, lifting and pushing them together. When he grazed the straining peaks, she couldn't stifle a moan.

"How about this?" He pinched a throbbing bud between finger and thumb. "Did you think about me touching these lovely nipples? Licking them?"

"Yes."

She nearly protested when he stopped touching her. Then he brought his fingers to her lips.

"Lick them, sweetheart."

She darted her tongue out and tentatively wetted his thick digits. The act felt shockingly provocative. Apparently, it aroused him too, for his manhood wedged against her bottom like an iron bar.

"Open up and take more of me," he urged.

When he pushed his fingers into her mouth, she let him in. He thrust them in and out, every pass heightening her feverish need. She licked his invading digits the best she could, and when she felt the tips hooking her inner cheek, she instinctively sucked.

"Christ, you're delightful," he rasped. "I can't wait to be inside this hot little mouth."

Before she could puzzle out what he meant, he pulled out with a *popping* sound that made him groan. He palmed her breasts, rubbing the stiff nipples with his slick fingers. Sparks of pleasure traveled outward from her breasts, igniting her nerves and gathering between her thighs. Moaning, she let her head fall back against his shoulder.

"When you thought of me licking you here"—his hot words entered her ear—"did you get wet?"

Blood surging to her cheeks, she nodded.

"Are you wet now?"

He didn't need an answer because he was unfastening her waistband and sliding his hand down her belly. When he touched her intimate cove, they both exhaled.

"What a good girl, so wet and ready for me," he crooned. "Did you think about this, Gigi? Did you fantasize about me diddling your pussy and making you come?"

Since she hadn't understood the concept of "diddling" until this moment, the answer was no. Yet desire was no longer a game but a burning need that threatened to consume her. All that mattered was how good he was making her feel, how necessary the pleasure was.

"Don't stop," she moaned.

"Like being frigged, do you, sweetheart?" His voice was dark and wicked, like temptation itself whispering in her ear. "Do you want to come?"

"*Yes.*"

Hooking her knees over his own, he spread her wider, exposing her fully to his touch. He found the hidden bud of her sensation, the slick sounds of his rubbing filling the carriage. As the flames raged out of control, she arched her back.

"Come for me, Gigi," he growled. "All over my hand. Right now."

With a gasp, she did.

Devil and damn, his passionate little nymph never did anything in half-measure. Feeling the slickness on her thighs, Conrad was harder than he'd ever been in his life. Bestial need took over, and he eased his limp treasure off his lap, laying her across the carriage bench. Going down on one knee—which wasn't the easiest, given the stiff ridge in his trousers—he yanked off her boots and pants.

Gigi raised her head, looking at him with bliss-dazed eyes. "What are you doing?"

"This," he growled.

He buried his face in her pussy.

Gigi's yelp of surprise melted into a moan as he hungrily licked up her cream. She was delicious—a dish he wanted to have every day for the rest of his life. Her smooth thighs quivered around his head as he ate her. She surrendered to the pleasure, gasping and clutching his hair. When he tongued her tight opening, pushing inside, he was rewarded with another squirt of ambrosia. He lapped greedily, and when he gauged she was ready, slid a finger inside her.

At the snugness of her passage, his forehead beaded with sweat.

By Jove, to bury my cock inside this perfect little hole—

"*Conrad.*" She came up on her elbows. "Are you certain you should be doing that?"

"You're mine, inside and out," he said hoarsely. "I want to know what your cunny feels like when you come."

Before she could argue, he resumed eating her pussy. He focused on her pearl, and from her breathless cries, she appreciated his attentions. All the while, he moved his finger inside her, feeling her lushness and sweet pulses in his cock. Knowing she was close, he redoubled his efforts, determined to get his due. And, bloody hell, she gave it to him. Chanting his name, she gushed another climax, this one straight into his greedy mouth.

Randy beyond measure, Conrad staggered to his feet. He was so hard he could barely work his trousers off his hips. When his cock fell into his palm with a heavy smack, Gigi's lips formed an enticing rosy ring.

A treat for another time, when I'm not about to explode like a steam engine.

Grabbing onto the carriage strap with one hand, he fisted his cock with the other. His fingers barely encircled his burgeoned shaft as he frigged himself.

"Can I, um, do anything?" Gigi whispered.

He ran a possessive gaze over her: his perfect nymph, wanton and lovely and sweet. Languid with pleasure that he, and no other man, had given her. She was *his* completely. And he had so much more to show her...

"Watch me, sweetheart," he gritted out. "I'm going to come for you—"

The climax gripped him by the stones, driving molten pressure up his shaft. He took aim, roaring as his seed spewed from him. She twitched as he marked her belly and thighs, crisscrossing her pristine skin with hot streaks, spending harder than he ever had in his life. Finally, shuddering and wrung dry, he dropped into the seat beside her. He dragged her close, tilting her head back to gaze into her eyes. They were bright and adoring, sparkling with newly discovered naughtiness.

"Are you all right?" he asked huskily.

"Quite." Her smile was bashful. "But you've made a mess of me."

"I did, didn't I?"

As he ran a finger across her slippery thigh, primal satisfaction filled him. Instead of wiping his seed away, he rubbed it deeper into her skin. Feeling her shiver, he smiled.

"It's only fair," he said. "For from the moment we met, you've made a mess of me."

After seeing Gigi back to her brother's manor, Conrad told his driver to head home. In the darkest hour before dawn, he experienced a heady rush: everything was once again going his way. Gigi had forgiven him, and they'd shared a sizzling night of pleasure.

She was going to be his...even if she hadn't fully admitted the fact to herself. Before they parted, she'd asked him to delay making their courtship public.

"Just until after Miss Letty's opening gala," she'd promised. *"After Xenia saw us the last time, my brothers refused to let me return to the spa. I managed to change their minds, and I don't want to jeopardize that before the opening. Will you wait until the spa is launched before making your suit known to my family? By then, my papa will be back, and you can speak to him directly."*

He'd agreed to her reasonable request and made one in return. While he would refrain from making his courtship public, he wanted to continue their private rendezvous.

"I want that too," she'd whispered.

She'd blushed, looking so shy and sweet that he'd burned to kiss her again. Knowing that he was tempting fate, he'd refrained and instead watched, heart pounding, as she nimbly ascended the tree to her bedchamber.

Yes, things were going as planned—

"Oy! You're driving too fast," his driver yelled. "Get out of the way, you bounder—"

Shoving aside the curtain, Conrad looked out the window and saw a dark shape approaching. A black carriage led by four black horses. Hooves thundered, and it picked up speed on the narrow road, coming straight at his carriage.

"What's going on, Ainsley?" Conrad demanded.

"Bastard's not slowing. Hold on, sir," Ainsley shouted.

Conrad grabbed onto the carriage strap an instant before the impact. Terrified neighing filled his ears. The world rocked wildly and overturned, and he tumbled into darkness.

Chapter Sixteen

"Bloody bumpkins," Redgrave muttered. "Can't drive worth a damn."

It was the following afternoon. Conrad was meeting with Marvell and Redgrave, the head manager at Godwin & Co., in his study at Honeystone Hall. Given the cut on Conrad's cheek, the two had naturally asked what happened.

"Ainsley took a knocking," Conrad said. "Luckily, he is fine. If it weren't for his expert handling of the reins, the results could have been far worse."

Redgrave cocked his head. "Did you see the other driver?"

Auburn-haired and beefy, with some of his muscle gone to fat, Redgrave was Conrad's former prizefighting coach. Since Redgrave had proven a dependable ally to have in one's corner, Conrad had kept the other on when he'd founded Godwin & Co. Redgrave assisted Conrad in making important decisions and kept the other men of business in line. He had the same winning instincts in this role as he'd had in the last.

Conrad shook his head. "It was too dark. All I saw were four horses—black, I think."

"Did you report the accident to the local constables?" Marvell asked.

"I am not sure it was an accident."

Redgrave's bushy brows shot up. "You think this was a deliberate attempt on your life? By whom?"

"I don't know the answer to either question...yet." Conrad addressed his solicitor. "What have you discovered about Mrs. Denton?"

After discovering Isobel skulking around in his study, he'd instructed Marvell to look for any financial ties she might have to his competitors. As Marvell withdrew a file from his briefcase, he had the look of a haggard mole. The tip of his pale nose was reddened, and his eyes were watery as he squinted at his notes. Nonetheless, he launched into an efficient summary of the facts he'd unearthed.

"I could not find any monetary transactions involving Mrs. Denton and either Trowbridge or Smedley," Marvell said. "However, I did find some social connections. Mrs. Denton apparently attended a showing at Her Majesty's Theatre and was seated in Mr. Trowbridge's box. It was a large party, and there were no reports of intimacy between the two during or after."

"A passing acquaintance or something more?" Picking up a pen, Conrad tapped it against his blotter. "Ever since I outbid Trowbridge for those factories, he has been itching for retribution. I would not put it past him to employ a woman to spy on me."

"A disagreeable fellow." Marvell blew discreetly into a handkerchief. "As for Smedley, he and Mrs. Denton have attended several of the same social events in the last year. Two balls and a house party, to be exact. Again, I could not find any gossip surrounding the two, and Smedley's wife was also present at those gatherings."

Conrad drummed his fingers on the padded arm of his chair. "This isn't much to go on."

"Would you like me to keep digging?"

At Marvell's blinking inquiry, Conrad felt his lips twitch.

"No," he decided. "While I don't trust her, at worst she's a pawn in someone else's game."

"What about the incident last night?" Marvell asked. "Should I hire Foxworth and his men to look into it?"

Given the dog-eat-dog world of Conrad's business, information was key. He kept investigators on retainer to stay abreast of industrial developments and the activities of his competitors.

"It wouldn't hurt. But I don't know for certain that the carriage struck us deliberately. I could have been run off the road by a drunken or careless driver."

"Plenty o' those about," Redgrave agreed.

"Regardless," Marvell said. "Any event that threatens your life is not to be taken lightly."

"I agree." Opening a drawer, Conrad removed the latest model Manton percussion pistol and set it on his blotter. "I will not be caught unprepared."

"Just like the old days, eh?" Redgrave said fondly. "You never backed down from a fight."

"Is that wise?" Marvell's brow wrinkled. "A man is more likely to be injured by his own weapon than—"

"Quit flapping your gums, Marvell." Redgrave rolled his eyes. "Only an idiot would shoot himself, and Godwin's no idiot. He can take care o' himself."

"Let's move on." From experience, Conrad knew to cut off the pair's bickering. "Redgrave, did you follow up on the Pearce matter?"

"Aye. It was as you said. The bloke's ripe for a plucking. According to my sources, Abel Pearce visited Jonah Westfield's office and inquired about the railway scheme you recommended. Westfield lured him in with the promise of unending profit, and Pearce invested his remaining assets. *All* of them. When that railway bubble bursts, and my sources say it will happen soon, *poof*"—Redgrave wriggled his thick fingers—"the dumb, greedy bastard will lose everything."

"I want to be the first to know when it happens."

Redgrave canted his head. "What did Pearce do to you, anyway?"

The memory flashed of standing behind his mama in Pearce's ostentatious study.

"I'm afraid I cannot help you, ma'am," Pearce had said.

"Have mercy, sir," his mama had pleaded. *"We are kin, after all. Our great-grandpapas were both sons of Langdon Pearce. According to this deed, given to me by my papa, there is a small cottage here in Chudleigh Bottoms that belongs to the descendants of my line—namely, me and my son. We are in desperate need of shelter and—"*

"When your great-grandpapa left this village, he abandoned his right to that cottage. Deed or no deed." Pearce had irritably waved aside the paper. *"As it happens, the cottage of which you speak is no longer habitable. It will soon be demolished and tenements built in its place."*

Stricken, his mama had begun to weep. *"Please, help us. We have nowhere else to go—"*

"There's nothing I can do. I'm sure you understand."

Then Pearce had turned his back on them—literally and metaphorically.

Conrad reined in his rage. "The bastard is getting what he deserves. We'll leave it at that."

"As you like," Redgrave said. "Now that Pearce is all but done for, and you ain't got a need for the spa, I wager you're chomping at the bit to get back to London, eh?"

"I won't be returning quite yet."

"Why not?" Redgrave peered at him. "Don't tell me you've taken a liking to this mudborough?"

"Chuddums has its merits."

The main one being Gigi. Even though they'd parted mere hours ago, Conrad missed her. He thanked God that she hadn't been with him when his carriage got struck. If anything had happened to her... His chest knotted. It was a good thing she'd asked to keep their relationship private for now. He would use the time to take care of any trouble...and to execute the final steps of his vengeance.

"I wish to speak to Marvell alone," he said.

After Redgrave departed, Conrad said, "Fill me in on Grantley."

"I have been monitoring His Grace's situation, as you requested. His health continues to fail, and his physicians suspect he won't survive more than a few months. Some of his debtors are panicking and calling in his debts."

Due to his gambling and general profligacy, Robert Beaufort, the Duke of Grantley, owed a staggering amount. Not only had His Grace emptied the considerable coffers of the duchy, but he'd also left nothing behind for his wife, Lady Katerina, and their five daughters. At this point, he had but one card left to play.

"What about the betrothal of Grantley's eldest, Lady Anne?" Conrad asked.

"As to that—" Marvell cut off, sneezing violently.

"What ails you?"

"Apologies, sir. It's the blasted London fog." Marvell wiped his nose. "It's brought about this dreadful bout of catarrh. I'm hoping that the country air will relieve my symptoms."

"You are welcome to stay the night. There's plenty of room."

"That's kind of you, sir. Very kind," Marvell said gratefully. "As for the betrothal, I learned that a colleague of mine was tasked with drawing up a contract between Grantley's eldest, Lady Anne, and her distant cousin, Harold Stockton, the duke's presumptive heir. No promises have yet been made. However, the Grantleys have sent out invitations for a ball in two weeks' time. Given His Grace's health, he has rarely been seen in public, which leads me to a conclusion."

"You think Grantley plans to announce the betrothal of his daughter to his heir."

"Yes, sir. Such a match would benefit both parties. Mr. Stockton comes from a branch of the family that has wealth from trade but little social standing. Lady Anne has the opposite problem. From what I've gathered, the duke has negotiated with Mr. Stockton to pay off his debts upon marriage and settle dowries upon his remaining daughters. In exchange, Mr. Stockton will have a wife who was born to play the role of duchess and will show him the ropes—socially speaking."

"Stockton will lose enthusiasm for the match when he learns that he isn't Grantley's heir," Conrad said pensively.

Anticipation simmered as he contemplated claiming his rightful place. All along, he'd been planning to destroy his older brother Robert…and now he had the perfect opportunity and venue to execute the final blow. The bastard was going to die knowing that Conrad had control of the duchy and the futures of his wife and daughters.

I am going to show Robert's family the same mercy he showed me and my mama.

He wondered how Gigi would react when he revealed the truth, because if things continued the way they were going, his new status would undoubtedly affect her. He told himself she wouldn't mind: people, in his experience, didn't tend to look a gift horse in the mouth. Moreover, she was loyal. He would focus on courting her—on binding her to him heart, body, and soul. Once he accomplished that, he could count on her to weather any storm with him.

"Get me an invitation to the ball, Marvell," he said.

"The reopening is going to be a disaster," Letty wailed.

Gigi exchanged a worried look with Xenia, who was chaperoning as promised. Owen had escorted them, and to Gigi's delight, her brother seemed less withdrawn. Not only that, but he was also putting his skills to use. At present, he was working on the spa's garden.

"All will be fine," Gigi soothed. "The road to success always has a few bumps."

"While these individual incidents could be called molehills," Letty said, wringing her hands, "they are adding up to be a veritable mountain of disaster."

She wasn't wrong: the bath had suffered an unfortunate series of setbacks. First, the discovery of the caldarium had apparently disturbed a nest of rats. The vermin had started invading the bath yesterday. Panicked, Letty had hired the local ratcatcher, a copper-haired lad by the name of Todd Cobbins. Cobbins, aided by his terrier Bobby, was currently waging war with the vermin. While the duo was undeniably fierce, they were outnumbered. Gigi had last glimpsed the pair holding back a furry tide in the pump room.

"Cobbins seems to know what he is doing," Gigi said with determined positivity.

"Even if he manages to eliminate the rats before the opening, there is still the damage left behind by the deer," Letty said glumly.

It never rained but poured. Deer had somehow found their way into the gardens, wreaking havoc on the hedges and shrubbery.

"Owen will take care of it." At least, Gigi *hoped* he would. "He worked on the gardens at Bottoms House, and the groundskeeper says he has a natural flair for outdoor design."

"What about the champagne?" The usually composed spinster looked ready to bite her nails. "I shall have nothing to serve my esteemed guests."

This was the cherry atop the bad luck cake. Expecting the delivery of the bubbly today, Letty had instead received an apologetic message from the London merchant. Apparently, thieves had ransacked his warehouse, making off with the crates of champagne meant for her.

"We'll think of something," Gigi said. "Maybe Mr. Thornton could help us?"

"He's never served champagne at the Briarbush Inn." Letty snorted. "According to him, champagne is a French conspiracy to sell overpriced grape cider."

"We have some bottles in the cellar," Xenia offered. "You are welcome to them, Miss Letty."

"Oh, Lady Harrington, I couldn't possibly—"

"Thank you, Xenia." Gigi gave her sister-in-law a grateful look. "That is generous of you."

"Think nothing of it. I only wish we could do more. A few bottles won't be enough for the crowd expected at the gala."

"What if we served mineral water instead of champagne?" Gigi mused. "It's bubbly. And more healthful."

"An excellent idea," Letty said darkly. "If we wish for the guests never to return."

Gigi sighed. "We have five days left. I am sure we will think of something."

"First the rats, then the mangled garden. Now this. Sometimes I am afraid that...that..."

"What are you afraid of, Miss Letty?"

"That this village *is* cursed."

To Gigi's astonishment, her stalwart friend burst into tears.

"There, there, dear." Gigi patted the other's shoulder while Xenia rummaged for a handkerchief. "You've a case of pre-opening jitters. There is no curse."

"Are you saying that you do not believe in the legend of Bloody Thom?" Letty sniffled.

Gigi thought of her dreams and hesitated. "Well, no. Not exactly."

"Ever since Thomas Mulligan died, the village and this business have been going downhill." Letty dabbed at her eyes with Xenia's handkerchief. "Now I know the haunting business at Bottoms House a few months ago was a hoax, but that doesn't mean the rest of the legend is a sham. I've lived here my entire life, and believe me when I say, Bloody Thom *is* real."

"I believe you." Xenia's expression was thoughtful. "I have felt his presence at the manor."

Guilt stabbed Gigi. Xenia had shared the dreams she'd had about Thomas and Rosalinda, which had coincided with her and Ethan's courtship. Yet now Gigi was having dreams of her own, which she hadn't disclosed. She was afraid of revealing too much to her perceptive sister-in-law. If she told Xenia about her dreams of the ghostly lovers, Xenia might put two and two together and realize that Gigi was engaged in a secret affair.

At the thought of Conrad, Gigi felt a dreamy tingle. While it wasn't easy being discreet, it was necessary. If her brothers found out about her clandestine trysts, they would call Conrad out and put her under lock and key for the rest of her existence. Moreover, she was enjoying the freedom of courtship without external pressures. Conrad was a complex fellow, yet he was letting her in bit by bit, and their burgeoning intimacy thrilled her.

She liked how she felt in his presence: free and wholly herself. Other suitors saw her as a prize to be won. When they looked at her, they saw her wealth, social position, and superficial charms. Conrad was different. He was rich and didn't need her money. He didn't treat her differently because of her background. While he had no qualms about letting her know about his physical attraction to her—and, oh my stars, the feeling was mutual—he praised her other qualities too. He thought she was clever, brave, and resourceful. He treated her like an adult worthy of trust...like his equal.

"While Bloody Thom might have taken a hiatus from wreaking havoc upon our village, I fear he is back," Letty was saying. "You know the poem about him and how it ends."

The verse, known by all the local children, was haunting and enigmatic, especially the last stanza which had recently been rediscovered:

Beware, beware the rattling chain
The flapping robes stained red and bold
Beware the moans and wails of pain
For 'tis Bloody Thom they do herald.

He brings death to all who cross his path
Be they creatures with feathers, fur, or skin
Green will wither and fortunes dwindle until his
    wrath
Is quenched by a true reckoning

He plays a mournful ballad of blame
Shaking the manor with his ire
His cry for justice is like a flame
Scorching all with unholy fire.

Alone, alone in his manor of sadness
Bloody Thom does howl, trapped by rage
Alone, he curses the village in his madness
Until love's seasons free them from their cage.

"By discovering the truth about Thomas and Rose, that they were lovers, not enemies, I thought we had laid his spirit to rest," Xenia said somberly.

"There remains much we do not know." Thinking of the dream she'd had of Thomas and Rosalinda, trapped in their sanctuary of stone as fire raged around them, Gigi shivered. "For instance, we don't know who murdered him and why and what became of Rosalinda."

"Until then, I think Bloody Thom will continue to have a hand in our misfortune," Letty said. "Chuddums will not find peace until he does."

"Perhaps we can help him find absolution." Xenia gnawed on her lip. "Solving the hoax of his sightings shed light on the real

Thomas and Rosalinda. We discovered Rosalinda wasn't a witch who cursed him but a beautiful young traveling woman. In my dreams, she and Thomas were lovers, a fact Wally later confirmed through his recollections of them as a young boy. And since those facts came to light, things *have* improved. Personally, I was lucky enough to marry the man of my dreams—"

"Ethan was equally lucky to have found you," Gigi cut in. "My brother was a curmudgeon until you came along."

"He and I are both fortunate." Xenia blushed. "And Chuddums seems to have benefited as well. Since we chased that nasty gang of Corrigans out of the village, the economy is improving, and people have hope again."

"You're right." Gigi brightened. "Perhaps these drawbacks at the spa are merely signs."

Letty's forehead pleated. "Signs of what?"

"Signs that we need to discover the rest of Thomas and Rosalinda's story. Perhaps Bloody Thom is causing trouble because he wants us to dig deeper—to find out the truth about what happened to him and Rosalinda. Once we do, we may free him from his rage, and he will leave the village alone."

"Ethan and I fell in love during autumn," Xenia murmured.

Gigi tilted her head. "Beg pardon?"

"I was just thinking about the phrase *love's seasons*," Xenia explained. "What if it literally refers to a season when a couple, who has parallels to Thomas and Rosalinda, falls in love?"

"That is an interesting theory," Letty said.

"There are four seasons, which may mean four couples need to fall in love to lift the curse." Xenia turned twinkling brown eyes to Gigi. "With winter in full swing, I wonder whose turn it will be to find their soulmate?"

Chapter Seventeen

"Where have you brought me? May I look now?"

"Not yet, duchess. Keep your hands over your eyes. I want this to be a surprise."

As he led her to his lodgings, Conrad hid a smile at Gigi's sigh of impatience. He'd picked her up again, and this time he'd parked himself beneath the tree outside her bedchamber in case she required assistance. She didn't. She'd descended the tree as gracefully as if it were a grand staircase. In the process, she'd treated him to a view that would provide fodder for his fantasies in the years to come.

On the ride over, she'd asked about the cut on his cheek, and he'd had to tell her about being run off the road. Her concern had warmed him, but he didn't want to spend the precious hours they had together talking about the darker side of life. He'd been weaned on pain, violence, and retribution. Tonight, with her, he had an appetite for finer things. Thus, he'd chalked the incident up to a mere accident.

"What have you planned for us this evening?" Gigi asked.

Only with her did he find wheedling endearing. Then again, he was finding he liked most everything about her. He liked their banter, especially now that it was playful rather than antagonistic. While she could be as sweet as honey, her personality had spice, too. He was never bored in her company and liked the games they played. It was a novel experience to desire a woman *and* have fun with her.

"We're here," he said. "See for yourself."

She dropped her hands, her eyes widening as she took in his temporary abode. Honeystone Hall was a handsome property located not far from the spa. In the moonlight, the limestone walls had a pristine, almost ethereal glow. The slate roof and decorative gables glimmered with a hint of frost. Woodsmoke wisped from the chimneys before melting into the black velvet sky. The mullioned windows beckoned with a cozy glow.

"You brought me to Honeystone Hall?" Gigi's eyes were more brilliant than the stars. "I have passed this place many times but never been inside. I understand it is quite grand but has been vacant since the squire passed."

"Come have a look." He offered his arm.

She bit her lip. "I would like to. But the servants—"

"I brought my staff from London. They are all longtime retainers, and you may rest assured when it comes to their discretion. I would never let harm come to you or your reputation, Gigi. Trust me?"

Nodding, she allowed him to lead her into the house. Since he'd only moved in a week ago, the décor remained that of the prior occupant. Luckily, he approved of the squire's taste. The oak furnishings, brass fixtures, and forest-green upholstery created an ambiance of rustic luxury. There were well-appointed public rooms on the first floor and a dozen bedchambers on the second, as well as a separate servants' wing.

Gigi looked around with open admiration. "What an agreeable home."

Conrad found himself absurdly pleased that she liked it. Then and there, he decided to acquire the property. It would make a splendid wedding present for his new bride. He didn't know when he'd started thinking of Gigi as his future wife. Once the idea had taken root, however, there was no resisting it. Their last steamy carriage ride had cemented it for him: he'd never felt that close to a woman, that crazed with desire for her. The notion of waking up next to Gigi every morning didn't fill him with dread but anticipation.

At the same time, he sensed that Gigi wasn't as certain about him. That was the way of nymphs: they tended to be elusive and mischievous, a bit flighty. If you didn't secure their loyalty, they would run roughshod over you and flee with your heart. Thus, his strategy was to use everything in his power—passion, intimacy, gifts, whatever it took—to bind Gigi to him.

"Allow me to give you a tour," he said.

He took her through the main rooms, enjoying her appreciation. Her delightful artlessness and buoyant spirit spoke of a nurturing upbringing, which fit what he'd learned about the Harrington clan. Her parents, the Marquess and Marchioness of Blackwood, were famous for their enduring love match, and her father was a war hero from his days of fighting Boney.

There was some gossip about her brothers: the middle one, a musician, had been injured in some accident which had ended his career as a maestro, and the youngest brother had gone missing for years after the disastrous military defeat in Kabul. However, the entire family seemed to have converged in Chuddums, and the locals credited their presence with the village's reversal of fortune.

"The billiards room is marvelous," Gigi exclaimed.

This room was his favorite of the manor, and he'd been so sure that she would share his opinion that he'd had the refreshments laid out here. She gazed rapturously at the coffered ceiling and dark paneled walls, trailing her fingers over the cognac leather seating before approaching the majestic billiards table that occupied center stage. Cushioned by an Aubusson, the mahogany table had carved acanthus leaves and other detailed foliage adorning the apron and legs, and the green baize surface was as smooth as glass.

Her eyelashes fluttered as she inhaled, taking in the scents of wood, leather, and cigar smoke. Watching her, Conrad felt heat rush into his groin. She was a sensual, unaffected creature, and there was a world of carnal delights he wanted to show her.

Down, boy. Play the proper host first. There is plenty of time for lovemaking.

That last thought was novel. With his other lovers, swiving had been at the forefront of his agenda. God knew he couldn't keep his hands off Gigi, but with her, he wanted more. Her conversation and laughter, the way she'd made him feel when she said he was more than what others believed him to be.

"Would you care for refreshment?" he asked.

He gestured to the table set up by the hearth. Crystal, fine china, and silverware gleamed in the firelight. A tiered cart offered a savory collation and assorted desserts, and a bucket of iced champagne stood at the ready. When she went over to inspect the offerings, he saw her gaze linger on the squares of rose-flavored Turkish delights. Her blush was everything he'd hoped for and more.

"You think of everything, don't you?" she mused.

"I do not believe in leaving things up to chance."

"Some might say you have controlling tendencies."

He thought she might be teasing him, but he'd never been one to shy away from the truth.

"Some would be right." He lifted the bubbly from the bucket. "Champagne?"

"Yes, please."

After filling a flute for her, then himself, he raised his glass. "To getting better acquainted."

Smiling, she pinged her glass against his, and they sipped in companionable silence, broken now and again by a snap and crackle from the hearth.

"This is nice," she said.

"What is?"

"Being in a normal situation, chatting over champagne." Her voice was playful. "Not being trapped in a sweltering caldarium."

He smiled. "Have you played billiards?"

She canted her head, her thick braid flopping over one shoulder. "Once or twice."

Recalling she'd said the same thing about tree climbing, he knew better than to trust her modesty. Moreover, the impish curve of her lips gave her away...thank God. While courting Vicky, Conrad had played with her a few times. Vicky had been a mediocre player at best, and the experiences had been deadly dull. His juices rose at the prospect of competitive play. Setting down his glass, he strolled over to the cue rack, and Gigi followed suit.

"First to fifty points?" he asked.

"Splendid."

She was examining the cues with an expert eye. She tested a few before selecting a shorter, lighter stick made of polished ash. It was the cue he would have chosen for her based on her height and build. The way she handled the shaft, running her fist along the length, made him stifle a groan. He snatched a longer, heavier cue with an ebony inlay on the handle.

As she set up the three balls, he said, "Why don't we make this more interesting?"

She paused, her fingertips resting on the red object ball. "In what way?"

"A wager." He smirked. "Don't worry, I shan't take all your pin money."

She studied him. "All right, I'll wager with you...but not for money."

Depraved visions danced through his head.

He cleared his throat. "What, ahem, are you proposing?"

"Whenever one makes a shot, which must be called in advance, one may ask a personal question of the other."

Intrigued, he asked, "I may ask anything of you?"

"We may ask anything of each other," she said with beguiling confidence. "This way, we will be growing two plants with one seed: enjoying the game and getting better acquainted."

He turned the proposition over in his head. There were plenty of things he wanted to know about the little minx. And he didn't mind trading confidences with her…to a degree. Intimacy was necessary to strengthen their bond; look at how she'd accepted his courtship after he'd disclosed a few facts about his prior lovers. If he didn't want to provide an answer, he would omit or gloss over certain details. In the boxing ring and in life, he'd mastered the art of evasion.

"Why not?" He waved at the table. "Ladies first."

"Thank you, sir. I shall pot the red."

Bending over, she positioned her cue and took her shot. Her cue ball hit the side of the object ball, sending the latter neatly into a pocket. He felt his brows rise.

She straightened, her eyes bright and smile enchanting.

"Tell me more about your childhood," she said. "I know your parents passed when you were young, but do you have any siblings? You mentioned a guardian. What was he like?"

"I had half-siblings whom I was not close to," Conrad said. "They're no longer living. As for my guardian, he didn't want anything to do with me. He sent me to boarding school, where I spent my childhood and adolescent years."

At the succinct summary, Gigi felt a shock of surprise, which turned into a throbbing ache. While her family had their share of travails and conflicts, they'd always had each other. She couldn't imagine having no one…being so alone.

"You have no family at all?" she asked softly.

"None I consider my kin."

"Conrad...I'm sorry."

"There's nothing to be sorry about, sweetheart." He circled the table, his eyes on the surface. "I got used to being alone. Truth be told, sometimes I prefer it."

No, you don't.

His casual manner didn't fool her. Shadows wisped through his gaze, and the tautness of his jaw gave him away. As she thought of his earlier admission—that he expected to be left to his own devices—her heart cracked a little more. Fierce desire welled in her to show him that he didn't have to face this world alone because now he had *her*.

The realization flowed through her with a breath-stealing rush.

I'm falling in love with Conrad Godwin.

With love as a Harrington tradition, she'd never doubted that she would one day find her soulmate. Yet none of her suitors had stirred that depth of feeling in her. No fellow had...until Conrad. The discovery didn't scare her. On the contrary, it felt like she was finally fulfilling her destiny.

"*Four couples need to fall in love to lift the curse.*" Xenia's words drifted into her head. Could Gigi and Conrad be one of the couples? Were they fated to meet—to restore Chuddums's fortunes?

"Cannon, left corner," Conrad said.

She focused on the game as he executed the shot the way he did everything else—with unflinching expertise. She found his confidence ever so attractive. When she played billiards in genteel social settings, she had to keep herself in check. Trouncing gentlemen was generally not conducive to holding their admiration, and as her mama oft reminded her, showing off wasn't seemly for a young lady. With Conrad, however, she didn't have to hold back. He seemed to admire her competitive spirit and enjoy challenging her.

"Well done," she said. "What do you wish to know?"

She expected him to ask about her family.

"You're such a good girl, Gigi. I want to know something naughty that you've done."

At his husky request, butterflies swarmed her chest.

"You already know the naughty things I've done. Since you were a part of them."

"A deed that doesn't involve me, then," he amended with a grin. "Something recent. I don't want to hear about how you filched a biscuit when you were a tot."

"Well, there is something." She drew a breath, wondering if she could confide. "Something I haven't told anyone."

His Viking's eyes glittered. "Go on."

"I lied to my family," she blurted. "Not a lie of omission—like being here tonight—but an *actual* lie."

"Tell me more."

"It's a long story," she warned.

"We have time."

"You know that I have three older brothers?" At his nod, she said, "The youngest of them, Owen, fought in Afghanistan. He was there when the army was decimated at the Khyber Pass."

"It's a miracle he survived it," Conrad murmured.

"Yes. He went missing for three years, but my family never gave up hope, never stopped searching for him. Although they wouldn't let me help, I prayed every night for his return." Even now, thinking of those years clogged her throat. "Eventually, they found him and brought him back. But he wasn't the same. After the ordeals he suffered, he had...he *has* demons. They haunt him, even in his sleep."

Recalling Conrad's unrestful dreams, she paused, wondering if he would say something about his own experiences. When he didn't, she decided not to press and continued.

"In the past, Owen has imbibed too much, indulged in a variety of vices, and at times, been aggressive. One such incident led to him wounding my middle brother, Ethan. As Ethan was a piano maestro, the injury to his hand was the worst thing that could have happened, even if Owen didn't mean to cause it.

"Ethan's spirits darkened, and there was nothing any of us could do to reach him. Owen was beside himself with guilt, but any time he and Ethan were in a room together, conflict would escalate. Ethan retreated to Bottoms House and pushed everyone away. Owen got worse, and my parents had to take him to recover at the country estate." Her voice hitched. "My family is close. The Harrington motto is *Ad Finem Fidelis*, which means 'faithful to the end.' But we were fracturing and there was nothing anyone could do to stop it."

Conrad came over and put an arm around her shoulders.

"Until you came up with a solution?" he asked. "Something that involved an untruth?"

She peered up at him. "How did you know?"

"Because I know you, duchess." His gaze was tender. "You cannot stand to let the people you love suffer. And you're a schemer."

"I am not a schemer," she protested.

"The Chuddums love potion? The escape from the caldarium?" He raised his brows. "Our midnight rendezvous?"

"While I may possess a certain ability to make things happen—"

"Aye, and you're a masterful schemer at that." He chucked her under the chin. "I should know, since like recognizes like."

She cast her gaze heavenward. "There's no point in arguing with you."

"Because I'm right."

"Do you want to hear what I did or not?"

"I'm listening."

"Since no one could get through to Ethan, I decided to take matters into my own hands." Seeing Conrad's smug look, she sighed. "Fine, I came up with a plan to get the family together again. I staged a situation at a ball. Nothing too scandalous, but enough so that I had an excuse to leave London and seek out Ethan."

Conrad angled his head. "What was this *situation*?"

"I told Ethan I was accidentally cornered by a fortune hunter in the garden without my chaperone. But the truth is I went out there on purpose. I knew the fortune hunter was lying in wait, but I didn't plan to stay long enough to get compromised; I just needed a whisper of gossip to justify seeking out my brother."

"Hold up." He drew his brows together. "You *deliberately* risked your reputation?"

"It was a calculated risk. The fortune hunter was in his fifties and rather podgy. I didn't expect him to give chase—"

"The bastard *chased* you?" Fury flashed in Conrad's gaze. "Give me his name."

"It's irrelevant. *I* engineered the situation. Moreover, nothing happened because I was faster than him, even if I did trip and tear my dress in the process." Seeing the gathering storm in Conrad's expression, she said hastily, "Do not make me regret sharing this with you. The point is that you said I'm a good girl, and I'm not. At least, not always. I misled Ethan so that he would let me stay."

"Did your ploy work?"

"Yes," she admitted. "Ethan took me in. James, my eldest brother, came to visit too. I wrote my parents, who brought Owen. Soon we were together again and more like we used to be. The moment I came to Chuddums, I knew there was something healing about the place."

"There is something healing about *you*."

"I wish that were true," she said wistfully. "My family still has conflicts. But at least we are together and not facing troubles on our own."

"No one could feel alone with you in their corner."

The longing in his voice stirred her own.

"And yet my family doesn't always accept my help. Even when I offer it." She studied the baize. "They love me, but to them I'll always be the baby girl who must be sheltered and protected. They do not seem to realize that I am an adult."

"You should be protected." Conrad tipped her chin up. "But you should also be respected for who you are and all you have to offer. I meant what I said before, Gigi. You have courage in spades and the spirit and competence to take on anything."

"Thank you for listening. For...for seeing me," she said tremulously. "You're the only one I've shared this with."

"I am honored."

Her eyes heated, and he gave her a handkerchief and a moment to recover herself.

"Do you wish to continue the game?" he asked.

Their intimacy was so enchanting that she'd forgotten they were playing. Never one to quit before a winner was declared, she nodded. Drawing a breath, she surveyed the table, calling and scoring another cannon.

"Tit for tat." Wanting to lighten the mood, she said, "Tell me something wicked you've done. Something you've never shared with anyone."

He canted his head, and his slow, sensual smile made the tips of her breasts tingle.

"I'll do better than that, sweetheart," he said. "I'll show you."

Chapter Eighteen

With quivering anticipation, Gigi watched Conrad reenter the room. He'd gone to fetch something, refusing to tell her what it was. To her surprise, he had brought in a book.

"This is something I haven't shown to anyone," he told her.

When he set the tattered blue volume on the billiards table, she felt her brows rise.

Slanting him a look, she said, "*The Naughty Naiad*?"

"At the boarding school I attended, one of the lads smuggled it in. He rented it out, and I was rather fascinated by it. A few years ago, I managed to secure a copy."

He didn't appear at all embarrassed to be sharing these facts with her. She found his comfort with sexual matters intriguing and arousing. Was there anything more attractive than a fellow who was confident in his own skin? The fact that he was baring his darker side was, frankly, rather thrilling. She liked his honesty—liked that he didn't try to shield her from who he was.

Moreover, she'd never seen an erotic book before and was dying to take a peep.

"Go ahead and take a look," he said.

At the roguish challenge in his eyes, she couldn't resist.

She flipped open the cover, and as she turned the pages, her cheeks flamed. The story featured a beautiful nymph named Pearl and a brawny satyr named Prickonus, and illustrations accompanied the bawdy story. Detailed sketches depicted the pair engaged in all manner of debauchery. The opening chapter, entitled "The Meeting," was about their first encounter, when Prick caught Pearl spying on him while he bathed. The image of the naked satyr emerging from the pond, water dripping from his massively erect member, sent a thrill of recognition up Gigi's spine.

Conrad was standing behind her, reading over her shoulder. She was acutely aware of his nearness and heat. His masculine scent tightened a coil in her belly.

"Remind you of anything?" he murmured against her ear.

"The day we met at the stream," she said breathlessly.

"Uncanny, isn't it? The moment I laid eyes on you, I saw my fantasy come to life."

She shivered as he covered her breasts with his large hands. Beneath her shirt, her nipples budded and throbbed at his proprietary touch.

"Keep reading," he said in a low voice.

She turned the pages, her senses reeling at the depraved words and images. The plot of each story was the same: naughty Pearl would tease the randy satyr until he was beside himself with lust. She would flee, and he would pursue her, hampered by his enormous erection. In the end, he captured her because, Gigi suspected, the clever naiad wanted him to.

Then the truly wicked games would begin, all of them described and drawn in exquisite, titillating detail. Trembling with arousal, Gigi felt Conrad sweep aside her braid, his mouth hot against her neck. He undid her shirt, button by button.

"Enjoy the stories," he said huskily. "Don't mind me."

Her shaky laugh melted into a moan as he caressed her bare breasts, his calloused fingers teasing the stiff tips. It was difficult, but she directed her attention back to the book, flipping through images that steamed up her brain.

There was the one of Prick holding Pearl captive against a tree. In one large hand, he pinned her wrists above her head while he impaled her upon his thick staff. Pearl's back was arched, her expression one of wild ecstasy.

In another picture, Prick had Pearl bent over a rock. Only this time, it wasn't his member inside her but his tongue. He stabbed that long, pointed organ inside her with voracious rapture as her dew dripped down his face. She returned the favor in the next drawing, in which she was kneeling, her eyes wide as she took the satyr's rod down her throat.

Image after image bombarded Gigi. Pearl bouncing atop a supine Prick, riding his thick shaft. Prick atop Pearl, her knees hooked over his shoulders, his bulging stones pressing tightly against her mound. The nymph and satyr entwined on the grass, their heads between the other's thighs, sharing the most lascivious of kisses.

The pair coupled in ways that stretched Gigi's imagination to its very limits. Yet their joining, while unabashedly physical, wasn't just that. In each of their locked gazes, she saw a reflection of the other. Their primal need for connection had led them to their true mate, and they no longer had to wander the woods alone. Thinking of Conrad's dark past, of how lonely his journey must have been without family or people he could count on, she understood why this story had captivated him.

Overwhelmed, Gigi felt Conrad unfasten her trousers, pushing them past her hips. Then he was touching her where she ached. Her head fell back against his shoulder as he fingered her slick crease.

"My own little nymph," he said hoarsely. "I've searched so long for you. And here you are, beautiful and wanton, perfect for me."

Her breath whooshed from her lungs as he lifted her, setting her on the table facing him. He removed the rest of her clothing, and wild with desire, she helped him. Because, she realized, she'd found her true mate, too.

As Gigi perched on the billiards table, naked and blushing, she was his every fantasy come to life. The lush sweep of her lashes, the rich vibrancy of her irises, her intoxicating form—he'd never seen her match and knew he never would. But it was more than that. He'd shared his private, filthy fantasies with her, and despite her innocence, she'd accepted them. Been *aroused* by them. What had started off as a game turned into a moment of startling recognition.

I've fallen in love with Gigi.

He wasn't meant to lead a solitary life: he'd just been waiting for Gigi to wander into it. Gazing into her luminous eyes, he felt hunger, pain, and pleasure all at once. With her, he let himself feel everything.

Slowly, so slowly, he bent his head and kissed her.

It was like sinking into a bed of flowers. He took his time, enjoying the indescribable pleasure of kissing his mate. In the tender press of their lips, he felt the sealing of his future. When she sighed with yielding sweetness, he greedily staked his claim. He thrust his tongue so deep that it was a wonder she didn't choke. Instead, she welcomed him with an excited little moan, and Christ, *Christ*, he had to have more of her. He tumbled her onto the table, and the sight of her lying on the field of green, her hair coming loose from her braid and her arms languidly stretched above her head, made him savage with lust.

He gathered her delicate wrists in one hand, pinning her for his pleasure. A breath puffed from her lips, but her dewy eyes shone with excitement.

"You're mine," he said with rough wonder.

Since nymphs were independent creatures, he set about proving the statement in ways that even Gigi couldn't argue with. He strung a necklace of kisses around her throat, feeling her pulse throb beneath his lips. Her scent intoxicated him. She smelled like sex in a meadow of flowers, like making love to a sprite in her natural habitat.

Eventually, he moved onto her breasts. Firm and round, they had an irresistible jiggle.

"You have the most perfect tits," he said.

Her shy giggle felt like a caress against his balls.

"You are original, I'll grant you that." Her cheeks pink, she peered up at him through her lashes. "That is the first time I've been paid that particular compliment."

"Trust me, it's not the first time a fellow has thought it," he said dryly.

Because the notion of another man ogling her breasts caused his vision to flash red, he focused instead on the bounty in front of him. Reverently, he palmed one smooth tit, perfectly designed to fit his hand, and felt her shiver. Hell, he shivered too. When he grazed a thumb over her plump nipple, her breath hitched.

"There's my favorite treat," he murmured. "It's better with nothing between us, isn't it, sweetheart?"

He meant more than her shirt, and the way she ran her fingers along his jaw, with a tenderness that made his throat flex, conveyed that she felt their intimacy as well.

"Yes, it is," she said.

The softness of her expression roused his darkest hunger. He nuzzled the crevice between her breasts as he rubbed both nipples. He breathed in her scent while her pillowy tits surged against his cheeks. She slid her fingers into his hair, holding him close. He shut his eyes, every fiber of his being pleasured by her touch. He turned his lips to the curve of her breast, exploring the silken mound. He spiraled toward the straining peak and gently flicked it with his tongue. She gasped, her spine bowing off the table as he took his time enjoying his treat. He teased her nipples until they were swollen and lewdly wet, until she was panting his name.

"I love how sensitive you are," he said thickly. "Will you come for me while I lick your tits?"

It was a rhetorical question, for she was clearly teetering on the edge. He sealed his lips around her nipple, sucking hard. When she cried out, he cupped her silky thatch. She was sopping wet. He rubbed the heel of his palm against her pearl, growling when she rewarded him with a gush of dew and arched wantonly into his touch.

Devil and damn. A man could only take so much.

Straightening, he unbuttoned his shirt and yanked it off. Too impatient to deal with his shoes, he shoved his trousers past his hips, grunting as he freed his erection. It slapped heavily into his palm. He groaned as he fisted himself, pumping slowly.

Gigi propped herself up on her elbows. "May I, um, help?"

"Yes, sweetheart," he said hoarsely. "There's nothing I would like more."

He helped her sit up on the edge of the table and wrapped her hand around his straining rod. Her breathy sound of excitement made him leap within her tender grip. The sight of her elegant fingers encircling his veined shaft enhanced his arousal. He closed his hand over hers, showing her what he liked.

"Frig me like this, duchess," he said.

"With that much pressure?" she asked, eyes wide.

"Harder, if you can manage it."

His words were filtered through his teeth because her touch, while inexperienced, was the most pleasurable he'd experienced, bar none. She gauged his response with sweet concentration, her bottom lip caught beneath her teeth, her gaze flitting between his face and his erection, which swelled in her fist. Her desire to please stroked the neediest part of him, the part he'd exposed to no one else.

"You're touching me so well," he told her. "See how hard you've made me?"

"Yes," she breathed.

But she faltered when a drop of seed oozed from his tip. Reaching between her thighs, he fingered her dewy slit, smiling when she whimpered.

"The wetness makes everything feel even better, doesn't it?" he murmured.

When she rubbed her thumb over his flaring dome, he thanked his lucky stars that she was a quick study.

"Do you like that?" she asked, her voice sultry.

He thrust into her fist, letting her feel every pulsing inch of appreciation. "What do you think?"

"I think that is a yes." She looked adorably pleased with herself.

Soon she was using both hands, her torturously gentle pumping bringing him to the edge...and keeping him there. He knew she wasn't doing it on purpose, but she was prolonging his orgasm, building his lust to an almost unbearable degree without taking him over. His chest heaving, he watched his glossy cockhead push through the hole of her fist again and again. Suddenly, she used her other hand to tenderly cup his balls, and primal need took over.

Pushing her back onto the table, he aligned his cock with her slit and thrust it against her plush folds. Bliss sizzled through his veins at the bare contact.

She gasped. "Conrad, we shouldn't—"

"I won't go inside, love," he promised. "I just want to feel this sweet pussy against my cock. Doesn't this feel nice?"

When she bit her lip, he gripped his cock, thumping the tip against her bud.

"Yes." She writhed, her eyes glazed. "Don't stop."

He thrust against her pussy, making sure his shaft grazed her needy little pearl. Her dew lubricated the friction, and soon they were panting, straining against each other. He bucked his hips, reveling in the lewd, wet sounds made by his pistoning cock.

One of his favorite scenes flitted through his head. He hooked her knees over his shoulders, exposing more of her cunny. Gripping her bottom, he plowed her furrow with bestial abandon. She arched, coming again with a breathless cry that triggered his own release. He drove against her, exploding with a roar, mashing his balls against her pussy until every drop of pleasure was wrung from him.

Panting, he dropped his forehead to hers.

"Was that wicked enough for you?" he murmured.

Her impish smile was the stuff of fantasies.

"I suppose it was." Brushing her lips against his jaw, she added in a whisper, "For now."

Chapter Nineteen

The opening gala was a smashing success.

With Letty beside her, Gigi surveyed the packed pump room, which served as an elegant assembly area. The chandelier sparkled, and the circle of Roman deities on the upper floor turned beneficent smiles upon the guests. The crowd was a mix of villagers and visitors from London, and many were whirling to the strains of a local quartet. Letty had also hired a dozen waiters for the event. Dressed in crisp black uniforms and white gloves, they circulated with trays of drinks and assisted at buffet tables, which included delicacies provided by the Leaning House, the Briarbush Inn, and Mr. Khan.

"Thank heavens for Mr. Godwin," Letty said in an undertone. "I don't know how we would have managed without his help. We cannot keep the champagne fountain filled quickly enough, and the spa is shipshape, inside and out."

After their steamy billiards game, Gigi and Conrad had relaxed in front of the fire, enjoying refreshments and a cozy chat. She'd told him about the problems at the spa, to which he'd replied, *"I'll take care of it."* As they'd gone on to discuss other things, she hadn't thought much about it. Until a day later, when a cart bearing crates of champagne had arrived at the bath's doorstep.

"*There's enough to float a battleship!*" Letty had nearly done a jig.

Soon thereafter, workers had started arriving. According to Cobbins, the team of ratcatchers from London was famous. They'd brought a pack of compact, white-and-brown dogs—"*Descendants of Billy, the greatest ratting terrier of all time!*" Cobbins had breathed in awe. He and his canine Bobby had trailed the team, picking up tricks. Within a day, the vermin had vanished.

Meanwhile, at the back of the spa, a half-dozen gardeners had assisted Owen. Apparently, the fellows worked with Joseph Paxton, the esteemed designer of the Crystal Palace and notable landscaper. The leader of the group had praised Owen's design, declaring it "a triumph of balance between nature and man." He'd invited Owen to stop by the firm when he was in London, and Gigi had been thrilled to see the rare smile that lit up her brother's gaunt features.

Everything was going smoothly, in no small part because of Conrad. Gigi hadn't had a chance to thank him in person yet, but his generosity had prompted her to take the next step. She'd sent him a note via Kenny (who'd finagled ongoing lessons from Conrad and thought he walked on water). In her message, she'd asked if Conrad would like to meet her family at the gala. A part of her fretted that it was too soon, but his reply had reassured her:

Say the word, sweetheart. I am ready when you are.

Gigi had strategized the best way to make the introductions. Good thing she was a schemer.

She turned to Letty. "Should we review how you will introduce Mr. Godwin to my parents?"

"Don't fret, my dear." Letty tapped her gloved fingertips against her temple. "I have it all up here. I am to make the introduction seem casual and say he is a friend of the spa, which is the truth. I am indebted to Mr. Godwin…and to you. Your friendship and happiness mean everything to me, and I will not let you down."

Gigi squeezed her friend's hand. "Thank you."

"Thank *you*, dearest. Now enjoy yourself, and I will bring your handsome devil to you and your parents after he arrives."

Gigi circulated, chatting with friends from London and extolling upon the virtues of the spa and local businesses. During a lull, she enjoyed a break with her parents, who'd arrived yesterday. She stood with them in an alcove, watching as guests lined up at the pump to sample the famous water straight from the source.

"I am proud of you, dear." Resplendent in an indigo gown that complemented her curves and upswept raven hair, Mama said warmly, "Your gala is a smashing success."

"The credit belongs to Miss Letty," Gigi demurred. "I merely helped with a few details."

Mama's violet eyes twinkled. "Well, whoever decided to incorporate souvenirs into the décor was a genius."

Building upon the success of her marketing scheme, Gigi had decorated with the theme of romance in mind. She'd ordered figurines of the star-crossed lovers from the local potter and sprinkled them throughout the room. The menu cards at the buffet table were written on a lovely cream cardstock engraved with a sketch of the lovers. The tinted pink glasses used to serve the water came from a nearby manufacturer. Guests who admired the items could find them all in the gift shop, along with other merchandise made by Chuddums's artisans.

Gigi smiled with satisfaction. "Thank you, Mama. I learned from the best."

"You certainly did." Papa, whose formal evening wear suited his austere handsomeness, put an arm around Mama's waist. "Your mama isn't London's most sought-after hostess for nothing."

"You are exaggerating, Marcus," Mama protested.

"Pandora, my love, there are two things in life that are impossible to exaggerate—your social acumen and your beauty."

Papa gallantly kissed Mama's hand. While Gigi was accustomed to her parents' open affection, her recent experiences gave her a new awareness of their intimacy. Papa's head remained bent over Mama's hand a moment longer than necessary, and although his expression was stoic, there was a glint in his steel-blue eyes that she hadn't noticed before. Mama, for her part, was blushing like a newlywed.

Eww. Stop noticing your parents flirting.

Gigi thought of Conrad, her pulse quickening. Introducing him to her parents was a big step, yet it felt...right. At the very least, it didn't make her feel like running for the hills. Anyway, if she ran, Conrad would undoubtedly give chase. A depraved image from *The Naughty Naiad* fogged her brain, heat blooming inside her. She still couldn't believe that Conrad had shown her the erotic book...or how titillating she'd found it.

Realizing that her father was addressing her, she tamped down a guilty blush.

"You have inherited your mama's charm, Gigi," he said. "How fetching you look."

"Thank you, Papa. This dress is courtesy of Mrs. Sommers." She beamed at him. "And it will require only the *teensiest* supplementation of my pin money this month."

Papa raised his brows. "Define teensiest."

"Now, darling," Mama said. "You know how important it is to support local businesses. Moreover, Mrs. Sommers charges a fraction of what the modistes in London do, and that dress makes our Gigi look like an angel. Don't you agree that the effect of the silver netting over that water-blue satin is exquisite?"

The dress *was* heavenly, with its demure off-the-shoulder neckline, fitted bodice, and wide, frothy skirts. Colette had secured Gigi's hair in a topknot, leaving dangling ringlets to frame her face. Fresh flowers, white silk gloves, and a pearl necklace completed the look. When Mama gave her a subtle nudge, Gigi performed a graceful pirouette.

"I am no arbiter of fashion, but as a former military man, I avoid fighting losing battles," Papa said wryly. "Which is all battles where the two of you are concerned."

"In that case, Papa." Gigi extended one elegantly shod foot. "I hope you do not mind that I ordered matching shoes as well."

"Those buckles are exquisite," Mama exclaimed. "I shall have to order a pair myself."

Papa's sigh was that of the long-suffering. "Since I risk becoming a pauper if this conversation continues, I shall make myself useful and fetch some champagne."

"That would be lovely, darling," Mama agreed.

After Papa strode off, Gigi looked at her mother, and they burst into giggles.

"Don't mind Papa," Mama said. "You know he enjoys indulging us."

"I know." Seeing the glow on her mother's beautiful face, Gigi felt her heart lift. "You look well. The time away did you good."

"As usual, Papa had the right of it." Her mother's smile turned wistful. "I did need some time to collect myself after Sister Agatha's passing."

Last year, Sister Agatha, the abbess at the Society of St. Margery and one of Mama's closest friends, had passed away peacefully in her sleep. Although Gigi had only met Sister Agatha a handful of times, she'd felt the strength of the bond between her mother and the older lady with the kind brown eyes. The loss had hit Mama hard; for weeks, she hadn't seemed herself. Finally, Papa had insisted on taking her on a relaxing trip to the Cotswolds, and Gigi was relieved to see the return of her mama's sparkle.

"I have missed you, dear." Mama squeezed her hand. "And your brothers. You shall have to catch me up on the latest developments."

All her life, Gigi had confided in her mama. However, her relationship with Conrad was complicated. As understanding and loving as Mama was, she was also a paragon. She was everything a true lady ought to be, and Society revered her for it. Unfortunately, that made it more difficult for Gigi to confess her own improper inclinations.

Luckily, she was interrupted by Ethan and Xenia. Ethan cut a dashing figure in his stark evening clothes. He was the perfect foil for his wife, who was as bright as a flame in a gown of crimson velvet.

"That dress is most becoming, Xenia, dear," Mama said with a smile. "Ethan, you shall be fighting off gentlemen who wish to dance with your wife."

Ethan looked rather smug. "Xenia promised her dances to me."

"You mustn't monopolize your wife," Mama chided. "No more than two dances—*at most*."

"But I don't wish to dance with anyone but Ethan." Unused to the intricacies of Society's rules, Xenia looked puzzled. "Why can I only dance twice with him?"

"Any more dances and people will say you are overly devoted and living in each other's pockets," Gigi explained.

"Oh." Xenia's brown eyes widened. "Is that a bad thing?"

"No," Ethan said.

"Yes," Gigi and Mama said at the same time.

Papa returned with the champagne.

"Marcus, do tell Ethan he mustn't monopolize Xenia's dances," Mama begged.

"Relinquishing one's favorite dance partner is a necessary fact of life, son." Papa distributed the glasses. "However, I do have a suggestion."

Ethan raised his brows.

"Claim the waltzes," Papa advised. "The longer, the better."

"Really, darling. What kind of example are you setting?" Blushing, Mama said, "Has anyone seen Owen?"

"We saw him when we were coming in," Xenia said. "He was fiddling with the hedges. Said they weren't quite right."

"Some deer trampled Miss Letty's garden, and Owen fixed the damage," Gigi clarified. "He was quite the hero."

Papa cleared his throat. "It's nice to know the lad is making himself useful."

"Owen always preferred being outdoors." Mama's smile was poignant. "He loved climbing trees and was fascinated with how things grew. Remember how he used to follow the groundskeeper around at the country seat?"

"I had forgotten," Ethan replied. "James and I teased him, calling him 'Capability Harrington.'"

Gigi had been too young to remember those days. With a pang, she wished she'd had more time with Owen before he'd gone off to war. Better yet, she wished he *hadn't* gone to war...wished he could be the happy, carefree, and rambunctious boy he'd once been. Yet confiding in Conrad had given her greater clarity when it came to her family. There were things she could not change. But she would always be there for them, should they seek her help.

James sauntered over. As ever, he was the epitome of the perfect heir with his precise cravat and elegant tailoring.

"Congratulations on your latest project, little sister," he drawled. "Once again, you've outdone yourself."

Before Gigi could thank him, Mama cut in.

"Dearest, who is that lady in green?" she asked casually. "The one you were chatting with by the pump. I do not believe I am acquainted."

Gigi hadn't noticed James talking to anyone, but now she darted a glance over to the water station. A statuesque brunette in emerald-green taffeta was sipping on a glass of water as a circle of gentlemen vied for her attention.

Above his pristine collar, James's jaw turned slightly ruddy. "Her name is Lady Morgana Vernon. I just met her myself. She had difficulty with the pump, so I offered my assistance."

"Naturally," Mama murmured. "You are a gentleman like your papa."

A sudden visceral awareness gripped Gigi, and she swung her gaze toward the entrance. Sure enough, there was Conrad. Despite the striking elegance of his black-and-white attire, he looked like a Viking surveying the spoils of a raid. His marauder's gaze locked boldly upon her, and she experienced the primal instinct to run: toward or away from him, she wasn't entirely certain.

He strode to Letty, bowing over her hand. Even from a distance, Gigi could see the blush on her friend's cheek. Then the pair headed over.

She drew in a deep breath. *Relax and act naturally.*

"My lords and my ladies," Letty said formally. "May I have the pleasure of introducing Mr. Conrad Godwin. He is a supporter of the spa, and no small part of tonight's success must be attributed to his generosity."

"It is an honor to make your acquaintances, Lord and Lady Blackwood." Conrad bowed to Gigi's parents before turning to her brothers and Xenia. "And yours, my lords and my lady."

"Your reputation precedes you, Mr. Godwin." Papa's expression was impassive. "The London papers are full of your exploits."

Gigi tensed, and that was before Ethan spoke up.

"Exploits that have no place in our village," her middle brother said in a dangerous tone.

Gigi shot Xenia a worried look. Her sister-in-law's slight shake of the head confirmed that she hadn't informed Mama and Papa about Gigi's encounter with Conrad at the spa. Nonetheless, Ethan's hostility might give away the game if Gigi didn't intervene.

"Such talk is often exaggerated," Conrad replied.

He did not seem the least bit intimidated by Ethan's scowling countenance.

"I wonder what interest a rustic village like Chuddums might hold for a man of your reputation," James said coolly.

"I am aware that some have questioned my business methods." A hint of brusqueness entered Conrad's tone. "However, what they call ruthlessness, I call ambition. I make no apologies for being a fellow who knows what he wants and goes after it."

To Gigi's thrill and dismay, he looked directly at her. Ethan, James, and Papa were all glowering at him. Flustered, she racked her brain for some way to defuse the tension.

"Did I miss something?"

Joining the group, Owen looked confused. His evening wear looked rumpled on his lanky form, and there were traces of soil on his cuffs. In one hand, he clutched a trio of white camellias.

"Owen, we were wondering where you were." Gigi leapt at the opportunity to change the topic. "Are those flowers from the garden?"

"The camellia bushes needed trimming, and I thought you, Xenia, and Mama might like these for corsages." Owen's stormy grey gaze was fixed on Conrad. "Who are you?"

"This is Mr. Godwin." To Gigi's relief, Mama stepped in, her manner smooth and gracious. "He has been helping Miss Letty with the spa. Mr. Godwin, this is my youngest son, Lord Owen Harrington."

"A pleasure, sir," Conrad said.

"Likewise," Owen returned.

"The camellias are lovely, dear." Smiling at him, Mama said, "Why don't you help Gigi with hers while Ethan attends to Xenia? Marcus, I shall require your assistance."

As the men set about their duties, Gigi gave her mother a grateful look. Mama nodded, but the glint in those maternal eyes implied that they would be talking later.

While Owen pinned the bloom to her bodice, Gigi risked a glance at Conrad. His jaw was taut, his gaze distinctly proprietary. For an instant, she feared he might tear the flower from her brother and insist on pinning it to her himself.

So much for a casual introduction.

"It is almost time for my speech," Letty said hastily. "Mr. Godwin, may I bother you to help me assemble the guests?"

Conrad gave a reluctant nod. "It is no bother, ma'am."

He went with Letty, sending a smoldering look back at Gigi.

Things are not going as planned, Conrad thought broodingly.

He was seated on a small dais, waiting for Miss Letty's speech to begin. Rows of guests faced the stage, and he fought to keep his anger from showing. He had to give it to Gigi: she knew how to put on a good performance. The statues of the Roman gods along the upper gallery lent gravitas to the event. Directly above him was Mars—fitting, given his pugilistic mood.

While Conrad knew it was important to make a good impression on Gigi's family, he had no talent for pouring on the butter boat. Her menfolk hadn't hidden their disdain, and he had a lifelong habit of never backing down from snobs. It stung that they'd judged him because of his origins. Because they believed him to be a social climber who wanted to get his grubby hands on Gigi.

Once they know who I really am, they will be singing a different tune.

He comforted himself with the knowledge that he wouldn't have to keep his secrets much longer. Justice would soon be his, and after that, the damned Harringtons would be falling over to welcome him into their family. He glanced at Gigi. She was seated on the other side of the stage, having an animated conversation with her brothers. It was clear that the Harringtons were a close-knit bunch, and Conrad wasn't certain that even the strongest passion would convince Gigi to choose him over them.

If you don't bind her fully to you, you will lose her.

He felt a flash of panic, which was quickly subsumed by righteous anger. Gigi was *his*. She'd shared physical intimacies and confidences with him. Though they hadn't spoken of love, he was quite certain that she was falling for him as he'd fallen for her.

Maybe he needed to hasten things along by getting her to admit to her feelings...

Miss Letty took center stage, clutching a roll of parchment. "To my esteemed guests, thank you for your patronage. If I may, I would like to say a few words." When she untied the paper, it unraveled, brushing the ground. "I shall start with a brief history of this remarkable building."

As Letty waxed on about Tobias Caldecott's vision, Gigi cast covert glances in Conrad's direction. He appeared to be politely interested in the speech, but his rigid posture revealed his true state of mind. He was furious. While she understood his reaction, she was annoyed too.

Did he have to be so heavy-handed with my family? Especially after I warned him to take things slowly. Now I must fix the damage he's caused with his boorish behavior.

As she cast her gaze upward in disgust, a movement caught her attention...a flicker in the shadowed second-floor gallery, behind the statue of Mars. Concerned that a guest might have ventured up into the area, which was cordoned off due to needed repairs, she craned her neck, but she couldn't see beyond the God of War's looming figure.

She blinked. Had the grim-faced statue *teetered*? It must have been a trick of the light... Then she caught the flash of something black and white against the stone back, and Mars pitched forward with ominous momentum. With jolting terror, she registered the statue's deadly trajectory and leapt to her feet.

"Conrad, move!" she cried. "The statue is going to fall!"

He looked up just as Mars toppled.

Chapter Twenty

Hearing his name, Conrad blinked. It took him a moment to register Gigi's face above his. He was lying in a bed, and she was perched by his side.

"Oh, Conrad." Her eyes shimmered with worry. "How are you feeling?"

"I'm fine—"

A blinding pain shot through his head, blurring his vision. He groaned, and just when he thought it had passed, an undertow of nausea pulled him under.

Bloody hell, I'm going to be sick.

"Move, Gigi," he said urgently.

"Do as he says," a male voice commanded. "I will turn his head so that he doesn't choke."

"I'll do it," Gigi insisted.

Conrad felt her hands cupping his jaw, but before he could protest, his insides surged, and he couldn't hold back the inevitable. An instant later, supported by Gigi, he puked his guts into a conveniently placed bucket. Afterward, he lay back, shuddering and humiliated. He hated being sick—hated how defenseless it made him feel. He'd learned early on that the weakest were culled. At Creavey Hall, being sick meant being exposed: other boys would steal your food or meager belongings or target you to prove their superior strength.

"I'm sorry," he muttered.

"Don't be, dear." Gigi's tenderness tightened his throat. "The physician said this might happen. You are lucky the injury was not more severe."

"The injury…?"

It all came back. Gigi's shout of warning, the massive statue hurtling toward him. He'd dove out of harm's way, hitting the ground as it rumbled beneath him. Then something heavy had knocked his head, and he didn't recall anything after that. Tentatively, he touched his temple and felt a bandage. Beneath the swaddling, pain pulsed.

"Where am I?" he asked.

"At Bottoms House," a male voice said.

Lord Ethan emerged behind Gigi.

"Why did you bring me here?" Conrad tried to sit up.

"Do have a care," Gigi said. "You could disturb your wound."

She pressed on his shoulders, and to his surprise, he didn't have the strength to resist her. He fell back against the pillows with a grunt.

"I'm fine—" he began.

"That refrain is getting tiresome, Godwin," Lord Ethan said. "Given that it is categorically untrue. The reason you are here in my home is because my sister insisted upon it."

"Someone needed to keep an eye on you," Gigi cut in. "You were lucky to dodge the statue, but part of Mars's helmet broke off and hit your head. Beneath that bandage, you've a cut on your temple and a lump the size of an egg. Luckily, that appears to be the extent of the damage. The physician says you've a hard head."

"Speaking of a hard head, my sister insisted upon staying by your side." Lord Ethan sounded irritated. "The rest of us had to take turns chaperoning her through the night."

Gigi stayed with me...all night?

Seeing the smudges of exhaustion under her vivid eyes, Conrad felt a surge of emotion. He couldn't recall the last time anyone treated him with such care—at least, anyone he didn't employ to do so. Gigi had lost sleep over him, taken care of him, out of genuine concern.

She cares for me. I knew it.

Despite the megrim muddling his thoughts, he felt his chest expand...with wonder, maybe. Or joy. As he wasn't well acquainted with either emotion, he couldn't be sure. At the same time, he was aware of the humiliating stench of his disgrace and the weakness of his position. He did not like being indebted to anyone...least of all, a man who thought him unworthy of Gigi.

"I apologize for the inconvenience," he said stiffly. "I'll summon my servants to bring me home."

"Stuff and nonsense," Gigi said. "You are staying put. According to the physician, you oughtn't move about for at least a couple of days. He said that recovery from a head injury can take unexpected turns, and fainting spells are not uncommon."

"I have never fainted in my life," Conrad scoffed.

Lord Ethan snorted. "How would you know if you're unconscious? Which you were for several minutes after being knocked in the noggin."

Conrad narrowed his eyes. "Being unconscious and fainting are two entirely different—"

"For heaven's sake, *stop it*." Gigi shot to her feet. "Both of you."

Conrad didn't reply because her movements had rocked the mattress and set off waves of queasiness. He concentrated on breathing and not spewing his guts again.

"Ethan." She glared at her brother. "Mr. Godwin nearly lost his life and is in his sickbed. You will cease baiting him, or I shall never speak to you again."

"Would that I could be so lucky." His lordship rolled his eyes but said nothing more.

"And you."

Gigi turned to Conrad. While it was a cliché that women were beautiful when they were angry, in Gigi's case, it was also true. She looked adorable while spitting mad. This led to the welcome discovery that while his head might not be in full working order, his other head was. When she wagged a finger at him, he had to subtly adjust the blanket to hide his burgeoning appreciation.

"You will cease being pigheaded," she scolded. "You nearly lost your life and are in no shape to go anywhere. You are staying put until I say you are ready to go."

Now he really did want to swive her. Wanted to pull her down into the bed and memorize the sweet concern in her eyes while he plowed her to an inch of their lives. Unfortunately, she was right: he *was* in a weakened state and could barely lift a finger.

"Fine, I'll stay," he said. "But I insist upon compensating your brother for the inconvenience."

"I am hardly going to charge you room and board," Lord Ethan grumbled.

"You should rest now."

Gigi laid a hand on his cheek, and her touch felt so good that he relaxed. He felt groggy, as if he couldn't keep his eyelids open another moment. Suddenly, he remembered that there was something he had to mention, something important. Something he ought to ask about... The thought dissolved in the wave of tiredness that crashed over him.

"I'll be right as rain by tomorrow," he mumbled.

"Sleep, my dearest. We'll talk when you awake," were the last words he heard before he went under.

He was back at Creavey Hall.

Back in the headmaster's office.

Back bending over the punishment bench, his trousers down around his ankles. A sheen of cold sweat covered his bare back, on fire with welts...and it was only the first round. Shivering, he tried to breathe through the pain and nausea—to not let fear get the better of him.

Grimshaw preys on fear. It makes him even more vicious. Don't give him the satisfaction.

When he felt the presence looming behind him, a whimper escaped despite his best efforts.

"What was that, Christian?"

That was his old name...the name of the boy he'd once been. This had to be a dream, but Obadiah Grimshaw's voice was too real, too convincing. The soft, pious tones did not disguise the sadistic rasp beneath, which became more pronounced whenever he carried out his "holy duty." Which, when it came to Christian, was often. The headmaster preyed on the weakest boys—the poor and sickly ones, the ones with no family...or family who specifically instructed that they be "reformed."

"N-nothing sir. I-I didn't say anything."

Christian bit his lip to prevent crying out as Grimshaw traced the tip of the birch along a welt. When the headmaster pushed, breaking through the skin, he tasted blood.

"The devil hates liars, you know."

Rounding the bench, Grimshaw gripped a handful of Christian's hair, yanking his head back until he had no choice but to meet the headmaster's gaze. It was like being buried in a coal cellar —like being suffocated by the dark filth heaped upon you.

"Only the guilty avert their eyes," Grimshaw admonished.

"Y-yes, sir."

"Now you will confess your sins."

"But I-I haven't done anything," he said, his voice hitching.

Grimshaw rose, his *tut-tutting* raising the hairs on Christian's nape. The headmaster made a show of rolling up his sleeves to reveal pale, hairless arms. He took his time adjusting his grip on the rod until his fingers curled comfortably, lovingly, around the bundled birches.

"Another six of the best, then," he said, smiling.

Christian trembled as the headmaster disappeared behind him. Even though he knew it would do no good, he braced. When the blow came, slicing into him like a red-hot knife, he swallowed the salt and rust of his pain. Even as heat spilled from his eyes, he resorted to his old trick. He fixed his gaze on the maker's mark engraved on the bottom rung of the bench, repeating the word like a talisman. Or a curse.

While she was no physician, Lady Pandora, the Marchioness of Blackwood, knew the fever that gripped Conrad Godwin came from more than the wound in his flesh. She'd experienced this agony herself and knew it came from a deeper place: the soul.

"Poor fellow," she murmured. "Whatever happened to you, let it go."

He shuddered, releasing a pitiful sound that tore at Penny's heart. In that moment, he seemed more like a lost boy than the merciless magnate he was reputed to be. It reminded her of the strength of demons. The ones she'd conquered, the ones she'd watched her middle child battle and beat, the ones that mercilessly plagued her youngest son. The ones her eldest had yet to face.

And she knew there was only one solution.

"Rest now." She swept a soothing hand over Godwin's damp brow. "You are not alone."

Returning to her chair, she kept vigil over the man in the bed. Maternal protectiveness for her daughter warred with compassion for this stranger as she watched his restless sleep. She consoled herself with the thought that, of all her children, her youngest was the one who seemed to know her own mind—and her own heart—best. Gigi seemed to have marched out of the womb with a purpose and a plan.

My dearest girl, I hope you know what you are about. For if this is your heart's desire, you shall have your work cut out for you.

Chapter Twenty-One

At her mama's insistence, Gigi left Conrad's side to have a lie down. She refused at first, but when Mama had promised to look after him, she gave in. Climbing into bed, she wondered how she could ever fall asleep, rattled as she was. One concern overshadowed the rest.

Did someone try to murder Conrad?

She flashed back to the white glove and black sleeve—had she imagined it? Given the poor lighting of the second-floor gallery, it *was* possible. Yet there was also the other incident, when Conrad had been run off the road. Too many coincidences, her intuition told her, and she was taking no risks where Conrad was concerned. He meant too much to her: the moment when she'd almost lost him had made her feelings crystal clear.

Thus, she'd shared her suspicions with her family. Ethan had organized his footmen to keep watch and sent word to the local constable, Rawlins, who would be coming by this afternoon for an interview. Due to Conrad's condition, Gigi hadn't informed him of the developments. Knowing him, he would jump out of bed and start hunting down potential suspects when what he needed to do was rest and let others take care of him.

Conrad, she reflected, wasn't a man who relinquished control easily. She knew enough about his past to understand why. He was too used to handling everything on his own, and he wasn't going to like that she'd kept her suspicions about the falling statue from him.

I shall deal with that later. After I close my eyes for a bit...

When Gigi awoke, afternoon sunlight was slanting through a gap in the curtains. She got out of bed and rang for her maid.

"What time is it, Colette?" she asked.

"It is nearing two o'clock, my lady. Lady Blackwood said not to disturb you."

"But the constable will be arriving soon," Gigi fretted. "And I wanted to speak with Mr. Godwin before the interview. Is he awake?"

"I'm not certain. Would you like me to check?"

"No, I will go see him myself." Gigi hurried to the dressing screen. "Please help me get dressed."

With her usual efficiency, Colette helped Gigi into a lavender walking dress and was putting the finishing touches on a simple coiffure when Mama and Papa came in.

Gigi twisted around at the dressing table. "Constable Rawlins hasn't arrived yet, has he? I haven't told Mr. Godwin about what I saw, and I ought to speak to him before—"

"The constable isn't here, but Papa and I wished to speak with you," Mama said.

Mama's tone brooked no refusal. While Gigi had been expecting a parental interrogation—honestly, she was surprised they'd waited this long—she nonetheless dreaded it.

She strove for nonchalance. "What about?"

"Conrad Godwin," Papa stated.

Lieutenant-Colonel Marcus Harrington, commander of battalions and defeater of Boney, had emerged full force. It had been said that Papa's implacability had intimidated soldiers into confessing the truth, and even Gigi felt a bit of trepidation. As much as she wanted her parents to support her relationship with Conrad, gaining their approval was not going to be easy. He hadn't exactly made a sterling first impression.

Gigi turned to face her parents, who, as usual, stood shoulder to shoulder. A united front.

"What about Mr. Godwin?" she asked brightly.

"Who is he to you, Georgiana?" Papa said.

Uh oh. Being addressed by her full name was never a good sign.

"He's a friend," she said. "As Miss Letty mentioned, he has been a generous benefactor to the bath—"

"I do not give a damn what Godwin has done for the bath." A muscle ticked along Papa's firm jaw. "I want to know what is going on between him and you."

"We spoke to Ethan and Xenia," Mama added. "We know about your earlier incident with Mr. Godwin."

"Nothing happened." When making excuses, Gigi had learned that consistency was important. "I slipped, and he caught me before I fell into the pool—"

"Then why do you care what happens to this fellow?" Papa demanded.

"I would care about anyone who was almost quashed like an insect by a falling statue."

"Gigi, that is enough."

Hearing the steel in Mama's voice, resignation filled her.

I'm doomed.

"Stop prevaricating and give us the truth."

"The truth is..." Gigi fiddled with her skirts. "I like Mr. Godwin."

Papa's jaw tautened. "How well do you know this fellow?"

"Well enough." Drawing a breath, she said, "We, um, ran into each other on several occasions. At first, I disliked him because I thought he was a heartless financier intent upon buying Miss Letty's spa—"

"That is Godwin's reputation," Papa said coldly. "He is an opportunist. He made his fortune buying failing railway stocks at a fraction of their original value, then selling them for exorbitant sums when the market recovered. You did not misjudge him."

"But I did," she said earnestly. "You see, I thought he only cared about money and profit. Yet when I made him understand what the spa meant to Miss Letty and the village, he changed his plans. He has given up pursuing the spa—and, as you heard from Miss Letty herself, he is now a generous benefactor."

"Perhaps he saw a better opportunity. Perhaps he realized there was more to be gained by pursuing you than the spa." Papa's shoulders were rigid, his hands curled at his sides. "Have you made any promises to him, Georgiana?"

She bit her lip. "Nothing, um, irrevocable."

Papa's eyes blazed. "By Jove, if the scoundrel has extracted *any* promise from you, then he has taken advantage of your kind heart and innocence. I shall call him out—"

"*No*, Papa."

Gigi shot to her feet while Mama put a staying hand on his shoulder.

"Marcus, darling," Mama murmured. "Let us not overreact."

"Overreact?" Papa thundered. "This bounder has had the audacity, the sheer insolence, to prey upon our daughter."

"That isn't true," Gigi said beseechingly. "Mr. Godwin did not prey upon me. He wants to court me. Our mutual attachment surprised us both."

"You have formed an attachment, then?" Mama did not sound surprised.

"Yes," Gigi said in a small voice.

"Bloody hell," Papa bit out. "You are too young to know your mind when it comes to men like Godwin. You've seen too little of the world—"

"And whose fault is that?" Her hurt bubbled up and spilled

over. "I *wanted* to go with you to Afghanistan. I wanted to help you find Owen. I want to help this family, but I am always told I am too young, too naïve, too useless to do anything!"

Papa frowned. "What relevance does Afghanistan have in this conversation? And no one in this family has ever called you useless."

He was right, of course. Yet, rationally or not, she had *felt* that way each time her family had left her behind. She wanted them to see that she was capable and to be taken seriously—the way Conrad saw her.

"Hyperbole aside," her father admonished. "My point is that you are a sheltered young lady, and men like Godwin know how to take advantage."

"*My* point is that I do know my own mind, and I know exactly the sort of man Conrad Godwin is." She squared her shoulders. "While he might seem ruthless, he has a caring side once one gets to know him. Moreover, he respects my independence and treats me like his equal."

"You may think you know him, Gigi, but you do not," Papa insisted. "A man like Godwin has no sense of honor or integrity. He does as he pleases, and I wouldn't be surprised if he brought about this murder attempt through his own actions. He does not belong in our world—"

"I belong wherever I damn well please."

Gigi whirled, her breath hitching at the sight of Conrad standing in the doorway. She had no idea how long he'd been there or how much he'd overheard. He was fully dressed, last evening's elegance an incongruous contrast to the bandage wrapped around his head. Otherwise, he looked much recovered...and furious.

Hastily, she tried to head off another confrontation between him and her parents. "Mr. Godwin, I am glad to see you improved. However, the physician advised that you stay in bed."

"Thank you for the hospitality," he said with icy civility.

"However, I will not stay where I am not welcome. Before I go, however..."

He stared at her father, who stared stonily back.

"What is this about a murder attempt?"

Chapter Twenty-Two

A quarter-hour later, Conrad found himself in the drawing room with the rest of Gigi's family. The Harringtons had closed ranks around Gigi. She sat on a settee between her mama and sister-in-law. Ethan Harrington stood behind his wife, the Marquess of Blackwood behind his. James, the Earl of Manderly, and Lord Owen occupied adjacent wingchairs.

Conrad stood on the periphery, his shoulder braced against a wall. The position provided a good vantage point of the Harringtons and Rawlins, the local constable, who was preparing to address the group. Rawlins's rumpled, sleepy-eyed appearance and the way he was fumbling to find his notebook did not inspire confidence.

Conrad had considered skipping the meeting, but as the topic concerned an assassination attempt with him as the target, he thought it prudent to stay. When he'd expressed his annoyance that Gigi had failed to mention that the falling statue had been no accident, her parents had stiffened, but she'd simply rolled her eyes.

"*Please. You had just suffered a concussion and needed rest, not additional stress. Anyway, I have everything in hand. The constable will be by shortly, and if you are ready to get off your high horse, you are welcome to join."*

Despite his foul mood, Conrad admired Gigi's spirit and begrudgingly conceded her point. He trusted her, and from what he'd overheard, he was right to. Gigi had stood up to her parents on his behalf: she'd admitted their mutual attraction *and* called him "caring." It was not the adjective he would have chosen to describe himself, but he wasn't about to look a gift horse in the mouth. His bond with Gigi was growing stronger day by day, and he no longer had any doubt that they belonged together.

Yet her family remained an obstacle. Conrad was still fuming over the marquess's characterization of him, although he ought to have expected it. All his life, he'd dealt with snobs who deemed him unworthy. Robert and his other half-brothers had shunned and tormented him because of his mama's working-class origins. Robert had further instructed the headmaster of Creavey Hall to "rehabilitate"—in other words, to abuse and prey upon—Conrad in whatever fashion the sadistic bastard saw fit.

As a prizefighter, Conrad had fought his way to the top, yet his triumphs and popularity had been accompanied by an awareness that his admirers viewed him as nothing more than a source of entertainment. Even his lovers—Isobel and her ilk—saw him as some exotic beast they wanted a turn riding or a supplier of whatever worldly goods they wanted.

Yet Gigi was different. She cared about him. While they'd butted heads as often as they'd made love, she treated him like a flesh-and-blood man, capable of feeling. She angered and amused, teased and tormented him. Sometimes, he didn't know if he wanted to fight or fuck her...or do both at once. All he knew was that he wanted her in his life, permanently.

And, hell, he might owe his life to her.

If not for her cry of warning, he might have met his end beneath a pile of rock.

Christ. He was going to have to find some way to deal with the

Harringtons. As much as it galled him, to secure Gigi's hand in marriage, he needed to convince the marquess and marchioness that he was worthy of their daughter. Apparently, his fortune held no swaying power...which left the other card he had to play.

Which I will reveal. When the time is right.

The constable made a clearing sound in his throat. "If I may. I would like to begin by expressing my sincere wishes to Mr. Godwin for a speedy recovery."

"I'm fine," Conrad said curtly. "But I will be better when the bastard who did this is apprehended."

"Understood, sir." Despite the puffy bags under his eyes, Rawlins's gaze was keen. "I share your concern. This village has suffered enough mayhem. In recent months, a nefarious gang of thieves and cutthroats called the Corrigans were expelled by the good people of Chuddums. We are still hunting down some of the gang members as well as their remaining stash of stolen goods. The last thing the villagers need is more bad news. Unfortunately, last night's disaster has led to fresh talk about a curse."

"Oh no," Gigi breathed. "Are people blaming Bloody Thom for the falling statue?"

Her sister-in-law reached over, and the two ladies gripped hands.

"Regrettably, that is the rumor," Rawlins said in somber tones. "The bath is closed for the day while Miss Letty deals with the damage, which leaves many of her genteel guests with free time in Chuddums. Combine their reports of the gala with the villagers' tales of the curse, and *voila*. Bloody Thom rises again."

"This could undo the progress the village has made."

Xenia Harrington bit her lip, and her husband placed a hand on her shoulder.

"We've come so far," Gigi moaned. "All of Miss Letty's hard work could come to naught if people believe a murderous ghost is lurking at the spa. Moreover, I *know* what I saw. The villain was no specter."

"I am in agreement, my lady, and hope that our interview today will lead us to the real culprit," the constable said. "Criminals have no place in Chuddums."

Conrad cut in. "I place my faith in deeds, not words. What are you doing about it?"

"I would like to start with a review of facts." Rawlins took the challenge in stride. "This morning, my men and I went to surveil the spa, and I believe Lady Georgiana was correct in her belief that this was no accident, but sabotage. We found traces of muddy footsteps on the second-floor gallery—fresh, but not identifiable, I am afraid. However, I discovered more compelling evidence when I examined the statues. They are attached to their respective columns by thin metal bands...all of which have been cut."

Gigi gasped. "Any one of the statues could have fallen?"

"With a determined push, yes," Rawlins confirmed. "My theory is that the assailant was not entirely certain where his target would end up. Thus, he needed a variety of options."

"Diabolical," Lord Ethan muttered.

"Indeed, my lord. The fact that the assailant chose to deploy Mars strongly supports that Mr. Godwin was the intended target, for he was the one directly in the line of fire."

"A few days ago, there was another attempt on Mr. Godwin's life," Gigi blurted. "It cannot be a coincidence."

Of course, she would make the connection. After the head injury, Conrad's grogginess had prevented him from thinking clearly, but he'd awakened this morning with the same conclusion blazing in his head.

Someone wants me dead. Who?

"What's this?" Rawlins asked.

With no choice, Conrad gave a terse summary of the carriage collision.

"You should have reported the incident, sir," the constable said, frowning. "We could have taken precautions for your safety. Perhaps this latest attempt could have been avoided."

"I've taken precautions, including hiring investigators to look into it."

Brows knitted, Gigi didn't look happy that he'd failed to mention his plan. But she couldn't say more with her kin breathing down their necks. Given that they were supposed to be mere acquaintances, she shouldn't know about his business.

"I handle my own affairs," Conrad said. "Tell me about this latest attempt. Do you know who was behind it?"

"Not yet, I'm afraid," Rawlins replied. "However, thanks to Lady Georgiana, we have a clue. She saw that whoever pushed that statue was wearing a white glove and black-sleeved jacket, which matches the uniform of the waiters. The cutting of the metal bands indicates the villain had advance access to the spa. As the waiters helped to set up for the gala a few days before, this lends further credibility to her theory. To that end, I obtained a list of the serving staff from Miss Letty and conducted interviews with the five who live in Chuddums."

"You have been busy," Conrad said with grudging approval.

"As my mama was wont to say, never put off until tomorrow what can be done today. After speaking with those five fellows, I do not believe the culprit is among them. However, this leaves seven candidates to interview, some of whom are scattered throughout the county. In the interim, I wanted to ask present company if anyone noticed anything unusual last night. Even seemingly unimportant details might lead to a clue."

Glances were exchanged around the room.

"This probably doesn't mean anything, but since you mentioned muddy footprints...well, Lord Fiddleston arrived with mud on his shoes." Lady Blackwood pursed her lips. "I only know this because he was complaining so much. His carriage got stuck—an axle broke, I believe—and he had to help his groom push and ended up soiling his favorite footwear. However, he was wearing a blue evening coat and no gloves."

"Thank you, my lady." Rawlins jotted in a small notebook

before turning to Conrad. "To your knowledge, would Lord Fiddleston have reason to wish you harm?"

"Not that I am aware of," Conrad replied. "The fellow is not one of my company's clients, and I am not acquainted with him personally."

"If Fiddleston had it in for anyone, it would be Lord Valmont," the marquess said dryly.

Rawlins paused, pen poised above his notes. "Why is that, my lord?"

"Valmont and Lady Fiddleston have been rather indiscreet," Lady Blackwood explained. "They were flirting by the pump."

"Ah." Rawlins crossed something out. "Any other instances of note?"

The discussion continued, with the Harringtons sharing a plethora of observations. Given Gigi's cleverness, Conrad was unsurprised by her family's acuity. The Earl of Manderly overheard a pair of lordlings expressing curiosity about the cordoned-off upper gallery, while Lord Ethan reported that one of the ladies had been caught filching one of the souvenir figurines. Xenia Harrington, who'd apparently been her husband's housekeeper before their marriage, was particularly observant about the staff.

"There was this one waiter who captured my notice," she mused. "A good-looking fellow with brown hair."

Manderly shot her husband a devilish look. "Better watch out, old boy."

"Very amusing," Lord Ethan muttered.

"It was because of how the fellow carried himself," Xenia protested. "He oozed confidence but was terribly incompetent at serving."

"Around six feet tall?" Lord Owen said suddenly. "Thick eyebrows?"

"You noticed him too," Xenia said with an eager nod. "Flirting with the ladies appeared to be his main skill. He kept spilling drinks and mixing up requests from the guests."

"That wasn't why I noticed him."

"Oh. What grabbed your attention?"

"He had the eyes of a predator."

At the shadow that came over Lord Owen's face, Conrad felt a chill seep through his veins. Apparently, he had something in common with this brother of Gigi's. Once one looked into the eyes of a brute, one never forgot.

Rawlins was writing busily. "This waiter does not sound like one of the men I interviewed thus far. Did either of you catch his name?"

"I think it was John," Xenia said.

She looked to Lord Owen for help, but his gaze had shuttered.

"Two Johns remain on my list, and I shall prioritize them," Rawlins said. "Thank you all for your contributions. Now, I have one further question, and it is for Mr. Godwin."

Although Conrad knew the question, he waited.

"Do you know of anyone who might wish you harm?"

Competitors, a former lover, family...take your pick.

"I am a powerful man," he said evenly. "Powerful men have enemies."

Rawlins's gaze sharpened. "Are you aware of specific enemies?"

When he did not reply, Gigi said, "*Do* you know of people who would try to harm you, Con—I mean, Mr. Godwin? If so, you must tell the constable."

If he were alone with Gigi, he would share his secrets...at least some of them. When the time was right, and she was his, he might even tell her everything. The long and sordid history of what—and who—had shaped him into the man he was today. He would not, however, expose any of this in public. Doing so would compromise the plans he'd meticulously laid out and jeopardize his long-awaited vengeance against the two bastards who'd wronged him.

"The constable has enough to do," he said. "Rawlins, after you have interviewed the remaining suspects, I expect to be apprised of your findings."

"Certainly, sir." The constable's face was grave. "But if you know of any threats to your well-being, I must advise you to share them."

"We want to help," Gigi said haltingly. "You trust us...don't you?"

I trust you. But only you.

He hated how crushed she looked. Yet he saw her papa's rigid disdain and her mama's worry. Her brothers were ready to pound him to a fare-thee-well. Anything he had to say to Gigi would have to be done in private.

"Rest assured, I will be returning to London shortly to handle the matter." Conrad bowed to the group. "Again, I thank you for your hospitality. If you'll excuse me."

He exited before the shock and hurt in Gigi's eyes could change his mind.

Chapter Twenty-Three

"He didn't," Duffy breathed.

"He did." Gigi gave the pink satin she was examining an annoyed twitch. "He said he's going back to London to 'handle the matter' and left the room without another word. Who knows if he'll even say farewell? At any rate, I am done with the bounder."

"You don't mean that. And I'm certain he will contact you before he leaves."

Duffy cast a discreet look around his shop, and Gigi did the same. After Rawlins shared yesterday that talk of the village's curse had been reignited, she had decided to visit Chuddums and try to put out fires. Mama had joined her on the mission. When they ran into friends from London at the tea shop and the milliner's, they'd laughed off the curse as an old wives' tale used to scare small children. Gigi had emphasized the true moral of the story: the love between Thomas Mulligan and his Rosalinda. With any luck, their efforts were paying off. At present, Mama was a few rows down, chatting with another acquaintance.

"What makes you so certain about Mr. Godwin?" Gigi asked.

"I've seen the way he looks at you. Like you're the only thing worth seeing and he resents having to tear his gaze from you for even an instant. That fellow is as head over heels for you," Duffy said quietly, "as you are for him."

"I am *not* in love with him."

When Duffy arched a brow, she huffed out a breath.

"All right, I was *beginning* to fall for him and thought we were coming to an understanding. But that is over now." She buried the pain beneath indignation. "Clearly, he has been keeping secrets from me. There have been two attempts on his life, and he will not even tell me who his enemies are."

Although Mr. Rawlins had cautioned that it was best to refer to the incident as an "accident" for now, she had shared the truth with her friend, whose discretion could be trusted.

"Perhaps Mr. Godwin has issues with trust," Duffy said.

"*Perhaps*?" Gigi squinted at him.

"I was trying to be optimistic. Have you confronted him about it?"

"Since I foolishly told my parents that Mr. Godwin and I had formed an attachment, they are watching me like hawks," Gigi muttered. "They'll never let me be alone in his company. The only reason they let me out of the manor today was because of exigent circumstances."

"The talk of Bloody Thom is everywhere," Duffy confirmed. "I've had half a dozen ladies from London ask if I've seen him myself."

"What did you say?"

"I told them that the actual legend is about the healing power of love."

"A perfect reply. How did they respond?"

"Well, I've had two proposals to elope to Gretna Green."

At her friend's wry expression, Gigi giggled.

"I think the only blacksmith's anvil you wish to visit is the one here in Chuddums," she said in a teasing whisper. "During the gala, I saw you and Mr. Keane crossing paths at the pump."

Her handsome, charming, urbane friend turned a telltale shade of red. "We, er, talked."

"It went well?"

"Rather."

"Oh, Duffy. I am so happy for you."

She gave his hand a squeeze, and they exchanged giddy smiles.

"I had best be on my way," she said. "Even with the clean-up completed, Miss Letty is having trouble convincing guests to return. Mama and I thought that if we spent the afternoon at the spa, others might follow suit."

"A splendid idea," Duffy said. "I shall spread the word that the bath is fully operational. It will take more than a curse—or attempted murder—to keep Chuddums down."

Mama suggested walking to the spa, and even though Gigi knew what was coming, she agreed. They strolled through the village green, where the obelisk dedicated to Abel Pearce cast a long and gloomy shadow.

"I cannot believe Ethan contributed to that monstrosity," Mama said.

"He regrets it." Shivering, Gigi felt the monument's darkness pass over her as they walked by. "He was merely trying to get rid of Mrs. Pearce."

They continued along the square. A few enterprising villagers had set up barrows to sell goods to tourists, and the air was scented with roasting chestnuts and freshly baked pies. Outside the Briarbush, Mr. Thornton was doing brisk business selling cups of steaming mulled cider. Wally, wearing an eye-catching fuchsia coat, stood on a crate giving free lectures about "historic sites," including the old churchyard and the abandoned mill on the outskirts. Now and again, Gigi and her mama stopped to exchange pleasantries with acquaintances, making sure to share where they were headed. When they turned onto Spring Lane, the crowd had thinned and it was just the two of them.

"What has happened to us, Gigi?"

The non sequitur caught her off guard.

"How do you mean, Mama?" she asked warily.

"You used to trust me."

Gigi could manage Papa's sternness. Being the youngest and his only daughter, she knew he had a soft-as-pudding spot for her. Yet she had no defense against the hurt in her mama's eyes.

"I do trust you," she said.

"Then why will you not confide in me about Mr. Godwin?"

Because I do not think you will approve. Because my feelings are too confusing. Because I think...I think I've fallen in love with him, and I don't know if it is a mistake.

"It is complicated," she hedged.

"Trust me when I say that I am capable of understanding complicated matters of the heart."

"But you and Papa have the perfect marriage."

To Gigi's surprise, Mama laughed. "Nothing is ever perfect, dearest."

"You two are," she returned. "All of Society says you are soulmates, destined to be with one another. I am certain neither you nor Papa have ever doubted your love for one another."

"While it is true that I fell in love with your papa the very first time we met"—Mama's mouth curved with nostalgia—"like any road worth traveling, every relationship has its bumps. I have always fancied myself a modern mama, the kind a daughter would unburden herself to. I hope I have not been harboring a delusion."

"You haven't. You are the most accommodating of mamas."

"Then talk to me, dearest girl, as you always have."

After a moment, she blurted, "Do you think it's wrong for me to like Mr. Godwin?"

"When it comes to relationships, right and wrong are seldom

simple." Her mama's expression held no judgment. "Does he return your feelings?"

"I think so—or thought so, rather." She nudged a pebble aside with her shoe. "Since this recent attempt on his life, he has been increasingly distant. You were there: he will not even discuss his suspicions concerning people who might want him dead."

"His tendency to keep secrets is worrisome."

Hearing the flatness of her mama's tone, she said hastily, "Mr. Godwin is not always like this. In fact, he can be quite open."

She thought of their easy, natural intimacy during the billiards game. She'd told him things she hadn't told anyone else. She couldn't reveal her forbidden trysts to her mama, however...and *especially* not the naughty secrets she and Conrad had shared.

"How much do you know about Mr. Godwin's past?"

"He has shared some of it." She glanced at her mama. "Promise you will not judge him by his origins."

"When have you known me to be a snob?" Mama looked a bit miffed.

"Well, Papa did say that Mr. Godwin doesn't belong in our world—"

"What Papa meant was that Mr. Godwin lives by a different set of values," Mama explained. "To your father, nothing is as important as a man's character. Any suitor of yours must be a gentleman of *honor*. It is Mr. Godwin's reputation as a man of ruthless ambition that concerns Papa, not his lack of a title."

Ashamed, Gigi said, "I ought to have known that is what Papa meant. I am sorry I misunderstood."

"I share your father's concerns, my dear. As it stands, Papa has taken a dislike to Mr. Godwin, and it will take much convincing to change his mind."

"And you, Mama?" Gigi asked in a small voice. "Could you bring yourself to like Mr. Godwin, even a little bit?"

"I do not know him well enough," Mama said frankly. "And my concern is that he has not been honest with you."

"He hasn't lied to me," Gigi protested.

"Lying by omission is still lying, my dear. He failed to mention the intrigues he is embroiled in. His presence in your life puts you at risk, and you were not even aware of it."

"He would never endanger me. He is very protective. As for the other details...it takes him a while to trust, that is all. He has been fending for himself for most of his life, and it is a difficult habit to change."

"If Mr. Godwin's mistrust is a result of his past, then I believe that habit can be changed," Mama allowed. "*If* he is willing. What do you know of his background?"

"He doesn't have much family to speak of. His parents passed when he was young, and his guardian put him in boarding school. His siblings are deceased. When he became an adult, he found success as a prizefighter—that was how he got his stake to begin investing."

"That explains the scars on his hands," Mama murmured.

Of course, Mama would notice; she noticed everything.

"He also told me that he'd suffered a romantic disappointment," Gigi disclosed. "But he thinks I am different. He says I am loyal, brave, and resourceful."

"It is a positive sign that he values your finer qualities. But what about him? Are his intentions honorable, Gigi?"

"They are. Which is why, um, I asked Miss Letty to introduce you at the gala."

"I had a feeling you were behind the introductions. In the future, you may skip the machinations and come straight to Papa and me."

"I shall," she said contritely. "Would you...would you approve of Mr. Godwin's suit?"

"Of all my children, you are the one who has always known her own heart," Mama said after a moment. "Since you were a little girl, you knew exactly what you wanted. Now that you are a woman, how could I trust your instincts any less?"

Warmth flooded Gigi.

"However, this is your future we are discussing, and I will do everything in my power to ensure that you are making a fully informed decision. If Mr. Godwin wishes to have an audience with Papa and me, he must first meet a condition."

She tilted her head. "What condition?"

"He must be willing to disclose his secrets."

Knowing Conrad's guarded nature, she asked uneasily, "You mean about his enemies?"

"About *everything*," Mama said emphatically. "As you've noted, Mr. Godwin is a complicated fellow with an unconventional history. It should come as no surprise to you that he harbors demons from his past."

While many attributed Mama's social success to charm, Gigi knew it was, in fact, rooted in perspicacity. She thought of Conrad's nightmare in the caldarium, the pain and terror that had oozed from him. Of his apology and admission that he hadn't expected her to return for him. Were those demons of mistrust contributing to his distant behavior now?

"I shall convince him to share more with me," she said.

"He must share it all," Mama said severely. "If I know anything about demons, it is this: they thrive in secrecy but cannot survive in the light."

A shadow passed through Mama's eyes, and Gigi thought she must be thinking about Owen. Of the period her brother still refused to talk about—that fueled his nightmares and destructive behaviors.

"I am not afraid of demons," Gigi said softly. "I would take them on for the people I love."

"You have always been the brightest of flames, my dear girl." Mama cupped her cheek, looking her in the eye. "However, Mr. Godwin is not another one of your projects. Whatever happened in his past, he is an adult now, and it is up to him to make the right choices. The ones that would make him worthy of you."

At the spa, Mama declined to use the caldarium.

"Go on without me, Gigi. At my age, the last thing I wish to subject myself to is an episode of overwhelming heat." She gave a delicate shudder. "I shall content myself with swimming and lounging."

Thus, after changing into a linen shift, Gigi entered the caldarium alone. It was cozy and warm, comfortably lit by several new wall sconces. She settled on the stone platform, and the heated surface melted away some of her tension.

Nonetheless, worries whirled.

What secrets is Conrad keeping from me? Would he be willing to lay all his cards on the table? What if my family refuses to accept him...what will I do?

Eventually, she drifted into a state of drowsy unrest. Half-formed images filled her head: a letter crumpling in a fist, tears rolling like rain, shadows falling and falling. Feeling darkness cover her, she trembled, but warm knuckles tenderly brushed her cheek. With a sigh, she leaned into the masculine touch, and the instant she did, it went from comforting to arousing. He fingered the line of her throat, and when he grazed the tip of her breast, pleasure spilled through her so convincingly that she opened her eyes.

And blinked.

"What are you doing here?" she blurted.

Chapter Twenty-Four

"I want to talk to you," Conrad said. "Before I leave for London."

At least, that had been his initial intention. His motives had taken a different turn the moment he found her napping and having what appeared to be an exceedingly naughty dream. Her shift had ridden up her hips, and the steam had rendered the material nearly transparent. Her nipples enticed like candied cherries, and his mouth watered at the glimpse of the dark triangle between her thighs.

The dreaminess vanished from her eyes. Shooting to her feet, she tugged down her shift—pity, that—and glowered at him.

"How did you get past Miss Letty and my mama?"

"The vent, remember?"

She looked nonplussed. "Should you be running around when your life is in danger?"

"Worried, sweetheart?" He flashed a grin, and when he received a narrow-eyed stare in return, he sighed. "I can take care of myself. And I brought reinforcements."

He showed her his pistol.

Looking unimpressed, she crossed her arms. "Why are you following me?"

"I was patiently awaiting the opportunity to speak with you."

"Really? You were hardly in the sharing mood the last time we were together. For all I knew, you had already left for London."

"Still miffed about that, are you?"

"I am not *miffed*. I am furious. There is a difference."

He wished she wasn't so adorable when she was angry. It didn't bode well for her in their future arguments. Instead of getting her point across, she was making him harder than rock.

"Look, duchess, it wasn't that I didn't trust *you*," he began. "But I wasn't about to expose my secrets to a room full of strangers."

"They aren't strangers. They are my *family*."

"They are strangers to me." He rubbed the back of his neck. "I will admit that I did not handle the situation well. After the near collision with a thousand-pound statue, I was not at my best. Overhearing your papa's opinion of me made matters worse, but I had no excuse for going in with fists swinging."

"No, you did not." Gigi paused. "But thank you for the apology."

"Do you forgive me?" He moved toward her.

"Not so fast."

She planted her hand in his chest, and even that small touch set him afire. The close brush with death had made him re-evaluate his life, particularly the part involving Gigi. After a day to think, he'd concluded that he wasn't falling for her...the deed was done. He was in love with Gigi. There was no other explanation for the way she made him feel. For the way he craved her loyalty and tenderness. The way he wanted to claim her smiles, tears, and everything in between. She was the one he wanted to go through life with, to grow old with, to build a family with.

Yes, he loved his little nymph. This was convenient because he wanted to screw her senseless as well, and even he wouldn't stoop to debauching a virginal lady. He would marry her, the sooner the better.

All he had to do was get her to say yes.

"There is more to talk about," she said firmly.

"I love you, Gigi."

Her jaw slackened. "I beg your pardon?"

"You heard me. I've been struck by Cupid's arrow. I've succumbed to the gentlest affliction."

"Are you comparing me to a sickness?" She drew her brows together.

"Well, you are like an ailment, aren't you?" He gave her a slow, wicked smile. "You make me so hot I feel as if I've come down with a fever."

"Smoothly done, Godwin." A smile tugged at her lips.

"I was going to wait until I returned from London to do this, but I think I must ask you now. Will you marry me, Gigi?"

Seeing the bright longing in her eyes, he felt a burst of triumph. She hadn't said it yet, but he knew he had her heart. Her kinfolk hadn't been able to wrestle that from him, no matter how hard they tried.

She drew a breath. "It depends."

"Name your terms," he said confidently. "I'll meet them."

"I want answers to my questions."

Since he was prepared for this, he said, "Fire away, sweetheart."

"Do you know who is trying to kill you?"

"No," he said candidly.

"Do you have suspects in mind?"

"Yes."

"Who are they?"

He gave her a piece of the truth. "I have two business rivals, Smedley and Trowbridge. On several occasions, I gained success at their expense, and they've held grudges."

"You think these competitors would try to murder you?" Gigi said, aghast.

"Industrialists are like sharks," he said candidly. "They're vicious, and if they smell blood, they'll go after it. After I outbid Trowbridge on some factories, he came to my office and issued threats."

Gigi's eyes were huge. "What sort of threats?"

"The usual kind." Conrad shrugged. "I would pay for what I'd done, he would destroy me, etcetera."

"Did you report him to the police?"

"Idle threats are common in my line of work. There was nothing to report. As for Smedley, I fed false information to the spies he'd planted in my office, and he lost a small fortune because of it. A few weeks later, my office was set on fire. Although I have no proof, I know Smedley was responsible."

"Heavens." Gigi wetted her lips. "Are there other suspects?"

Tread carefully.

"There was a woman I was involved with." He cleared his throat. "She didn't take it well when I ended things."

"When was this?"

"Before I came here."

She bit her lip. "You ended an affair a few weeks ago?"

"Duchess, it meant nothing." He nabbed her hand, pulling her close. "We both had an itch to scratch and scratched it with one another."

Gigi tugged at his hold, but he didn't let her go.

"There were no promises or feelings involved," he insisted.

"Then why would she bother trying to end your life?"

"I don't think she is the guilty party," he said. "But it would be remiss not to mention her as a possible suspect. Her motive would likely be injured pride...hell hath no fury, after all."

"Perhaps if *you* had ended things on a more positive note," Gigi said tartly, "she wouldn't feel scorned."

Conrad was starting to get annoyed. "First of all, our understanding did not involve commitment, which means there was no bad way to end it. Either of us could have gone our own way at any time—and we frequently did, even when we were seeing one another."

"Oh." Twin lines appeared between Gigi's brows.

"Second, the reason things did not end well was because of her actions, not mine. I caught her snooping in my study."

"Snooping? For what?"

"Most likely for confidential business information, that sort of thing. It's possible that she was working for Smedley or Trowbridge. Or maybe she thought to unearth something scandalous she could use to get revenge."

Gigi frowned. "Do you have scandalous secrets?"

Sweetheart, where to begin.

While he was in love with Gigi, he saw no need to compromise his vengeance by giving away unnecessary details at this juncture. After they were wed and she was bound to him, he would tell her all...especially since his two biggest secrets would affect her. He'd heard from Marvell that Grantley's health had taken a turn for the worse. The title and revenge would soon be Conrad's.

"She didn't find anything she could use against me," he said neutrally.

"How could she betray you, her own lover?"

Gigi looked adorably indignant on his behalf.

"The fact that you ask that question is what makes you different from her. From any of the females I've associated with," he said intently.

"How many women have you, ahem, *associated* with?"

Bespelled by her pure violet gaze, he felt trapped. While he'd never been ashamed of his hot-blooded nature, he wished he hadn't been quite so prolific in this area of his life. He realized that the need that had driven him hadn't just been lust. He'd hungered for connection...the kind he'd found with Gigi. He'd wanted someone who would stick with him through thick and thin, who would care if he lived or died, who he could trust with his secrets and the deepest yearnings of his heart.

Since he'd failed to find that, fucking had served as a distracting alternative. He'd told himself that he didn't want commitment, that he had no time for it...but maybe he'd been making excuses. Maybe what he truly felt was that he wasn't deserving of devotion. Certainly, no one had bothered to offer it to him before Gigi. Although she hadn't given him any promises, she'd made him feel worthy of care and attention in a way no one else had. The emptiness of his life before her struck him like a visceral blow.

"Is it taking you this long to count your lovers?" Gigi asked incredulously.

"No."

You are making a hash of this, Godwin.

"That is, I wasn't doing that."

He wasn't easily unnerved. Yet now the decades of success and domination seemed to melt away. Suddenly, he was once again that scrawny, desperate, unloved boy.

Bloody hell, man, you've bought and sold half of England. You've never backed down to anyone. Are you honestly afraid of being rejected by this little minx?

He was no namby-pamby. To prove it, he put his hands on Gigi's waist, steering her backward. She emitted a squeak of protest as her spine hit the wall.

"What are you doing?" She struggled futilely. "Unhand me."

"Not until you listen to what I have to say."

She glared at him. "I can listen without your hands on me."

"I talk better when I'm touching you," he muttered. "You asked about my lovers, and I don't want to lie. I haven't kept a tally, but I also haven't deprived myself of company when the need arose. Call me a rake, if you must—"

"If the shoe fits."

"But I have been responsible and taken precautions. My future wife will have no worries about Venus's curse or the existence of any by-blows."

Gigi's long lashes fanned. He saw the moment she comprehended what he was telling her. Even in the dimness, he saw the rosy tint of her cheeks.

"Isn't that lucky for her?" she retorted.

"It is lucky for *you*. Because you are the woman I intend to marry."

"What if I don't want to marry you?"

He took the hit because he deserved it. And because her pout told him she hadn't decided *not* to marry him...she just wanted convincing. He was happy—nay, eager—to provide the sweetest persuasion. His eyes holding hers, he went down on one knee.

"What are you doing?" she asked suspiciously. "It will take more than a few flowery words on bended knee to sway me."

"Then it is a good thing I had other uses planned for my mouth."

He bunched her shift in his fists, yanking it up past her thighs. At the sight of her glossy little nest, hunger raked his gut.

"What are you doing?" she squeaked. "My mama is just outside—"

Her protestations melted into cock-hardening moans as he swiped his tongue up her juicy slit. Her flavor saturated his senses and made his head spin. To give himself better access, he pulled one of her slender limbs over his shoulder, fitting her pussy snugly against his mouth. He feasted on her, grunting with enjoyment. If the way she clenched his hair was any indication, she didn't mind that he was a messy eater.

"When we're married," he said thickly, "I'm going to start every day by having you for breakfast."

"Conrad, that is wicked—"

"Duchess, if you think that is wicked, I wonder what you will think of this."

Running his middle finger down her crease, he found her entrance. He eased his finger in, sweat beading on his brow. Devil and damn, she was tight. One day soon, he was going to claim this snug passage, and anticipation made his cock leap in his smalls.

Until then, there were plenty of other delights to explore. He pressed deeper, feeling the resistance of her unused muscles.

"Let me in, sweetheart," he rasped. "Let me pleasure you."

He leaned forward, tickling her pearl with his tongue. She gasped, and his self-control suffered a blow when he felt wetness gush around his digit. Bleeding hell, she was so ripe for fucking. He thrust his finger as he licked her, greedily lapping up her nectar.

"Conrad, don't stop," she pleaded.

Her twitching thighs told him she was close, and he knew how to catapult her over the edge.

"Help me, sweetheart," he urged. "Play with those pretty breasts while I eat your pussy."

She hesitated, looking bashful...well, as bashful as a lady being gamahuched against a wall could look.

"You know you want to." Feeling her sheath softening, he added another finger, driving deeper. "Your nipples are straining against your shift. Rosy as Turkish delight and just as sweet. Let me see you touch them, duchess."

Slowly, she released her hold on his head and brought her hands to her heaving tits. To encourage her, he redoubled his oral efforts. He was rewarded when she moaned and cupped her breasts, her graceful fingers plucking at the engorged tips. It was the stuff of fantasies, his captive nymph pleasuring herself while he made a feast of her cunny.

"Pinch them," he said roughly. "Do it hard."

She obeyed, trapping those naughty buds between finger and thumb. At the same time, he shoved two fingers as deep as he could and sealed his lips around her pearl. He sucked, and she yelped his name, flooding his mouth with cream.

A gentleman would have probably left it at that, but he wanted more from her. Wanted everything...and he wasn't stopping until he got it.

Still trembling from her climax, Gigi's breath caught as Conrad suddenly spun her around. He covered her back with his chest, pressing her against the wall. The rough stone abraded her nipples, setting off sparks of pleasure. One would think she would be satiated, but when he reached between her legs, desire surged anew.

His mouth hovered by her ear.

"Don't make me wait until I get back from London," he coaxed. "Give me your answer now. Say you'll marry me."

She tried to be rational. While he had apologized for his behavior and disclosed more of his past, she was realizing how many secrets he held. Her heart told her to trust him, but her head was yelling at her to be more sensible.

"We don't know each other well enough," she began.

"You know everything important about me," he asserted. "I will be a good husband."

She bit her lip, thinking of what he'd revealed about his last relationship.

Either of us could have gone our own way at any time—and we frequently did.

"What is it, love? You don't believe me?"

"I believe in fidelity," she blurted.

"Gigi." Moving his head, he stared into her eyes. "I would never betray you in that fashion. I will be faithful and expect you to be as well. How could you think otherwise?"

"You said...with your last lover..."

"She meant nothing," he said bluntly. "You, on the other hand, are everything. Not only will I be true, but I will also protect you with my dying breath. These are vows I've never given to any woman. Never wanted to, until I met you."

Oh, he was persuasive. And that was to say nothing of what he was doing with his hand.

"You keep secrets from me," she persisted. "I don't even know what you'll be up to in London, how long you'll be gone—"

"I'll be hunting down the bastard who tried to kill me. I've hired Foxworth & Co., a highly reputable agency, to assist with the investigation, and we will have the culprit in no time. Then I'll come to you a free man—the man you know you're destined to marry."

She flashed to Thomas and Rosalinda making love in the caldarium. Lovers brought together by destiny. Could the same be true of her and Conrad?

"I don't know that." Her protest sounded weak to her own ears. "How can I think when you...oh my *stars*."

He continued to circle her hidden peak with his middle finger. She could feel how slick she was. He pressed and rubbed, rubbed and pressed, making her pant against the wall.

"Once you're mine, I am going to do such wicked things to you." His husky promise made her shiver. "And you will love it all."

He rubbed harder and faster. Her eyelids drooped as passion consumed her. With his other hand, he caressed the length of her spine, his thumb pressing blissfully down her vertebrae and against the small of her back. When she felt him delve lower, between the swells of her bottom, her eyes popped open.

"Not there, surely," she said in shock.

"You didn't read to the end of the book. When the satyr finally claims his little mate," he said, his voice guttural, "he does so everywhere. He takes her so completely that she will never again think of leaving him."

What he did next was so depraved that she had no words for it. He pushed against a forbidden opening, and her body resisted, but he pressed steadily until she felt the tip of his finger enter her *there*. A place where she was certain nothing was supposed to be.

The sensation was unbearably naughty...and titillating.

"You're mine, Gigi," he rasped. "Admit it."

He owned her pleasure, diddling her pearl while teasing her sensitive pucker. Before passion robbed her of her wits entirely, she twisted her head, needing to see his face. And that decided it for her. For despite his commanding tone and carnal games, his brows were drawn…and his marauder's gaze revealed something he'd never shown her before.

Naked, desperate longing.

His need punched through the barriers of her heart, flooding all the chambers. In that instant, she knew she loved Conrad Godwin—knew she wanted a future with him.

"I'm yours," she whispered.

Triumph glittered in his eyes. "Promise you'll marry me."

"I can't. Not yet. I need to get my parents' approval first—"

"You have until my return from London," he growled. "If you cannot convince your parents by then, I will go to them myself."

He slammed his mouth on hers, the forceful thrust of his finger taking her over the edge.

As she keened her pleasure, he said fiercely, "That's right, duchess. Remember how good this feels. How I'll make you feel all the time once you're mine."

Chapter Twenty-Five

Leaving Chuddums took longer than Conrad expected. After settling matters with Gigi—as much as one could settle anything with a nymph—he'd planned to pack up and go, but he hadn't accounted for the visitors that arrived at Honeystone Hall. They came in a stream, villagers bearing gifts and well wishes for a speedy recovery after his "accident." Mrs. Pettigrew and Mr. Khan arrived first, the former with a dish of her famous Bloody Knights of Windsor pudding (whatever that was) and the latter with a box of assorted confectionary. Then came Mr. Thornton with a pot of his wife's chicken soup and a jug of his own "kill-devil," which he claimed would cure any ails.

More and more of the Chuddumites showed up, until it resembled a damned party in Conrad's drawing room. Some of them had visited Honeystone Hall in the past, and they regaled him with tales of the old squire's hunts and house parties.

"It's lovely to have a gentleman residing here again," said some lady whose name he hadn't bothered to remember. "We couldn't have asked for a better new neighbor."

Conrad had no idea why the villagers were being so welcoming. He wondered how they would feel after he took over Abel

Pearce's properties and sold them off to the highest bidder. More to the point, how would *Gigi* feel? Unease crept over him. At first, he'd thought that sparing the spa would be sufficient to appease her, but her affection for the village as a whole had become increasingly obvious.

Yet once he took possession of Pearce's holdings, he would have no choice but to divest them...preferably for a large profit. It wasn't as if he could invest in Chuddums: that would be a risky venture at best and ruinous at worst. The capital required to preserve the village's future would strain even his deep pockets, with little hope for returns in this lifetime. A man might as well dump his money in the Thames. Only a complete fool would attempt such a thankless task.

More importantly, destroying Chuddums was an essential part of Conrad's vengeance. Pearce deserved to reap what he had sown. He'd devastated Mama by demolishing the cottage that was hers by birthright. Conrad was simply returning the favor by tearing apart Pearce's legacy.

Tit for tat.

As for Gigi, she would understand after Conrad explained things. She would take his side because she was loyal and loving. Hell, if she wanted, he had properties elsewhere he could profitably develop. He could build her a square ten times nicer than Chuddums's, and he could employ her friends to run the shops. What more could she want?

Satisfied with his solution, he was about to announce that the festivities were over when two new faces appeared.

"Mr. Godwin!" Kenny dashed over on skinny legs. "May I have one more lesson before you go? Please?"

"Where are your manners, Kenneth?" Wally chided. "Mr. Godwin's a busy man and might not have the time."

That fact didn't dissuade you from giving me a half-dozen tours, you old codger.

"But, Great-Grandpapa, Mr. Godwin has time for a *short* lesson, doesn't he?"

Hands clasped together, Kenny turned huge, shimmering eyes upon Conrad. Above the boy's freckled nose, faint traces of the shiner lingered.

Christ.

"A short lesson." Conrad sighed. "In the garden."

"Hooray! I'll see you there, sir," Kenny sang as he darted off.

"It's kind of you to take an interest in my great-grandson," Wally said. "Lord knows his own papa doesn't."

"He's a fine lad," Conrad said gruffly.

"Not much of a fighter, though."

"It doesn't matter. Survival is what counts. That was my first lesson to Kenny: if you can't win, you run or hide."

"A good lesson. You're like him, you know."

"You, er, think I am like Kenny?"

"No, Thomas. Thomas Mulligan."

Wally had a faraway look, as if he'd drifted into the past. During the tours, this had happened a few times, and Conrad knew the old fellow would eventually find his way back.

"He had fought battles before arriving here," Wally said dreamily. "They scarred him, I think. But, like you, he was a survivor, and in the end, he found his peace."

"In Chuddums, you mean?"

"With Rosalinda. He wasn't looking for love, but he found it anyway."

I know what that is like.

"If only he'd trusted her sooner, the curse could have been averted," Wally said sadly.

Conrad drew his brows together. "Wait. What are you talking about?"

After their steamy interlude, Gigi had told him her theory that their meeting was somehow tied to the local legend. She'd shared her dreams and belief that their relationship might play a part in undoing the curse. Amused by her fanciful reasoning, he'd chucked her under the chin and told her that if the legend convinced her to marry him, then he would invite Bloody Thom to the wedding himself.

Now Wally reminded him that the legend wasn't just a ghost story. During their tours, the nonagenarian had told Conrad that he'd known the real Thomas and Rosalinda. As a young boy, Wally had seen the lovers together by the stream…the stream where Conrad had met Gigi.

A tingle crossed Conrad's nape.

Wally blinked. Once, twice.

"Isn't that something?" Chortling, he scratched his ear. "I don't remember what I was saying."

Conrad left for London early the next morning. He'd informed Redgrave and Marvell of his schedule, and he arrived to find them waiting.

They'd barely settled in his study before Marvell blurted, "It's happened. The Westfield railway bubble burst this morning. Soon it will be all over London."

Conrad clenched his hands. "The price of the shares?"

"Worthless," Redgrave confirmed. "Westfield fled town because he's afraid of rioters coming after him."

I have Pearce. Finally, I have him.

"Call in Pearce's debts," Conrad said. "Every last one."

"And when he cannot pay?" Redgrave raised his thick brows.

"We claim the collateral. His land in Chuddums."

Redgrave nodded, smiling with satisfaction. "With the right buyers, Godwin & Co. stands to turn a tidy profit. I know of several fellows hungry for land to build factories—"

"Or we could take our time," Marvell cut in. "Look for the right sort of investors."

"Right sort?" Redgrave stared at his colleague as if the fellow had sprouted another head. "The only investor we care about is the one willing to pay the highest price."

"There are other considerations."

"Considerations other than profit?" Redgrave turned to Conrad. "Are you hearing this?"

"I am. And I'm curious what Marvell has to say," Conrad said coolly.

Marvell took a nervous sip—not of tea, which Conrad had offered. Instead, he held a familiar-looking bottle of water. The solicitor had become a proponent of the Chuddums cure, which he insisted had relieved his allergy symptoms.

"Chuddums has unique properties." Marvell pushed his spectacles up his nose. "In addition to the healthful springs, there are bountiful natural resources, including woods and streams—"

"Which make it an ideal place to set up factories," Redgrave pointed out.

"Moreover, the local folk are charming." Marvell tunneled determinedly toward his point. "They are friendly and boast a plethora of traditions not found elsewhere. And there is the curse."

Redgrave's brows shot toward his hair. "Curse?"

The solicitor filled him in, with sufficient detail to earn a considering look from Conrad. Maybe there was something in Chuddums's water after all. It had transformed his solicitor from a sensible, pragmatic fellow to one who spouted tales of ghosts and star-crossed lovers.

"Utter tommyrot," Redgrave scoffed. "Don't tell me you actually believe in that nonsense, Marvell."

"Whether or not one believes the legend, one cannot deny the fascination it holds," Marvell said primly. "There is a reason why it has persisted for nearly a century. Why villagers, to this day, blame any shortfalls on the curse. There is, for lack of a better word, a *magical* feeling in Chuddums. It is wholly unique and, when properly harnessed, gives the village excellent potential for profit. The success of the Chuddums Potion proves this."

"Finally, you are talking sense again," Redgrave said. "For a moment there, I thought you believed in that ghostly fiddle-faddle."

"What I believe is irrelevant. What is important is that the legend's compelling nature makes it a draw for tourists. With the right leader at the helm, one who understands Chuddums's distinctive charm, the village could prosper and enrich all involved."

To Conrad's consternation, Marvell was looking straight at him.

"It's too risky," he said flatly. "The investment required is too high and the returns, if any, too far in the future."

"Leave the business of saving villages to coves who don't mind losing their shirts," Redgrave said. "We take things apart and sell them for quick profit. That's what we do."

"As you say." Pressing his lips together, Marvell lapsed into silence.

"Let's move on to another matter," Conrad said.

He disclosed the second attempt on his life.

"The carriage collision wasn't an accident, then," Redgrave said grimly. "You need security, Godwin. I know some blokes, former prizefighters, who work as guards—"

"Bring them on," Conrad said. "Hire guards for me and for the office. Tell our employees to stay alert and report any potential threats. I do not wish for a repeat of what happened at the Manchester office."

"Shall I fill in Mr. Foxworth and his investigators?" Marvell asked.

"Do that," Conrad said. "Any developments concerning Trowbridge or Smedley?"

"I do have some news," Redgrave said. "According to my source, Trowbridge had a fit of apoplexy last month. He's been keeping a lid on the matter because he doesn't want his competitors to know he's in a weakened state. While he's been spreading rumors that he's been traveling and looking for new projects, he has, in fact, been recuperating at his country manor. Apparently, he's in a bad way and can barely fend for himself."

"Which makes it unlikely that he is the mastermind behind these attacks," Conrad said pensively. "Good work, Redgrave."

His chief manager nodded. "If there's nothing else, I'll see to the guards."

After Redgrave's exit, Marvell said, "I have news about Smedley."

"Oh?"

"Last year, he was involved in a project with several other investors, one of whom was Harold Stockton."

Interesting. A connection between Smedley, my competitor, and Stockton, the man I will be usurping in the line of inheritance.

However, Robert had covered his tracks well. Conrad doubted Stockton knew that Robert had a half-brother with a claim on the duchy. Without that knowledge, Stockton would have no reason to want Conrad dead. But if Stockton—or, indeed, Robert—knew that Conrad was alive, then both men had ample motivation for murder. After his escape from Creavey Hall at age seventeen, Conrad had covered his tracks well and taken on a new identity. Robert had never come knocking, and Conrad assumed that his brother believed he was dead.

"Is there any indication that the Duke of Grantley knows I'm alive?" Conrad asked.

"Not to my knowledge, sir. As you requested, I've had his activities monitored for the past year, and he hasn't hired investigators or the like. His illness has kept him confined to his bedchamber, and his mental state has deteriorated significantly. Reports have described him as 'childlike.' To be frank, I am not sure how much he remembers of his past. I doubt he has the wherewithal to find you and organize an attack."

"Noted," Conrad said. "Did you secure the invitation to the Grantley ball?"

"Yes, sir. From what I understand, His Grace's physicians are advising him not to attend. He is insisting upon it, however, saying that he will make this appearance even if it is his last."

Anticipation swirled in Conrad like a wintry wind. He would give Robert a proper send-off. His brother would go to hell knowing that Conrad had brought about his destruction.

Chapter Twenty-Six

After Conrad's departure, Gigi's parents went to visit with James and Evie at Grove Hall for a few days. Xenia and Ethan decided to accompany them, but Gigi had begged to stay in Chuddums under the pretense of helping Miss Letty. Surprisingly, her family had agreed...probably because Conrad was gone. In addition, with Owen also staying behind, they probably thought it would kill two birds to have her and her brother looking out for each other.

Gigi had an ulterior motive for staying. While Mr. Rawlins was investigating the attacks and Conrad had hired professionals in London, she wanted to do her part. As both incidents had occurred in Chuddums, someone in the village might have noticed something. People had a natural wariness when it came to authorities, and perhaps they would find it easier to talk to her than the constable. At any rate, it wouldn't hurt to try, and Gigi was determined to assist Conrad however she could.

Thus, she dragged Owen to the village. They did the usual rounds, and she shopped, chatted, and visited with friends. During the conversations, Gigi made it known that she was interested in information regarding the opening gala. Anything people had seen or heard, no detail was too small. By week's end, she'd listened to various theories about what had caused the statue to fall—including Wally's far-fetched proposition that Fenwyck, a neighborhood feline known for mischief, had cut the wires with his claws. She was giving up hope on discovering anything useful when she received a note from Mrs. Sommers.

Arriving at the dress shop, Owen took one look at the neat but crowded interior and announced that he would wait outside. Gigi hurried in and found Mrs. Sommers waiting for her.

"You said you might have some information?" Gigi asked breathlessly.

"Yes, my lady." Mrs. Sommers's expression was somber. "It's best you hear it from the source. We'll talk in the back."

Gigi followed the dressmaker to the workroom, where Mattie was waiting. The young brunette was twisting her skirts, looking unaccountably nervous.

"Mattie, you must tell Lady Gigi what you told me," Mrs. Sommers said.

"Oh, but it's shameful, Aunt Henrietta." Mattie's bottom lip quivered. "I can't speak of it."

Concerned, Gigi said, "You can talk to me, dear. I shan't judge."

"Promise?"

"I promise."

"All right." Mattie took a deep breath. "Do you remember I mentioned my new follower, milady?"

Gigi nodded.

"I met him when I was running an errand in Chudleigh Crest. He was a gentleman, opening the door for me and carrying my basket. He was handsome, too, with thick brown hair and the most charming manner."

Recognition sizzled through Gigi. "Was he a waiter at the gala? His name was John?"

"He told me his name was John Brown," Mattie said with a

small nod. "He'd been a waiter in London, and Miss Letty had hired him for that evening. He said he planned to stay on in Chuddums and look for more work because…because…"

"Yes, dear?"

"He said he fell in love with me at first sight. He said he wanted to marry me. And I…I believed him. Because I did, I allowed him liberties. Oh, milady, I'm so ashamed!"

Mattie burst into tears while Mrs. Sommers put an arm around her.

"It's not your fault," Gigi said quietly. "He used his charm to manipulate you."

"When the constable was asking around the village for information about him, I couldn't come forward." Mattie's voice hitched. "I didn't want there to be talk about me."

"Mattie is a good girl," Mrs. Sommers said. "While she's had her followers, it's always been a bit of girlish fun. She's never acted improperly."

Given her relationship with Conrad, Gigi was hardly going to judge poor Mattie. And she understood the importance of protecting the young woman's reputation.

"We'll keep your name out of this," she promised. "What else can you tell me about Mr. Brown? Any details would be helpful."

"We met a handful of times at an abandoned cottage. We didn't, um, talk much." Her cheeks red, Mattie said, "He told me our meetings had to be secret because he wanted to protect my reputation. He said he would speak to my parents, but he had to improve his prospects first."

A likely excuse. As likely as the name John Brown.

"He was supposed to meet me the day after the gala, but he never showed. Then I heard that he'd left Chuddums, and I knew. I knew that he'd been lying, that he…he used me."

Fresh tears dribbled down Mattie's cheeks.

"Oh, my dear." Reaching out, Gigi squeezed the other's hand. "You deserve so much better."

"Do you think John...do you think he pushed the statue?" Mattie asked. "People are saying it wasn't an accident, and that is why the constable is looking for him."

Gigi wasn't surprised the villagers had figured it out. "Yes, that's true."

Mattie drew a shaky breath. "Then I have something that might help."

Reaching into her skirts, she pulled out a slip of paper and offered it to Gigi. Gigi saw that it was a pawn ticket for a pair of cuff links. Unfortunately, the ticket was torn where the shop's address would have been. The only clue to the location was the bottom half of a word, which she quickly deciphered: Spitalfields.

This is a clue. A way to track down the assailant.

Her heart thumping, Gigi asked, "Where did you get this?"

"John, or whatever his real name is, dropped it the last time we met. I had planned to return it to him." Mattie sniffled. "Now I am giving it to you, in hopes that something good will come from my misfortune."

That night, Gigi penned a letter to Conrad and enclosed the pawn ticket. The discovery filled her with excitement and apprehension. In truth, since he left, anxiety had gnawed at her: What if he was attacked again? What if he was hurt? Would she even know? Although he'd assured her he was taking every precaution—and he was, admittedly, a man who could take care of himself—their separation fueled her worries.

She couldn't shake the feeling that she ought to be by his side. Yet her parents would never permit it, and she needed to work on winning their approval of Conrad's suit. She would redouble her efforts when they came back in a few days, and in the meantime, she would send Conrad the clue. She told herself that progress was being made.

She went to bed, intending to send the letter off first thing in the morning.

In the moonlight, her hands were shaking. Even though she'd washed off the blood, she felt the warmth of her beloved's life seeping through her fingers. She stifled a sob, but there was no one to hear her in the dark woods. She was alone.

He should have never gone off by himself. We should have been together—protecting one another. I failed to trust our love, to keep him safe...and now it is too late.

It was too late—for regrets, for anything but one final act.

Thomas was gone, and soon they would be after her. She would have to flee, but she had one thing to do before she left. Before she pulled up stakes and found her destiny on the road, as her ancestors had done for centuries. Shunned by her family, she would now have to travel alone, but she wasn't afraid. Her heart was too full of pain and grief and fury to feel anything else.

On the road, she would lose herself. But she would lose other things as well—the first lesson of traveling was to surrender the idea of possessions.

What you own is not who you are, her da used to say. If you possess nothing, then nothing possesses you.

Her eyes welled. She wanted that freedom again. Needed it to bandage her shattered soul. Yet there was one treasure she had to keep safe, and she'd come here to the place where Thomas had declared his love and asked her to marry him.

The rush of the stream told her she'd arrived. In the silvery light, she examined various hiding places, a poignant certainty filling her when she ran her fingertips over the ancient bark. Thomas had made love to her against this tree, whispering his adoration as she writhed in bliss against the sun-warmed trunk.

Taking the oilskin pouch from her pocket, she removed the paper one last time and reread it through blurry eyes. Then she refolded it, pressed it to her lips, and sealed it in the waterproof casing. Ascending the tree, she hid the pouch in a hollow obscured by branches.

"I know you're here." The predator hunted her in the darkness. "Come out, or I'll drag you out by the hair!"

Quickly, she descended. A cloud shifted, and as the moon caressed her face, she felt power quicken inside her. For the first time, she was unafraid to meet her destiny. He caught her by the edge of the stream, wrapping her hair around his fist, yanking her against him. He clamped a beefy hand over her mouth, his voice pouring into her ear like poison.

"He's gone. I killed him. Now it's just you and me, Rose."

"Wake up, Gigi. *Wake up.*"

Gigi bolted upright, her mouth open mid-scream. It took her an instant to recognize Owen's worried face. He was standing next to her bed.

"Wh-what happened?" she said shakily.

"I couldn't sleep and heard you shouting. You were having a nightmare." Owen raked a hand through his shaggy hair. "I thought my dreams were bad, but you...you were screaming bloody murder."

Murder. That's what I saw. But it was no dream.

"You are going to think I'm mad," Gigi said hoarsely.

Owen's mouth twisted. "Given the madhouse I reside in, I am hardly going to cast stones."

"I didn't have a dream. It was a vision...like the kind Xenia was having."

Owen's gaze was searching. "About Mulligan and Rosalinda, you mean?"

"Yes. And I need you to help me with something. Please."

"All right."

"Get dressed, and I'll meet you downstairs in ten minutes."

Owen cocked his head. "Where are we going?"

"I'll explain on the way."

Sunrise was painting the sky as Gigi and her brother rode to the woods. Tying up their horses, they headed for the stream, leaving footprints in the frost. The giant yew stood by the water as it had for centuries. As it had when Rose had come looking for it. Gigi surveyed the tree, looking for the hidden hollow.

"I think it's behind those branches up there." She pointed at a spot about sixteen feet off the ground. "I'm going to need a boost up."

She removed her velvet mantle, beneath which she wore an outfit suitable for climbing. Owen helped her onto his shoulders. She touched the lowest branch. After testing its strength, she pulled herself onto it, using it to access the next branch, and so on until she arrived at her destination. Pushing aside the dense, evergreen needles, she found the hollow she'd seen in the vision. She reached inside, feeling around in the darkness, her pulse speeding up when her fingers closed around a packet.

"I found it," she called breathlessly. "The pouch Rosalinda left—it's still here."

"Splendid," Owen returned. "Will you come down before I have to explain to everyone how you broke your neck?"

Tucking the pouch in her pocket, she descended nimbly. With Owen peering over her shoulder, she opened the oilskin envelope and pulled out a fragile, yellowed piece of paper. Her breath snagged as she read the faded but visible script.

"Oh my stars," she breathed.

Owen's brows pinched together. "Mulligan and Rose were married?"

The special license confirmed their legal union. Staring at the dark smudges along the edges, Gigi knew what they were. Even more than his shaky signature, Thomas Mulligan's fingerprints, inked in his own blood, told of what he'd sacrificed for love.

He should have never gone off by himself. We should have been together—protecting one another. I failed to trust our love, to keep him safe...and now it is too late.

Certainty blazed through Gigi, vanquishing doubt and fear. She wouldn't make the same mistake as Rose. She believed in her love and would do whatever it took to protect him.

"Owen." She turned to her brother. "I have another favor to ask."

Chapter Twenty-Seven

Late that afternoon, Gigi, accompanied by her brother, arrived at Conrad's London town house. It was an imposing Palladian in an excellent square not far from her parents' residence. The butler seated her and Owen in the drawing room, which was as fashionable as the exterior and decorated in rich jewel shades.

Conrad strode in. "Gigi?"

Seeing her lover looking robust and handsome in his shirtsleeves and a grey double-breasted waistcoat, a neckcloth of celadon silk knotted beneath his chin, she let go of the anxious breath that had been trapped inside her since the dream. If they were alone, she would have run into his arms. She had to settle for his possessive grip as he took her hand and kissed it.

"You're a sight for sore eyes," he said. "But what the devil are you doing here?"

"I had to see you," she said tremulously. "I convinced Owen to bring me."

"I am obliged, sir." Conrad extended a hand to her brother.

After a moment, Owen shook it.

"It wasn't my idea," Owen said. "If I didn't escort her, Gigi threatened to come alone."

"Let us sit," Conrad said. "I'll ring for refreshment, and you'll tell me what this is all about."

Given the day of traveling, Gigi was famished. So was Owen, for he wolfed down several plates of the sweet and savory teatime delicacies the butler brought in. Conrad sat, tea untouched, as she told him about the pawn ticket. True to her word, she kept the identity of her source anonymous, merely noting that the suspect who went by "John Brown" had seduced an innocent girl.

Conrad studied the slip before looking up at her with warm eyes. "Clever and resourceful, like I said. No one should ever underestimate you, Gi—I mean, my lady."

Gigi beamed at the compliment. And the fact that he was trying to make a good impression. Not that Owen noticed—he was busy inhaling a selection of Gunter's delectable iced cakes.

"Do you think the pawn ticket will lead us to John or whatever his name is?"

"With this clue, my investigators will track him down." Conrad paused. "But you could have sent the ticket and spared yourself the trouble. Your parents—"

"Won't even know we came," Gigi assured him. "Owen and I plan to return to Chuddums immediately. But I had to see you—to make sure all was well."

"I'm fine, duchess. Now that you are here."

Conrad's intense regard sent pleasant tingles over her nape.

"Owen, would you mind giving us a few moments?" she asked.

Her brother frowned. "Even I know that's not proper."

"Please," she beseeched. "Just a few minutes?"

"One would think I would be immune to your wheedling by now." Sighing, Owen rose, brushing crumbs from his trousers. "You have ten minutes and not a minute more."

The instant the door closed behind him, Conrad pulled Gigi into his arms.

"Christ, I've missed you," he said.

He sealed his mouth over hers, and his kiss was more expressive than words. With hammering joy, she tasted his hunger and desire for her. Yet it was more than lust. His tender grip on her jaw, as if he were holding something infinitely precious, made her melt against his hard length. She wrapped her arms around his neck, sharing all the love in her heart.

He broke the kiss, resting his forehead against hers.

"You are so bloody sweet," he said raggedly. "If we don't stop, I'm going to have you on this settee. And your brother will be back soon."

Through the haze of passion, she said, "There is another reason why I had to come."

"What is it, sweetheart?"

"I had a vision of Rose last night. She had blood on her hands...belonging to Thomas. It must have been right after his murder, and she knew the villain was after her too. In the dream, I saw her hide a piece of paper inside the hollow of a tree. The yew tree where you and I first kissed. Do you remember it?"

"Of course." Conrad's grin was lazy. "I've entertained several fantasies involving you and that tree."

Blushing, she said, "Owen and I went there, and we found the paper."

He raised his brows. "What is on it?"

"It's a special license. Rose and Thomas were married in secret, and guessing from the bloodstains on the paper, they gave their vows just before he died."

"That is incredible," he murmured.

"I think Thomas had been asking Rose to marry him, but she was afraid because of their differences in station. In my vision, I *felt* her regret—how she wished she'd said yes earlier. How she yearned to go back and change her decisions. Because she should have trusted in their love, you see."

"Would that have made a difference?"

"Perhaps," Gigi said earnestly. "Perhaps if Rose had married Thomas, she could have convinced him to take her away from Chuddums and start anew. But she was afraid of the differences between them, afraid of how others—her family and the villagers—would react. So she waited until it was too late. By then, Thomas had become convinced that the only way to gain her hand was to battle her past for her. He went to deal with the danger alone, when they should have faced it as a pair, and...well, you know the rest."

"I think I understand, but I want to hear it from you." Conrad's gaze blazed with urgency. "Tell me why you're here, Gigi."

"I needed to know that you were safe," she confessed. "I've been so worried since you left. I kept thinking, '*What if something happens, and I never told Conrad...*'"

"Tell me now," he coaxed.

Although his words were soft, his face was carved with passionate intensity. All his focus was on her, and instead of being afraid, she gloried in it. Because he was everything to her, too.

"I love you."

They were the easiest three words to say because they were true. Certainty filled her that no matter what the future held, she was meant to face it with this man. Her love, who was holding her hands tightly as if he feared she might flee or change her mind.

"I love you, Gigi," he said. "So damned much."

"I didn't give you an answer before because I was afraid. But now I'm not," she said. "I know what I want: a future with you. So the answer is yes...yes, I will marry you, Conrad."

"You have made me the happiest of men."

Seeing the smolder in his eyes, she tipped her head back for his kiss.

"Hold the thought. I'll be right back."

Bemused, she watched as Conrad hurried out of the room. He returned shortly, and before she could ask where he'd gone, he went down on one knee. Her heart fluttered when she saw what he held: a ring. And not just any ring—the most beautiful, extraordinary, extravagant ring she'd ever seen.

The center stone was a cushion-cut sapphire of at least three carats. What made it unique wasn't just the clarity and size but also the color: deep violet with hints of royal blue. The rare, vibrant stone was complemented by dazzling, pear-shaped diamonds on either side. Only the finest craftsmanship could have produced the ring's gold filigree setting, which had a delicate floral pattern. Then she saw the inscription inside the band and gurgled with laughter.

"'*For my sweet affliction*'?"

"One for which I will never have a cure," he said tenderly.

"This ring must have cost a fortune."

"More or less," he said dryly.

"I adore it!"

"I had a feeling you would." His expression was intent, as if he were memorizing this moment. "Georgiana Flora Aileen Harrington, will you marry me?"

"Yes," she breathed. "Yes, please."

He slid the ring onto her finger. A perfect fit. Then he rose, drawing her close, and the fit of their lips was even more sublime. In fact, it was so sublime that she lost track of everything.

"Today, sweetheart?"

"What about today?" she asked dreamily.

"Will you marry me today?"

She blinked. "Today? That's too soon—"

"I want you to be mine," he said firmly. "There is no point in waiting."

"Even so, it is impossible—"

"I have a special license." He cradled her cheek. "I wanted to be prepared for the moment you said yes."

Just like Thomas, who'd had a license waiting for Rose. The feeling of inevitability coursed through Gigi, making her heart thump faster.

This was meant to be. I've felt it from the beginning. This is fate.

She bit her lip. "But my family..."

"We can have a grand affair for them later, if you wish." He brought her hand, the one wearing his ring, to his lips. "I will wait if I must, Gigi. But I am ready to start our forever today."

Her head put up arguments. Would her family forgive her if she said yes? What would this do to her reputation? What would her friends and Society think?

Her heart, however, gave her the answer.

Trust in your love. Protect it. You belong with Conrad.

Giddy with love, she said, "In that case, so am I. Let's get married."

Chapter Twenty-Eight

After Gigi consented to marry by special license, Conrad went to find Owen. The news sent her brother into a state of shock, and she couldn't blame him. It was sudden and unexpected...yet it was also the *rightest* thing she'd ever done.

"You ought to wait." Owen dragged a hand through his hair. "You must speak to Papa and Mama—"

"I want this," Gigi said softly. "More than I've wanted anything."

"They are going to *murder* me." Owen's gaze had a frantic gleam. "It was bad enough that you convinced me to escort you here. Now you want to get *married*—"

"I know it isn't fair to put you in this position," Gigi said. "I will accept responsibility for my actions."

"As will I." Conrad stood beside her...a united front. "You have my word that I will look after your sister, Lord Owen. That I will love, honor, and cherish her for the rest of my days. She will want for nothing, and I would lay down my life for her."

Owen stared at Conrad. Then he braced his hands on his hips, his gaze directed at the ceiling while Gigi's heart beat like a wild drum.

"You've made up your mind," her brother said suddenly. "I cannot stop this, can I?"

Slowly, Gigi shook her head. "I am following our family tradition and marrying for love. I hope that you can understand...or forgive me, if you cannot. Either way, I know this is the path I'm meant to be on."

Owen expelled a long breath.

"Who the devil am I to tell you what path to take?" he muttered. "You've never been lost a day in your life. Unlike me."

"Owen—"

"Promise me this."

He took her by the shoulders, and in that moment, he was the brother he'd been before the war. His grey gaze was focused, his posture alert. A man ready and able to protect the people he loved.

"Promise me you're going to be happy," he said solemnly. "The happiest of brides, as you deserve to be."

Her voice quivering, she said, "I promise."

"Then you have my blessing, little sister." He kissed her forehead gently. "For what it's worth."

"Thank you, Owen. It means everything!"

With a squeal, she threw her arms around her brother, and heat pricked her eyes when he hugged her back.

"Enough of that." He extricated himself. "Now that you've gained my approval, you have bigger problems to worry about."

"I haven't a worry in the world."

She looked happily at him, then at Conrad, who smiled tenderly back.

"Really?" Owen asked. "What are you wearing to your wedding?"

Her eyes widened.

It is happening. Gigi is going to be mine.

As Conrad stood waiting for his bride by the darkening window, he was overcome with elation. Somehow, he'd captured the heart of the little nymph who was everything he'd fantasized about and more. For so long, he'd been focused on vengeance, and while justice was going to be undeniably satisfying, what he was feeling now was sweeter.

I am going to have everything.

Gazing around the room, he decided to give his staff a raise. With short notice, they'd managed to transform the drawing room into a hothouse bursting with bouquets of white roses and lilies, swathes of tulle and glowing candles adding to the romantic ambiance. The rector he'd hired stood at the ready, Bible in hand.

"You didn't think to mention you'd found yourself a wife?" Redgrave muttered beside him.

His chief manager was serving as his groomsman. Redgrave looked like a brawler stuffed in his Sunday best. His greying beard was neatly trimmed, and a white rose was tucked into the buttonhole of his lapel.

"There was nothing to mention. Gigi hadn't yet accepted my offer."

"But you *had* offered for her, and you didn't tell me."

Conrad drew his brows together. "Are you sulking?"

"Grown men don't sulk," Redgrave retorted. "I just thought I'd earned your trust."

"It is not about trust. It was a private matter. You know I do not like my affairs to be bandied about."

"That is my point. You can trust me not to wag my tongue like a damned fishwife."

"If I didn't trust you, would you be standing with me at my wedding and holding the rings?"

Redgrave looked slightly mollified. "You have always held your cards close to your chest, Godwin. Been that way since you showed up at my office all those years ago, looking to be a winner. Even though I didn't know the first thing about you, I didn't regret shaking on that deal then, and I don't now."

"As I recall, your office was a tavern," Conrad said. "You were three sheets to the wind and forgot you'd agreed to train me until I hunted you down at another tavern the next day and dragged your drunken arse to a boxing club."

"Those were the days, eh?" Redgrave said fondly.

Although Conrad rolled his eyes, he felt a twinge of unease. He *was* in the habit of holding his cards close, and soon he would have to reveal some, if not all, of them to Gigi. The Grantley ball was in two days, and he'd planned to reveal his identity there. While he'd been focused solely on how his brother Robert would react, now he had to think of his soon-to-be wife.

From Gigi's perspective, the revelation ought to feel like a bonus. It would elevate her status and strengthen his position with regard to her family. When all was said and done, he didn't think she would mind…but he ought to prepare her ahead of time. After their wedding night, he decided. When he'd staked his claim and she belonged to him fully. Then she would take his side, no matter what.

The drawing room door opened. Conrad, who would have scoffed at anyone who called him sentimental, felt as if time drew to a halt. As he laid eyes on Gigi, he stopped breathing, his senses absorbed by the perfection of her and this moment.

She exceeded his deepest fantasy, and her clothing had nothing to do with it. Truth be told, he preferred her with none at all. Yet his Gigi was a fashionable chit, and he'd wanted her to remember her wedding day with pride. Earlier, he'd pulled a few strings, and a modiste named Madame Dubois had arrived with trunks and an army of assistants in tow. When Gigi had bubbled over with excitement, telling him that she'd been on a waiting list for an appointment with the exclusive dressmaker, he knew he'd made the right choice.

Madame Dubois had brought a selection of wedding dresses, and after Gigi had chosen her favorite, the assistants had worked on the fitting. Conrad had informed the modiste that Gigi was to have carte blanche for a trousseau as well, including a ball gown for a special occasion. He left the ladies to it, his lips twitching when he heard Gigi's exclamations of delight through the closed door.

Seeing Gigi now, Conrad knew the modiste was worth every penny. The pristine, off-the-shoulder ivory dress looked exquisite on Gigi's slender frame. Trimmed with the finest lace, tight in the bodice and fluffy in the skirts, the gown gave her the appearance of a demure princess. Her hair had been fashioned into a shiny coronet and studded with orange blossoms. The tender length of her throat was bare—an oversight he would remedy soon—yet she needed no ornament beyond the ring that marked her as his.

As magnificent as the sapphire was, it was no match for Gigi's eyes. He felt as if he could drown in her gaze—in the love, mischief, and loyalty that, from this day on, would belong to him. He would no longer be a lonely beast roaming the earth alone. He had won his mate, body and soul, and now he would bind her to him.

Escorted by her brother, Gigi glided the short distance to Conrad. She smiled at him and placed her hand in his. His chest expanded with pride and wonder as the rector began the ceremony that would join them forever.

Chapter Twenty-Nine

I am married, and it's my wedding night.

The thought ought to have made Gigi nervous. Instead, it gave her a giddy thrill. She felt grown-up and adventurous, ready to explore one of the great mysteries of womanhood. Since she and Conrad had already started down this path and her mama had explained the basic facts of life, she knew what was about to happen tonight.

A pang struck Gigi as she thought of Mama and the rest of her family. Their absence was the only thing that marred her happiness. She'd written a letter, explaining everything and begging their forgiveness. She sent it to Bottoms House so that they would receive it upon their return. Once her family saw the love between her and Conrad, she was certain they would understand and support her marriage.

In the meantime, she couldn't wait to be alone with her new husband.

After the wedding ceremony, which had been simple yet beautiful, Conrad had hosted a decadent feast. The eight-course meal was an extravagant display of haute cuisine: sturgeon caviar on toast points, turbot in a delicate lemon sauce, beef braised with truffles, and roast pheasant stuffed with raisins and fennel were just a few of the delicious offerings. For dessert, the butler had wheeled in the chef's *pièce de résistance*: a *croquembouche*. Balls of puff pastry stuffed with cream had been stacked to form a towering pyramid and drizzled with caramel to create a show-stopping finish.

Over supper, Gigi had enjoyed getting to know Conrad's partners. Mr. Redgrave had shared rather bawdy tales about Conrad's time as a prizefighter that made her eyes grow bigger and bigger... until Conrad cut him off. She liked Mr. Marvell, too, who shared her fondness for Chuddums and was an aficionado of Letty's bottled water. Conrad, for his part, had been at his charming best. He'd managed to draw out Owen, discussing landscaping projects he'd undertaken at his various estates (which made Gigi wonder how much property her new husband owned). At one point, her brother even let out a rusty laugh.

After the party ended, Gigi had gone up to her sumptuous new bedchamber. One of the maids helped her change into the bedtime outfit supplied by Madame Dubois. Used to voluminous night rails, Gigi felt daring and sophisticated in the sleek ivory negligee and peignoir. The peignoir was sheer and flowy, with scalloped lace edges and a delicate ribbon belt. Beneath it, the silk negligee clung to her curves, and panels of lace provided racy, peek-aboo views. Her hair cascaded down her back in loose waves.

At the knock on the adjoining door, Gigi's heart sped up.

"Come in," she said.

Conrad entered, and her pulse stuttered at his magnificence. His black silk dressing gown accentuated the blatant virility of his form. He raked his gaze over her.

"Devil and damn," he said in a raspy voice.

"Is it too much?" Flustered, she pressed her hands to her warm cheeks. "Madame Dubois said such sets are all the rage in Paris."

"It's definitely too much. But I have a solution for that."

Prowling over, he took hold of the peignoir's belt and gave it a swift tug. The robe parted, and he pushed it off her shoulders, letting it pool on the floor. He had seen her unclothed before, yet Gigi felt strangely more exposed in the lacy negligee. Her nipples, stiff and rosy, peeped beneath the lacy bodice, and the high slits revealed her upper thighs.

"There now, that's better." Proprietary pride gleamed in Conrad's eyes. "I planned to be gentlemanly and ease you into our wedding night with conversation, love. But I think I cannot wait to have you."

His impatience mirrored her own. She placed her palms on his chest, feeling his thumping vitality. Wonder filled her that this magnificent man was hers.

"I want you too," she whispered. "I cannot wait for us to belong to each other completely."

Tenderness transformed Conrad's harsh features as he sifted his fingers through her hair.

"You're mine," he said roughly. "And I'm yours. For the rest of our days."

When he bent his head, she rose to meet him. Their lips clung in the sweetest of kisses. The joining felt like a culmination of every kiss they'd had: from the first at the stream when they were strangers to the most recent when the rector had declared them man and wife. It was gentle and scorching, exploring the complexity of the desire that bound them.

She sighed when he kissed her ear and neck. The beginnings of his night beard abraded her decolletage, and it was an exquisite sensation. His large hands palming her shoulder blades, he pulled her roughly against his mouth. She whimpered as he licked her breasts through the negligee. He swirled his tongue until the swollen buds were fully visible through the wet lace. When he sucked a throbbing peak into his mouth, she swayed.

The next instant, he was carrying her to the bed. He lay her across the mattress, and she felt like a princess sinking into the feathery softness. He fingered the ribbon strap of the negligee before grabbing the delicate bodice. She gasped as he tore the garment down the middle.

"That negligee was *expensive*," she sputtered.

"I'll buy you more." He raked a smoldering gaze over her exposed form. "Humor me, sweetheart. I've always wanted to do that."

She scowled at him. "To do what? Destroy my wardrobe?"

"No, little nymph. I've fantasized about having my wicked way with you."

At the rasp in his voice, a delicious quiver worked up her spine. Having leafed through *The Naughty Naiad*, she understood the nature of his desires. Her husband was undeniably hot-blooded, but beneath his primal depravity was also a yearning for connection: the longing of a lonely satyr for his mate. His fantasy stirred her own need to be desired with savage intensity—to be important, everything, to the man she loved.

"I'm yours," she said softly. "To do with as you wish."

The look that came into his eyes made her tremble with anticipation...and a wee bit of fear. Not of him—she knew he would never do anything against her wishes—but of her own desires. Of the unexpected vein of wickedness that ran through her own soul. All her life, she'd striven to be the perfect daughter, the girl no one had to worry about. She'd concerned herself with the needs of others more than her own.

With Conrad, she was recognizing what she wanted. And it didn't matter if it wasn't proper or good. She had only to be herself, and the recognition incinerated her inhibitions.

"You are a bloody gift," he marveled. "And you're all mine."

In a rapid movement, he pinned her hands above her head. Feeling the possessive strength of his grip, instinctive panic shot through her. Her first instinct was to tug free, but he held her fast. As her lungs pulled for air, she saw that his gaze was fixed upon her heaving breasts. His pupils were dilated, his features sharpened by hunger.

The satyr...my husband.

Desire thrummed in her blood and guided her actions. She went slack in his grip, surrendering to the fantasy. To his seductive dominance.

"Now that you've captured me." The tremor in her voice was not entirely feigned. "What do you intend to do with me?"

His eyes lit with astonished lust. His nostrils flared.

"Anything I want," he growled.

He fell upon her like a ravening beast. She writhed as he used his mouth on her. He grunted with enjoyment as he licked her breasts. When he bit the soft underside, she jerked, then moaned when he tongued away the small hurt.

"That's going to leave a mark," he murmured.

"You don't sound too sorry about it," she said breathlessly.

"I'm not." His smile was sensual and unapologetic. "Before the night is done, you'll bear my mark in more ways than one."

He took his time licking her nipples. All the while, he anchored her to the bed for his ravishment, his hands still holding her wrists, his hips pinning hers down. His cock felt like a steel bar against her thigh. Wantonly, she strained against him. His restraint heightened her sensations until she felt as if she might burst out of her skin.

"Rub that needy little pussy against me until you come," he instructed.

He nudged her legs apart with his knee, and she was so aroused that she didn't think twice about obeying his carnal command. She arched her hips, sliding her throbbing sex against his hard thigh. The motion made a lewd, slick sound, but it felt so good that she didn't care. He sucked her nipple deep into his mouth, and when she felt his teeth, she flew over the edge.

"Devil and damn, you're gushing like a fountain." Beneath his heavy lids, his eyes shone with lust. "Keep your hands where they are, sweetheart. I *have* to taste you…"

Releasing her wrists, he slid down her body and buried his face between her legs.

Conrad grunted with pleasure as he ate his wife's cunny. She was more delicious than the chef's *croquembouche*. With her, he was insatiable, and it wasn't just the way she squirmed and sighed, squirting cream onto his greedy tongue. It was also how she obeyed his command, keeping her hands above her head. The sweet sounds she made and the purity of her surrender. Having pledged herself to him, Gigi was giving him everything.

The thought made him crazed with desire. He redoubled his efforts, circling her pearl with his thumb and tonguing the virginal hole he would soon breach. He worked a finger inside, panting at her tightness. Beneath his robe, his turgid cock pulsed with the imperative to claim his bride, but he wanted her to be ready—to be as wild with need as he was.

He licked her to another orgasm, sucking her pearl while she squealed his name. Only then did he mount the mattress, kneeling next to her head. Fisting a handful of her luxuriant tresses, he guided her lips to his dripping erection.

"Suck it, sweetheart," he said huskily. "Make it nice and wet. I don't want to hurt your snug little cunny when I take you."

Her vivid eyes, the color of a dream, widened at this new demand. After a brief hesitation, she wetted her lips and parted them. Pride and lust pounded in his chest.

"Such a good little nymph," he crooned.

He pushed the wide head past her rosy opening, letting her get used to the feel of him. He went slowly, watching his veined shaft disappear into her mouth. Gratitude filled him as she gracefully took what he offered.

"Your tongue feels like velvet against my cock," he said with approval. "Mind your teeth now because I'm going to give you more."

He thrust deeper, enjoying her muffled gasp. Little by little, he fed her more. Pulling out and pushing in, he got her accustomed to the feeling of taking him this way. He didn't get all the way in—not even halfway—but when she moaned around her first mouthful of cock, the blissful reverberation took him too close to the edge. He withdrew, and seeing the garland of spit that hung between her lips and his engorged dome tested his limits.

He gathered her atop him, kissing and kissing her.

"Are you ready for me, sweetheart?" he asked.

Her hair rippled like a dark river over her shoulders. "Make love to me, darling."

Needing no further encouragement, he reversed their positions and rolled on top. Parting her thighs, he brought his cock to her pussy. He took an instant to memorize the image of his florid tip nudging her virginal gates before driving home. The fit was snug, delightfully so, but her dew eased his path. Fire blazed up his spine at the indescribable joy of claiming her—his mate, his wife.

Noticing that her bottom lip was caught beneath her teeth, he halted. "Are you all right?"

Brows pinched, she wriggled a little. Her movements felt so bloody good that it required all his willpower to remain still while she came to a decision.

"I'm fine," she announced to his everlasting relief. "As fine as one can be with something that, um, sizeable lodged inside one, that is."

"Sizeable, am I?" He leaned down, rubbing his nose against hers. "You might not realize it yet, but size has its advantages."

"Really?"

She looked so unconvinced that he had to smile.

"I'll show you," he murmured.

He started with a leisurely pace until he saw her discomfort fade. When her hands fluttered over his bunched biceps and gripped onto his shoulders, he increased his tempo. As he plunged into her lushness, he kissed her until she was panting. He strummed her rosy nipples as he thrust harder, deeper, grunting when her sheath clenched around him. When he planted himself all the way to the root, she gasped.

"Conrad." She gazed at him in wonder. "I feel so...so full."

"You were meant to take my cock," he said roughly. "And I was meant to be inside your sweet pussy. Now follow my lead."

He began to move—really move. He drilled into her tight hole, angling his shaft to graze her needy peak. She whimpered, her fingers digging into his shoulders as he rode her. Pleasure unleashed his inner beast. He wanted to take, take, take—to pound himself into his sweet nymph until he was a part of her.

"I've wanted you for so long," he said between harsh breaths. "Finally, you're mine."

"I belong to you, darling. And you belong to me. Forever."

With her words, Gigi tore his heart from his chest and took it into her keeping. His vision blurred, and he slammed into his wife, growling as he ground his balls against her plump folds. Over and again, he staked his claim, stroking her pearl as he shafted her. As she panted and moaned, her eyes never left his. The adoration in her gaze was a gift beyond measure, one he would cherish until the end of his days. When she convulsed around him, there was no resisting the summons.

Release roared through him, erasing everything he thought he knew about pleasure. The scorching bliss went beyond physical. Even as he spewed hotly inside her, the connection transcended their bodies. He was transported to that glowing meadow where nothing could hurt him, where he was no longer alone, where nothing mattered but being joined to the mate of his soul.

She brushed a lock of hair from his forehead, and he shuddered with pleasure at this, the simplest of touches. He was still hard, rocking inside her while she sighed.

"I'm so glad you're my husband," she whispered.

"That's just as well. Because we're bound together," he said huskily. "Now and forever."

Chapter Thirty

Gigi woke up to a strange sensation. At first, she thought she was dreaming, but then she felt the heated glide of familiar lips along her neck, the prickle of stubble. Her lips curved as she registered that she was lying on her side, her spine nestled against Conrad's chest. He had an arm slung over her hip, and his hand was busy doing wicked things between her legs. When he played with her little button, she sighed, pressing back against him.

"Good morning, husband," she said breathlessly.

"A very good one at that, wife," he agreed.

Feeling his erect member against her bottom, she giggled.

"Do you wake up like this often?"

"Every morning."

Her eyes widened, and she twisted her head to meet his amused eyes.

"We get to do this every morning?"

He flashed a grin. "A man can only hope. However, being the considerate bridegroom, I must ask: are you sore, love?"

After a quick assessment, she said regretfully, "A little."

He rolled her onto her back, kissing her on the nose. "I was too greedy last night."

He hadn't been the only one. She'd lost track of how many times she came, the night a blur of ecstasy. After he'd taken her the first time, they'd refreshed themselves with champagne and fed each other leftover cream puffs. He'd teased her for getting cream on her nose, then licked it off. When he bit into a cream puff, filling had squirted out and landed squarely on his member. Warmth flooded her as she thought of her boldness. Of the way she'd bent down and teasingly licked the cream from *him*...

"Although I wasn't the only one with an appetite, was I?"

Conrad's knowing smirk made her blush even harder.

"You need time to recover. Moreover." He cleared his throat. "There is something we need to discuss."

His somber expression gave her pause.

"This sounds serious."

"It is rather. Here, allow me to see to your comfort first."

As he arranged the pillows for her, her wariness grew.

She sat up. "Have I done something wrong—"

"No."

He pressed her gently against the fluffed pillows before settling against the headboard beside her. He took her hand, interlacing their fingers.

"The only thing you've done is to make me the luckiest bastard alive," he said.

While that was reassuring, she sensed his brooding tension. "Then what do you wish to discuss?"

"I have something to tell you. It will not change anything between us, but it...it will change things. In general, I mean. And for the better, I hope."

Conrad was nervous, she realized. As he was rarely so, her anxiety increased.

"Just tell me," she begged.

"The truth is, Gigi...I am not who you think I am."

Startled, she said, "Would you care to clarify?"

He drew a breath. "I was not born Conrad Godwin."

Alarm jolted her. "Then who are you?"

"I am going to tell you all of it, I promise," he said earnestly. "But I must start at the beginning for this to make sense. Please bear with me, sweetheart. You have my word that you have nothing to worry about—"

"Nothing to worry about?" Her voice trembled. "The morning after my wedding, the man I married is telling me he isn't who he claimed to be!"

"I *am* Conrad Godwin. It's just that I am...well, I'm someone else, too." He tightened his grip on her hand. "When you asked about my family, I told you my parents died when I was young, and all of that is true. My mama was a beautiful but poor commoner. She was hired to be a nurse to an older gentleman who was her senior by three decades. The two fell in love, and despite the objections of the gentleman's three sons from his first marriage, he married her. A year later, I was born."

Gigi absorbed the information. "You are the son of a gentleman?"

"I was born into your world," he confirmed. "However, I did not see much of it. My papa had a frail constitution, so Mama and I spent our days cloistered on his country estate. I wouldn't have minded it, except my half-brothers also resided with us. They resented Papa's new marriage and took out their hatred on Mama and me. The eldest, Robert, was in his twenties at the time, and he led the charge. He and my other half-brothers bullied me at every opportunity. They said my mama was a whore and that I was another man's bastard. They beat me where no one could see the marks, destroyed things that were valuable to me. I was a child and could not fight back against any of it."

Despite her bewilderment, empathy pulsed through Gigi.

"How could they be so cruel?" she murmured. "Did you tell your parents?"

"Papa was too weak to do anything about it. Even if he could, he was an indulgent father and would not believe his own flesh and blood capable of such meanness. Mama was afraid that stress would worsen his ailing health and kept most of it from him. She told me she would handle it. She couldn't, of course. When Papa died—I was seven at the time—things went from bad to worse."

"What happened?" Gigi asked.

"Robert inherited everything. Now that Mama and I were dependent on him, he showed his true colors. What he'd done before had been but a taste of the cruelty of which he was capable. By his orders, my mama and I subsided on meager meals and wore castoffs that the servants would not touch. Everything we had, we had to beg for. Sometimes he made us kneel and kiss his ring as a sign of fealty and respect."

Shock filled Gigi at the despicable treatment Conrad had received at the hands of his own brother. With a tremor, she remembered his nightmare in the cavern—had that been of Robert abusing him? She squeezed his hand, wanting him to know that she was there with him as he revisited the shadows of his past.

"I was prideful, and I didn't want to do it." He curled his free hand into a fist. "But Mama told me to keep my head down and do as Robert wanted. She would find a way out for us, she said. I just had to be patient. We had each other, and that was what mattered."

As Conrad wrestled with his demons, Gigi waited, patient and anxious.

"About a year after Papa's death, Robert called us into the study. He informed my mother that I was to be sent away to boarding school. A remote place called Creavey Hall, where the upper classes sent their troublesome sons to be reformed. Mama begged him not to separate us, but that only made him gloat. I still remember his words."

Conrad's throat rippled, his voice emerging with foreign malice.

"'I have the power to do whatever I please,' my brother said. 'And it pleases me to see you suffer. To take away everything that means anything to you.'"

"What an evil man," she exclaimed. "To hurt his own kin—"

"He enjoyed our pain. My two other brothers were afraid of him and followed his lead. My mama wept, vowing that we would run away and live in a village where Robert couldn't find us. Even then, I knew she had no power to follow through on her promises. I was eight when they took me away to Creavey Hall. My mama sent letters full of plans for our future together, but I never saw her again. She died a few months after I arrived at Creavey. Her spirit and heart had simply been...broken."

"I'm so sorry." Overwhelmed by the tragedies that he had suffered, Gigi cuddled closer, wrapping an arm around his torso. "I cannot imagine what it must have been like to lose your mama and your home."

He put an arm over her shoulders, holding her close.

"It wasn't easy, but I learned to survive."

Peering up, she saw the ice in his eyes and shivered.

"Were the boys at Creavey Hall...were they bullies like your brothers?"

"Some were. Others had been housed there because they were not like other boys, and their families wanted them kept out of sight. A few were like me: sent there to be 'reformed' by Creavey Hall's system."

Gigi's nape prickled. "What did the system involve?"

"Punishment," he said succinctly. "Administered by the headmaster, Obadiah Grimshaw. He was a sadistic bastard who hid his proclivities behind a guise of piety. He enjoyed pain—enjoyed inflicting it on young boys. In his mission to 'reform' those in his charge, he had all manner of tools at his disposal: birches, paddles, a cat-o-nine-tails. His system involved beating you until you admitted guilt, even if you hadn't done a bloody thing. Most boys learned to confess to sins they hadn't committed. I was one of the hard-headed ones. That was how I earned these scars."

He sat up, twisting to show her his back. It stunned her that she hadn't noticed them before...that he'd somehow kept them hidden from her. That he'd felt the need to. Pale lines of knitted skin crisscrossed his strong, sculpted back, and her heart cracked with the knowledge that he would forever bear the marks of his abuse.

"You asked me once how I learned to be a prizefighter. This is how. Thanks to Grimshaw's lessons, by the time I escaped that hellhole at age seventeen, I'd learned to tolerate pain better than most. I could take a beating and still give a good fight."

At his shrug, anger welled inside her.

"Don't you *dare* make light of this." Her voice trembled. "No boy should ever suffer the abuses you did. Grimshaw ought to be put behind bars—"

"He got his comeuppance. Don't you worry about that."

The mildness of Conrad's tone made the statement somehow more menacing.

"What happened to him?" she asked.

"It was a few years after I absconded from Creavey. Grimshaw had retired to the countryside. One day, he returned home from his duties as a church deacon and discovered neighbors thronged around his cottage. They were gawking, whispering, pointing to the pages papering the outside of his home—pages taken from the books in his hidden stash. Entire volumes of pornography depicting extreme acts of sadism covered every inch of those walls. His favorite mementos from his days as headmaster—the whips and birches, the paddles and rods—were hung like decorations for all to see."

Gigi swallowed. "I suppose that is what one calls just deserts."

"No, just deserts was when Grimshaw took his own life," Conrad said coolly. "When he discovered he couldn't bear being a pariah, the old hypocrite hung himself."

Gigi shivered at his ruthlessness. At the same time, she couldn't bring herself to feel pity for Grimshaw. The bounder had abused vulnerable children in his care, and he'd reaped what he'd sown. Thinking of the damage he'd caused—of the suffering he'd inflicted on Conrad, a vulnerable boy who had no one to look after him—made her sick to her stomach. Finally, she understood the root of Conrad's issues with trust: he'd been betrayed by those closest to him. His brothers, Grimshaw, even his past lovers.

"When I escaped Creavey at age seventeen, I changed my identity so no one could find me. Do you know why I adopted the name Conrad Godwin?"

She shook her head.

"I chose Conrad because it sounded strong. Like a man bullies would think twice about taking on. And Godwin..."

At the faraway look in his eyes, she whispered, "Where did Godwin come from?"

"It was the name of the furniture maker that built Grimshaw's punishment bench," he said flatly. "Every time I was forced to submit to his beatings, I would see the maker's mark. And I would repeat it to myself to distract from the pain. One could say *Godwin* helped me to survive, so that is who I became."

Heat pushed behind her eyes, words failing her.

"Does knowing this piece of history make you think less of me?"

Conrad's features were impassive, yet his eyes burned with emotion. He'd laid himself bare in a way he never had before, and it horrified her that he might mistake her reaction for anything other than what it was.

Fury at his abuser. Admiration for him. Most of all, love.

"Quite the opposite." She pushed through the hitch in her voice. "To know that you've survived this, it...well, it quite breaks my heart. You didn't deserve any of it. Not the treatment from your brothers, not the abuses from Grimshaw. I wish your mama could have protected you and herself, even though it wasn't her fault that she could not."

"No," Conrad agreed. "The fault was not hers."

"I've always admired your strength of will. Even when it drove me mad. But now I am grateful because it helped you to survive a past that would have brought others to their knees. While I am sorry beyond words that you had to go through such travails, it made you the man you are today: Conrad Godwin. The man I love with all my heart."

She touched his jaw, feeling its rigidity. The tension of everything he'd held back.

"Thank you for sharing this with me. Given all you've survived, I understand now why trust does not come easily. Why it has been difficult for you to share your secrets."

"I trust you," he said roughly.

His declaration felt like the greatest gift.

"That bodes well for our future," she said softly. "We are bound now, and as husband and wife, there shouldn't be any secrets between us."

"About that." Conrad tucked a stray lock behind her ear. "Do you recall how I started this conversation?"

Lost in the warm, green pools of his eyes, she had to cast her mind back.

She tilted her head because it suddenly occurred to her. "What was your birth name? Who was your papa?"

"I was born Christian Beaufort," he said. "My papa was Hugh Beaufort, and my eldest brother is Robert Beaufort."

She blinked as the names sank in. "The Duke of Grantley…he is your brother?"

"He is. And I am his heir." Conrad's gaze glittered. "Despite his attempts to destroy me, I survived. My middle brothers died one by one, and Robert's wife, Lady Katerina, has given him only daughters."

She tried to comprehend what he was saying. "You're going to be a duke one day?"

"Within weeks, according to my sources. Robert is dying of syphilis, and he doesn't have long. Soon I will be the Duke of Grantley." He lifted her hand, kissing it. "And you will be my duchess."

As she digested that information, a thought struck her.

"Since we met, you've been calling me duchess," she said, bemused.

"Yes," he said tenderly. "Every time I did so, I was actually calling you *mine*."

Her heart melted. "Why didn't you tell me this before we were married?"

"Would it have changed your decision to marry me?"

"No. But was it because you didn't trust me fully...until now?"

"Sweetheart, when you showed up on my doorstep yesterday, I wasn't thinking about my past. My primary objective was to make you mine before you changed your mind. And to get you into bed as quickly as possible."

"I am not going to change my mind," she said softly. "*Ad Finem Fidelis*, remember?"

"I remember." He cupped her cheek, his eyes intense. "It was selfish of me, dragging you into this situation with danger still swirling—"

"That is the point of being faithful until the end. From now on, we stick together through thick and thin, the good times and the bad. No matter what the future brings, we face it together."

"My brother might be trying to kill me."

She gawked at him. "You think Grantley hired someone to push that statue?"

"I don't think he knows I am alive. But if he does," Conrad said matter-of-factly, "I am a threat."

"How so?"

"He's been working to broker a marriage between his eldest

daughter, Anne, and his presumptive heir, Harold Stockton. Stockton is our distant cousin, and he's made a fortune with mills, which is a good thing because Grantley has emptied the duchy's coffers. He needs Stockton's money to provide for his wife and daughters after he is gone, and he has convinced Stockton that the marriage would be mutually beneficial. Coming from trade, Stockton has little experience with high society, and having Anne to guide him would ease the transition. When Stockton discovers that the title won't be going to him, he will renege on the engagement for Anne has neither looks nor a dowry to recommend her."

"That is unkind," Gigi said. "I am acquainted with Miss Beaufort, and she is an intelligent and agreeable lady. In fact, she purchased a crate of Chuddums water."

"At seven-and-twenty with no offers in sight, she probably thought that was her only hope of finding a husband," Conrad said wryly. "She takes after her mama, whom Grantley did not marry for looks."

"She is your niece. Or half-niece anyway," she said hastily when Conrad's jaw tautened. "Shouldn't you be nicer toward her?"

"She is the daughter of my enemy. The man who sent my mama to an early grave and me to an institution where I was beaten daily. And you expect me to be *nice*?"

"While Robert deserves your animosity, his wife and children do not," Gigi said gently. "They are innocent and not to blame for his dastardly behavior."

"Then it is their misfortune to bear his name." Conrad's chest heaved. "Tomorrow, Grantley is giving a ball to announce the betrothal. I plan to use the opportunity to reveal who I am, and the outcome could get ugly."

Seeing his agitation, she knew further argument would be futile. Conrad was a fair man; once he was calmer, he would listen to reason. And maybe she could help smooth things over between him and Robert's wife and children.

She squeezed his hand. "I'll go with you. You will need the support."

"I had hoped to have this business behind me before we married. But know this: I would lay down my life to protect you. At the same time, you must be aware of the danger. My family is not like yours. There is no love between me and them. Now that you are my wife, you must be vigilant—you must trust me to know what is best, even if you don't understand."

"I do trust you," she said.

"You are the dream that sustained me through my darkest days," he said fiercely. "At the same time, you are better than any fantasy. Now that I have you, I cannot lose you, Gigi."

She touched his jaw. "I'm here. And I am not going anywhere."

Something primal flashed in his eyes, then his mouth crashed onto hers. His hunger was insatiable and fueled her own. He shoved aside the bedclothes, her spine arching against the headboard as he kissed his way down her body. He touched and tasted her with a wildness that made her blood rush. Pushing her thighs apart, he examined her sex with wolfish approval.

"Just what I wanted for breakfast," he said.

She expected him to bend his head. Instead, he flipped onto his back. Clamping his hands on her hips, he maneuvered her, positioning her over him so that she faced his toes, her pussy hovering over his mouth.

"This way?" she said in shock. "Are you certain…oh my *stars*."

He'd yanked her down on his face. His hot licking forced a moan from her lips.

"That's it, sweetheart," he said thickly. "Ride my tongue."

Heat washed over her as she did exactly that. She abandoned herself to the pleasure of her husband's masterful loving.

"Your pussy is my favorite meal. Can you feel my tongue inside you?"

"That's so wicked," she panted.

"But you love it, don't you?"

Speared upon his tongue, she gasped her agreement. She balanced herself on his hard torso, grinding against him, decorum vanquished by mindless delight. She gazed at her husband laid before her like a buffet: his sculpted chest, sinewy legs, and long, thick cock. Strings of desire tugged at her core, releasing some inner floodgate. Despite the heady bliss, she was embarrassed by her gushing response and tried to dismount.

He held her fast.

"I'm licking my plate clean, duchess," came his muffled growl. "But if you are hungry, feel free to have your own feast."

At his suggestion, her gaze flew to his massive member. Did he mean that she could…that they could do this *simultaneously*? The image from the book flashed across her mind's eye. Before she could lose her nerve, she inched forward, circling her fingers around his shaft. His cock was so hard that she had to pry it from the ridges of his abdomen. The head was red and swollen, lustrous with his essence.

Leaning forward, she licked the dripping tip.

"That's it, sweetheart," he rasped. "Suck me."

With a hum of excitement, she did. He was delicious—salty and male, so hot and hard in her mouth. His earthy words of encouragement, muttered against her own quivering flesh, emboldened her. She took him deeper, urged on by his guttural praise.

"What a hungry little nymph I married."

Delirious with desire, she wriggled against his mouth as he slid inside her own. He pushed her forward, impaling her mouth on his spear even as he filled her with his tongue. She pumped his shaft, sucking and sucking as he ate her pussy. The pleasure built and built, and when she felt his finger breach her forbidden entrance, she let out a squeak.

"All mine, remember?" he said thickly. "Even here."

What he was doing felt too naughty, too good. With feverish

abandon, she cupped his stones, and his growl spilled like honey through her veins.

"You have the sweetest touch," he gritted out. "The sweetest mouth..."

She tried to take more of him as her pleasure reached a zenith.

"*Christ*. Move, Gigi. Or I'll spill in your mouth—"

The notion was enough to send her over. She pulled him from her lips with a *pop*, pumping his shaft with jerky movements as ecstasy rolled through her. A heartbeat later, he roared and exploded...thick, milky fluid jetting from him. It splattered her cheeks, chin, and lips, and she reveled in his hot pleasure. She nuzzled his still-hard cock while he kissed her thigh. They rocked together, taking and giving, until the crisis passed.

Afterward, they lay face-to-face.

"I didn't shock you, did I?" he asked.

"Which part are you referring to?" She felt oddly lighthearted. "The fact that I married a duke's heir, or what we just did?"

He laughed.

"I should have known you had hardy sensibilities." His eyes brilliant, he ran his thumb over her bottom lip. "If I live to be a hundred, duchess, I will never have enough of you. You are my deepest fantasy...and more."

Chapter Thirty-One

"Nervous, duchess?"

"A bit," Gigi whispered back. "I have friends and acquaintances here tonight. They are already looking at us and talking."

She wasn't wrong. They'd arrived at the Grantley residence mere moments ago and were waiting to be announced. Standing at the top of the staircase, Conrad felt the heat of curious gazes from the ballroom.

"Let them look."

As Conrad lifted her hand to his lips, her ring caught the light and blazed with purple fire. If that wasn't sufficient proof of his claim, the matching sapphire-and-diamond necklace draped around her throat surely was. The modiste had dressed Gigi in violet taffeta, which heightened the contrast between her raven hair and fair skin, bringing out her vivid eyes. The elongated bodice clung lovingly to her slender torso, the full skirts swaying with her graceful movements. Gigi looked every inch the duchess she was, the kind of woman who made a fellow stand tall with pride to have her by his side.

"By the end of the night, the only topic of conversation will be how beautiful you are," he murmured. "And what a lucky man I am."

"I think your announcement might compete for attention."

Hearing the ruffle of anxiety in her wry words, he said, "You do not have to do this with me. If you wish to go back to the carriage—"

"I am not letting you do this alone." Looking adorably outraged at the very idea, she straightened her shoulders, which were rimmed by sensual black lace. "I am ready when you are."

She squeezed his hand, and he gripped hers. They were next to be announced, and when it was his turn, Conrad gave their names to the steward. At first, the fellow looked confused, but when Conrad gave him a commanding look, the fellow shrugged, probably assuming the name was a coincidence or that he was some distant relation.

"Lord Christian Beaufort and Lady Georgiana Beaufort," the steward boomed.

Gasps and whispers erupted as Conrad led Gigi down the stairs. The moment they reached the dance floor, they were swarmed by guests buzzing with the need to know who he was and why Gigi, one of their own, bore his last name.

He ignored them, steering her through the throng toward his destination: a small group standing by a potted palm. Well, not all of them were standing. Conrad's gaze was fixed on the man sitting in a grand, wheeled chair. Fashioned to look like a throne, it appeared to function like a gilded cage. Despite getting regular reports on his brother's condition, Conrad felt a brief shock at the changes.

Robert's once stately figure had shriveled. He was slumped in his seat, a blanket draped over his withered lap. His thick hair had been reduced to a few oily strands combed across his skull. The disease had carved into his flesh, leaving scars and collapsing his features. His nose, half-dissolved, left a gaping shadow where an arrogant, hawkish edge had once been. Yet his eyes were the same.

Even though they were now covered in a dull film, Conrad saw recognition flare in those pitiless depths.

Robert's wife, Lady Katerina, stood at his side. Dressed in an unflattering shade of pink, she was a tall, plain brunette who looked as if life had sucked the marrow from her. Deep lines were etched around her eyes and mouth. She watched Conrad like one watches a tiger escaped from its enclosure. Her eldest daughter, Lady Anne, was a younger, less depleted version of her and stood on the other side of Robert's chair. Next to her was Harold Stockton, a short, balding fellow whose tailoring attested to the universal truth that wealth could not buy taste.

The final member of the cozy group…well, that was a surprise.

"Mr. Godwin." Isobel Denton's light laugh was no doubt intended for the surrounding guests, all of whom were avidly eavesdropping. "If this is meant to be a prank, it is far from amusing. You are interrupting an important occasion, the betrothal between Lady Anne and Mr. Stockton—"

"That is precisely why I am here," Conrad said. "I couldn't miss such an important family occasion, could I…brother?"

He was ready for Robert to deny their connection. His Grace's refutation would be meaningless, for Conrad had documents, meticulously compiled by Marvell: parish records and eyewitness testimonies that established who he was.

Robert bared his chapped lips, revealing teeth rotted at the roots.

"I always knew you would come back." His words were raspy and effortful. "Like any mongrel, you are a survivor."

"I've done more than survive," Conrad said coolly. "I believe you are acquainted with my wife, Lady Georgiana Beaufort?"

Looking uncertain, Gigi nonetheless played her part with disarming charm.

"It is a pleasure to see you again, Your Graces," she said. "Lady Anne."

"It is lovely to see you, Lady Gigi." Lady Anne's mouth pulled into a tight smile. "I haven't yet thanked you for introducing me to the Chuddums Water Cure. It has worked wonders."

When Gigi gave her a friendly nod, Conrad's mood darkened. His family did not deserve kindness from his wife.

"Do you know why I am here?" Conrad asked.

Robert's gaze darted, but even if he could run, there was no place to hide.

He grunted. "I suppose you've come to claim what is yours, brother."

At the acknowledgement, gasps went up around the room.

Knowing he had won, Conrad expected to feel some sort of satisfaction. Instead, what he felt was coldness and rage. The wrongs Robert had committed against him crowded his head, banging against his skull. His temples pulsed. On the verge of regaining what was rightfully his, he found it wasn't enough.

I must have justice. An eye for an eye. Your blood for every drop you took from me.

"As your heir and the soon-to-be Duke of Grantley, I came to apprise you of my plans," he said. "For you see, *brother*, I will show your family the same courtesy you've shown me."

He heard Gigi inhale. Her presence anchored him—kept him from driving his fist into Robert's face and caving in what was left of it.

"You...you leave them out of this," Robert hissed. "This is between you and me."

At the spark of Robert's old fire, Conrad was glad. He wanted a fight—a rematch now that he wasn't easy pickings. His hands curled.

See how Robert enjoys being the weak one. The vulnerable one. See how he enjoys being powerless while I grind my boot into his neck.

"You treated my mama worse than a servant. You separated her and me. She died trying to find a way to fix what you broke." Fury cleared his head and numbed him. "I will have justice, which means I will take from you what you took from me. I will treat your family like you treated mine. In other words, when I am duke, I will see to it that they have *nothing*."

He towered over Robert, who shrank back in his chair.

"Please, sir." The timorous plea came from Lady Anne, who had turned as white as her dress. "Whatever has happened in the past, this is a conversation best had in private—"

"I've held my silence long enough," Conrad snapped. "Unlike your papa, I have nothing to hide."

When Lady Anne pressed a hand over her mouth, her mama took a step forward.

"There is nothing to be gained by airing dirty laundry in public, sir," the duchess said. "Our family's reputation affects you as well. Let us reconvene upstairs—"

"I've said what I had to say. Except this."

Conrad aimed his stare at Stockton, who looked like a cornered hare.

"Stockton, I am Robert's heir. If you choose to marry Anne, know this: whatever Robert promised you is now void. When I control the duchy, she will have nothing from me."

Lady Anne let out a soft whimper.

"I am sure what my husband means is that, um, renegotiations will be necessary." The unwelcome interruption came from Gigi. "He will handle things differently than his predecessor, I am sure—"

"When I say nothing, I mean nothing."

At his growled words, Gigi stiffened but kept her polite smile in place.

"Darling, why don't we discuss this in private?" she said.

He resented that she was siding with Lady Katerina, the wife of his enemy. Yet Lady Anne was openly weeping, her mama huddling next to her, and the pitiful sight gave Conrad pause. He was aware of the onlookers circling like sharks, eager for a taste of blood.

Maybe Gigi is right. I've gone in for the kill. I can finish this off elsewhere.

Before he could speak, Robert raised his hand. Conrad froze at the sight of the ring. Now loose on his brother's bony finger, the circle of gold and its winking ruby ripped a scab from his soul.

How does it feel to be on your knees, Robert? This time, you will be the one kissing the ring. The one to say you're sorry for existing.

Wheezing, Robert pointed a finger at him. "You...you are not fit to be the next Grantley."

Rage flooded Conrad. "But I will be the duke. And when I am, your bloodline will pay for your sins."

As Robert sputtered, Conrad turned to Gigi, who was gazing at him, wide-eyed.

"Let's go," he said tersely. "This family reunion is over."

Grabbing her hand, he dragged her away.

Chapter Thirty-Two

Gigi found the emotion that filled the carriage foreboding, to say the least. As was the fact that Conrad had chosen to sit in the opposite corner, his mood dark and brooding. Even though the curtains were drawn, he was staring at the window. He hadn't said a word since they left the ball, and she could bear the silence no longer.

"Do you want to talk about what happened?" she asked.

After a moment, he trained his gaze on her.

"Don't do that again."

His icy manner chilled her. At the same time, his churlishness rankled. Reminding herself of the distressing ordeal he'd gone through, she managed to stay calm.

"A lot happened tonight," she said quietly. "What are you referring to?"

"Do not contradict me. Do not put words in my mouth. Above all," he said through clenched teeth, "do not *ever* take their side over mine."

His dictatorial tone challenged her patience, which she held onto by sheer force of will.

"The only side I am on is yours," she said. "I was trying to support you through an understandably difficult moment—"

"It was not difficult," he said coldly. "I had everything in hand before you interfered."

"That is unfair." His accusation stung. "While your brother deserves your animosity, his wife and children do not. They are blameless, victims as you are—"

"Do not compare them to me." His snarl ripped through the cabin. "Katerina, Anne, and the rest of Robert's bloodline are nothing like me. They were not beaten within an inch of their lives by him. They were not separated from the only person who cared about them, then locked away for nearly a decade of unspeakable abuse. They do not know the first thing about suffering and pain. They've lived in the lap of luxury, and the only price was to pledge their allegiance to a monster."

While Gigi knew that Conrad could be ruthless in business, she hadn't until this moment realized he could be heartless in relationships. Certainly, he'd discussed his past lovers with a degree of indifference, but she'd believed those relationships had been transactional and nothing more. She'd also believed him when he said he felt differently about *her*. Love, she'd told herself, would make all the difference.

Unwelcome thoughts crept into her head.

How well do I know him? After all, he has kept secrets from me...

Her love and knowledge of his past tempered her doubts. Robert Beaumont *was* a vile man who'd inflicted unimaginable suffering on Conrad. It was only human for Conrad to want justice. Although he had kept secrets from her, he had eventually trusted her with facts that were not the easiest to share. Over time, he *was* opening up to her.

"Robert's wife and daughters had no part in what he did to you," she said gently. "They likely didn't even know of your existence."

"My mama was equally blameless," he shot back. "As was I.

That didn't stop Robert. Now, he will reap what he sowed. The people closest to him will suffer for what he did. *He* is the one causing them pain, not me."

"While Robert is responsible, you would be making the choice to hurt innocent people, too. You would be acting like him—"

In the next instant, Conrad was leaning over her. His hands planted on the cabin walls, he caged her. His savage expression reminded her of the satyr's. Her heart thumped...not entirely because of anxiety. Her husband's nearness, his intensity, stirred a primal response.

"Do not compare me with that bastard," he said in a low, dangerous tone.

"I know you are not like Robert." She wetted her lips. "Nonetheless, his wife and daughters...they are your family."

Conrad's gaze was fixed on her mouth. The tension between them sizzled, even as it took a different form.

"*You* are my family, Gigi," he said. "Your loyalty, your love—all of you belongs to *me*."

"That isn't the point—"

"I think it is. I think you need to be made aware of what those vows you gave me mean. I think you need to be shown who you belong to."

When he shoved himself from the wall, she didn't know whether to be relieved or disappointed. Then his hands went to his waistband. Casually, he unfastened his trousers. Hard and swollen, his cock jutted from the fine wool like an angry beast. The stiff truncheon swayed when the carriage went over a bump, and he grabbed the strap to steady himself. She knew this was no way to end an argument; they ought to sort out their problems. When he began to pump his fist along his impressive length, however, she grew mortifyingly wet.

"What do you think you are doing?" The breathiness of her voice betrayed her. "We have matters to discuss."

"I'm done discussing. I have a better use for that lovely mouth of yours."

He brought his cock within an inch of her lips. The dome was flared and dripping. She smelled his unique musk, and her mouth pooled.

She looked up at his glinting gaze. "How does this solve anything?"

"It will make me feel better," he said in gravelly tones. "As my wife, don't you want to see to my needs?"

She could have denied him, and maybe she ought to. Yet his domineering attitude, while annoying, was also arousing, stirring an instinctual desire to please. And she didn't doubt that he needed soothing. While his words spoke of lust, the emotions radiating from him spoke of other needs as well.

A need to bind her to him with passion. To stake his claim on her loyalty and heart.

While she could have told him that those things were *fait accompli*, she saw in his shadowed expression that he wasn't in a place readily reached by words. He wanted action...of the most carnal kind. Her blood thrummed with the recognition that she wanted it too.

"We are talking after," she told him.

"After." Triumph sharpened his features. "Now open wide for me, love."

Trembling, she acquiesced to the lewd command, and a heartbeat later, his cock was a heated weight upon her tongue. His salty essence saturated her senses even before he pushed in. Given their earlier practice, she expected the inexplicably exciting sensation of having her mouth filled, yet there was a difference this time. Before, Conrad had let her explore as she wished.

Now he was setting the pace.

He thrust in, going deeper than he ever had. When she tried to close her hand around the base of his shaft, he prevented her from doing so. To her surprise, he placed her gloved palms, one by one, onto his thighs.

"Keep them there," he ordered. "Let me use your lovely mouth as I wish."

The word "use" set off a wicked tingle. In her mind's eye, she saw Pearl kneeling before Prick with her hands just so while he took his pleasure. While all the drawings had been provocative, Gigi had found this one particularly arresting. For the satyr had sheathed himself so completely that the nymph's lips had kissed his stones. With his fingers curled in her tresses, his eyes rolled back in bliss, he'd looked completely and utterly undone. In truth, he had been the one brought to his knees.

Could I do that to Conrad? Unravel his self-control? In opening myself to him, am I opening him up to me?

The notion intrigued and aroused, but Gigi didn't have time for contemplation. Her hands curled around his sinewy thighs as he drove deeper. Her lips stretching to accommodate his girth, she had to breathe through her nose, so fully did he occupy her.

"Such a good little wife," he growled. "Letting me swive your mouth. But you like it, don't you? Beneath that pretty gown, is your pussy full of cream?"

Oh my stars.

Squeezing her legs together, she felt the slickness smearing her thighs. Her nipples were throbbing points. She moaned, the sound muffled by the shaft stretching her lips.

"That is a sweet sound, duchess. Let me feel you moan around my cock."

She couldn't disobey him if she tried. She was too aroused, too lost in the filthy thrill of what they were doing. Conrad slid a hand in her hair, scattering pins. His grip was rough, just tight enough to elicit an arousing discomfort. Yet it was the control this gave him that stirred her the most. The way he held her head in place so that he could take her as he wished.

He drove his hips, and she felt a thrill of panic as he went farther than he had before. So far that he nearly cut off her air. Through eyelashes dewy with effort, she saw that she hadn't even taken all of him.

"Relax, love. I will take care of you. Give yourself to me."

His tender words, uttered while he plunged his cock even deeper, caused her heart and her pussy to flutter. She had joined her life with this man, for better or worse...*Ad Finem Fidelis*. Even if she disagreed with his path to revenge, she trusted him to make the right decision. Once he was calmer—once the wounds ripped open by the meeting with Robert had healed—he would listen to reason. Until then, she would soothe the beast, and in doing so, surrender to her own passions.

The instant she let go, tension left her. She relaxed into the hand cradling her skull, the relentless incursion of his cock. His taste and touch felt essential, and she wanted to be what he needed: a vessel for his pleasure, a companion for his loneliness, a mate for his soul. She craved the intensity of his attentions, the way his gaze was riveted to her face as he pushed deep inside.

"Just so, love." Pleasure roughened his voice. "Relax your throat and take all of me."

Somehow she was doing it. Controlling her natural reflexes and letting him in. She drew a breath through her nose as he breached her throat. He withdrew then plunged, and she felt the shocking sensation: the press of his stones against her lips.

"Christ, I'm a lucky bastard. I married the best little cocksucker."

His rude praise made her whimper, eager to earn more. Wetness coated her chin as he buried his cock again and again, grunting with bliss. His gaze remained locked on hers, smoldering with a heady mix of love, lust, and pride.

"Mine," he said.

He lunged his hips, the tip of his cock nudging muscles that clenched around him. Groaning, he drew out while she sputtered, but then he slid back in, pairing his thrusts with panted words.

"You're not theirs. You're mine. Say it, Gigi."

He yanked out, the wide dome of his cock hovering by her mouth, glossy from her kiss.

Knowing what he wanted, she gave it to him. "I'm yours."

"My nymph." He shoved inside, claiming her in action and in words. "My wife and my mate. You'll never leave me."

"I won't leave," she gasped when he gave her the chance. "Trust me, Conrad."

His eyes blazed with emotion. "I do. More than anyone. *I love you.*"

"I love you," she whispered back.

Her words unleashed an animalistic frenzy. He mated her mouth, cramming himself inside. She felt his possession everywhere, her pussy clenching at his filling thrusts. He was close, she could tell, his girth stretching her to her limits, his stones slapping against her lips.

"I want to spend inside," he growled.

The notion flashed heat across her senses. He'd stilled, his body rigid with the effort to hold himself in check. He was waiting for permission, she realized. When she nodded, his nostrils flared, and with no hesitation, he took what she offered. He pounded into her mouth, his hand a vise in her hair, his eyes glowing with dark adoration.

"I am going to come so hard," he rasped. "Every drop is for you, Gigi."

Suddenly, he held, grinding against her lips. He came with a savage shout. His pleasure flooded her in hot, salty bursts, and mindless with need, she swallowed what she could. The rest spilled over her lips and down her chin.

His chest heaving, he collapsed onto the bench, gathering her onto his lap. He kissed her slowly, thoroughly, not seeming to mind that she tasted of him. In fact, he seemed to like it, and the thought made her squirm with arousal against his hard thighs.

"Thank you, my love." While her husband exuded satisfaction, the hunger in his eyes was far from satiated. "Now it's your turn."

Chapter Thirty-Three

When Conrad awoke, he was instantly aware that Gigi was not beside him. This was displeasing. However, he was reassured by her lingering scent, which told him she hadn't been gone long. Perhaps she needed a moment alone after the intensity of last night.

Perhaps he did, too.

Fitting his hands behind his head, he stared into the dark, swirling canopy of his bed. He'd tested her limits last night. At first, he'd worried that maybe he'd gone too far: that he ought to have waited before coming down his near-virgin bride's throat. What he'd discovered between Gigi's sleek thighs had relieved his concerns. Her pussy had been so swollen and ripe that it had required only a few licks before her sweet juice filled his mouth.

That had been in the carriage. When they arrived home, he'd carried her to his bedchamber and made love to her through the night. They'd fallen asleep, entwined and momentarily appeased. Now thoughts of their intimacies—including how she'd cried her climax into the pillow while he'd shafted her from behind—had given him a morning cockstand that tented the bedsheet. He thought about hunting Gigi down and giving her another injection of marital bliss...yet something stopped him.

I must talk to her first. I must tell her about Pearce.

Unease slithered through him as he recalled her reaction to his plans for Robert's family. The way she'd taken *their* side instead of his. His dominant behavior in the carriage had stemmed partly from a need to reinforce their bond—to show her how fully she belonged to him. He needed to know that, come what may, he could count on her loyalty.

While they hadn't yet discussed the ball, he knew she didn't agree with his method of justice. If Gigi had any faults, it was that she was too tender-hearted. Her empathy and sheltered upbringing blinded her to the harsh realities of life. The duchess and Lady Anne might weep at the prospect of having their lives of privilege and luxury ripped away, but that was too damned bad. They'd made their bed and now they had to lie in it. Moreover, the argument that they were "family" held no water. If the situation were reversed, if Conrad needed help from Lady Katerina, she would probably spit on him.

Vengeance was the goal that Conrad had been working toward for decades—that defined him not as a victim but as a victor. He'd expected Gigi to see his point of view, yet she'd advocated for his enemy. This did not bode well, especially as it pertained to his plans for Abel Pearce. All along, Conrad had told himself that once she was his, she would understand why he needed to destroy that which Pearce most cared about. Why selling Chuddums off piece by piece until there was nothing remaining of Pearce's legacy was a necessary act of justice.

Worry gnawed at him. Maybe he should have told Gigi earlier, but the time had never felt right. He hadn't felt certain enough of her love...until now. Last night, she'd surrendered to him so sweetly, and if she could trust him to have his depraved way with her, then surely she could take his side against Pearce.

In his head, he prepared concessions. He would spare Miss

Letty's spa. If Gigi's other friends needed work, he would see to it that they were not left in the cold. He would toss out his idea to develop a bustling square for them...just not in Chuddums. Truth be told, he'd avoided this conversation long enough. News of Pearce's misfortune might have hit the village by now, and Conrad wanted to be the one to break the news to Gigi.

When she didn't return to bed, he rang for his valet and got dressed. He found her downstairs in the drawing room. Sunlight streamed through the window, gilding her upswept raven locks and rich burgundy dress. She was scribbling at the escritoire but smiled at him as he approached. Tipping her chin up, he gave her a thorough morning kiss.

"You look hard at work," he murmured.

"I felt uncommonly energized this morning." She gave him a teasing look from beneath her long lashes. "Which is odd, given how little I actually slept."

"Blame yourself." He ran a thumb along her cheekbone. "You are quite the distraction, love."

"The feeling is mutual."

He was about to kiss her again when Owen stalked into the room.

"Good morning," he said. "Hope I'm not interrupting."

"Actually, I need to speak with my wife—" Conrad began.

"You're not," Gigi said.

Since they'd spoken simultaneously, Gigi tipped her head at him.

"Was there something you wished to discuss?" she asked.

No. Yes. Bloody hell, stop being a namby-pamby and tell her about Pearce.

"As a matter of fact, yes. In private."

Owen was retracing his steps to the door just as the butler opened it. One look at the old retainer's visage, and Conrad's gut tightened.

"What is it, Yardley?"

"Lady Georgiana's family has arrived, sir." The butler cleared his throat. "And they are demanding to see her. *Immediately.*"

Gigi braced herself as Mama and Papa entered, followed by Ethan and James. Her family's grim expressions heightened her guilt and anxiety, and she hurried toward them.

"Hello, everyone. How did you get my letter so quickly? I thought you would still be at Grove Hall—"

"Is it true, Georgiana?" Papa thundered. "Did this blackguard trick you into marrying him?"

She'd never seen her father so enraged. The steel in his eyes flashed, his posture rigid and hands fisted for battle. Behind him, James and Ethan had similar stances.

"Conrad didn't trick me into anything," she said quickly. "Did you read my letter? In it, I explained—"

"We did not read your letter."

Mama's gaze was narrowed upon Conrad, who stood beside Gigi. Tension came off him in waves, adding to her fears that this encounter with her family would go even worse than the last. She couldn't let that happen.

"Then how did you know that Conrad and I are wed?" she asked.

It was the first time she'd confirmed the status of her marriage. Seeing its effect on her kin—her papa looked staggered, her mama pale—she almost wished she could take it back. But it was the truth and the path she'd chosen to take.

"It's all over London," James said tersely. "The town is abuzz with how you showed up at the Grantley ball with Godwin—or Christian Beaufort or whatever the blazes his name is. There is wild speculation about what prompted your marriage and whether you had our support. I was swarmed the moment I set foot in my club this morning."

"I will explain everything, I promise. However." Gigi drew her brows together. "What are you doing in London? I thought you were at Grove Hall for the week."

"We came to London because we were concerned about Godwin's interest in you," Papa said tightly. "James felt, as I did, that something was not right about Godwin's appearance in Chuddums. Why would a man of his financial stature be interested in a sleepy village? We came to London to investigate the issue."

"You investigated me?" Conrad's voice was low and menacing.

"We will do anything that is required to protect Gigi." This came from Ethan, whose countenance was stormy. "Marriage can be undone. You wed her under fraudulent pretenses, which is grounds for an annulment."

"Gigi knows who I am," Conrad fired back. "And you will be laughed out of the courts if you claim my deception, as it were, harmed her in any way. Not only am I rich, but I am also going to make her a duchess before long."

"Do you think we care about a bloody title?" Papa roared. "It is your character, sir, that makes you unfit for my daughter. You have deceived an innocent girl at every turn, and when she finds out your true nature, she will leave you."

"The hell she will—"

"*No.* No more fighting."

Panicked, Gigi moved in between Conrad and her father.

"Please, Papa," she begged. "Conrad hasn't deceived me. He didn't even know I was coming to see him. I found a clue, you see, concerning the attempt on his life. As it was important, I felt I should deliver it personally, and Owen escorted me—"

"To be clear," Owen muttered. "I did not volunteer."

"Fine, I *dragged* Owen here. When I arrived, Conrad and I came to an understanding. While unexpected, it was not in any way coerced. He asked me to marry him, and I said yes. Willingly. Because I love him." She gazed beseechingly at her family. "We Harringtons have always married for love, and I promise you I have upheld that tradition. I know I should have waited for your permission and hope in time you will forgive me, but, well, love can make one impetuous. I didn't want to wait a moment longer to be Conrad's wife."

"Oh, Gigi." The pain in Mama's expression stabbed her heart. "Oh my dear girl, do you know the man you have married?"

Gigi slanted an uncertain look at Conrad. He was impassive, his eyes as cold as a winter sea.

"It is true that Conrad didn't tell me his identity until after we were married. But he had good reasons for it," she said quickly. "Reasons that are his to share, if he wishes, but which I can assure you make perfect sense. Moreover, none of that changes how I feel about him."

"Did he tell you about his dealings with Abel Pearce?" James asked.

Her brother's inquiry slid like a cool droplet down her spine.

Frowning, she said, "What about Mr. Pearce?"

"Do you want to tell her, Godwin?" James lifted his brows. "Or shall I?"

When Conrad said nothing, his jaw tight, Gigi felt a pulse of fear.

"What is it?" she whispered. "What involvement do you have with Mr. Pearce?"

"I'll explain everything," he gritted out. "In private—"

"There is no way in hell I am letting my sister be alone with you," Ethan snarled. "Nor will she want to, after she discovers your plans for Chuddums."

Chuddums? Why would Conrad have plans for the village?

Her heart thudding, Gigi said, "Please. Someone tell me what is going on."

James took pity on her. "A few days ago, the bubble burst on a railway scheme engineered by a fellow named Jonah Westfield. It's all over the papers. Investors have lost everything."

"That is horrible, but how is that relevant—"

"Abel Pearce was among the investors. He went all in, and now he doesn't have a penny to rub together. Even worse, he was already up to his eyebrows in debt. His properties in Chuddums are mortgaged to the hilt, and suddenly his loans were called in. The news spread like wildfire through the county. When I heard, I had a suspicion that I could only confirm in London."

Gigi glanced at Conrad, and his stony expression sent her anxieties spiraling.

"What suspicion?" she asked, her voice trembling.

"The timing of Pearce's downfall with Godwin's appearance seemed more than coincidental," James said matter-of-factly. "My man of business knows the head clerk in Westfield's office, and he was able to find out more about Pearce. Apparently, Pearce was a recent investor, and the clerk remembered how he'd bragged about being referred by 'the famous Conrad Godwin himself.'"

"Conrad?" Gigi stared at her husband. "Is this true?"

"Pearce asked my advice, and I gave it," he said flatly. "Look, there are things you don't know. Things I will explain when we are in private—"

"So that you can tell my sister further lies?" James's mouth curled in a sneer. "No, Godwin, she will hear the truth. Not only did you deliberately entice Pearce into investing in a faulty scheme, you had an ulterior motive for doing so. I had my man of business investigate Pearce's debts. Apparently, one by one, his loans were bought up by a holding company called Sterling Capital. The company has remarkable legal scaffolding to hide its owner, and I almost stopped digging until I discovered Sterling Capital owned a company I was familiar with. One that Gigi once asked me to look into: Empire Investment. The firm that tried to buy Miss Letty's spa."

Sucking in a breath, Gigi turned to Conrad. "You own Empire Investment. Do you own Sterling Capital as well?"

"I do," he said curtly. "That is what I wished to discuss with you this morning. Before your family's unannounced arrival."

"What were you going to say?" Her head was spinning. "That you deliberately ruined Mr. Pearce so that you could take over Chuddums?"

"No, my grievance is with Pearce," he stated. "He wronged me, Gigi—grievously so. Gaining control of Chuddums was part of my plan to gain justice."

"This is about revenge...again?"

She stared at him, seeing the Viking in a gentleman's suit. Everyone had told her he was a ruthless man, and she'd seen the evidence herself. Yet she'd made excuses and willingly let herself be deceived. Fissures spread through her heart as she looked at her husband and wondered if she knew him at all.

She took a breath. "What are you planning to do to Chuddums?"

Conrad hated being backed into the ropes. It was a weak position, where you found yourself defending against blows until one finally knocked you out. In this case, he wasn't just facing his supposedly loyal wife: the entire Harrington clan was taking jabs at him.

Stay calm. You knew Gigi would find out eventually. Just explain everything, and she will understand.

As much as he resented having to share his past with anyone but Gigi, he had no choice.

"I am related to Abel Pearce," he said. "On my mother's side."

Gigi stared at him, her lips pressed together.

"You'll recall that my papa died when I was not yet eight. My brother Robert became my guardian and decided to send me to Creavey Hall."

There was still no response from Gigi, but he heard the marchioness exhale. He wouldn't be surprised if she'd heard of the school. It had a notorious reputation.

"My mama didn't want us to be separated," he said gruffly. "I told you she promised to find a solution, and that is where Abel Pearce came in. He and my mama were descendants of Langdon Pearce's sons; their great-grandfathers were brothers. Abel's family stayed in Chuddums, while my mama's left. Nonetheless, my mama's branch of the family retained the deed to a local cottage, and my mama was so desperate that she took me to see Pearce.

"She told him our situation. Begged him to honor the deed that had been passed down to her so that we might have shelter from Robert's cruelty. At the time, Pearce was a wealthy man, and it would have cost him nothing to save my mama's life and mine. But he refused."

"Why?" Gigi said quietly.

"Because of indifference." The dark undertow of fury sucked at him. "Because he was too busy, too important, to give a damn."

"He wronged you," Gigi said.

"He bloody well did," Conrad agreed. "That is why he is getting what he deserves. I am going to take away what he took away from me: everything. I am going to destroy his legacy by selling it off piece by piece. By the time I am finished, no one will even remember the name Pearce."

"In the process..." Gigi's violet gaze held his. "You will destroy Chuddums."

"I will not touch Miss Letty's spa," he assured her. "I promised you that, and I am a man of my word."

"What of the other villagers? Have you thought about them?"

He didn't like the accusation in her eyes.

"They are not my problem," he said brusquely. "The way

Pearce was managing his affairs, it was only a matter of time before he would have to sell off the square—"

"Mr. Khan isn't your problem? The Thorntons? Mrs. Pettigrew and Wally?" Gigi's voice rose.

He strove to hold onto his patience. "If they need work, I'll find them jobs elsewhere. Maybe I'll develop a square in a more profitable place than Chuddums—"

"The villagers are not cattle to be herded from one place to the next!" She balled her hands. "Do you know what the irony is? All of them speak of you with *admiration*. They say you are a fine addition to the village and hoped you would take up permanent residence at Honeystone Hall. Yet this entire time, you were a wolf in sheep's clothing. No, I take that back. You didn't even bother to wear a costume. I pulled the wool over my own dashed eyes!"

"Gigi—"

"You lied to me, Conrad. Time and again. And before you argue"—she held up a hand—"lying by omission is still *lying*."

Feeling the ropes biting into his back, he reacted as he always did: by going on the offensive.

"I have never hidden the kind of man I am," he shot back. "Yet you came to London to find me. You let me put my ring on your finger, and you gave me your vows. Which means your loyalty belongs to me—not to Grantley's family, Pearce, or those bleeding Chuddumites."

"This isn't about loyalty, you bounder," Gigi cried. "Not mine, anyway. You are the one keeping secrets. You are the one hiding things from *me*."

"I've told you my reasons," he snarled. "I've explained myself to you and your goddamned family, and that should be bloody enough."

"It's not."

Her tone felt like a slap.

"I beg your pardon?" he said icily.

"To ruin your enemies, will you sacrifice the lives of innocents?

Do you care nothing about the good and decent folk who will be caught in the crossfire? For the sake of revenge, are you willing to become like those men who hurt you?"

"Do not compare me with those bastards! You know what they did to me. What I suffered—"

"Yet you are willing to inflict suffering on blameless villagers? Listen to me." Gigi was as stern as he'd ever seen her. "You have the opportunity to be different from those who hurt you. Instead of destroying lives, you could save them. Chuddums has much to offer. Look how far my scheme with the water has gone. You could use your wealth and skill to help the economy grow—"

"You are wasting your breath, daughter." The marquess regarded Conrad as if he were vermin. "A leopard does not change its spots. Godwin has, and always will be, a man without ethics or principles. He is not good enough for you."

The pressure shot up in Conrad's veins. "You know nothing about me, you judgmental bastard. I have my reasons—"

"Do *not* speak to my papa that way." Her eyes flaring, Gigi set her shoulders back. "I don't care about your reasons. All I care about now is what you will do with Chuddums."

She doesn't care about my reasons? What I've gone through? She cares more about those stupid villagers than me—her own husband?

His vision flashed scarlet.

"You wish to hear my plan? Here it is. I am going to sell that place off to the highest bidders, brick by brick," he said concisely. "I will make a tidy profit, but the true returns will come from the satisfaction of wiping Abel Pearce's legacy from the face of this earth."

"If you do this, you are not the man I believed you to be. The man I thought I married would never choose vengeance over everything...over love." Her voice wavered, but her resolve clearly did not. "If you destroy Chuddums, our marriage is over."

It had been a long while since anyone dared to give him an ultimatum. To be issued one from Gigi, the one person he'd trusted with his darkest secrets, felt like a knife between the shoulder blades—like the inflicting of all the scars on his back combined. Worst of all, he felt panic whirling inside him. The closing in of the dark forest.

Chest heaving, he jabbed a finger at her. "You do not get to make that decision."

"I am leaving," Gigi said. "If you change your mind, you know where to find me."

She turned her back on him.

Turned. Her. Back.

A moment later, she walked out.

Chapter Thirty-Four

"Certain I can't persuade you to stay in the carriage, guv?"

The question came from Adrian Foxworth, the investigator hired by Conrad to find the cutthroat who'd tried to kill him. In his late forties, with thick salt-and-pepper hair and tilted hazel eyes, Foxworth had come through for Conrad in the past, and this time was no different. He'd traced the pawn ticket Gigi had found to a shop in Spitalfields and persuaded the owner to give up the client's name and address. As it turned out, "John Brown" was an alias of Gregory Johnson, who lived in a nearby tenement.

When Foxworth informed Conrad of the development, Conrad had decided to go along. Currently, he, Foxworth, and three of the latter's men were monitoring Johnson's tenement. Foxworth and Conrad were parked in a carriage in the lane behind the building, watching the rear gate. People had come and gone, none of them matching the description of the waiter at the gala.

Taking out his pistol, Conrad checked that it was ready for use.

"If Johnson shows up, I can handle myself," he said.

"I don't doubt it." Foxworth was gazing through a slit in the curtains. "But I make it a policy not to put clients in danger."

Truth be told, Conrad wouldn't mind a little violence. Since Gigi left yesterday, he'd teetered between rage and despair, and he craved an outlet for his roiling emotions. A few moments when he didn't have to feel the swirling emptiness inside him. When he didn't have to see the hurt in Gigi's eyes...as if he had somehow betrayed her. While he could concede that he probably ought to have told her his plans earlier, her reaction had been proof positive of why he hadn't.

She claimed to love me. Yet when push came to shove, she left. Just like everyone else.

He couldn't believe that she had given him an ultimatum. That she would make him choose between her or his revenge. He despised manipulation and yet... Now that his temper was cooling a little, he also felt prickling unease.

For the sake of revenge, are you willing to become like those men who hurt you?

He wanted justice for what had been done to him. His intention wasn't to hurt innocent people...and, he thought righteously, he was willing to give the Chuddumites jobs. He'd even offered to build them a square. But that wasn't good enough for Gigi. No, she wanted...what the hell did she want, anyway?

You are the one keeping secrets. You are the one hiding things from me.

The feeling of discomfort grew. While Gigi had given him an ultimatum, she wasn't trying to manipulate him for her own gain. What she wanted was honesty and trust...things she had a right to ask for in a marriage. Things that he, himself, valued. She wanted him to do right by the people of Chuddums who, for some godforsaken reason, had welcomed him into their odd little fold. He thought of all the well-wishers who'd interrupted his packing, of Kenneth pestering him for lessons, of Wally's interminable tours... and Christ.

For the first time in a long time, he felt...ashamed.

"Eyes up, guv. We 'ave movement."

Shoving aside his jumbled thoughts, Conrad looked out the window. A man with his cap pulled low and a scarf hiding his face had exited the tenement and was headed in their direction.

"Is that the cove?" Foxworth said.

"I didn't notice him at the gala, but his height and build matches what the others described."

"Let's have a chat wif 'im, then. I'll go first, so as not to scare 'im. If it looks like I need help, you back me up."

Before Conrad could argue, Foxworth alighted from the carriage and approached the man.

"Afternoon, sir," Foxworth said. "I was looking for a friend o' mine who lives near—"

The man pulled out a pistol and fired. The rest seemed to happen in slowed time. Foxworth fell to the ground. The driver shouted something from the perch, and the man fired at him before turning and running down the alley in the opposite direction.

Shaking off his paralysis, Conrad leapt from the carriage. He checked on Foxworth, who gasped, "Bullet passed through my shoulder. I'm fine—"

"I've got him." The driver rushed over.

Conrad took off after the suspect. If the bounder escaped into the maze of streets beyond the back lane, they would never find him. Conrad pumped his arms, gaining ground. Just as the bastard reached the mouth of the alley, Conrad sprang. He tackled the other, dirt spuming as they hit the ground. They wrestled; Conrad's opponent was strong, refusing to be subdued. The man's hat flew off, revealing brown hair and a visage with prominent eyebrows that fit the description of Gregory Johnson.

Just when Conrad thought he had Johnson pinned, the man kneed him in the groin. The dirty move made him see stars and momentarily lose his grip. The other threw him off and made a run for it. Conrad caught Johnson by the shoulder, but the other's coat tore, leaving him with a handful of fabric. The man escaped into the street, narrowly missing an oncoming omnibus. The vehicle trapped Conrad in the lane and blocked his pursuit of the suspect.

"Move," Conrad yelled. "Get out of the way."

"Bugger off," the omnibus driver yelled back. "Can't you see there's a block-up ahead?"

By the time the omnibus moved, Conrad knew it was too late. He raced into the congested street, surveying the snarl of people, carriages, and carts. Seeing no sign of the suspect, Conrad let out a string of oaths.

I almost had him. I was this bloody close.

Turning back, he bent to pick up the section torn from the suspect's coat. The brown kersey was thin and cheap, and when he searched the fabric for clues, he felt a lump in the inner pocket. Reaching in, he retrieved a small drawstring bag. He loosened the tie and poured the contents into his palm.

He stared at the familiar object, one he would know anywhere. The oval ruby upon the ornate gold band winked with secrets. It was Robert's ring...the one Conrad had seen on his brother's hand last night.

"What is the meaning of this?" Robert cried. "Who are you? How dare you invade my home!"

"I am a constable of the Metropolitan Police, Your Grace," the man in the dark-blue uniform said. "I am here to arrest you under the suspicion of attempted murder. You must come with me to the station at once."

"Can't you see my husband is very ill?" Lady Katerina stood by Robert's wheeled chair, pale and trembling. "Clearly, he is not capable of what you are accusing him of—"

"We believe that this was an attempted murder by hire."

The constable showed the duchess the ruby ring that Conrad had recovered.

"Do you recognize this, madam?"

"I...well, yes. I think I do."

Lady Katerina cast an uncertain look at her husband, who was swatting at the surrounding constables.

"It looks like Robert's ring." Her voice held a tremor. "The one given to him by his father."

"Indeed, your husband's initials are inscribed on the inside of the band," the constable informed her. "This ring was found in the possession of a man named Gregory Johnson, who we suspect tried to murder Mr. Godwin."

"Lies! Lies!" Robert shrieked.

"There...there must be some mistake." Lady Katerina turned to Conrad. "I beg of you, sir. I know there is bad blood between you and Robert. Whatever he did to you, look at him now. Surely, he is paying for his sins. If that is not sufficient atonement, you will soon be the Duke of Grantley. My daughters and I will be at your mercy. Are you not satisfied?"

Staring into those lifeless eyes, Conrad felt a spike of pity.

"There is nothing I can do, ma'am," he said. "Robert must pay for his crime."

"You're a lying bastard!" Spittle clung to Robert's cracked lips, his sunken eyes glowing with hatred. "You're behind this. You want to destroy me!"

Staring at the pitiful, shriveled, and decaying man, Conrad expected to feel some sort of emotion. Some satisfaction, maybe relief. Instead, he felt nothing.

"I did want to destroy you," he said. "However, you saved me the trouble and did it to yourself."

Robert was still yelling as the constables wheeled him away.

Chapter Thirty-Five

"Shopping is a lovely distraction," Xenia said brightly. "Thank you for suggesting it, Evie."

"You're welcome." James's wife, Evie, the Countess of Manderly, smiled in her shy way.

Gigi was strolling along the square with her two sisters-in-law. A curvy, bespectacled blonde, Evie preferred her studies to socializing. According to James, she was happiest in the greenhouse he'd built her, where she conducted experiments with plants. Gigi was touched that Evie had made the trip to check up on her.

Three days had passed since Gigi's return to Chuddums, and she'd spent the bulk of it weeping in her bedchamber. She was grateful that her family had forgiven her for her reckless behavior... if only she could forgive herself as easily. She'd been a fool to entrust her heart to Conrad. Despite all the evidence pointing to his ruthlessness—his business dealings, sabotage of the spa, plan for revenge against his brother—she had given him the benefit of the doubt.

Over and again, she'd made excuses. She'd rationalized that he had a good heart, and because of his past, he merely needed time to trust and love again. She saw the extent of her self-deception. He'd been manipulating her, lying to her about his motivations this entire time. Now, because of her, the fate of Chuddums hung in the balance.

"Truth be told, my motivation was a bit selfish," Evie said. "Since this is my first visit to Chuddums, I wanted to see the square myself. James has spoken highly of it."

"You might as well see it now. While you still can," Gigi said bleakly.

"Oh, my dear." Empathy and worry shone in Xenia's eyes. "Do you think Mr. Godwin intends to go through with his plan?"

"I don't know what he is going to do. In his letter, he did not mention specifics."

Gigi had received a note from Conrad this morning, which she'd shown her sisters-in-law.

Dearest Gigi,

Much has happened since we parted. Due to the pawn ticket you found, a connection was made between the assailant at the gala and my brother. Robert is now in police custody. As his days are numbered, he will spend the rest of his life behind bars.

The threat to my life is over. I have given orders to my guards that you no longer require protection, and I breathe easier knowing that my presence in your life does not compromise your well-being.

There is much left unsaid between us, and I ask that you grant me an audience so that I may better explain my behavior and the actions I have taken. I will return to Chuddums in a week's time to discuss our future. Despite our separation, you are in my thoughts, and it is my greatest hope that we will soon come to a mutual understanding.

Your husband,
C.

"As someone who has not met Mr. Godwin, I know I am not the best judge of his character," Evie said. "But I thought there were hopeful aspects to his letter. For example, he seems quite concerned for your welfare."

"I was surprised to learn that he had guards following me," Gigi admitted.

She wasn't sure how she felt about it. On the one hand, his tendency to take covert actions and keep things to himself played a large role in their marital conflict. On the other, maybe it was his way of showing that he cared.

"Conrad's protectiveness probably doesn't mean anything," she went on with a sigh. "He would act that way toward anything he considers a possession. To him, I'm no different from a piece of property."

That, she realized, was what hurt the most. She'd fallen in love with him, but to him, she was just part of some plan. He wanted a nymph who would soothe his lust and a duchess who would enhance his prestige.

He never took me seriously—never saw me for who I am. He was just using me. And I was foolish enough to give him my heart.

Evie pursed her lips. "Don't you think it is a good sign that he wishes to come to an understanding with you?"

"The problem is that his version of an understanding and mine are different. I've told Conrad what it will take to heal our marriage, but I know him. He is used to getting what he wants. He thinks he can negotiate his way out of this. That he can appease me with some trifling offer."

"Building a square elsewhere for the villagers is not exactly a trifling matter," Xenia said dryly. "But I see your point. He does not understand what Chuddums means to you and, more importantly, to the people who live here."

"Precisely." Gigi gave a morose nod.

Xenia hesitated. "This may not be my place to say…"

"Do speak freely, dear."

"As a woman married to a man who likes to, ahem, dig his heels in—"

"Ethan can be as stubborn as an ox," Gigi said. "You might as well say it."

"Well, your Mr. Godwin strikes me as a man who is similar in this regard. And from personal experience, I can say that issuing an ultimatum to an obstinate fellow is unlikely to be productive," Xenia said earnestly. "Your threat to end your marriage might have led Mr. Godwin to feel backed into a corner. Therefore, he attacked you when, instead, he should have tried to work out a compromise."

Gigi mulled over the confrontation.

"I was hurt and angry," she confessed. "Because of that, I wasn't the best of listeners. And I think…I think I did lash out at him."

"You had reason to feel as you did," Xenia said.

However, the more Gigi reflected upon her behavior, the more she regretted it.

"Conrad is obstinate, but he learned to be that way because of his past. He's had to fight to survive. People—evil people—have had him against the ropes time and again, and only his determination saved him."

Oh my stars. Did I corner Conrad, emotionally speaking? Did I escalate our conflict?

"Once cooler heads have prevailed, it will be easier to have a constructive conversation," Xenia said. "You may come to an understanding yet."

"I hope you are right." Gigi sighed. "Do you want to know the greatest irony? I thought that he and I were like Thomas and Rosalinda. That, despite our differences, we were destined to be together…destined to meet here in Chuddums. I even thought that…that…"

"Yes, dear?" Xenia murmured.

"I thought that maybe our love was going to help break the

curse." A tear slid down her cheek. "Yet instead of saving Chuddums, I have helped to destroy it."

Xenia put an arm around her shoulders. "Speak to Mr. Godwin first. Wait until he tells you his intentions before jumping to conclusions."

"And if my fears come to pass?" she asked tearfully. "If Conrad chooses his vengeance over our marriage?"

"Then you will deal with that if it happens. With your family by your side."

"*Ad Finem Fidelis.*" Evie passed her a handkerchief.

"Thank you both." Drying her cheeks, Gigi summoned a smile. "I don't know what I would do without you."

The trio wandered through the square, which was ominously quiet. Since the news had broken that Mr. Pearce had lost everything, including his properties in Chuddums, anxious despair had gripped the village. Gigi knew the feeling. She felt as empty as some of the shop windows, as cold as the breeze that swirled up dried leaves and deposited them along the base of the now obsolete monument.

To distract herself, Gigi focused on Evie. While lovely, Evie wasn't the chattiest of ladies, which made it difficult to ascertain the situation between her and James. Moreover, when the conversation veered toward more personal topics, Evie deftly redirected it to her work. Gigi was getting an earful about the critical role of pollination when Mrs. Sommers came hurrying toward them.

"Is something amiss, Mrs. Sommers?" she asked.

"Forgive my manners, but I am afraid there is." The modiste darted her gaze over the square. "Have you seen Kenneth? He was supposed to come back to the shop for lunch, but he did not show."

"We haven't seen him," Gigi said. "But we would be glad to help you look."

"Thank you. Ordinarily, I wouldn't intrude, but my poor boy has been targeted by bullies—"

"Say no more," Xenia said. "Let us split up to cover more ground."

Xenia paired with Mrs. Sommers and Gigi with Evie. After seeing no sign of Kenny on their side of the square, Gigi led the way to the streets behind it.

"Conrad once caught bullies beating Kenny in one of the back lanes," she said anxiously. "Maybe the poor lad was cornered there again."

They searched a couple of alleyways to no avail. As they explored a third, Gigi had to cover her nose to block the stench coming from the large piles of rubbish. Suddenly, a figure materialized at the end of the lane. Gigi's heart raced as he came closer and she recognized him: the waiter from the gala. He held a gun.

"Run, Evie," she gasped.

She and Evie turned—but another man had emerged, blocking that path. Beefy and menacing, he, too, aimed a pistol at them. They were trapped.

"The first one to make a peep gets a bullet through her brains," he said.

Gigi was about to scream anyway when she was grabbed from behind, a cloth shoved in her face. Sickly sweet fumes choked her. An instant later, she tumbled into oblivion.

When Gigi came to, she found herself sitting on the ground. She tried to move but couldn't. Looking down, she saw ropes circling her arms and torso, binding her to a column. Groggy and confused, she tried to figure out where she was and how she'd come to be here. Panic swelled when she made out beastly shapes lurking in the dimness and the flutter of ghostly forms. Her cry of fear was muffled by her gag.

"Look who is awake," said a strangely familiar voice.

A woman holding a lamp approached, her face hidden by the hood of her cloak. As she traversed the high-ceilinged space, the lamp illuminated passing objects. The shadowy forms weren't animals but old machines...broken looms and spinning mules once used to produce textiles. And the hovering ghosts were remnants of cloth left on the looms.

I'm at the old mill. In a flash, everything returned to Gigi. *Evie and I were looking for Kenny when those bounders kidnapped us. Dear heavens, where is Evie now?*

Looking wildly around, she spotted her sister-in-law bound to another pole. Evie was slumped over, her blonde hair loose and falling over her face. The slow rise and fall of her chest showed that she was alive—*thank heavens.*

The woman stopped in front of Gigi. Crouching, she pulled down Gigi's gag.

"Don't try to scream," she said. "I have a pistol, and I am not afraid to use it."

Shock percolated through Gigi as she stared at her captor.

"Lady Anne?" she said hoarsely. "I don't...I don't understand. Why have you done this?"

"Because my papa is too ill to act and my mama too weak." Anne rose in a graceful movement. "Your husband is trying to destroy my family, and I cannot allow that to happen."

"You...you were behind that falling statue?" Gigi asked in disbelief.

"If the numskull I hired had done his job properly, then Mr. Godwin's death would have looked like an accident. In a perfect world, the knowledge of his claim to my family's title would have died with him. Instead, I had to deal with a botched murder attempt and an uncle who threatened to take away everything from me."

Anger overcame Gigi's fear. "Conrad has a right to the title. Your papa was the one who tried to take away his birthright." A thought occurred to her. "How long have you known that Conrad is your papa's brother?"

"For some time," Anne said mildly. "During bouts of delirium, Papa spoke of his younger half-brother Christian. He confessed his sins—the beatings, the sentencing to Creavey Hall. Mama insisted it was Papa's illness talking, that he would never be capable of such malevolence. Making excuses for him is one of her hobbies. I, however, have never been one to bury my head in the sand. I sold off my jewels to hire an investigator. His discovery that Conrad Godwin was my long-lost uncle coincided with the latter's arrival in London. I knew that Godwin must have some plan up his sleeve."

"Did you tell your father about this?"

"Why would I bother?" Anne said coldly. "The entire situation is of his making. Even before his illness, he never protected me, my mama, or my sisters from harm. He emptied the duchy's coffers, spending it on whores, horses, and cards, with never a thought for us. For anyone but himself. Now he will die alone in a cell, ravaged by a disgusting disease—fitting, I suppose."

Anne's indifference raised the hairs on Gigi's nape.

"He is your papa. While he has committed unpardonable sins, have you no feelings for him?"

Anne tilted her head. "Not really, no. During my time on the marriage mart, he complained about every expense, watched every penny. He called me a 'bad investment' because he claimed I lacked the beauty, charm, and wit to attract a suitor." She scoffed. "What I really needed to land a husband was a dowry, but Papa would rather spend money on the harlots who gave him syphilis than the daughter who could give him grandchildren."

When you put it that way...

Gigi pitied everyone who had the misfortune to be born into Robert Beaufort's sphere.

"I even came up with a plan to save us all. I was the one who approached Mr. Stockton and planted the idea of becoming his wife. I was the one who endured his tedious conversation. I even allowed his advances since they were accompanied by secret gifts I could sell to fund my campaign against Mr. Godwin." Anger blazed in Anne's eyes. "Yet the instant Mr. Stockton learned he would not be duke, he reneged on his promises. He abandoned me, just as Papa did."

"That is Mr. Stockton's fault, not Mr. Godwin's," Gigi pointed out.

"They are both to blame."

Anne's crafty expression sent a chill down Gigi's spine.

"After I have dispensed with Mr. Godwin, my original plan will come into play. Mr. Stockton will become the duke, and I his wife. And if he were to have an accident a few months after the wedding..." Anne trailed off delicately. "I must confess that the life of a wealthy widowed duchess holds a certain appeal."

She means it. She is mad and means to kill anyone she perceives as an obstacle—including Conrad. You cannot let that happen.

Gigi swallowed. "Dispensing with Mr. Godwin will not be as easy as it sounds. After all, you already failed once—"

"Twice, actually. Do not forget the carriage collision," Anne said. "Mr. Godwin is indeed a formidable opponent. I suspected that he must have something nefarious planned for me and my family, for why else would he have kept silent on his claim to the duchy? I enlisted my dearest childhood friend, Isobel, to discover his plans. Alas, even she, who has a talent for manipulating men, could not uncover his scheme. I could not take any chances, which led to the two, and unfortunately failed, attempts on his life.

"When Mr. Godwin came to the ball and unveiled his plan to destroy my family, I nearly panicked. But then I realized that all was not lost. When I saw you and Mr. Godwin together, I knew I had found his Achilles' heel. His one weakness—you."

Gigi remembered Conrad's impassioned declaration: *You, on the other hand, are everything. Not only will I be true, but I will also protect you with my dying breath. These are vows I've never given to any woman. Never wanted to, until I met you.*

Her heart raced because she knew that while Conrad had lied about other things, he hadn't lied about loving her. He would come after her. And he would do whatever was necessary to save her...including risking his own life.

"Don't do this—"

Anne retied the gag, smothering her words.

"Enough talking now," Anne said. "Your husband will be here soon, and I must prepare for his arrival."

Chapter Thirty-Six

From the cover of trees, Conrad regarded the old mill. Moonlight gave the building an eerie, Gothic appearance; with its boarded-up windows and crumbling stone walls, it looked like a residence fit for Chuddums's famous ghost. Conrad had secured his horse farther downstream to make his approach as stealthily as possible. Otherwise, he'd followed the kidnapper's instructions to the letter:

> *If you want to see your wife alive, meet me at the old Chuddums mill at midnight. Come alone, or she will die. Slowly and unpleasantly.*

The note had been accompanied by a lock of Gigi's hair and her engagement ring.

Afraid to risk Gigi's life, Conrad had made the trip from London alone. Traveling by train to Reading, then by horseback to Chuddums had allowed him to arrive just in time. He hadn't informed Gigi's family: if they came charging to her rescue, there was no telling what might happen. It was clear to Conrad that he was the true target. It was a fair exchange: his life for hers...one he would make without hesitation.

Given the choice, however, he would rather they both lived. There was so much he wished to say to his wife, amends he needed to make. He told himself there would be time for all of that...later.

He focused on his plan. In his surveillance of the place, he'd seen four men, armed, patrolling the building. A clearing separated Conrad and them, the distance too great for him to pick them off by gunfire. Sneaking around back was likewise unfeasible, given that the mill backed onto the stream.

His only path was through the guards.

So be it.

He recognized one of the brutes as Gregory Johnson and cursed himself for not capturing the bastard the other day. And for removing the guards he'd put on Gigi. He'd believed the danger was over when the real villain had been lying in wait.

Another figure emerged. A woman. Christ, he recognized her too.

"Any sign of him?" Anne asked.

Like father, like daughter. Of course, my niece would be behind this. What a bloody family I was born into.

"No, milady," one of her lackeys replied.

"Keep your eyes sharp. Godwin's wily as a fox. If you wish to get paid, you must shoot him on sight. Understand?"

Hell, Robert's daughter might be worse than he was. While he was a malicious bully, his offspring was capable of cold-blooded murder.

"Yes, milady."

When she cast a look in Conrad's direction, he quickly retreated behind a tree. Heart thudding, he hoped that his hiding place and the darkness kept him concealed.

"Well, don't just stand there, gawping like idiots."

Even from a distance, Conrad could hear Anne's contempt.

"You two—patrol the surrounding area. Godwin could be

hiding beneath our noses. I will keep watch here with Johnson and Heller." Anne pulled a pistol from her skirts, her voice dripping with disdain. "If one wants a thing done, one must do it oneself."

Conrad risked another look. Johnson and a mountain of a brute who had to be Heller flanked Anne. The other two cutthroats were fanning out, one headed in his direction.

Perfect.

Conrad returned his firearm to his pocket. He had to attack swiftly and quietly—Gigi's life depended upon it. He concealed himself behind foliage, listening as the heavy steps approached.

"Uppity bitch." The cutthroat was muttering to himself. "It'll be a miracle if I don't strangle 'er before the night's over—"

Conrad moved. Lunging from the shadows, he wrapped his arm around the brute's throat, preventing the other from releasing more than a muffled sound. With his forearm, he crushed his foe's windpipe, locking the hold with his other hand. As the cutthroat thrashed, clawing at his arm, he held on with determined strength.

Eventually, the brute stopped struggling. Conrad felt the telltale jerking—the signal that the cutthroat was down for the count. He held on for a minute longer before letting the dead weight sag to the ground. The bastard wouldn't be getting up anytime soon.

Exhaling sharply, Conrad rolled his shoulders.

One enemy down.

He slipped into the night, in search of the next.

"Evie, wake up. Please."

When Evie's lashes finally lifted, Gigi could have cried with relief.

"What is going on?" Evie asked groggily. "Where...where are we?"

"We were taken by cutthroats hired by my husband's niece,

who wants him dead." It was the fastest explanation Gigi could give. "They tied us up but, luckily, not very well. I managed to get us loose. Now we need to escape before they use me to barter for Conrad's life."

Evie's pupils were dilated, and she was trembling. Before shock could take over, Gigi gave her sister-in-law a ruthless shake.

"Swoon later, dear," she said. "I have a plan and need your help."

She tugged Evie toward the back wall, where the sound of rushing water was unmistakable.

"There are guards outside the doors, but I've found another way out. See that opening up there, where the board has fallen off?"

She pointed to the small window about twelve feet off the ground. The frame was empty of glass. The moonlight illuminated a thick branch just beyond.

"I don't understand. How will we escape through there?"

Evie sounded strange and unlike herself. Her voice was oddly devoid of emotion.

Dear Lord, please help Evie hold it together until we escape.

"I can reach the window if I climb on your shoulders," Gigi said. "Once I'm out the window, I'll use the tree to climb down. My plan will work—I've done it before."

"But what about me?" Evie whispered. "Are you going to leave me here?"

"Of course not, dear. You are going to climb out after me. Once I get to the tree, I will secure a rope, which you may use to climb up."

"Where are you going to get a rope?" Evie looked at her with frightened eyes.

"We are going to make one," Gigi explained. "See the cloth on the looms and worktables? Help me gather some pieces and we'll tie them together. Quickly now."

She went off to collect the remnants, and Evie did the same. The fabric was tattered but strong enough, and soon they had a rope. However, they quickly realized that their clothing would hinder their ability to climb. They helped each other unhook their skirts and petticoats, letting the heavy layers drop to the ground. Dressed in their bodices and drawers, they were ready to make their escape.

Winding the rope over her shoulder, Gigi said, "Ready to give it a go?"

Evie gave a tentative nod.

To Gigi's relief, Evie was stronger than she looked and managed to keep her balance while Gigi climbed onto her shoulders. Straining, Gigi tried to reach the edge of the window but came up a few inches short. At the same time, Evie wobbled, and Gigi teetered, her arms windmilling, before the former steadied her stance.

"Sorry," Evie said breathlessly.

"You're doing splendidly." Perspiration dotted Gigi's brow, her heart thumping. "Can you manage to give me a boost?"

"I shall try my best." Gritting her teeth, Evie bent her knees in readiness.

"On the count of three," Gigi said. "One, two, *three*."

Evie pushed, and Gigi used that momentum to propel herself past those final inches. She grabbed onto the edge, holding on despite the pain slicing into her right palm. Straining with effort, she pulled herself up and through the opening, grabbing onto the branch. Thank heavens, it was sturdy. She glanced below, and seeing no guards, eased herself onto the limb, then crawled toward the trunk. She secured the rope and crept back toward the window, tossing down the loose end.

"Your turn, Evie," she called softly. "You can do it."

Looking scared but determined, Evie grabbed the rope. Gigi's breath stuttered when her sister-in-law slipped a few times, but Evie braced her feet against the knots and kept on climbing.

"You're almost there," Gigi encouraged. "Stay toward the left. There's some jagged glass on the right side of the window."

Nodding, Evie followed the instructions, and when she reached the opening, Gigi pulled her onto the branch. When the wooden limb creaked in protest, Gigi scooted toward the trunk.

"Follow me," she said.

She descended nimbly, landing on her feet. Evie's movements were slower and less confident, and she lost her grip on the last branch, falling a few feet and landing with an awkward stumble.

"Are you all right?" Gigi helped her up.

Wincing, Evie said, "I twisted my ankle. But I think I can walk."

"Lean on me. We'll try to get to the woods, hide there until—"

A shot rang out.

Gigi's blood chilled as Anne's voice rang with triumph.

"I got Godwin. I killed that bastard at last."

Conrad had only seconds before his maniacal relation discovered his ruse.

After subduing the second cutthroat, he'd bound the man's hands with his neckcloth and gagged him with a handkerchief.

"Run back to the mill." He'd waved his pistol in front of his quarry's wide eyes. "Run as fast as you can, or I will put a bullet through you."

The bounder had taken off. He'd barely made it out of the woods before Anne took aim and fired. The cutthroat fell, landing face down.

Two down, two to go.

"I got Godwin. I killed that bastard at last," Anne gloated. "Johnson, verify that the dead body is Godwin's."

Conrad crept forward, his pistol at the ready. Once Johnson

was in range, Conrad would shoot the bastard. This would leave one cutthroat to deal with, plus Anne...who was probably deadlier than all her hired ruffians combined. Johnson neared, and Conrad tightened his finger against the trigger.

At that moment, he saw a movement at the side of the building.

Christ...it was *Gigi*.

Even as his heart leapt at the sight of her, she dashed toward the fallen body and into the line of fire.

"Conrad," she cried.

"Grab her, Johnson!" Anne screamed.

"Gigi, get down," Conrad shouted. "*Now.*"

Gigi came to a halt. Obviously confused, she paused...then dropped to the ground.

Conrad pulled the trigger, and Johnson gave a pained cry, hitting the ground a few feet from Gigi. Breaking cover, Conrad sprinted toward her. She lifted her head from the grass, and even in the moonlight, he saw the bright relief in her eyes.

"You're alive," she breathed.

"Stay down!"

An instant later, he was there with her. He kept his pistol aimed at Anne and Heller, who remained by the mill.

"Stay in the woods and head toward the stream," he said tersely. "I've a horse waiting about a mile away. Go for help while I take care of these two."

"I can't leave—"

"I'll be fine."

"I'm not worried about you. It's Evie," Gigi burst out. "James's wife. When I thought you got shot, I told her to hide behind the building while I came to you."

Bloody hell.

He stiffened as Anne moved. Not toward them but to the side of the building...

"I'll fetch Evie. You get to the horse. Go."

He took off in a run. When he was close enough, Heller let off a shot, which he dodged before firing his own pistol. He hit the other in the shoulder, but the brute charged at him like an enraged bull, tackling him. Hitting the ground, he lost his grip on his weapon. When Heller crushed his windpipe with a massive hand, Conrad delivered a solid punch to Heller's jaw. Heller's hold slackened, and Conrad dug his fingers into his foe's wound. Heller howled, and Conrad reversed their positions, smashing his fists in the brute's face until the other lay still.

Retrieving his pistol, Conrad held it at the ready as he hunted down Anne. He found her by the stream's edge. She was using a blonde woman as a shield, her pistol pressed against the other's temple.

"Throw down your weapon," Anne said. "Or I'll shoot her. Don't think I won't."

The blonde whimpered, her eyes blank with terror.

"I want your word," Conrad said. "Your word that you will let her go."

"You have it."

He didn't trust Anne. But what choice did he have? He couldn't let an innocent woman die.

Maybe after Anne takes her shot at me, Evie will have a chance to make a run for it.

"Be strong, Evie," Conrad said. "Tell Gigi I love her."

Slowly, he lowered his pistol, tossing it in front of him.

"Goodbye, Uncle," Anne said.

The shot pierced the night.

Chapter Thirty-Seven

Braced for impact, Conrad flinched at the blast of gunfire.

A heartbeat later, when the pain didn't come, he looked down at himself and saw no gaping injury. His gaze went to Anne, whose smug smile was still in place as blood trickled from her nose and mouth. She fell forward, a wound at the back of her head. Rooted in place, Evie stared down at the dead woman.

"Evie, are you all right?"

It was Gigi's brother, James. Dropping the smoking pistol, he ran to his wife.

Then Conrad lost track of everything else as Gigi dashed toward him. He caught her against him and just...just held on.

"I was so scared." Her voice was muffled against his waistcoat. "When I saw you throw away the gun, I thought Anne was going to—"

"I'm all right, love. Are you?"

"No." She shook her head against his chest.

Tipping her head back, he gazed at her beautiful, tear-stained face.

"You will be," he said huskily. "You're the bravest woman I

know. I love you, Gigi, and I was afraid I wouldn't be able to tell you. Afraid that I would leave this earth without having the chance to apologize. To tell you that I was wrong: vengeance isn't the most important thing to me—you are. I would do anything for you. Nothing else matters."

"I do love you so," she blurted. "And I'm sorry for my part in our fight. I shouldn't have given you an ultimatum. I should have listened and tried to understand—"

"I shouldn't have kept secrets from you. And I won't do it again."

He sealed his promise with a kiss, pouring his emotions, everything he felt for her, into it. She kissed him back with equal fervor, her love shining through the dark forest and showing him the path home. Home to his wife, his Gigi.

Finally, he registered the voices in the background. Reluctantly, he lifted his head and saw that they had gained an audience. The entire Harrington clan and some of the villagers were present. The Marquess of Blackwood had his arms crossed and was staring at Conrad through slitted eyes. Lord Ethan had a similar stance. Lord Owen and the ladies weren't quite as unapproachable, but they weren't exactly welcoming either. The only friendly face belonged to Gigi's friend, Duffield, who stood next to a brawny, dark-haired fellow with an eye patch.

The draper gave Conrad an encouraging smile before saying to the crowd, "Let us see if the constable and his men need help and give the family their privacy."

After the villagers dispersed, Gigi nudged Conrad.

"Don't just stand there," she whispered. "Go greet my family."

Right. You've been given another chance, man. Do not make a mull of it.

Yet he was already off on the wrong foot, given that his crazed niece had kidnapped Gigi and Evie. Then there was the fact that his in-laws had just caught him with his tongue down Gigi's throat. The only thing that might save him was that James appeared to be doing the same to Evie, with a passionate intensity Conrad wouldn't have expected from the proper, buttoned-up earl.

He sighed. Delaying helped nothing. Keeping a firm hold on his wife's hand—if he had to do this, he wasn't doing it alone—he went over.

"Good evening, my lords and ladies." Clearing his throat, he strove for a conversational tone. "How did you know to come here?"

"Kenny Sommers." The unexpected answer was supplied by Xenia. "Apparently, he was being pursued by bullies and was hiding in a pile of rubbish in the alley. By the by, he attributed the 'run and hide' technique to you, Mr. Godwin. He says it has saved his hide more than once."

Conrad glanced at the Blackwood patriarch, who didn't look too impressed that Conrad had taught the lad to hide in a heap of garbage. While some might consider the tactic cowardly, from Conrad's perspective, it was better than Kenny getting beaten to a pulp.

"I only suggested that strategy in the instances when Kenny couldn't win a fight," he muttered. "Unfortunately, in Kenny's case, that might be in every instance."

"In this instance, it proved fortunate," Xenia said. "For Kenny saw the brutes take Gigi and Evie and managed to get a good look at the carriage. He told Mrs. Sommers, who sent word to us. We contacted Constable Rawlins—he and his men are here, taking care of the cutthroats out front—and together we canvassed the village for information. Everyone wanted to help. By piecing together observations made by Mr. Thornton, Mrs. Pettigrew, and others, we were able to ascertain the direction the carriage was headed. Then Mr. Duffield, who has a keen eye, noticed that the muddy tracks left by the carriage had a reddish tint—"

"Duffy is a genius with color," Gigi said fondly.

"And Mr. Keane—he's the blacksmith, in case you haven't met

him—recalled getting that same sticky, red mud on his boots when he went fishing in the stream. That brought up the question of what the kidnappers might have been doing by the stream, and Wally, who knows Chuddums better than anyone, thought of the abandoned mill. He had a hunch that the kidnappers might be using it as a hiding place, *and* the carriage was last seen heading in its direction. We came to investigate, and the rest, as they say, is history."

Conrad wondered why Xenia's convoluted account made perfect sense to him.

Devil and damn. I might owe these Chuddumites. Even more than I realized.

He drew a breath. "I owe an apology. To everyone."

The marquess gave him a hard stare. "It is late. Anything that needs to be said can be said in the morning. Come, Gigi—we're going back to Bottoms House."

"I am going home with my husband," Gigi blurted.

What did I do to deserve her?

Conrad's chest *hurt* with the love he felt. Seeing her papa's brows lower, however, he cut in.

"I have acted dishonorably," he said. "I have kept secrets from Gigi when I should have trusted her. My thirst for vengeance has put her and others in danger, and I will never forgive myself for that. Never."

"Conrad—" Gigi began.

"No, love. Let me say this." He blundered on. "Despite the mistakes I've made, there is one thing I've done right. I fell in love with Gigi—the bravest, kindest, and most resourceful woman I've ever met. Somehow, I managed to win her heart and her hand, and while I deserve neither, I will do everything in my power to be a husband and a man who is worthy of her. For nothing is more important to me than my wife's happiness. I will gladly spend a lifetime earning her forgiveness...and yours. Because you are her family, and she is mine."

Someone gave a swoony sigh. Conrad didn't know who because his gaze was now on his wife, who was smiling at him, her eyes luminous pools in the moonlight.

"Gigi, when I say I will do anything to make you happy, I mean it," he said intently. "The reason it took me a few days to get here is because I was arranging a surprise for you: a plan to revitalize Chuddums. You were right. The village is worth investing in, and I will dedicate myself to ensuring its prosperity and future. In truth, I would be repaying a debt, for Chuddums has given me everything I've ever wanted. It gave me *you*."

"Oh, darling!" Gigi clasped her hands together. "That is the best surprise ever!"

"Just when I was beginning to find you tolerable, Godwin." Ethan's look was wry. "How is any husband going to top the gift of a bloody village?"

Conrad took the male ribbing as a sign of progress.

"I also purchased Honeystone Hall," he told his wife. "Consider it a wedding gift."

At Gigi's squeal of delight, both Ethan and Owen snorted.

Then James came forward, and Conrad braced. If the earl wanted to plant a facer on him, he would take it. He deserved it for endangering the fellow's wife...and Gigi. Hell, he had half a mind to plant a facer on himself.

As James regarded him, Conrad hunched his shoulders.

"You have my thanks," James said.

Conrad stared at the hand being offered to him.

"I don't understand. Your wife was kidnapped because of me—"

"Your lunatic relation abducted Evie. And you were willing to exchange your life for hers. For that, you have my everlasting gratitude."

Hearing the taut emotion in the earl's voice, Conrad understood. Maybe he had something in common with Gigi's kin after all. He shook the other man's hand.

"And I owe you," he said quietly. "For doing what needed to be done."

Although James had made the only choice he could to save his wife, Conrad suspected that killing someone—even a scheming, cold-blooded murderess—would not sit well with his honorable soul.

James's nod was gruff.

The marquess put a hand on his heir's shoulder. "I think we've all had enough," he said firmly. "What we need now is a good night's sleep. Let us return to Bottoms House. And Gigi…"

"Yes, Papa?" she asked with a hint of worry.

"We shall expect you and your husband in the morning."

Even though the statement was not directed at him, Conrad felt a burst of hope. This was the first time the marquess had acknowledged his relationship to Gigi. Her happy nod confirmed his optimism.

"We'll be there, Papa," she promised.

They were heading to the carriages when they encountered Rawlins, emerging from the mill.

"My lords and my ladies." The constable's usual lethargy was replaced by an air of palpable excitement. "You will not believe what we discovered."

Chapter Thirty-Eight

"Rose..."

"No, don't talk, my love," she wept. "Save your strength."

"Too late for that." Despite the stain blossoming over his bandage, Thomas smiled. "It doesn't matter, my darling. I have already evaded death once, and I have no fear of what is to come. There is only one thing I must do so that I may go in peace..."

"Tell me. Whatever it is, I will see it done," she vowed.

"Marry me, Rose."

How much more could a fractured heart bear before it was crushed into smithereens?

"I want to," she said between hitched breaths. "More than anything. All those times you asked me before...I wish I had said yes. I wish I had had the courage to follow my heart. Now it's too late."

"It's not." He lifted a shaking hand to cup her cheek.

Regret and sorrow clogged her throat. "There isn't time to make such arrangements—"

"In my desk, there is a special license. I never gave up hope that you would say yes. And finally, you have."

The glowing contentment in her beloved's eyes released another flood of tears.

"All we need n-now..."

He started coughing, and panic gripped her until the spasms eased.

"Go fetch the rector," *he said.*

"I...I cannot leave you, Thomas," *she whispered.* "I want to stay by your side."

Gazing into her eyes, he said solemnly, "I vow to you that I will not leave this earth until you are mine, and I am yours. Until we are joined in name as we are in body and spirit. I will not rest until the world knows the story of our love."

"Gigi, love. Wake up."

Slowly, she opened her eyes to find Conrad gazing down at her.

"You were having quite the dream." Concern creased his features. "Was it a nightmare?"

"No." With a trembling hand, she brushed aside his stray forelock. "It wasn't a nightmare."

Curling into the crook of her husband's arm, she described her dream.

"In the end, Thomas and Rosalinda conquered all odds and found happiness," she said tremulously. "He died knowing that he had won the woman of his heart. And wherever she went, she took with her the knowledge that she was worthy of the man she loved."

"Theirs was a love story, just as Wally claimed," Conrad mused.

Gigi had to laugh. "You listened to Wally?"

"I didn't have much choice, did I? There's no escaping the old codger." He paused. "Since he played a part in saving my hide last night, I suppose enduring his tours is the least I can do. In fact, I was thinking of consulting him on the plans for revitalizing Chuddums."

"If you do that, Wally will love you nearly as much as I do," she teased.

"Minx."

He pulled her atop him, his kiss slow, adoring, and heated. When they'd arrived home mere hours ago, they'd bathed and tumbled naked into bed. They'd traded kisses and sweet promises until they fell asleep. Now desire leapt between them, bright as a flame, and she writhed against her husband, reveling in his virile strength.

"Devil and damn, I've missed you," he said ardently. "But we can't."

She blinked at him. "We can't?"

"I promised your papa that we would be there in the morning," he reminded her. "It is nearing noon. We cannot be late."

She furrowed her brow. "Why do you care if we're late?"

"Because they are your family and are important to you. Therefore, they are important to me. My goal is to win them over—which I won't do by showing up late."

She stared at him. "You are serious?"

"My success wasn't an accident," he said earnestly. "I believe in efficiency: in setting goals and following strategies to achieve them. Before, I had my sights set on revenge. But now..."

Understanding made her heart feel so full she feared it might burst.

"Now your goal is love," she said softly.

"Precisely. Given my past transgressions with your family, I must do things right this time. I must do right by *you*." He cupped her cheek, regret in his eyes. "Now be a good girl and climb off. We only have...*Christ*."

She tightened her grip, stroking his turgid shaft. He was as ready for her as she was for him. When she nipped his bottom lip, he groaned.

"Make love to me, darling. Knowing how efficient you are," she murmured, "I am certain you will manage to do so and get us there in time."

Chapter Thirty-Nine

They arrived at Bottoms House a bit past one. Luckily, everyone had gotten a late start, and James and Evie had yet to make an appearance. Seated beside his wife in the drawing room, Conrad was trying very hard to focus on what Constable Rawlins was saying. Gigi's nearness kept distracting him. One would think that their quick, but passionate tumble this morning would have sated him. Instead, it had the opposite effect. He had a raging appetite for his wife, and it didn't help that her fragrance teased his nostrils and the sight of her pretty mouth crowded his head with filthy thoughts.

He reflected that one thing hadn't changed between them and probably never would. When it came to Gigi, he would always be a beast. He was lucky that she liked their games as much as he did. In fact, he had new amusements he was dying to show her...

Catching the Marquess of Blackwood's gaze fixed upon him, Conrad hastily shoved his thoughts back into the gutter from whence they came. By Jove, his father-in-law was like a bloodhound trained to sniff out impropriety. If he were perfectly honest, he found Blackwood slightly intimidating. He hadn't met many men who were loving husbands and doting papas, who conducted themselves with honor in their public and personal lives. In truth, he'd never had what he would consider a role model. He wouldn't mind learning a thing or two from Marcus Harrington.

"Now, then," Rawlins was saying. "As I mentioned last night, during our sweep of the mill, my team and I discovered a hidden chamber filled with valuables. This morning, I matched those valuables to the list of unrecovered goods stolen by the Corrigans. I interrogated the gang members currently serving sentences, and one of them sang like a bird. Apparently, that stash was supposed to be their pension after they were released from gaol. Moreover, the hiding place of the goods wasn't random; it was the result of an agreement between their leader and Abel Pearce."

"Mr. Pearce was abetting the Corrigans?" Gigi said with a gasp.

Rawlins nodded. "In exchange, he received a small percentage of the profits. Based on this information, I wish to search Pearce's former properties...with your permission, Mr. Godwin, as the new owner."

"You have it," Conrad said.

"I cannot believe Mr. Pearce was in cahoots with those dreadful Corrigans, who wreaked such havoc and destruction in Chuddums." Xenia huffed with outrage. "Wait until the villagers hear about this—"

"The news has already spread." Rawlins cleared his throat. "As we speak, there is a melee in the village square."

Gigi canted her head. "What is going on there?"

"As an officer of the law, I cannot condone the destruction of public property. In this case, however, it could be said that the public is acting in its own best interest and removing what many consider an eyesore."

"The monument to Pearce," Conrad said, bemused. "They are removing it?"

"That is one way to put it, sir." Rawlins raised his brows. "I believe the goal is to smash it to smithereens and use the granite bits to pave a new path through the green."

I'll be damned. Maybe there is justice after all.

After Rawlins headed off, Gigi patted Conrad's arm.

"See, darling?" she said brightly. "Things have a way of working out as they ought to."

"I'll say." He smiled slowly. "Is it bad that I shall enjoy walking over Abel Pearce every time I cross the green?"

"Better than the alternative of allowing that monument to stand." Ethan grimaced. "I thought I would never hear the end of it, especially from James."

"Speaking of James," the marchioness said. "Has anyone seen him or Evie this morning?"

Everyone shook their heads.

Conrad had an inkling of what was delaying the couple, but as he was currently courting the family's favor, he thought it wise to keep it to himself.

"Well, it is nice to see them together." The marchioness smiled. "To see all my children happy."

When she included Conrad in her warm, maternal gaze, he felt a pleasant jolt.

"I couldn't be happier," Gigi piped up. "Wait until you see the plans Conrad has drawn up for Chuddums—"

"You deserve the credit, love." He kissed her hand, seeing with satisfaction that his ring was back where it belonged, sparkling upon her finger. "From the start, you recognized the potential of Chuddums and have been its steadfast champion. Your scheme with the water has already brought recognition to the village, and I am merely following your example."

"A toast," her mama proposed, raising her teacup. "To Gigi, who is, and has always been, a force to be reckoned with."

Gigi glowed as they clinked their cups in her honor.

"Thank you," she said. "But, truly, you must see Conrad's vision for the village. He plans to clean up the docklands and build a theatre—"

"A theatre? Really, Godwin?" Ethan gave him an exasperated look. "Is there no limit to your husbandly generosity?"

"Not when it comes to Gigi," Conrad said. "There is nothing I wouldn't do for her."

The Marquess of Blackwood sighed, addressing him for the first time today.

"A word of advice."

"Yes, sir?" Conrad said warily.

"There is nothing wrong with indulging one's wife. But mind you don't spoil the chit," the marquess said severely.

"Papa," Gigi protested.

But Conrad took the gleam of amusement in her papa's eyes as a good sign.

At that moment, James came in. He was alone.

"Good afternoon, dear. Where is Evie?" the marchioness asked.

Conrad didn't know James very well, but he was no stranger to male frustration.

"Evie's gone," James said in flat tones. "She left early this morning."

Epilogue

"Come out, come out, wherever you are."

Stifling a laugh at Conrad's exaggerated growl, Gigi raced merrily through the maze of hedges. The balmy summer night was made for adventures such as these. The sky was a stretch of black velvet, and the moon was round and bright, lighting her path. Owen had done a spectacular job with the landscaping at Honeystone Hall, and the labyrinth, in particular, was garnering him acclaim. Gigi followed the twists and turns until it took her to the heart of the garden where, at her request, Owen had left an ancient oak standing at its center.

Anticipation sizzled through Gigi when she saw that Conrad had beaten her to their meeting place. He must have taken a shortcut, for he awaited her by the tree, hands braced on his hips. With his shirt untucked and open at the collar, his eyes gleaming in the moonlight, he looked deliciously primal. Her husband, her duke, her mate who owned her heart, body, and soul.

Which was just as well since he'd entrusted her with his. Since their marriage, their bond had only grown stronger. Their love had given them the confidence to share their deepest dreams and desires with one another...and to play out those desires, no matter how wicked they were. To Gigi's delight, being married had given her more freedom, not less. Her husband encouraged her to shed her inhibitions, which was why she'd suggested their game tonight.

Remembering her role, she pressed her hands to her chest.

"You found me!" she gasped.

She saw Conrad's lips twitch.

"I'll always find you, little nymph." He crooked a finger at her. "Come here."

She tried to escape (or pretended to, at any rate). It was great fun darting around the tree, keeping just out of Conrad's reach. By the time she let him capture her, she was breathless and barely holding back her mirth.

"We'll see who has the last laugh," Conrad said.

His sternness made her giggle even as he backed her into the tree. She wore a plain chemise—there was no point in wearing anything more extravagant, given her husband's troglodytic tendencies when it came to her clothing. When Conrad trapped her against the trunk, she trembled at the sensation of being sandwiched between the trunk and his hard length.

"You're a naughty little tease," he admonished. "Making me chase you through the garden."

She batted her eyelashes. "What will you do now that you have me?"

His gaze was smoldering. "Whatever I want."

Never one to disappoint, he pinned her wrists above her head with one big hand. With the other, he grabbed the neckline of her chemise and tore the garment in half. As he raked a hot glance over her naked form, her nipples budded, her thighs squeezing together instinctively. He touched her with a casual propriety that never failed to stir her. Her breath quickened as he caressed the line of her throat, pressing slightly into the hollow at the base. When he palmed her breast, pinching her nipple between finger and thumb, she couldn't hold back a whimper.

"I think you enjoy the chase as much as I do," he said huskily. "I think you are wet, wanton, and ready to fuck."

Oh my stars. Her knees trembled at her husband's filthy language. At the filthy intent in his eyes. However, she'd discovered that the game was even more thrilling when prolonged.

"Unhand me, you beast," she said breathily.

"If I am wrong, I will eat my words."

With a knowing smirk, he reached between her thighs, and she had to bite back a moan as he took his time fingering her slick crease.

"On second thought," he murmured. "You should be the one to eat her words."

He held up his index and middle fingers. She blushed, seeing the glistening abundance of her arousal. When he pressed his fingers against her lips, she went hot all over.

"Open for me, love," he said.

He thrust inside, and the depravity of tasting her own wanton flavor made her squirm against the tree. Conrad's plunging fingers reminded her of the other way he used her mouth and the skills she'd learned. Hollowing her cheeks, she sucked on his invading thickness.

"That's it." Approval heated his gaze. "Suck my fingers like you would my cock. Show me how badly you want to be fucked."

Lost in the carnal fantasy, she obeyed, swirling her tongue around his digits. She applied suction, drawing on him, the wet, lascivious sounds making his chest heave. Soon she needed to be filled elsewhere, and her mate's ravenous expression told her she wouldn't have to wait long. Sure enough, he released her and unfastened his trousers. Her heart thumped as his thick, meaty shaft slapped into his palm.

In an easy movement, he lifted her against the trunk.

"This is all for you," he said in guttural tones. "Take me, Gigi."

He impaled her on his cock.

She moaned at the depth of his penetration, the totality of it.

He filled her until there was no room for breath, thought, or anything but the molten craving that forged them as one. He held her aloft against the oak, bringing her down on his massive pole while simultaneously thrusting upward. Her senses overwhelmed, she clung to his flexing shoulders, circling his hard hips with her legs, reveling in his power and stamina. Several strokes later, she came in a flood of bliss.

"Just so," he groaned. "I love it when you gush around my prick."

A heartbeat later, he maneuvered her onto the grass on all fours. He entered her from behind, grunting as her pussy continued to spasm around him. Gripping her hips, he pounded into her, the heavy slap of his thighs setting off fresh quivers. Panting, she had the vague thought that this degree of wanting, of passion for another, shouldn't be possible, but her husband had taught her to expect the unexpected. His strong, relentless drilling brought her pleasure to a crest. As she teetered on the edge, he pressed a wet finger against her secret pucker and pushed.

The incursion, illicit and exquisite, made her gasp and twist her head to look at him.

"I love you," he said fiercely. "My nymph, my duchess, my every fantasy come to life."

Her reply was lost as he screwed his finger deeper, the twin sensations of fullness pushing her over. Even as she tumbled into ecstasy, she kept her gaze on his. His lap slammed against her bottom again and again until he bellowed, inundating her with his hot essence. Afterward, he gathered her into his arms, and they floated on a sea of bliss, anchored body and soul, their hearts beating as one.

Steeped in contentment, Gigi gazed at the starry sky. Conrad placed a hand on the small swell of her belly, his touch gentle and possessive.

"I wasn't too rough, was I?" he asked.

"No, darling," she said dreamily. "That was perfect. As always."

His laugh was male and knowing. "Who could have guessed that being with child would make you even more wanton?"

She blushed but had no argument since he spoke the truth.

"Are you complaining?" she asked archly.

"To the contrary. I'm planning on keeping you pregnant so you'll continue having your wicked way with me."

She slapped his chest. "Do stop being a beast."

"Why? You love it." He captured her hand, kissing it. "Almost as much as you love me."

Hearing the need beneath his confidence, she stopped teasing.

"I adore you," she said softly. "And I was ever so proud of you today."

This afternoon, Conrad had formally presented Mrs. Sommers with the key to her renovated shop. He'd expanded the space to twice its original size and added windows to make it bright and airy. These improvements were among the many he had implemented in the last few months, making him a local hero. When the villagers proposed erecting a tribute in his honor, however, he adamantly vetoed the idea.

"To build success, one must have the proper foundation. My part was easy," he said with a shrug. "The rest is up to Mrs. Sommers."

"She is more than up for the task. As are the other good folk of Chuddums." Shifting, Gigi lay atop him and gazed into his gleaming eyes. "Everything is going so well. Do you think it is possible that we have broken the curse?"

"I know *my* fortunes have improved." He tucked a loose tress behind her ear. "Because of you."

"But what about Bloody Thom? Do you think he's gone for good? I haven't had a dream about him and Rosalinda for months."

"Who knows what the future will bring?" her husband said philosophically. "The only thing I know is this."

"What, darling?"

"I will love you in this life and beyond."

Her heart overflowed. "And I, you."

As they kissed, the moon banished the shadows of the garden.

From Grace's Desk

Dear Gentle Reader,

I had such great fun with Gigi and Conrad, and I hope you enjoyed their passionate, enemies-to-lovers romance as much as I did. These days, I crave a fictional escape, which is why I created Chuddums. While the village isn't perfect, it is filled with good and decent folk who treat friends and strangers alike with kindness, look out for each other, and believe there's room for everyone at the table.

Next up is James and Evie's story. If you've been following my books, you know I love a steamy second chance romance…especially when the couple is married ;-) James and Evie have a delicious, doozy of a tale, and I cannot wait to share it with you!

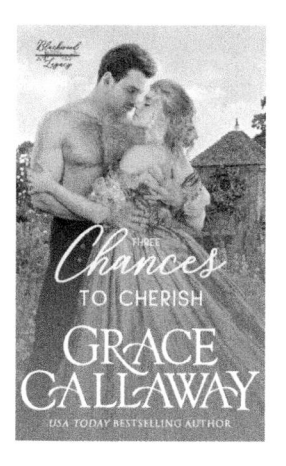

When a slow-burn marriage of convenience ignites, old vows are broken…and new desires forged.

Hugs and happy reading,

Grace

Author's Note

As Gigi candidly admitted, she borrowed her idea for the "Chuddums Water Cure" from the town of Malvern...as did this author. Located in Worcestershire, the hillside spa town of Malvern has been a popular tourist destination since the Victorian era, when people came from far and wide to sample the natural mineral springs. Much has been written about Malvern water and its medicinal effects. Dr. John Wall, for instance, published a pamphlet about its purity, in which he concluded that "the Malvern water is famous for containing just nothing at all."

In the 1840s, Drs. Gully and Wilson opened hydrotherapy clinics, which quickly became popular and attracted prominent patients including Charles Darwin, Florence Nightingale, and Lord Tennyson. It is said that Queen Victoria herself refused to travel without a supply of her favorite mineral water. The efficacy of the water "cure" was, of course, questioned by some, including Sir Charles Hastings, the founder of the British Medical Association.

As for the Chuddums Potion, is it indeed an elixir of love? It is hard to know when even its detractors have found themselves succumbing to the sweetest affliction. According to history books, Conrad, the Duke of Grantley, one of Chuddums's most famous residents, made it a habit to drink a glass a day. And he enjoyed a long and passionate happily ever after with his beloved duchess.

Acknowledgments

As always, I owe a debt of gratitude to my readers. My journey as a writer would not be possible without your support and encouragement. Thank you for championing my books and for loving my fictional universe as much as I do.

To my creative collaborators: thank you. My editor, Peter Senftleben, helped to make my vision for Gigi and Conrad come to life. My proofreaders Alyssa Nazzaro and Faith Williams polished this book to a shine. I was very much inspired by the beautiful cover art provided by Night Witchery Designs. And a special thanks to Jill Glass, who takes care of the things I forget to.

To my local writing buddies and my Carlsbad retreat pals: I'm so glad we're in this business together. Y'all inspire me, each and every day. And a special shout out to Annika, who figured out the falling statue on our first day at the beach :-)

To my family: you are my rock and my inspiration. I love you.

About the Author

USA Today & International Bestselling Author Grace Callaway writes hot and heart-melting historical romance brimming with mystery, adventure, and unforgettable characters. Her debut novel was a #1 National Regency Bestseller, and her subsequent books have topped national and international bestseller lists. She is a three-time winner of the following: the Daphne du Maurier Award for Excellence in Mystery and Suspense, the Maggie Award for Excellence in Historical Romance, and the Passionate Plume. She is also a recipient of the National Excellence in Romance Fiction Award, the Golden Leaf, and the National Excellence in Storytelling Award. Her stories have been translated into German, French, and Italian, and are available as audiobooks.

Born and raised on the Canadian prairies, Grace moved south to study at the University of Michigan, where she obtained a doctorate in clinical psychology. Currently, she and her family live near the beautiful San Francisco Bay. When she's not writing, she enjoys dancing, exploring cozy cafes with her rescue pup, and going on adapted adventures with her special son.

Keep up with Grace's latest news!

Newsletter: gracecallaway.com/newsletter

- facebook.com/GraceCallawayBooks
- bookbub.com/authors/grace-callaway
- instagram.com/gracecallawaybooks
- amazon.com/author/gracecallaway

Printed in Great Britain
by Amazon